BLOOD TIDES

C.R. STURGILL

This book is dedicated to my mother, Janet Sturgill, grandmothers June Sturgill and Dean Wilcox, and my grandfather Clifford Wilcox.

$\mathcal{T}$ABLE $\mathcal{O}$F $\mathcal{C}$ONTENTS

CHAPTER I

PIRATES

❧

"Sail ho!" a shrill voice cried from high overhead in the crow's nest.

"Can you make 'er?" Captain Fitzgerald called back, walking quickly to the port rail on the main deck. He shielded weathered eyes from the brilliant sun and squinted at the faint speck on the horizon.

Timmy, the skinny young sailor perched in the crow's nest, stared breathlessly through the long spyglass. "Frigate," he finally shouted down.

Blast! Please be navy. "Colors?"

It was several more minutes before the sailor could make out the flag attached to the main mast of the distant ship. He cursed under his breath and swallowed hard.

"Timmy?" Captain Fitzgerald called out impatiently.

"Black, white skull…red eyes."

"By the powers!" the captain shouted. "All hands on deck! Hard to starboard! Man the braces and lift every scrap of canvas!"

Sailors began to appear from all parts of the ship—some grabbing the braces and sheets and others scurrying up the ratlines—to ensure all of the sails on all three masts were raised, trimmed, and filled with wind. Slowly the ship turned and gained speed, heading away from the distant frigate.

"What is going on?" Peter Wellington asked, now standing beside the captain and staring at the approaching ship. "What kind of ship is that?"

Captain Fitzgerald quickly looked at the well-dressed businessman who was in great part funding the voyage from England to the New World with both his money and cargo. He thought briefly about lying, but it would do no good. They would all know the truth much too soon. "That's the *Bloody Seas*, captained by Captain Bloodstone—one of the fiercest pirates in the Caribbean. He's a little far north of his normal range."

"Pirate? Where's a pirate?" a six-year-old blond-haired boy inquired. He had broken off chasing his twelve-year-old brother across the deck with his wooden sword when he overheard the captain and his father's conversation. His shirtless chest and back were dark brown from exposure to the sun over the long journey.

"Not now, Henry," Mr. Wellington said, holding his hand out to his son. "Can we outrun him?"

"No," the captain responded soberly.

"I'll kill that mean old pirate and all of his crew!" Henry shouted, striking his sword against the rail. "James, come help me!"

"Can we fight?" Mr. Wellington asked, briefly glancing at James rushing over to the rail to stand beside his brother.

"I've only got twenty men and six guns. Bloodstone keeps ninety-nine men at all times and has thirty-six guns."

"So, what do we do?"

"Pray, Mr. Wellington. Pray."

The merchant ship had decent wind, and every sail was taut, but the pirate frigate steadily grew larger behind them. Mr. Wellington now stood at the rail of the quarterdeck, with his two children, sizing up the infamous pirate ship. The *Bloody Seas* was a large, three-masted ship painted pitch black. It was rare for a pirate to have a ship that large. Most frigates were warships used by the various navies. He could now see the black flag flying high above its decks. Although he couldn't discern the details of the skull yet, with its glowing red eyes, he felt an ominous chill nonetheless.

Mr. Wellington's heart raced and his sweaty hands clutched the rail. Henry continued to run about, waving his wooden sword before him, oblivious to the impending doom. James played some too, but frequently glanced up at the approaching ship. Mr. Wellington didn't take his eyes off of it. It could have sailed straight out of a nightmare.

This had been such an exciting journey. He was taking his two boys and moving to the New World. His wife had passed away from the fever the past winter, and he felt he and his boys needed a change. He owned a very profitable textile business in England and felt certain it would do as well in North Carolina. After a long journey, they were only a day from their destination. All three had been in such good spirits for the entire voyage. But now…

"Blast, that's a fast ship!"

Mr. Wellington turned to look at Captain Fitzgerald, who had walked up to stand beside him. The Captain's face was pale and gleamed with a thin layer of sweat. He looked tired—or sick. "Tell me about this Bloodstone."

Captain Fitzgerald studied the wealthy man's face and then glanced at his two fine boys running about the quarterdeck, impervious to the danger. He mopped his brow with the sleeve of his long blue coat. He was dressed more like a British naval officer than a merchant captain. He sighed. "Dreadful scourge, he is. Some say the devil himself. Supposedly started off just attacking the Spanish—for some kind of wrong they done him. Now he targets anyone and anything. He's a very sick and twisted man and very unpredictable. He's bent on becoming the most infamous and feared pirate ever."

"Obviously we cannot outrun him. What's your plan?" Mr. Wellington also wiped the sweat from his brow with the wide sleeves of his white silk shirt.

"If we resist, we'll all definitely die. I'll have to surrender and offer him our cargo. Maybe he'll be in a kind mood and spare most of us. But you and your boys need to hide in my cabin. Lock the door. If someone tries to get in, hide beneath the bed. Maybe they won't search my quarters."

If Mr. Wellington had been by himself, he would have insisted on facing the pirate with the captain. He wasn't much of a fighter, but he wasn't a coward either. Still, he had to try to protect Henry and James. "Boys, we are going to the captain's cabin for a bit," he said as he turned and walked toward the ladder leading to the main deck.

"No! I want to fight the pirates!" Henry said, stomping his foot in anger.

"Henry, come now!" Mr. Wellington commanded.

James grabbed his younger brother by the shoulder and helped guide him behind their father. Soon they were all three inside the modest captain's quarters, beneath the quarterdeck. Mr. Wellington left the door ajar six inches or so, and the three crouched inside, peering out onto the deck. They waited to watch what fate Bloodstone would choose for the ship.

Captain Fitzgerald watched from the quarterdeck until he could make out the pirates rushing about the deck of the *Bloody Seas*. It was evident even from this distance that they were readying weapons and guns for a battle. He cursed and quickly headed to the main deck. He ensured all of the sails were properly trimmed and taut and the ship was sailing directly leeward as he reviewed all of his options.

"They will catch us within a half an hour," first mate Richard Cook said as he joined the captain mid-deck.

"I know. I know," Captain Fitzgerald said softly.

"You aren't planning to resist, are you?"

The captain looked at the young first mate. He was a good man. A little raw, but he would make a good merchant captain someday, or maybe even achieve that rank in the Royal Navy. He had no doubt that he and all of his crew would fight bravely, and to the death, if he ordered it. But they were so overmatched; it was too futile to even contemplate. He then turned to look at the door to his cabin, sitting slightly ajar. He knew the fine Wellington family were huddled together just inside, peering intently at him.

"Nay. We'll pretend we haven't seen them and continue full speed ahead. When the devils come up beside us, I'll talk to Bloodstone and offer him the cargo. We're close to the coast. I doubt he wants to risk a long battle with the Yankee navy close by."

Richard nodded in approval and walked away to check on the helmsman.

Captain Fitzgerald made the rounds of the men milling about the main deck who weren't on the rigging and working the sails. He told them his plan. He didn't want a hero trying to fire a shot at Bloodstone or the other pirates. They seemed a little more at ease after his briefing.

"They're taking the wind out of our sails!" Timmy cried out, still manning the crow's nest.

"What in the blazes is he doing?" the captain said to no one in particular.

Suddenly, there was a roar behind the merchant ship. A moment later, there were the sickening sounds of ripping sails and splintering wood. Captain Fitzgerald turned to see shredded sails and pieces of the yard and mizzenmast falling to the deck. There was another explosion, followed by yet a third. The mizzenmast was snapped in two, and the top half fell back onto the quarterdeck. Several screams were mixed in with the crashing.

"Chain shot from the chase guns!" Timmy cried. He tried to hide his terror. The last pair of cannon balls, joined by a chain, kept going past the mizzenmast and struck the mainsail below him, ripping it nearly in two.

Timmy started to shout about the sails of a second frigate in the distance on the port side, but the fourth shot stuck the main mast, just below him. He clung tightly to the crow's nest railing as the top of the mast rocked forward and backward. He screamed helplessly when he heard the loud snap. The top of the mast, along with the crow's nest, tumbled to the deck with a loud crash, landing just before the forecastle.

There were no more explosions. The ship was suddenly eerily silent, except for what was left of the shredded sails flapping in the steady breeze and some soft moans. Captain Fitzgerald rushed to check on Timmy. A quick inspection confirmed the obvious. He then went back toward the quarterdeck to look for survivors. He had just reached the ladder when the black bowsprit of the *Bloody Seas* came into sight. With the loss of the mizzenmast and most of the mainsail, they were quickly overtaken. He walked back to the middle of the main deck and waited. Richard, pale and shaken, joined him.

The large frigate sailed up parallel to the merchant ship and then slowed its speed to match it. The pirate ship was truly a ghastly site. It was painted black from bowsprit to rudder and to the top of the masts. "Bloody Seas" was painted on the hull in bright, blood-red paint. Above the white sails, the large black flag flapped in the wind—the white skull, with glowing red eyes, sneering.

About half of the crew of ninety-nine lined the starboard side of the ship. They brandished a wide variety of weapons: cutlasses, axes, blunderbusses, and pistols. They growled, cursed, and grinned wicked grins at the unarmed sailors. Although not visible, Fitzgerald knew many more manned the guns below deck. He managed to hide his sheer terror. He appeared to wait calmly for a parley.

Finally, the mob of pirates parted, allowing an imposing figure to approach the rail. It was obvious this was Captain Bloodstone. He was a large man, well over six feet tall and weighing near 250 pounds. He was dressed in a long black coat with brass buttons, a red silk shirt, loose black breeches tucked into black leather boots that came to his knees. A large black belt with a brass buckle had at least four pistols hanging from it, as well as a cutlass and a dagger. A black tricorne hat completed the ensemble. Black curly hair flowed out from beneath the hat. His face, brown and leathered from years of weathering, bore a rough black beard. He closely resembled the late Blackbeard, one of the greatest pirate legends. Two other pirates followed close behind, probably the quartermaster and boatswain.

"Arrr! Who be the cap'n of this here ship?" Bloodstone called out in a deep, booming voice.

Captain Fitzgerald stepped forward. "It is I. Captain David Fitzgerald." His voice only shook a little.

"And what be ye haulin'?"

"Cloth—linen, cotton, a little silk. And some rum and provisions."

"Open your gangway and extend a plank. Get some hands haulin' your cargo up on deck," Bloodstone ordered as if it were his own crew.

Captain Fitzgerald shouted out orders. Most of his men rushed below deck through the open hatches and returned carrying crates of clothing, stacking them near the rail. A couple more removed the gangway and extended the gangplank from their ship to Bloodstone's. Several pirates lashed the two ships together with ropes, and a score or so rushed across the narrow plank and began grabbing crates and carrying them back to their ship. Several pirates stayed aboard the merchant ship to keep an eye on the captain, his first mate, and crew. All had flintlocks or cutlasses drawn.

When the cargo had all been transferred, Captain Bloodstone, accompanied by another pirate, walked across the plank. The other pirate was dark skinned and wore a black leather waistcoat with no shirt underneath and black leather pants. He wore a wide black slash around his waist, hung with pistols, and a black scarf on his head. A black patch covered his left eye. A scar extended above and below it. Although not as physically imposing, he was almost as intimidating. The other pirates moved aside to allow the two to reach the captain and his first mate.

"Ye been right helpful, Cap'n," Bloodstone said, now facing Fitzgerald. He then drew one of the pistols from his belt. "I'd like to let ye go to sail your empty ship back to the motherland. But that might hurt me reputation. Nothin' personal, ye see." He raised his pistol to the captain's head. Another pirate grabbed Richard as he started to move forward.

"Halt, you mean pirate!" a voice called out from beneath the quarterdeck.

Bloodstone and the pirates quickly turned to see the small, shirtless boy come rushing through the door of the captain's cabin brandishing a wooden sword. Bloodstone grinned as the boy ran across the deck, past the surprised pirates and sailors.

Suddenly, Captain Fitzgerald struck Bloodstone's arm with his hand, knocking the pistol away. Bloodstone stepped back just as Fitzgerald swung at his head with the other fist. The punch missed, but not that of Bloodstone's tanned companion. His fist crashed into Captain Fitzgerald's jaw, dropping him to the deck. Bloodstone leveled the pistol at the fallen captain's head and squeezed the trigger. The ball struck Fitzgerald in the top of the head, spraying blood and brains onto the deck and the boots of those closest to him.

"Frigate ahoy, bearin' hard from port!" a voice called out from the *Bloody Seas's* crow's nest. "'Pears to be navy."

"Blast it to Hades!" Bloodstone roared—a curse, not a command. By this time, Henry was almost to the pirate captain. Bloodstone turned to look at the boy and drew another pistol, dropping the empty one to dangle from his belt. The tanned pirate was closer to the boy and drew a long dagger. He made a step to intercept him.

"Hold, Diablo," Captain Bloodstone commanded. "Let's have a lookey at the swab."

"You killed the captain!" Henry shouted, pointing his sword at the huge pirate.

"He attacked me, swab. Just 'fendin' meself. But I like your spirit. Ye 'minds me of me at your age," Bloodstone said with a grin as the boy stopped before him, his sword a foot away from his stomach.

"Henry!" another voice cried from the captain's cabin. Mr. Wellington rushed out after his son.

One of the pirates reached out and grabbed him before he reached Diablo and Bloodstone. The wiry man wrapped his arms tightly around the businessman so he couldn't move.

"Do not harm my son! You have got the cargo. Please just leave us be!"

"The frigate's closin' fast," the pirate called out from the crow's nest.

"All this ruckus be ruinin' a good day! Hold him tight. Let me have a better look at this Henry." Bloodstone stared at Henry, who looked back and forth between his father and the pirate captain.

"Let my daddy go, or I'll run you through!" Henry yelled. The pirates laughed heartily at the boy.

"Well, blimey! Look at this. The boy be marked by the gods!" Bloodstone pointed to the dark birthmark on Henry's left chest. "Hmmm…looks like a bird. Maybe a hawk."

"Captain, we need to be leavin'," Diablo said, not impressed with the boy or his birthmark. He spoke with a slight Spanish accent.

"Aye. We be takin' this one with us though. He be marked and will be good luck. He's now the Hawk. Turner, take the boy to Wesley."

The tall, gangly pirate called Turner emerged from the throng and scooped Henry up. He threw him over his shoulder like a sack of grain. Henry yelled, screamed, kicked his legs, and tried to hit the pirate with his sword. Turner ignored the protests and quickly transported him over the plank and onto the pirate ship.

"That will give us one hundred men," Diablo stated, scowling after the Hawk.

"True enough, I reckon."

Bloodstone pointed his pistol at Mr. Wellington, cocked it, and pulled the trigger in one quick motion. The bullet struck him in the middle of the chest. He crumpled to the deck as the pirate holding him involuntarily released his hold. The pirate stumbled backward and looked down at his own chest. The ball had passed straight through Mr. Wellington and into him. A warm stream of blood ran down his white linen shirt. He dropped to his knees and looked up to see Bloodstone's slight grin. He finally collapsed forward onto the dead businessman, mouth and eyes still open.

"I count ninety-nine. Back to the *Seas*!"

James had watched the entire scene unfold, paralyzed in terror. His brother was taken by Bloodstone, surely to be tortured and murdered, and his father lay dead. He wanted to scream. He wanted to rush out and kill Bloodstone and the rest of the pirates. But he was frozen. Tears were the only things moving, flowing freely down his cheeks and onto his shirt as the nightmare continued.

Bloodstone and Diablo walked quickly back over the gangplank, followed closely by the dozen or so pirates left onboard. The ships were unlashed and the gangplank removed. The *Bloody Seas* began to drift away. The merchant crew stood in stunned silence. They were alive and were apparently going to survive the attack, but their captain lay dead before them, and all of their cargo, the source of their income, was gone. The ship was also dead in the water. Hopefully the approaching frigate belonged to the US Navy.

"We runnin' or fightin'?" Diablo asked Bloodstone once they were back aboard the *Bloody Seas*. They both walked quickly to the forecastle. The frigate clearly belonged to the fledgling US Navy. It was one of a half a dozen or so formidable warships built over the past few years.

Bloodstone emitted a deep growl and stroked his beard thoughtfully. "Blast 'em! We be sorely prepared for a battle like that. Plus the men be tired. And our belly is heavy with booty."

"What if they had to rescue innocent British sailors?" Diablo asked, glancing back at the merchant ship, its crew standing like statues.

"Well blow me down! Splendid idea it is!" Bloodstone clapped his quartermaster firmly on the shoulder. Diablo was several inches shorter, and much thinner, but solid muscle. He barely flinched. "Let's give 'em some fire to douse!"

Diablo grinned and quickly headed back down to the main deck, shouting orders as he went. "Give me all six guns of explosive shot and ready some granadoes." There was a flurry of activity as the pirates gleefully followed the orders. They all took great pleasure in being part of the most feared pirate crew of the era.

Bloodstone made sure the Hawk was below deck and then made his way back to the gangway. "Ho, first mate!" he called across to the other ship. First mate Cook made his way through the pirates to stand at his own gangway. "Ye may blame the US Navy for this. I wanted to set ye free." He turned back to Diablo. "Light the fuses."

Diablo shouted the orders to his men. The fuses on the eight explosive cannon balls were lit with slow matches most of the pirates kept in brass tubes strapped to their wrists or attached to their clothing and rolled into the cannon barrels. The men with granadoes likewise lit their fuses. "Fire away!"

A dozen granadoes were launched over the short expanse of water onto the merchant ship's deck. The sailors suddenly came to life and scattered, yelling and trying to avoid each other. The granadoes started exploding. Some sent shards of metal flying in all directions. Others contained burning cloth and tar, which set fire to the fallen sails and the deck. Next, the six cannons fired their explosive shells. The damage was massive, and bodies, and pieces of bodies, were strewn about the now flaming deck. Fire quickly engulfed the deck, masts, and sails.

"Bring 'er about. Strike the colors, hoist the sails, and steer 'er home!" Bloodstone shouted, turning away from the rail. The pirates quickly set about their sailing duties, and the *Bloody Seas* quickly distanced itself from the burning merchant ship. The screams eventually died out, either from the increasing distance, or the deaths of their owners. To Bloodstone's relief, the quickly approaching frigate steered directly toward the merchant ship to search for survivors.

CHAPTER II

PIRATE LIFE

"Well, what the devil you be doing here, little boy?"

Henry had been carried through an open hatch on the main deck, down a ladder, and onto the gun deck, where many pirates waited, ready to fire the cannons if ordered. He was carried across the deck and shoved roughly through a door into a small forward cabin. The only light came from a couple of small windows and an oil lamp burning on a table. It was sparsely furnished: a round table with several wooden chairs surrounding it, a bed with a small table beside it, and a large, high-backed cloth chair in the corner. Several shelves were built into the walls and were filled with well-worn books. Clothing was scattered carelessly about the floor.

The man talking was heavyset. He had a chubby red face, gray hair poking out from beneath a red scarf, a scruffy gray beard, and a pair of small round eyeglasses sitting halfway down his red nose. He sat in a chair on the far side of the table. He wore an old, stained, yellow-tinted, long-sleeved white shirt, unbuttoned halfway down to reveal curly gray hair on his chest, a pair of blue baggy breeches, and a brown sash that was tied around his waist for a belt. He had a brown, soft-leather, knee-high, boot on his right foot. His left leg was a wooden peg extending from the pant leg.

As Henry stared at the old pirate, the gravity of the events of the past two hours came crashing down on him. He was aboard a real pirate ship, with a pirate captain that had just shot and killed Captain Fitzgerald. A pirate held his father, and his brother was still in the captain's cabin aboard the other ship. Now an old man with a peg leg was addressing him. He dropped his sword, ran past the seated pirate, and dove onto the hard bed. He cried into the dirty pillow as hard as he had ever cried.

Henry heard the chair slide on the wooden floor and then the old pirate stand up and walk toward him. The clacking of the peg was slow and loud. He had no more bravado or fight left in him. If the pirates wanted to kill him, then so be it. He continued to cry and waited for a bullet or blade to enter him.

"What's that crazy pirate thinkin' now?" the old man asked as he settled heavily into the large blue-cloth chair on the other side of the bed. "What's your name, boy?"

Henry snuck a peak at him from underneath his hand, which covered the side of his face. He still sobbed, but the tears had mostly quit falling. "Henry," he said quietly.

"Well, I'm Wesley. I'm the cook on this heap o' boards. Don't s'ppose the cap'n told you what I'm to do with you, did he?"

"No. I hope he's dead by now!"

Wesley chuckled. "Don't reckon you'd be the only one. Maybe someday, lad, but I doubt today's that day."

"He killed our captain! And another pirate is holding my daddy. And my brother is hiding all scared in the captain's cabin." Henry turned over on his side, so he could look at Wesley. He wiped the remaining tears from the corners of his eyes. "He won't kill them all will he?"

"Hmmm. Cap'n Bloodstone's a hard 'un to figure, son. I've been sailin' with him for nigh ten years now and still can't make him. Maybe not…maybe not."

"What's he going to do with me?" Henry asked, now staring in fascination at the wooden leg.

"I reckon you'll be our swab. Cap'n must be fond of you though. Never took on a young'n before."

"What's a swab?"

"A swab cleans the decks and does other such dirty chores about the ship. Hard work, but not too bad for a healthy lad such as yourself."

Suddenly Henry heard loud booms. They sounded like they came from somewhere above them, but not from the cannons just outside the cabin. The ship rocked backward and forward from the force. Henry didn't know exactly what the sounds were, but he knew enough to not need to ask. He rolled back over and buried his face in the pillow.

Wesley walked back over to the table, sat down, and resumed reading his book. He wasn't sure what to do about young Henry, so he decided to let him cry it out until Captain Bloodstone came to enlighten him more about the plan.

The wait wasn't very long. The hulking captain soon came in and shut the door behind him. "Mr. Wesley, I assume ye met the Hawk?" Bloodstone walked over to the big chair and collapsed wearily into it.

"The Hawk, Cap'n?" Wesley turned in the chair so he could see the captain and Henry.

"Hawk! Stop your blubberin' and turn 'round here so Wesley can have a look at ye."

Henry slowly rolled over and sat up in the bed. He looked briefly through wet, reddened eyes at Bloodstone and then at Wesley.

"Now, don't that mark on his chest look right smart like a hawk?" Bloodstone asked.

Wesley leaned toward the small boy and looked over his gold-rimmed glasses. "Well, I reckon it do, Cap'n."

"What did you do to my father and brother?" Henry demanded.

Bloodstone stared at Henry, a little perturbed by the tone of his voice. "It's a right woeful tale indeed."

Henry's bottom lip rolled down, and his red eyes moistened again.

"Now, there'll be no more or your blasted cryin', Hawk! Wipe your eyes and listen to what I have to say."

Henry wiped his eyes and did his best to not cry.

"Well, me, your father, and the first mate were parleyin' right civilized like, when to me surprise we were set upon. A Spanish frigate had sailed right up to us and opened fire. Evil devils those Spaniards are! Me crew and I managed to get back aboard the *Seas*. But I'm afraid your daddy and brother and all of the other matey's on your ship didn't fare so well. We'd saved 'em all if we could, I swear to ye, but the scurvy dogs had us all dead to rights. We fired our cannons at the mangy curs and sent 'em runnin' like bilge rats, we did. But your ship was up in flames by then."

Henry's lip quivered again, and he quickly wiped at his eyes. "But I saw you kill my captain!"

"Be respectful, lad," Wesley interjected, before Bloodstone could.

"Ye also seen him attack me. Punched me sorely in me jaw he did. I never wanted to harm the man. Seemed like a right solid cap'n, he did. But I had no idea if he had a pistol stashed or a dagger meant for me belly. Had to shoot him, lad. It be him or me at that point. Just a sad day, all the way 'round, it is."

Henry stared at Bloodstone. The captain seemed like he was telling the truth. But Henry's mind was reeling. His father and brother were dead. He was all alone in the New World and now onboard a pirate ship. He was tired, sad, and scared. He couldn't speak.

"Keep your chin up, lad. Got ye a home right here, ye do. As we say, t'morrow be a new day. It'll be some right hard work, but there's lots of adventures and excitement on the open sea. Ain't that right, Wesley?"

"That definitely *ain't* a lie."

Bloodstone glared at Wesley. Henry looked back and forth between the two men, not understanding the gaze they exchanged. Finally, Bloodstone's face softened a little. "Mr. Wesley's gonna fix us all some dinner directly now. Ye can eat and then get some sleep."

Wesley brought Henry a plate of food a short while later. He thought it would be best not to have the frightened lad dine with the crew. They had been out to sea for a while, and after yet another successful battle, they were heading home. The men would be happy, rambunctious, and drinking lots of rum.

"Here you go, lad. It's some rough fare to be sure. We've been at sea for a while now. You can sleep in my bed tonight, and I'll sleep in the chair." Wesley set the plate and a glass of water on the table and headed back to tend to the rest of the hungry crew.

Henry crawled out of the bed and sat down at the table. The meal consisted of brown beans, salted pork, and hardtack biscuits. Wesley had told the truth about the food, but Henry was starving. He gobbled down the meal and washed it down with the dingy, warm water. He then climbed back into the big bed, covered up under the foul-smelling blankets, and quickly fell to sleep.

Shafts of light from the small windows illuminated the room the next morning. Henry quickly sat up, blinked hard, and looked around. He was disappointed to see that the previous day and night weren't a dream, and he was indeed on a pirate ship. The cabin door opened and Wesley limped in, once again carrying a plate of food and a glass of water.

While Henry ate breakfast—boiled eggs, salted beef, and hardtack—Wesley moved busily about the cabin, searching through piles of clothing on the floor. He finally pulled up a stained white shirt. He drew his dagger and began cutting and ripping on it. "Once you finish eatin', try this on."

Henry ate quickly and put on the shirt. Wesley had cut a foot or so off of the bottom and several inches off of the sleeves. It was still large, but not too much so. Henry only buttoned it halfway up, leaving his chest, and birthmark, visible. Wesley then tied a red scarf around Henry's waist. He picked up Henry's wooden sword off of the floor and stuck it underneath the scarf up to the hilt.

"Not a bad lookin' swab at all. Now, let's find you some work to do." Wesley knew the best thing for Henry would be to keep him busy. There was definitely a lot of work to be done and a lot to learn on a pirate ship.

Henry's thoughts turned briefly to his brother and father and all of the other people on the other ship—but only briefly. Wesley led him up the ladder to the main deck. It was much larger than the merchant ship he had sailed on from England, but the deck was laid out similarly. At the front of the ship—the bow—two sets of steep ladders, one on each side, led up to a deck called the forecastle. At the rear—the stern—two more sets of ladders led up to the quarterdeck. On this deck stood the large wheel that steered the ship, along with a binnacle that housed the compass. Captain Bloodstone's cabin was beneath the quarterdeck. Quartermaster Diablo's was beneath the forecastle.

There were three tall masts hung with lots of square sails. The ratlines, rigging, and shrouds that connected the sails, booms, yards, spars, and masts to the ship fascinated Henry. A number of pirates could be seen scampering up and down the ratlines at any given time, and there was a pirate, the topman, who stood in the crow's nest, high above the mainmast. Weapon racks and cannons lined the rails of all of the decks. A longboat was secured to each side of the main deck. Wesley said he would show him the lower decks once all of the pirates were awake and moving about.

Wesley found Henry an old mop and a bucket of water and set him to mopping all of the upper decks. There was quite a mess left over from the celebration the night before. A number of pirates milled about the deck, and some tended the sails, but most were sleeping off the celebration. Everyone seemed friendly, but they were mostly quiet and subdued.

Henry examined the weapon racks closer as he worked. There were a number of different types of guns, swords, spears, axes, and boarding pikes. Tarps were close by that covered the weapons in bad weather. Granadoes were stored in wooden chests. He wondered what it was like to shoot all of the guns. He also wondered if he could have a real sword or dagger to replace his own. He was really captivated by the big iron cannons—six on each side of the main deck, four on the stern and four on the bow—along with the different types of ammunition stacked around them. The sky was almost cloudless and deep blue, and the sun soon grew hot. There wasn't much of a breeze that day. To the starboard side of the ship, and at the limits of sight, he could see land. He wondered if it was the New World.

He quickly grew unhappy with mopping. He was already hot, tired, and sweaty. When he realized no one was paying attention, he quickened his pace and barely brushed over large sections. By the time he got to the forecastle, his bucket was empty, so he mopped with a dry mop.

Luckily, no pirates were close by. When he finished, he went searching for Wesley.

He found him in the galley—the large kitchen and dining area on the gun deck beside his cabin—cooking lunch. "I'm done, Mr. Wesley," he said proudly.

"Done, eh?" Wesley turned to look at the sweat-covered boy. His own face was red and shining with perspiration. "Guess it's time to show you the rest of the ship, huh?"

Henry frowned.

"It's a big job, lad, and dirty." Wesley took the bucket from Henry and filled it with water from a spout sticking out of a water barrel. He handed the heavy bucket back to the boy and led him out onto the gun deck.

This deck was full cannons and cannon balls. The cannons were chained to the walls and floor, with the balls stacked behind them in shot garlands. Rammers and swabbing sponger rods were fastened overhead. Buckets of water sat nearby, with linstocks propped against them. The air was comfortable here and the lighting good, since most of the gunports were open and allowed the breeze and light to enter. At the far end of the ship there were doors leading to the officers' cabins. Some of the pirates sat in the corners on the floor eating their lunches.

Another hatch and ladder led to the orlop deck. Most of the pirate crew was found here. Some were still sleeping in hammocks hanging from the ceiling, spaced only inches apart, but most were moving about rolling up their hammocks and storing them in the racks on the ceiling and walls. Many were climbing up the ladders to the upper decks. There were a couple of metal frames with handles on each side set into the floor. Wesley explained they were pumps used to clear the hold if they were taking on water. The stern side of the deck had doors leading into the infirmary. There wasn't much else on this deck other than a couple of open areas for dining and gaming. The air was hot and stale, with no windows or gunports, and smelled of sweat, unwashed bodies, and urine. Several lamps hanging from the ceiling provided the only light.

The last deck was the hold, in the very bottom of the ship. The hold was almost completely filled with casks and crates of food, water, rum, and loot they had taken, including the crates of clothing from Henry's cargo ship. He thought of his father and brother again and his eyes glazed over. There were also a couple of pens with straw on the floor inside. It looked like they had housed animals, although they were empty now. The air was thick, hot, humid, and difficult to breathe. It reeked of rotten meat and mold. Wesley had to duck to walk beneath the low ceiling. At the far end of the stern side of the deck was the magazine—full of casks of powder, fuses, and ammunition. Wesley told Henry to stay away from that area.

Wesley noticed Henry was quite and then saw his glassy eyes. "Watch out for the bilge rats down here. Big as cats! Once you finish, get some more water from that cask over yonder, and then swab the deck above. The crew should be out of your way by then."

Henry was a little scared after Wesley climbed up the ladder. There were no windows in the hold, or even gunports. A couple of hanging oil lamps provided the only light. They also created large moving shadows. He hoped Wesley was joking about the size of the rats, but he did hear a lot of scurrying and gnawing. He quickly mopped what floor was exposed, refilled the bucket, and climbed up to the next deck.

Once the mopping of all of the decks was complete, Henry returned to Wesley's cabin. Wesley fixed him hardtack and a bowl of what he called pirate stew—a watery broth with chunks of several types of meat—and let him eat in his cabin at the table. Afterward, Henry climbed into the bed and napped for several hours. The sun was low on the starboard side when Wesley woke him.

"Time to meet the crew."

Most of the pirates were scattered about the upper decks. One large group was gathered in a circle watching a pair throw dice in the middle. The crowd was loud and boisterous. Another large group was singing crude songs as an older pirate played a violin. Several smaller groups were scattered here and there, playing cards or other games of chance or telling stories. Wesley led him up the ladder to the forecastle. Captain Bloodstone stood there looking down on his crew below. Five other pirates were with him.

"There be little Hawk! How's your first day a piratin'?"

"Fine, sir. Hard work though."

The pirates, including Bloodstone, chuckled. "I s'ppose it is. Lot's o' good times too. I'd like ye to meet me officers. This here is Diablo, me quartermaster. He's mean as a snake, he is, but a good hand. All of the pirates answer to him."

Henry looked at Diablo. He was the dark skinned pirate that had almost grabbed him before he reached Bloodstone on the merchant ship. Diablo glared coldly at him with his one good eye, barely nodding his head. Henry didn't like Diablo.

"And Spider here is me bosun. He can climb like a spider. He handles the sails and riggin' and such. Makes sure we have as much or little sail as we need."

Spider was a short, wiry man. He stood a little hunched over, and his arms appeared too long for his body. He wore tight brown pants cut off just below the knees, a white cotton shirt with the sleeves cut off, and a red scarf tied around his head. A number of daggers hung from the sash around his waist. He grinned at Henry, a grin missing a couple of teeth. He seemed nice enough.

"Next be me gunner. Andre, we call him. He be a Frenchman, and you'll sure as not understand him, but he can sure as the blazes make some bombs."

Andre was dressed in fine clothes: white stockings leading up to tight blue breeches, a black belt, a blue doublet with brass buttons, a white silk shirt, and a blue waistcoat. He wore a scarf around his neck and a blue tricorne hat with a feather sticking out. He had shoulder-length black hair and a thin black mustache. He exuded an air of royalty. He removed his hat and bowed low. "My pleasure, Mr. Hawk," he said in a thick French accent.

"Next we have Mr. Bones. Bones is me surgeon and carpenter. If it needs a fixin', Mr. Bones is the man to fix it. Just ask Wesley and Diablo." Bloodstone chuckled.

Mr. Bones was tall, maybe as tall as Bloodstone. He was very skinny, but not in the strong wiry way that Spider was. He was dressed in fine black breeches that almost came to his ankles, a white ruffled silk shirt, and a bright red doublet with brass buttons. A black tricorne hat finished the ensemble. He smiled at Henry and gave a little bow. "A pleasure to make your acquaintance, Mr. Hawk." He spoke in a British accent. Henry liked Mr. Bones.

"Me navigator, Hobbs. He handles the charts and steers the ship. Never been lost a day in his life." Bloodstone clapped the navigator hard on the shoulder.

Hobbs was a short, heavyset man, probably not much younger than Wesley. His cheeks were puffy and red, and he wore a pair of small round glasses. His balding head was uncovered, and the setting sun reflected off the top. He looked out of place aboard a pirate ship. "Well met, young Hawk.

"Ye'll be workin' closely with me crew here. They're gonna teach ye all about piratin'. You're a swab for now, lad, but ye'll be a pirate one day—a good one too, I'll wager. Ye'll bunk with Wesley, and he'll teach you readin' and writin'."

Bloodstone detached a sheathed dagger from his belt. "Now, take this here dagger. Even a swab needs a blade for his chores. Just don't go cuttin' yourself." The sheath was shiny black leather, and the hilt of the dagger appeared to be ivory with a red gem in the middle. "Go ahead. Take it, boy."

Henry reverently reached out his little hands and took the dagger. It was almost a foot long and was very heavy. He slowly pulled it out of the sheath. The silver blade shone brightly in the rays of the setting sun. It looked like the knife had never been used. Bloodstone, Bones, Spider, Hobbs, and Wesley all laughed at the boy's amazement. Henry didn't notice Diablo's scowl and gaze that could have killed.

"Arrr!" Bloodstone shouted, as he turned from Henry and faced the pirates below. "Listen up, ye bunch of bilge rats!" he shouted. This time his booming voice stopped all of the noise. All eyes were upon the captain.

"This here lad is our new swab. Henry be his God-given name. But he be marked by the gods. Show 'em your mark, lad."

Henry looked at the imposing captain, handed his dagger to Wesley, and then unbuttoned his shirt all the way and spread it open. He retrieved his dagger and stared at the pirates below.

"That be a hawk, or I swear I've never seen one. From this day forward, he is the Hawk. He be a swab for now, but he also be learnin' to be a pirate. I gave him me prized dagger, I did, cause he's marked by the gods, I'm gonna treat him as good as if he be me own boy. And if anyone harms a hair on his head, they just as soon be harmin' me. Now, let's hear it for the Hawk!"

The pirate crew below started cheering, and then even started chanting, "Hawk, Hawk, Hawk." Some fired their pistols into the air; others drew their swords and waived them about. Henry was amazed. He looked up at Wesley, who reached down and rubbed his head. Henry then looked up at Bloodstone, who grinned and winked. Bones and Spider both nodded in approval. Diablo met his gaze briefly, and then turned away, a heavy scowl still on his face.

Henry turned back to the pirates, drew his dagger out of the sheath, and held it in the air. The roar grew even louder.

CHAPTER III

THE ROCK

The last week of the voyage passed quickly for Henry. Wesley made sure he stayed busy with plenty of chores. By the time dinner was over, and Wesley had read him some verses out of a big book called the Holy Bible, Henry would be fast asleep. Wesley had tied up a hammock for Henry in the corner of his cabin.

Henry learned much more than just swabbing a deck that week. He spent time with Spider, who taught him how to climb the ratlines, rigging, and ropes. Henry loved that. Spider compared him to a monkey. He quickly learned to go barefoot on the ship, like most of the other pirates, to aid with the climbing. He learned all about sails, booms, spars, gaffs, sheets, braces, and rigging. He soon knew about sailing with the wind, and tacking into it, and understood what made a ship move.

He also spent time with Mr. Bones. Not only was Mr. Bones the carpenter and surgeon, he also repaired sails. There were several holes to patch in the hull and a couple of sails to mend from the battles they had fought prior to capturing Henry. He liked the Englishman. He didn't seem to fit in with the rest of the rude and crude pirates and did indeed keep to himself most of the time. But he was friendly enough when engaged.

Andre showed him the workings of cannons and the many different types of cannon balls he could make: chain shot, canister shot, grape shot, explosive shells, hot iron shot, sangrenel, and regular round shot. He seemed to take great pleasure in devising new and deadlier weapons. He showed him how to make powder cartridges to load into the cannons and smaller cartridges for the other guns. He also made the granadoes and tended to all of the muskets, blunderbusses, and pistols.

Hobbs had a very interesting job. He stayed mostly on the quarterdeck, steering the ship with the large wheel, which turned the rudder on the stern of the ship. He also maintained charts on the waters and islands of the Caribbean and the Atlantic coast. He had a large compass housed in a binnacle, a ring sundial, an astrolabe, sounding leads, and a backstaff. He had to constantly know the latitude of the ship, the direction it was heading, the depth of the water, and where they were on the chart. His cabin was on the main deck below the sterncastle, next to Bloodstone's, so he could always be close to the helm. A couple other pirates could man the helm when Hobbs needed a break or sleep, although none were as skilled as him.

Henry didn't see Captain Bloodstone very much. He stayed in his cabin a lot of the time. He would come out and make a couple of rounds about the ship, speak to most of the men, and then disappear again. Occasionally he would poke his head into Wesley's cabin to speak to both of them.

The pirates were a strange collection. They were from all parts of the world and had many different accents. Some went by first names, some last names, some nicknames, and some just made up a new name upon joining the crew. A lot of them had unique ways of dressing too. Most of their clothing came from the ships they took. Some dressed like naval officers from the various countries—most common were England, Spain, and France. There were short breeches, long breeches, long coats, doublets, waistcoats, baggy clothes, tight clothes, shirts, and clothing made of leather, silk, cotton, velvet, and linen. Some of the pirates merely wore clothing made from canvas. Every color was represented, and many wore a mismatch of colors. Most wore hats or scarves on their heads. Some had scarves about their necks, and almost all wore a sash around the waist or a belt. Many wore earrings in their ears. Most went barefoot aboard the ship or wore rope sandals. Henry was told that boots were mainly for fighting. Weapons were plentiful. Most of the men had several pistols and daggers on their persons at all times.

Most worked hard about the ship during the day, and then in the evenings, after a steadily declining fare for supper, they enjoyed themselves on the top decks. They rolled dice and played cards and backgammon. Some sang and danced to the musicians playing fiddles, penny whistles, and lyres. The musicians were regular pirates by day and music makers at night. Storytelling was also a popular pastime. Most drank a foul-smelling drink they called rum. Henry knew it must be good though, because they seemed very happy when drinking it and got happier the more they drank. The ones that drank the most seemed to sleep the latest in the mornings.

All of the pirates treated him well. He spent most of his time with Wesley, Spider, and Mr. Bones. Diablo was the only pirate that frightened him. The quartermaster hardly spoke to him. When he did it was almost always to command him to move out of the way or fetch something. He tried his best to avoid him. He thought about his father and brother some, but he stayed so busy he didn't have a lot of free time to think. He followed the captain's orders and didn't cry again. All in all, he was content with his new life.

The pirates kept time by ringing a bell on the main deck every half hour—all day and night. Someone was always at the helm and several on watch. As the days passed, the pirates talked more and more about a place they called the Rock. It was an island that they considered their home. On the morning of the sixth day, Billy Hawkins—at about sixteen the youngest pirate after Henry—cried out from the crow's nest, "Rock ho!"

There was bustling about the ship that quickly grew louder and busier. Pirates began to rush onto the main deck from down below. Henry ran to the forecastle railing to see the source of the excitement. On the starboard side of the ship was a long strip of land, covered with thick brush and trees. The land rose up to a tree-covered ridge that stretched the length of it. They rounded the tip of strip and came to the mouth of an inlet. Another island, or possibly part of the same larger island, was on the port side, and the one they had just rounded on the starboard.

Most of the canvas was reefed, and they sailed cautiously into the inlet. Ahead of them, large trees blocked off the water, stretching across from each side. It appeared that the ship was going to crash into them. Suddenly, Diablo, who had walked up close to him, blew into a curved brass horn. He blew two quick bursts. There was a rustling sound from both landmasses, followed by a loud creaking. To Henry's amazement, the two large trees began to rise out of the water. Foot by foot they slowly raised until soon they stood on their respective beaches. The *Bloody Seas* sailed past the trees, which could be heard being lowered back into the water behind them. A sheltered cove lay beyond, closed in by land on three sides. A smaller, two-masted schooner was anchored close to the beach on the port side. Their ship sailed up beside it. An anchor was dropped off the stern and the sails fully lowered. Another group of pirates, probably fifty strong, was on the beach in front of them, waving and cheering enthusiastically.

The longboats were lowered into the water, and rope ladders were thrown over the sides of the ship. Pirates stationed themselves in a line that stretched from the hatches, across the deck, and down the rope ladders. They quickly went to work transferring cargo from the hold to the longboats. When a boat was full, two pirates rowed to shore where the waiting pirates quickly grabbed the crates, casks, and sacks, headed up the beach, and disappeared into the green vegetation. The boats were rowed back to the ship, and the process was repeated. There was a lot of cargo, but with almost 150 pirates working hard, the ship was soon empty. Then the longboats set about transferring the pirate crew to the shore. Eventually all of the pirates, including Henry and Wesley, were on dry land.

The pirates then picked up the remaining cargo and headed into the thick vegetation past the sandy beach. Henry grabbed a sack of grain and fell into line. A trail wound its way through thick bushes and growth that was taller than Henry's head. A sword would have been needed if someone wanted to leave the trail and explore. Most of the pirates held the crates and barrels on their heads or shoulders, above the vegetation. Gradually, the thick undergrowth gave way to a pine forest. Henry was instantly fascinated by this stretch of land. The pines limbs high above were thick and blocked out most of the sun's light. On the ground, the forest was mostly open.

"There's ol' Razortooth," Wesley said, huffing behind Henry.

The boy followed his gaze to a large round pond. After a moment, he saw the enormous alligator submerged just below the surface, about ten feet from the closest bank. Only its head was above the water. Its large, evil, unblinking eyes watched the pirates pass. "Does it ever bite anyone?" said Henry.

"Aye, we've lost a mate or two over the years. They got a little too drunk and wandered a little too close," Wesley said.

"Why don't you shoot it with your guns?" Henry asked, still staring back at Razortooth even though he was well past.

"The cap'n likes him. Calls him his pet." Wesley chuckled, but Henry didn't find the humor.

The land began to rise, and the soft, sandy ground transitioned to firmer dirt. Soon the pine trees gave away to older, taller oak trees. The forest wasn't as open here, but it still begged to be explored. They passed another couple of ponds, but Henry didn't see any alligators. As the land rose, it also became rockier, with large boulders strewn about. Then, suddenly, the trees were gone. Straight ahead was a huge clearing of tall grass, and tree stumps were scattered about.

In the middle of the clearing was wooden palisade. It was almost ten feet tall and made of the rough-hewn lumber from the trees that used to fill the clearing. Square gunports were cut out of the bottom half of the wall every ten feet or so. A cannon barrel could be seen in each. Other smaller round holes were cut about halfway up the walls, spaced in between the cannons.

The palisade was three sided. The fourth side was a rock wall—the base of a large, mostly barren, rocky mountain. The top of the mountain was flat, with only a few small bushes visible. Henry realized that must be the Rock. The trail led up to a wooden gate, which was open. He followed the pirates in, his mouth hanging open in amazement.

There were six small, thatched-roof huts standing in the right half of the enclosure and two large wooden buildings on the left. Straight back were two wooden doors set into the rock, their hinges bolted into the stone. Cannons lined the three palisade walls, and muskets and blunderbusses leaned against the wall in between.

The pirates split up and carried their spoils to various places. The barrels and casks went through the right door in the mountain, behind which was a cave. Some of the crates went into the smaller of the two buildings on the left and the remainder in the cave behind the other door in the mountain.

One of the large buildings contained the galley, dining area, and food storage, where Wesley kept an abundance of dry food, fruits, vegetables, and spices. Extra fruits and vegetables were stored in one of the cool caves. There was also a freshwater spring in that cave that supplied all the clean, cold water they needed. The island was a paradise for the pirates. The great meals and nutrition got them through the rough days on the sea.

One of the six huts was assigned to Wesley, and Henry continued to stay with him, still sleeping in a hammock. Bloodstone and his other officers occupied the other huts. Andre and Hobbs shared one. The remainder of pirates slept in hammocks in the other large building.

The next day, Bloodstone and about half the pirates took the schooner and sailed to a city called New Orleans to sell the loot they didn't need and to buy some items that they did. They were gone for a couple of days. Henry was glad that Diablo went with him. Mr. Bones and several helpers worked on careening the *Bloody Seas* in the harbor. They laid it on its side using large ropes tied to tree stumps and stakes, and the large anchor, to hold it in place. Then the pirates scraped off barnacles—which slowed its speed—repaired and replaced damaged boards, and applied a mixture of tallow, oil, and brimstone. Then the hull was repainted black. The sails were also repaired.

Henry loved life at the Rock. There wasn't near as much work to do, and the food was much better—fresher too. A group of designated

hunters, fishermen, and gatherers went out almost every day. The hunters came back with deer, wild goat, boar, rabbits, squirrels, turtles,
pheasants, and doves. The fisherman caught flounder, sea bass, perch,
and crabs. The gatherers knew where to find figs, limes, dates, papaya,
grapes, and wild onions.

Henry learned a lot more about pirate life at the Rock. The pirates
had a list of rules, called articles. They governed every part of being a
pirate, including how to divide up treasure: Captain Bloodstone got two
shares; Diablo, Wesley, Spider, Andre, and Mr. Bones got one and a half,
and the remainder of the pirates got one share each. Bloodstone also
gave Henry a share for his first voyage. He received one gold coin, called
a doubloon, and two silver pieces called pieces of eight. He was fascinated by the treasure and kept the coins in a small leather pouch, which
Wesley had given him, tied inside the sash around his waist.

The pirates also got together and voted on their next adventure.
Usually Bloodstone made his suggestion, and everyone else eagerly approved. They kept a record of which pirates were going to make up the
ninety-nine and which ones had to stay behind. The ninety-nine was
just a superstition that Bloodstone had. He said it was his lucky number. However, there were a number of pirates who no longer sailed.
Some stayed behind due to amputations and permanent injuries, others because they were too old. Some stayed behind only until their injuries healed sufficiently. Bloodstone, Wesley, Spider, Hobbs, Andre,
and Mr. Bones always went. The crew also periodically voted for captain. But Bloodstone always ran unopposed and was always reelected
unanimously.

Henry liked to go out with the hunters and gatherers and explore the
island. The pirates were the only people living on it. The only things that
scared him were the alligators. Several more of the freshwater ponds
had alligators in them, but none as big as Razortooth. If the pirates
were hungry enough, they would kill a gator, but that was a last resort.
Sometimes, Henry would wander off by himself, brandishing his dagger
in place of his wooden sword, attacking any tree or bush that got in his
way. He would also fling it at any animal within throwing distance.

He didn't totally forget about his father and brother, but their images, and the prior six years of his life, quickly faded into distant memories—almost dreams. His new life was good and exciting. He had chores to do, but he also had a lot of free time to do as he pleased. Bloodstone was stern and strict but didn't care about little things such as bedtime and if he were in sight at all times or not. He also knew that life would only get better when he was old enough to learn how to shoot guns and cannons, fight with swords and daggers, and capture Spanish ships.

In the evenings, Wesley taught Henry how to read and write. Most of the pirates could do neither. A lot of the reading came from the Bible. Wesley read passages to Henry, until Henry was old enough to read them to Wesley. He also had a number of other books, including the *Iliad*, the *Odyssey*, the *Aeneid*, *Robinson Crusoe*, *Don Quixote*, and countless others. Any time they captured a ship, the pirates would give any books found to Wesley and any charts and maps to Hobbs. Henry loved the stories of adventure and great battles most of all, but he didn't realize at the time that he was embarking on an adventurous life just as exciting as any of the books they read.

CHAPTER IV

FIRST BLOOD

When Henry was eight, he was taught how to use firearms. He learned how to load and shoot muskets, blunderbusses, and flintlocks. Andre was his teacher. Not only did he make and maintain the weapons, he was the best shot with each. The muskets were heavy and kicked hard, but Henry was a quick learner. After practicing on targets, he began to hunt with the hunters. He killed his first deer that same year. Most of the pirates were proficient with guns, but they didn't really practice. Most battles ended up being fought with swords, after the first rifle volley or two, so shooting wasn't a skill they honed. But since Henry wasn't allowed to fight in battles yet, he practiced shooting.

Captain Bloodstone himself taught Henry hand-to-hand combat. Bloodstone found him a cutlass that was shorter and lighter than most. It was still heavy, and Henry was limited in his ability, but he learned to wield it and the basic fighting tactics. He also practiced with axes and daggers. Most of his time at the Rock was now spent shooting, hunting, and sparring. He couldn't outfight anyone with a sword yet, but he soon surprised most of his sparring partners with his quickness and cunning.

Over the next few years, Henry got to go on most of Bloodstone's voyages. After everyone started referring to him as the Hawk, or Hawk, he eventually stopped thinking of himself as Henry. Henry was soon a distant memory, along with his family and prior life. He was now simply Hawk. He still swabbed the decks, but quickly became a helpful hand about the ship. He bounced around from Wesley to Spider to Andre to Mr. Bones to Hobbs. Diablo was the only one of the officers who didn't want his help.

He spent most of his time helping Spider with the sails and rigging. Spider was a kind, easygoing man. He liked to joke, laugh, sing, and entertain Henry and anyone else nearby. His singing was bad, but his songs were always entertaining. Spider was much older than Henry, but easily adjusted down to his level. He seemed to never have a bad day. Henry soon became the best ratline climber on the ship. He was usually the one that manned the crow's nest—the topman—to spot enemy sails. But when a battle was imminent, he had to go to Wesley's cabin until it was over. Bloodstone would hear none of his protests.

With Hawk's intelligence and reading skills, he also became a skilled chart reader and navigator under the tutelage of Hobbs. Bloodstone and Wesley told him that was an invaluable skill; not even Bloodstone or Diablo could navigate. If a navigator made a mistake and didn't know the bearings of the ship or where it was heading, the results could be disastrous. A reef below the surface could slice the hull open and sink a ship. Or a ship could ground on a sandbar or become lost at sea, resulting in starvation and dehydration when supplies ran out. Hawk could soon read the charts, use the navigation instruments, and read the stars at night.

They were successful in almost all of their battles. The only time they didn't take their prize was when a warship intervened. Bloodstone rarely engaged any of the navy ships of any country—he liked to take easy merchant prizes. After the battles, Hawk usually helped Mr. Bones patch up wounded pirates. Occasionally they had to amputate an arm or leg. That task consisted of giving the pirate some rum to drink, something hard to bite on, holding his good limbs down, and sawing off the injured one. Mr. Bones then stitched it closed with catgut. Afterward, the injured pirate received a sum of money from Bloodstone, depending on which limb was removed, as per the articles. Mr. Bones was also constantly stitching up minor cuts and bullet holes. There was also a good supply of ointments, tinctures, teas, and salves for any other sickness or disease in the infirmary. Medicine was something else taken from their "prizes".

Usually, a few pirates were killed in every battle. If they weren't close to the Rock, chain shot was tied to their legs, and they were tossed overboard to quickly sink to the bottom of the ocean. Wesley usually said a few words and a short prayer. Death was just an accepted fact aboard the ship. No tears were shed. New pirates were recruited, when needed, from the crews of captured ships or from slaver ships' cargo.

They were sailing the schooner on one particular voyage and had a much smaller crew than usual. "Hawk! Get your lazy bones out of your blasted hammock and out on the deck!" Bloodstone roared.

Hawk nearly fell onto the floor trying to wake up and extricate himself from the hammock. "Sorry, Captain," Hawk said, now standing before the imposing man. Hawk was large for twelve years old, already showing broad shoulders and some definition to the muscles on his naked upper body. But he was still dwarfed by Bloodstone.

"Can ye feel it, boy?" Bloodstone asked, ignoring the apology.

"Feel what, sir?"

"Feels like it be a good day for some killin'!"

"Killing? Do I get to fight today?" Hawk asked, his heart suddenly racing wildly.

"Aye. Least some shootin'. Now get ye dressed and meet me on the deck."

Hawk quickly slipped out of the baggy tan breeches he slept in and into his tight blue linen pair. He found the tight pants were easier for climbing the rigging. He tied a red sash around his waist, slipped his sheathed dagger into it, and pulled on a white cotton shirt. He left it unbuttoned, as was his want. He didn't wear a scarf or hat on his head, and his blond hair was still tussled from sleep.

As he emerged from the cabin, he felt something amiss. The ship was listing to port, like it was taking on water. The pirates that weren't manning the cannons were rushing up and down through the hatches, carrying various things in their hands. Hawk quickly climbed up to the main deck. He looked up to see the sails in total disarray, most torn or removed entirely. Men were taking sails and pieces of wood and placing them into empty barrels. There were at least four of these barrels spaced about the upper decks.

"What—?" said Hawk.

Suddenly there were two explosions from beneath the main deck. They were from cannons, but no ship was attacking. The schooner rocked hard to port then back to starboard. "What's going on?" he called out to Captain Bloodstone.

"The art of deception, me boy," Bloodstone replied with a wink. "Hoist the flag!" he called out to the pirate closest to the main mast. Hawk watched as the flag was raised. Only it wasn't theirs; it was a Spanish flag.

"I think this is the craziest scheme you have ever had," Mr. Bones said as he and Andre approached the two.

Bloodstone laughed. "Don't want me men to get bored, I reckon."

"Do you know how long it will take to repair the hull and sails? What is left of the sails, that is." Mr. Bones was as serious as Hawk had seen him.

"That be why we're in the blasted schooner, Bones," Bloodstone said, his temper flashing. "Besides, ye might not need to."

"What's going on?" Hawk finally demanded, looking back and forth between the three men.

"Our captain had the crew move all of the cargo to the port side, causing the ship to list," said Mr. Bones. "Then he had them destroy most of the sails. And he instructed Mr. Andre to shoot two cannon balls through the starboard hull to make it look like we were attacked. And I assume we are going to set those barrels of wood and sails ablaze shortly to make it look like we are on fire."

Hawk looked incredulously at Bloodstone. "Why are you doing all of that?"

"There be a Spanish galleon, belly bulgin' with loot, I wager, sailin' this way out of the Windward Passage. I imagine they'll stop to help a fellow Spanish ship in distress." A grin on Bloodstone's face replaced the scowl that Mr. Bones had earned. "Andre, ye be ready below deck?"

"But of course, my Captain." Andre was clearly excited at the prospect of another battle.

"Hawk, scamper up to the crows nest. Be ready with the muskets. Ye'll know what to do when the time comes. Aye, good day for some killin'." Bloodstone walked away seeking Diablo, shouting orders to any pirate he passed.

Hawk's heart started racing again. He was finally going to be in a battle! He was excited and scared. He had shot plenty of targets and animals over the past few years, but never a person. He scampered up the ratlines and climbed into the crow's nest. Four muskets stayed in it at all times. He confirmed they were all loaded and then waited nervously for events to unfold.

Lamp oil was poured into the four barrels, and then they were set on fire. The flames were fairly small, but the sails put off a thick black smoke. The pirates then started scurrying about with even more haste. Fifty or so grabbed blunderbusses and crouched below the railing on the port side, causing the boat to list even more. The remainder followed Andre below deck.

Hawk scanned the horizon and soon saw sails in the distance. The ship was a huge three-masted galleon. He had never seen a ship so big; it was easily three times as big as their ship. The wind filled the galleon's large square sails, and their schooner was anchored with no sails raised, so the big ship approached quickly. He crouched down inside the nest, barely peaking above the rail to watch the ship close. *How will we defeat that monster?*

On the bow of the Spanish galleon, Hernandez, the first mate, peered through the telescope at the disheveled vessel in the distance. "Captain Cortez, surely you're not heading to that sinking ship?"

"She is flying a Spanish flag and might still have Spanish sailors aboard," Cortez said curtly.

"It could be a trap, sir."

"Doubtful," said Cortez. "The pirate scum in these waters are not intelligent enough for ruses. And what pirate captain would cripple his own ship? Besides, we are a floating fortress. Have the men ready the main deck guns and the muskets just in case."

The Spanish captain now surveyed the ship with his brass spyglass. He saw several men aboard a longboat in front of the schooner waving their arms wildly, but no movement on the ship's deck.

"Sir, what about the lower decks? We just have eight guns on the main deck," said Hernandez, keeping a wary eye on the smoking ship.

"How many do you think we need for a sinking ship, First Mate Hernandez? You worry too much, my friend. This is not my first voyage."

Hernandez walked away, shouting orders to the crew. *I hope it is not your last.*

The large galleon closed quickly on the two smaller vessels. Cortez could now see the cannon holes in the schooner's hull, the shredded sails, and fires burning on at least four parts of the ship. It listed hard to port, away from his ship. The longboat had four sailors in it, and it bobbed helplessly in front of the damaged ship. "What say you now, Hernandez?"

"Something still does not seem right, sir. I'd be wary."

"Well noted, First Mate. But you still have a lot to learn before you earn your own ship." The galleon trimmed its sails and glided into a position broadside to the schooner, with the longboat in between.

"Ahoy in the longboat!" Captain Cortez called down to the boat almost directly beneath him. "What is your situation?"

"We were attacked by pirates—the devil himself, Bloodstone, no less!"

"And how did you escape?" Hernandez called down from beside the captain.

"We managed to get a couple of good shots in his hull. He was taking on water. With the condition of our ship, he didn't risk boarding." The speaker in the longboat was dark-skinned and wore black breeches, a black waistcoat, and black scarf on his head. A diamond-studded patch covered his left eye.

"Are you the captain, sir?" Cortez asked.

"Our captain was killed, with most everyone else. I am the quarter-master, Diablo." While they were speaking, the current was bringing the galleon closer. Soon it was only thirty feet away from the schooner, with the longboat crowded in between. "Can you have your men board the schooner and look for survivors? We only had room for us four. Also, if you'll throw down some ropes, we'll get off this boat before we're smashed to death."

"Hernandez, get everyone over here. The current will soon have us close enough for the gangplank." Cortez unfurled a rope ladder over the side.

Hernandez scowled but quickly shouted orders to the men on the main deck. They left their posts at the cannons, or sat down their mus-kets, and gathered together behind the captain. "What kind of name is Diablo, for an honest Spaniard?" he called down to the quartermaster.

Diablo stood up in the longboat. He spat into the water. "Never met an honest Spaniard," he replied, his hands on his hips, very close to two of his flintlocks.

"Those are some unkind words for someone seeking rescue," Hernandez said, looking at his captain.

"In fact, the only honest Spaniard is a dead one," Diablo said. No one noticed the other three pirates moving their hands to their pistols hilts.

"You go too far, friend!" Cortez shouted. "Another comment like that, and we shall leave you to die in that boat."

"I should think not." Suddenly Diablo's hands reached down, grabbed two pistols, and brought them up. He cocked the hammers in one fluid motion and fired both, one at the captain and one at his first mate. The captain was struck in his right shoulder. He staggered back-ward and grabbed for his own pistol. Hernandez wasn't as lucky. A gap-ing hole opened up in the center of his breastbone. He looked down in horror and then toppled backward on the deck.

As the men on the galleon started to react to the attack, six cannons from the schooner fired. Since the ship was listing hard to port, the cannons were aimed at the galleon's deck, despite being on the gun deck of the schooner. They were loaded with canister shot, which consisted of musket balls and nails. The deadly spray tore through the Spanish sailors.

As soon as the cannons erupted, Hawk grabbed a musket and stood up. He saw Captain Cortez, somehow missed by the shrapnel, lean over the rail with his pistol pointed at Diablo. Hawk quickly trained the musket on the man's chest. Although the adrenalin was rushing through his body and his heart was pounding, he had no time to think about missing the shot. He took a deep breath and then slowly exhaled. He squeezed the trigger, and a second later, the ball struck the captain on the left side of his chest.

Once again Cortez staggered backward, away from the rail. He dropped his pistol and clutched at the wound that was quickly soaking his white silk shirt with warm red blood. He turned to look up directly at Hawk. Hawk had grabbed another musket and was prepared to fire again. But he froze. The look on the Spanish captain's face wasn't one of anger, or fear; it was shock, horror, and sadness. Cortez's mouth opened as if he was trying to speak to Hawk, to ask why.

For Hawk, time was barely moving. The sounds of battle faded to a distant murmur. Pirates and sailors were just blurs on the periphery. It was now just he and the Spanish captain, locked in a death stare. Cortez dropped to both knees, still locked onto the young pirate's eyes. His hands dropped. Slowly, ever so slowly, he leaned over to the side, finally collapsing to the deck. He no longer stared at Hawk, but his eyes and mouth remained open—for eternity.

Hawk also collapsed to his knees. He was covered in sweat and felt dizzy, light-headed, and nauseated. Suddenly, he lurched forward and vomited onto the floor of the crow's nest. He finished and sat down, with his back to the battle. He pulled his feet up, folded his arms across his knees, and buried his head into his forearms. He cried like he hadn't since his first night on the *Bloody Seas*.

Below, the battle raged, but it was mostly one-sided. The pirates rushed from their crouching positions on the port rail over to the starboard rail. They fired their blunderbusses into the new wave of sailors that had emerged from the lower decks of the galleon. At this range, they were almost as deadly as the cannons. Once all of the pirates had fired, they dropped their blunderbusses and picked up loaded muskets that were lying on the deck in front of the rail. Dozens of sailors dropped.

Diablo and the other three pirates had now climbed the rope ladder to the galleon's deck. As soon as the pirates on the *Bloody Seas* finished firing muskets, the four pirates drew their cutlasses and set about slaughtering the stunned and panicked sailors. Another group of pirates had climbed the ratlines. They now untied some of the long rigging ropes and swung out over the galleon's deck. They dropped into the midst of the sailors, their drawn cutlasses quickly swinging.

The battle was soon over. The Spaniard's had no choice but to surrender, as more and more pirates swarmed the deck. If any more of the crew came up through the hatches, cutlasses immediately cut them down. The two ships were now almost touching. Spider put several pirates to lashing the two ships together with ropes. A gangplank was extended between the two.

"Arrr!" Bloodstone bellowed loud enough to be heard by all. "Any of ye Spanish dogs that wants to live can go over to me ship. She still be seaworthy. I be takin' this one. Me crew, grab all of your valuables and get your sorry hides over to our new ship."

The pirates came streaming over the gangplank, carrying weapons, crates, and their personal items. The Spanish sailors steadily filed over to the pirate ship. Once they realized the pirate captain had spoken the truth, they were relieved. They were going to survive one of the most feared pirates in the Caribbean.

Henry had managed to climb down from the crow's nest. He was weak and shaken and didn't share in the pirates' elation. He found Wesley, and they headed over to the galleon. They stayed clear of the other pirates and started moving their few possessions into the cabin closest to the galley below deck.

Bloodstone sent Andre and a large group of pirates below deck on the galleon. Another group was busy in motion about the main deck.

Soon the crews had completed the swap. Bloodstone had the galleon's sails hoisted. The other ship had now leveled off some, the sailors having repositioned the cargo in the hold. They'd also thrown the smoking barrels overboard and were working on getting some sails back into place.

"Ho, Spaniards! Ye forgot something. Don't let it be said that I be a selfish pirate. Mr. Diablo?" Suddenly, the cannons on the main deck fired at the schooner. A few seconds later, the ones on the gun deck fired. At that distance, they tore through the unsuspecting schooner from top to bottom. Some of the sailors were killed, but those shots were meant to destroy the hull. And they were successful. As the galleon sailed away, the schooner began listing to starboard; this time it wasn't a ruse. The hold was quickly filling with water.

"What's wrong, lad?" Wesley asked Hawk, who had run into the cabin and headed straight to a hammock. Wesley had been busy arranging his new cabin.

Hawk lay down in the hammock facing the wall. "I…I shot someone," he said, doing his best to hold back the tears.

"Ah, I see." Wesley sat down in a chair close by. The previous occupants had the cabin furnished well. "You never forget your first kill."

"It was horrible! I…I saw his face. He just stared at me. He looked… so sad."

"Killing ain't an easy thing to do, that's for sure. Gets easier though," Wesley said somberly. "And he would have killed you if he'd had the opportunity. It was a battle, Hawk."

"Why do we do it?" Hawk asked, rolling over to lie on his back and stare at the ceiling.

"Do what?"

Before Hawk could reply, the cabin door swung open. Captain Bloodstone strolled in. He was puffing on a long curved pipe, as he liked to do after a battle. Wesley stood up and vacated his chair for the captain. He went and sat down at a desk against the far wall.

"What be wrong with ye, Hawk? Heck of a shot out there. A captain no less! Saved Diablo too, I'd wager." Bloodstone sat down in the empty chair. He stretched his feet out, leaned back to rest his neck and head against the high back, and puffed the sweet-smelling tobacco smoke into the air.

"Why do we attack ships and kill innocent people and take their loot?" said Hawk.

Bloodstone suddenly sat up straight and leaned forward. Wesley cringed and turned away to look at a book on the desk. "Innocent people?" Bloodstone roared. "Innocent people? There ain't a cursed one of those Spanish curs innocent! They've killed, enslaved, and robbed from innocent people for two hundred years, ye can bet your life. All of the gold and silver they haul back to Spain is sticky with the blood of innocent men and women! They all lost their innocence the first day they left Spain."

Hawk sat up in the hammock, leaning his back against the wall. "Really?" He suddenly felt a little better.

Bloodstone breathed deeply and sighed. "They've killed thousands of natives that weren't even armed, me lad. Least those bilge rats were armed. They be on a ship prepared for battle. They knew the day they left Spain what they risked, they did. If they weren't stealin' loot from innocent people, they wouldn't be attacked by me or any other pirates."

"So, that captain had probably killed lots of innocent people?"

"Aye, Hawk, I'd wager hundreds, least had his men do it. Cowards those Spaniards are. Brave against unarmed men and women, not so brave against a crew of armed pirates. Ye done a right good deed today, Hawk."

Hawk managed a smile. "Thank you, Captain. Shot him right in the chest, I did."

Bloodstone chuckled softly. "Let me tell ye another story 'bout the bloody Spaniards." Bloodstone took a deep puff on his pipe. He blew out a smoke ring that hovered in front of his face for a moment before drifting up to the ceiling. "Ye see, me and me parents were on a voyage from New Spain to North Carolina. I reckon I be 'bout your age in those days. We were tryin' to get away from the Spanish Main. Our ship were set upon by a cursed Spanish warship. My father and the menfolk were slaughtered before our very eyes, they were. The women and children, being mostly Indian or part Indian, were set off to Cuba. We were forced to work in the sugarcane fields like dogs.

"My mother and me were there for a year or two. We were both beaten most daily, nearly starved to death too. Then one day, one of the devils drank too much. He started bullyin' me mother worse than usual, he did. Got right fresh with her. Then he started tryin' to rip her clothes off and have his way with her right there in the daylight. I had all I could take of the devil. I picked up a large smooth stone, charged him, and struck him in the side of the head. Blood spattered all over the three of us. He fell to the ground, and I set upon him. Smashed his skull in, I did.

"More of them dogs came runnin'. Me mother was shot and killed. I managed to smash another's one's skull and then fled. I ran as fast as me legs could carry me for hours. I finally reached a beach, and by the gods, a pirate ship be sailing close by. They spotted me, covered in blood, realized I wasn't a Spaniard, and picked me up. I still clutched that bloody stone in me hand. The pirates named me Bloodstone, and Cap'n Christopher White took me in, much like I did ye. And to this day I have been tryin' to pay those devils back for what they did to me and me family."

Hawk's eyes were wide and his mouth hung open as he listened to the captain's tale. He didn't notice Wesley, in the far corner, with the slightest of grins on his face. "Wow, that's some story! No wonder you hate those Spaniards."

"Aye, me lad. As should ye. Don't forget they killed your family too." Bloodstone stood up and walked out of the cabin.

Hawk never grieved for another dead Spaniard.

CHAPTER V

USS ENTERPRISE

ॷ

"Blast!"

"Not Bloodstone?" Captain Nathaniel Cord asked his lieutenant.

Lieutenant James Wellington lowered the spyglass. He had been excited when he saw the black ship. But Bloodstone wasn't the only pirate who painted his ships black. "No. How can we not come across that cowardly dog?"

"Ah, it's a big sea, my boy. But one of our fleet will eventually find him. The sea gets smaller each day."

"I just hope we get to him first. I want to personally make him pay," James said, his quick temper flashing.

"I hope so too—for the sake of all of the poor pirate scum that you encounter between now and then." Cord smiled at his junior officer.

As captain of the USS *Enterprise*, he had rescued James off of a burning British merchant ship some six years prior. James had impressed him from the start. He was very intelligent and eager to learn everything he could, especially when it came to combat. He also had a burning determination for revenge that never wavered.

Cord had immediately put him to work as a cabin boy. He had thought about finding a family to keep him in one of the states, but there was something special about James. And he deserved the right to try to avenge the death of his father and abduction and presumed death of his brother. James took it upon himself to finish his chores as fast as he could each day so he could learn everything else there was to know about the ship. He was soon one of the best gunners and fighters onboard. For most sailors, it was just a job. For James, it was his life. He also learned how to operate the sails and how to navigate. At sixteen, Cord promoted him to lieutenant. Cord worked on James's education, having him read any book they came across and maintain the official ship's log.

As part of the New Orleans Squadron, the USS *Enterprise* had most recently served the United States in the war with England from 1812 to 1815. They had patrolled the east coast and had numerous engagements with the British navy. It was there that James really cut his teeth and proved his worth as a fearless and cunning fighter. They had last fought in the Battle of New Orleans and helped end the war. They were now assigned to hunt pirates in the Caribbean, something James had desperately wanted.

The only concern Cord had for his lieutenant was that his rage sometimes got the best of him. He tried to help him control it. The navy wanted to capture pirate ships with as little fight as possible and then try the pirates in a courtroom. If convicted, they were hanged. James preferred to kill everyone aboard a pirate ship and then sink it. He said it saved a lot of time and money. There were two problems with that strategy. One, if the pirates knew that surrender was not an option, they would fight harder and to the death, causing more navy casualties. Two, there were usually a few pirates aboard each ship that were innocent of piracy. They were usually the skilled men—navigators, cooks, carpenters, gunners, musicians, and surgeons—forced to join the crew when their ships were captured.

Cord wanted to keep James engaged, help him maintain a good attitude, and continue to prepare him to be a captain someday soon. So every so often, he'd let him decide how to attack the pirate ship and the fate of the ship and its crew. This was one of those times. They were far from land, and there was no chance of anyone seeing the battle and outcome. The crew all liked James, as long as they continued to have success and few casualties. James did have an excellent military mind and came up with sound, although usually daring, plans.

"Well, Mr. Wellington, what say you?"

"Burn and slash. We should be able to catch her before she reaches shallow water. Let's load some chain shot in the swivel guns and shred her sails when we're within range. Load and man all of the starboard guns for a broadside soon after. Every hand on deck needs a granado or stinkpot, with a blunderbuss or muskatoon close-by. When the smoke and flames clear, we'll board."

Captain Cord decided to allow James's plan. It was just a schooner they faced. The *Enterprise* was one of a new class of navy frigates. It had three masts of square sails, fifty guns, and three hundred sailors. The schooner was no match, and most likely the pirates would try to surrender or escape. It would also send a good message to the pirates that a new era was dawning.

The *Enterprise* sailed with the wind, as did the pirate ship, but with three masts and larger sails, it steadily gained on the smaller ship. James stood on the forecastle, in between the five swivel guns. The ships were soon close enough that he could see the pirates scurrying about the deck. They had no trail guns though, so they could do nothing in their current position.

James gave the order to fire as soon as they were within range. The five guns fired, sending the chained balls hurling into the masts and sails. Most of the sails sustained at least some damage. The schooner slowed greatly as the sails flapped loosely in the wind. James's heart began to pound hard as the battle started. He loved when the captain gave him control. He lived for these moments—making the heartless, cowardly pirate scum pay the ultimate price. He hoped and prayed that one day it would be Bloodstone's ship he encountered.

"Hard to port! Ready the guns!" he shouted. His orders echoed through the men behind him until they had reached the navigator and the gunners below deck. The *Enterprise* turned to the port side of the schooner. With its superior speed, it began to overtake the floundering ship. The navigator had the front of the ship pointing at a forty-five degree angle to the port hull of the pirate ship. "Fire the guns!" shouted James.

The *Enterprise* was slightly behind the schooner and at such an angle that most of its cannons could be pointed at the pirate ship. Only a couple of the cannons near the stern of the pirate ship had a chance of hitting the bow of the frigate. Twenty cannons fired their projectiles into the schooner. Around fifteen balls struck the hull, rails, and deck of the ship. Pirate bodies went flying across the deck, and pieces of wood scattered in all directions. Screams rang out from above and below deck.

Two of the cannons on the schooner managed to return fire. One ball sailed harmlessly in front of the *Enterprise*. The other one hit halfway down the hull near the bow. James knew there were no men in that part of the hold. "Come along side! Throw granadoes at will."

The pirates hadn't had time to recover and find weapons before the granadoes began bouncing onto the deck. Some of the granadoes were filled with gunpowder and scraps of metal. The metal tore through the pirates as the gunpowder set fire to the deck. The others were stinkpots and emitted a thick smoke with a revolting smell that caused physical illness.

James grinned. Sometimes it was too easy. "Ready the blunderbusses!" The pirates who hadn't fallen ran about wildly in the smoke. Some coughed and vomited while others threw buckets of water on the flames. There was a stray shot or two fired, but none struck anyone on the *Enterprise*.

"Fire!" James yelled.

The blunderbusses fired their multiple musket balls into the smoke-shrouded pirates. More screams rang out; more bodies fell. Now the two ships were side by side.

"Grapple and prepare to board!" James commanded. He grabbed the two flintlock pistols that hung from his belt. The sailors threw ropes with iron grappling hooks tied to the ends. They struck the deck of the pirate ship and were then pulled up until they hooked into the rail.

The sailors pulled hard, drawing the two ships together. The ropes were quickly lashed to the belaying pins on the rail of their ship.

They waited momentarily for the smoke to begin to clear. Then James himself led the charge. He ran and leapt over the railing of both ships. Before he landed, he fired both pistols at dazed pirates. By the time his feet struck the deck, the pistols were bouncing by his side, and his cutlass was in hand. His blade was a silver blur. His crew quickly filled the deck beside him.

Many of the pirates tried to surrender, but James was recalling the images of his unarmed father being callously shot and the deaths of the captain and the rest of the good people on the merchant ship that day years before. He imagined what kind of torturous fate his brother Henry probably met. No, these pirates were not that same brutal crew of Bloodstone, but today they would have to do. The sailors steadily advanced to the far side of the deck. Soon all the pirates were dead, except for a few that had jumped overboard. Most of the pirates couldn't swim, and even the ones who could had nowhere to go.

James led his men down through the hatches and into the lower decks. There were a few more pirates to kill on the gun deck, but they didn't offer much resistance. Once all of the pirates were dead, the sailors went down to the hold and quickly grabbed any valuables and headed back up to the main deck and back to the *Enterprise*. The cannons had been reloaded by then and were angled down to the waterline of the schooner. They fired again. This time all of the balls struck the hull. The *Enterprise* sailed away as the pirate ship slowly disappeared into the depths.

"I'm glad you're on our side," Captain Cord said when James was back by his side watching the other ship sink. "That was brutally efficient."

"It's good to have the men get experience like this," said James, his face expressionless. "We barely took damage and didn't lose a sailor. They'll be ready when we find Bloodstone."

CHAPTER VI

A MAN AND A PIRATE

"Nice shot," Diablo said, after Hawk finally emerged from Wesley's cabin for dinner.

"Thank you," Hawk replied, shocked that Diablo was speaking to him.

"It's a little tougher when you're not perched one hundred yards away in the crow's nest. Oh, and by the way, you didn't save my life. He'd had my dagger in his throat a second after your bullet struck him." Diablo continued past, not waiting for a reply.

There was a great celebration aboard the galleon that night. It was a rare feat for a pirate to take a galleon, and unheard of with only one ship—a schooner at that. The cargo was also a huge sum of gold and silver bars, doubloons, pieces of eight, gemstones, and jewelry. It was the richest haul Bloodstone had ever taken. Even Wesley wandered out onto the deck to listen to the music and singing and watch the dancing. He drank some, but not to excess. Most of the other pirates crossed way over the line of excess that night. Bloodstone stayed out a little longer than usual, even dancing a quick comical jig in the midst of his crew. This was the shining gem in his treasure trove of a pirating career.

The huge ship barely made it past the trees in the lagoon before it had to anchor. The crew used several longboats to ferry the loot and themselves to shore. The party continued the first night back at the Rock, with the shore-bound crew getting their chance to celebrate. It was several weeks before the pirates sailed again, other than to sell the galleon to the British in Jamaica and buy another schooner and sloop with the money. The pirates also made many trips to New Orleans. Hawk still didn't know exactly what all took place in that legendary city, but he knew the men came back very happy and very broke. Most of the pirates also upgraded their wardrobes with their newfound wealth.

Soon after that time, the pirates stayed away from New Orleans for a couple of years. A war broke out between the United States and England, during which England tried to take the city. So Bloodstone and his crew visited other, more pirate-friendly, cities until things settled down.

Hawk continued to train with weapons and hunt over the next two years. He also continued to participate in battles. He was still confined to the crow's nest, but he quickly earned the reputation for being one of the best shots with a musket. He also shot multiple targets in the course of a battle. The first few people he killed still caused him to feel a little squeamish, but he no longer mourned for them. He would just remember Bloodstone's tales of Spanish brutality, and what Bloodstone told him the Spanish did to his own father and brother, and he was ready to shoot again. Soon he no longer felt anything. However, he did only target men that were attacking or threatening his fellow pirates. Even Spaniards deserved better than to be shot without cause or warning.

He kept five muskets in the crow's nest with a small cask of powder, a stack of cloth, and leather bag of balls for reloading. Occasionally, an enemy spotted him and shot back. But they were usually in the middle of a fluid battle and were trying to shoot high into the air without a proper rest. Only once did a ball strike the mast just below him.

His melee skills were getting honed too. Captain Bloodstone was still his trainer. The captain was getting older now, by pirate standards, but was still arguably the best swordsman. He was deceptively quick, and what he had lost in speed, he made up for in cunning and brute strength.

Hawk was quicker now, but couldn't match the mental processes honed by thirty years of fighting. Sooner or later he made a mistake, or fell into a trap, and Bloodstone made him pay. But he was getting closer and was fueled by the desire to be the best.

By age sixteen, he was growing into a man. He already stood six feet tall and weighed close to 180 pounds. His hair was still blond, and it hung down to his shoulders in the back. He usually wore his white cotton shirt unbuttoned, showing off his tanned, toned chest and stomach—and, of course, his birthmark. His sleeves were cut off above the elbow, showing arms muscled from years of climbing rigging, working the sails, and wielding muskets and cutlasses. His blue linen pants hung just below the knees, showing similarly muscled calves. He wore a red scarf about his waist for a belt and occasionally one around his neck.

The pirate life had matured him way beyond his years. His voice was deep now, and he carried himself with an air of command. As many of the pirate crew turned over, mostly through death and injury, the new men looked to him almost like a quartermaster—and a possible heir to Bloodstone. They ignored his age and respected his knowledge and skill. He was also intimidating from an intellectual standpoint—able to read books, write, and interpret maps and charts. From working with the officers, he knew the workings of the ship inside and out. The only thing he hadn't done was fight hand-to-hand.

"Come in, lad," Bloodstone called out from behind the large table in his cabin on the *Bloody Seas*.

Hawk walked in, shutting the door behind him, and sat down in a chair on the near side. "You wanted to see me, sir?" Despite living with pirates most of his life, Hawk didn't talk like one, unless he wanted to. Wesley had always tried to coach him on his manner of speech, and reading a wide variety of books helped.

"Aye. So ye think you're gettin' good with that cutlass?" Bloodstone looked up from his chart, relit his pipe, and stared at Hawk.

"Pretty good, sir."

"And I s'ppose you're itchin' to fight for real?"

Hawk leaned forward, his eyes widening. "Aye! That's the only way I can get better. There's only so much I can learn practicing."

Bloodstone chuckled. "I reckon' it be 'bout time. Can't protect ye forever. I'd killed twenty with a blade by your age, I'd wager."

"When can I fight?" Hawk asked eagerly.

"We be comin' up fast on a small Spanish merchantman. I figure she be as good as any to cut your teeth on. No trickery this time. We'll come up broadside, fire a few rounds, and then swing over. Stay back till the first wave is aboard, then drop in behind. Keep your back to the rail, or to our crew, and just fight one at a time."

Hawk stood up, trying to suppress his exuberance. "Yes, sir!" he said enthusiastically, and he went to prepare for his first battle.

The *Bloody Seas* was much faster, with its three masts fully rigged, than the two-masted merchantman. And they hadn't taken any ships yet on this voyage, so they were light in the hold. Normally, Bloodstone would have just hailed the ship, gone onboard, killed the officers, and took their treasure, marooning the remainder. But this attack was about Hawk. The men respected Hawk, but Bloodstone knew there were some who resented that he never had to get dirty in a fight. He merely stood in the crow's nest and picked off sailors from a distance. Bloodstone knew Hawk had all of the training he needed. He just had to get some real experience now. Since the Spanish ship wasn't a naval ship, it should be a fairly easy battle and a good learning experience.

The *Bloody Seas* sailed up broadside to the merchantman. The ship was fairly typical of a merchant carrier. It had two masts and sixteen cannons and was eighty feet long. There were only a dozen or so men on the main deck. Many times merchantmen only had twenty or thirty sailors, so they made easy targets for the pirates. Most didn't put up a fight. Almost all of the ninety-nine pirates, except for the ones manning the cannons on the lower deck, were gathered on the main deck or up in the rigging. Hawk was in the crow's nest.

"Ho, Spaniards!" Bloodstone called across to the other ship. Both ships had reefed their sails and slowed their speed. They were only thirty feet apart. "I wish to parley with your cap'n."

The man that stepped forward from the group of sailors was dressed like a Spanish naval officer, not a merchant captain. "I am Javier Ramirez, captain of this humble merchant vessel. And whom am I speaking with?"

"Cap'n Bloodstone it be. I s'ppose ye heard of me?" Bloodstone surveyed the merchant crew a little more closely. Something didn't feel right. There were some others among the sailors wearing military clothing. That was seen on a lot on pirate ships and warships, but not normally on merchantmen.

"Aye, I believe I have. I've heard that you are a cowardly man, though very brave against unarmed men, women, and children—a plague on the Caribbean and a black mark on humanity itself." Captain Ramirez stared unflinchingly at the huge pirate.

"Get ready," Bloodstone growled to Diablo. Diablo gave some nods and hand gestures to several pirates. One ran over to the hatch and disappeared below deck.

"Ye got a right sharp tongue there, Spaniard. And here I was in a kind mood." Bloodstone rested his right hand on a pistol handle and his left on the hilt of his cutlass. "But if ye'll give up your loot without a fight, I might be able to overlook your rudeness."

"A very generous offer indeed, Mr. Bloodstone. Let me confer with my men here and let you know our decision." Captain Ramirez turned to the three sailors close to him who were in similar uniforms.

"If he says anything but yes, open fire," Bloodstone whispered to Diablo. Most of the pirates waiting to board had their cutlasses or axes ready, and a few had pistols.

Ramirez finally turned back around to face the pirates. "We have reached a decision, sir."

"I figured ye'd be reasonable like," Bloodstone said.

"Fire!" Ramirez roared. He and the sailors closest drew their pistols and shot at the pirates. At the same time, eight cannons fired from the deck below. The balls from the pistols nearly all found a target, with the pirates grouped so close together. Ramirez's shot grazed Bloodstone's left shoulder. Several pirates were wounded and other's dropped to the deck. The cannon balls wreaked havoc on the gun deck and the cannons of the *Bloody Seas*. Screams and small explosions were heard from below deck as the hull was shattered almost directly along the line of cannon ports.

Hawk had watched the scene unfold from high up in his perch. He had developed an uneasy feeling early in the exchange. Something wasn't right about the uniformed men on a merchantman. The captain was also too calm and insolent. Hawk had already trained his musket on Captain Ramirez before he had given the order to fire. A second after the sailors fired their weapons, Hawk's musket ball struck the captain in the head. He was dead before he hit the deck. Hawk didn't allow himself to think about the horror of the situation, the pirates falling, or the screams below deck. He quickly grabbed the next musket and fired again, picking another man in uniform.

Captain Bloodstone roared with rage and began firing his pistols into the sailors. He had six hanging from his belt. Several balls found targets. He was a little upset that Hawk had stolen his opportunity to kill Ramirez, but there were plenty more targets.

The other pirates quickly recovered from the shock and rushed to the weapon racks against the rail. Soon the blunderbusses were roaring, doing great damage at that range. Sailors began dropping and scurrying for cover. A couple of cannons managed to fire from the gun deck, striking the side of the merchant vessel.

Bloodstone knew most of his cannons, and the pirates manning them, were unusable now and that the other ship would be ready to fire again soon. They had to get to the other ship and neutralize the enemy. "No quarter!" Bloodstone shouted, leading the charge. The pirates up on the ratlines and rigging began swinging over the water between the two ships and dropping onto the merchant deck. Others threw ropes with grappling hooks over to the other ship's railing. Those pirates pulled hard to bring the two ships together. Then they just climbed onto the railing and leapt over the narrowing gap.

More sailors were now coming up through the hatches on the merchant ship and joining their remaining comrades. Most had come from manning the cannons, since the pirates were boarding their vessel.

Sinking the *Bloody Seas* would leave the pirates no option of retreat, and they might fight even harder to take the merchant ship. The Spaniard's only hope was to repulse the pirates, inflicting enough injury and death to force them back to their ship. Some had pistols drawn, other cutlasses and sabers. The pirates now realized that many of the sailors were marines—trained soldiers that were frequently aboard warships but rarely aboard merchantmen.

The first pirates arrived in an enraged frenzy. Most had never been in a battle where they were hit so hard at the start. They occasionally lost men, but not like they had in the opening volley. They were used to Bloodstone using deception and cunning to place the odds in their favor before the battle even began. The length of the battle normally just depended on how long they wanted to play with their prey. Now they were in a real battle, and the outcome wasn't certain.

Hawk fired the remainder of the muskets, trying to help the first pirates to land safely. Although the pirates were well-armed, seasoned fighters, they were initially badly outnumbered as the Spaniards swarmed. He scampered through the rigging until he found a long rope that he quickly cut with his dagger. He then drew a pistol and launched himself through the air. As he flew, he cocked the pistol and shot down into the Spaniards, wounding one in the shoulder. He let go of the rope and fell the remaining ten feet, landing beside his pirate comrades.

He threw his pistol down and drew his cutlass. Then he froze. His heart was trying to pound out of his chest. His legs and arms were weak, his sword heavy. It suddenly struck him that he was in a real fight now. He would have died at the end of every practice battle with Bloodstone if they'd been fighting for real. Now it *was* real. He could get hurt. He could die. There was no margin for error now. Almost any lesson learned would be learned too late. Swords and axes swung and clanged all around him. Men grunted, roared, and screamed. The wounded still fought, while the dying and dead littered the deck.

"Not in the crow's nest any more, swab," a voice said from just behind his right shoulder.

He didn't turn to look. There was only one person it could be. His hesitation turned to rage. As he had grown into a man, he was getting closer and closer to standing up to Diablo. In a different situation, this might have been the day. But now he had to focus his anger somewhere else. A uniformed marine suddenly appeared around the left flank of the pirates. He spotted young Hawk not engaged and charged with cutlass raised.

Hawk quickly raised his cutlass to block the overhand blow. He then kicked his right leg out, striking his opponent's left knee. The marine stumbled backward, nearly falling. Any hesitation and nervousness in Hawk had ended with the first swing of the sword. Now he relied on his training and instincts. He slashed viciously toward the man's left side. The marine managed to block it, but barely in time. Hawk pulled his blade back and quickly swung at his other side. Again the sailor barely managed to deflect the blade. Hawk was driving him back and keeping him on the defensive.

Hawk next brought a powerful one-handed blow straight down at the sailor's head. The sailor blocked it, holding his weapon with both hands. Hawk swung one more blow straight down. This time, as soon as the blades made contact, Hawk reached his left hand down to his waist, drew his dagger, and plunged it into his adversary's side, right below the ribs. The marine saw it coming, but too late, with his sword locked overhead. He dropped his blade to clutch at his side. Realizing his fatal mistake, he looked up at his attacker, an appeal for mercy in his eyes. He found none. Hawk swung a final blow with his cutlass to the right side of the sailor's neck. He collapsed to the ground in a quickly spreading pool of red.

"Not bad, me lad," another voice said.

Hawk turned to see Bloodstone standing beside him. The pirates now gained the upper hand and began pushing the sailors and marines back toward the middle of the deck. The enemy still had the numbers—more came up from below deck—but most of the marines were dead. The merchant sailors all fought because they knew they would die either way, but they were overmatched.

Hawk engaged his next attacker. This one was dressed in regular seaman garb. Hawk almost felt sorry for him, but only for a moment. He knew many pirates lay wounded and dead back on the *Bloody Seas*. If Ramirez hadn't attacked first, most of the sailors would have been spared. Hawk swung a few wide blows, from side to side, forcing the man to block. After a couple of overhead blows, he feinted to the right, forcing the sailor to start moving his blade to counter. Then he stopped his swing and quickly ran his blade through the man's stomach and partially out of his back.

Hawk, Bloodstone, and Diablo fought side-by-side-by-side, and along with the now huge throng of pirates, quickly finished the grisly job. Hawk slew two more sailors before the battle was done. His training had paid off well. He realized that Bloodstone was truly an elite fighter. The fact that he hadn't ever defeated him in practice didn't mean he couldn't dispatch most anyone else. Bloodstone had emphasized the art of surprise, and using tactics like kicking, punching, and using two weapons. It worked well in an actual fight.

"Looks like I can manage OK out of the crow's nest after all," Hawk said to Diablo as he wiped his blade clean on a fallen sailor's shirt and sheathed it. For a moment, Hawk thought Diablo would attack him.

"I'd say you're still better with a mop, swab," Diablo said, and he walked away. The pirates quickly stripped the merchantman of any loot, which, other than some silver, a little gold, and some sugar cane, wasn't much. Then they returned to their ship to inspect the damage and help the wounded.

There were six dead pirates on the deck of the *Bloody Seas*. There was a crowd gathered around one. Hawk nervously pushed his way through the circle of pirates silently staring down. He gasped when he saw Spider lying on the deck, a hole in his left breast. Other than Wesley, Hawk had been closer to Spider than any other pirate—helping him with the rigging and sails almost every day. Tears instantly filled his eyes. He had seen a lot of dead pirates during his ten years with Bloodstone's crew but had never lost anyone close.

"Hawk, below deck," a pirate's voice rang out as he climbed up through the hatch.

Hawk quickly turned and headed to the lower deck. There were eight dead bodies strewn about the gun deck. He climbed down to the orlop, which was crowded with the wounded. He headed straight to the infirmary, brushing past the line of wounded waiting their turn, and entered the room. Mr. Bones was inside, his face pale and shining with sweat. On one of the tables lay Andre. Hawk quickly noticed that his right leg was mangled beyond repair. Andre was surprisingly calm, but obviously shaken.

"Great, now we'll have two peg-legs hobbling about the ship," Hawk said, approaching the table. "What a racket!"

"Aye, I will still be better than most, with only one leg," Andre said, smiling weakly. "Let's get it over with." He placed the leather-wrapped hilt of his dagger in his mouth and bit down.

Hawk held down his leg, and Mr. Bones quickly sawed if off and sewed up the stump. "Go get some rest. I'll fashion you a new leg as soon as I get everyone else mended up," Mr. Bones said. Hawk helped Andre up and, placing his arm around the Frenchman, assisted him out of the room and to an open hammock. He returned to help Mr. Bones take care of the rest of the wounded, including Bloodstone, though the captain's grazed shoulder was a minor wound.

The ship was badly damaged, but the holes were above the waterline. Diablo temporarily took over Spider's duties and got the ship moving again toward open water. There was no celebration for their victory. The bodies from below deck were brought up to the main deck and placed beside the others. Chain shot was attached to their legs, and they were prepared for their burial at sea.

Two hours later, once the wounded were patched up as well as possible, Bloodstone gathered all hands to the main deck. He addressed the somber crew. "Tis a sad day indeed, mates, and a black spot on our victory. By blasted treachery and deceit, we've lost fourteen brothers. One of them be our bosun, Spider. I take the blame for these deaths. T'was I that tried to parley right civilized like with a Spanish fork-tongued devil.

The cowards set a trap, with marines loaded aboard a merchant carrier. Won't happen again, I swear by the blazes! But when we be back at the Rock, ye can decide whether I deserve to be your cap'n or not. Now, Mr. Wesley, say a kind word for these poor souls."

Wesley stepped forward, standing in front of the bodies. "Ashes to ashes, dust to dust. God, please forgive these men for their wrongs and such. I'm sure they had good hearts and intentions. If it pleases thee, open the gate and let the sorry lot into Heaven. Amen."

The bodies were then picked up one by one and tossed overboard. They quickly sank into the murky water. Then the assembly each shot one pistol into the air in honor of the fallen. The group quickly disbanded, and the ship set sail for the Rock. Hawk and Wesley walked back together to their cabin.

Hawk sat down in the high-back leather chair and Wesley at the table. "Sad day," Wesley said, shaking his head.

Hawk fought back his tears. "Yeah, it is." The two sat in silence for a moment. "Wesley?"

"Yes, Hawk?" Wesley had only recently begun calling him Hawk, as opposed to lad or Henry."

"Do you think those men will go to Heaven, especially Spider?"

Wesley rubbed thoughtfully at his scruffy beard. "It's hard to say. They all did a might share of killin' and stealin' in their time. Not to mention cursin', lyin', gamblin', and adulterizin'. I'd say they all broke 'bout every law there is, and broke every commandment, a time or two. But such things aren't for us to decide. Only God knows what was in their hearts and souls."

"So if they don't go to Heaven, they go to hell?" Hawk was hoping for a better answer.

"Yeah. I reckon they do. I don't think there's much in between. But some of them might like one as well as the other." Wesley chuckled softly.

"Why do they all do it?

"What's that?"

"Pirating? What makes all of these men want to do this, when they can be killed, maimed, and go to hell?" Hawk and Wesley had many such conversations over the years. They both enjoyed each other's company, and none of the other pirates had similar deep thoughts about life and death.

Wesley thought it was a strange question, but then remembered that Hawk had known no other life but this one. "Times are tough all around the world. There aren't many jobs, 'specially for folks in the countryside. Money and food are hard to come by, and the workin' conditions are brutal if you can find a job. Most of these men were sailors workin' on merchant or navy ships. Many were forced into it through impressment. Life is hard on those ships, much harder than ours. They get very little pay and are frequently abused and even killed by their captains. Bloodstone is a hard man, 'specially on the Spanish, but if he takes you onboard, it's not a bad deal. You get plenty of loot, lots of freedom, and all the adventure you can stomach. You're free to take your money and leave whenever you want. So piratin' is a big step up of for many."

"How did you end up here?"

Wesley smiled and shook his head, "Now, that's a right long tale, and not for tonight."

The *Bloody Seas* returned uneventfully to the Rock two days later. That night Bloodstone called a meeting of all of the pirates in the middle of the fort. A huge bonfire was built, and the remaining pirates gathered around it. The mood had changed somewhat. Everyone had their time to grieve, and it had been several days without a good night of music, rum, and celebrating. Even Andre seemed to be getting along well with his wooden leg. Several other pirates had lost limbs after the battle, mostly hands and arms. Supper had been served and several barrels of rum were rolled down to the congregation. Excitement was building when Captain Bloodstone stepped inside the circle near the fire.

"Arrr!" Bloodstone growled, getting everyone's attention. "It's been a tough week, to be sure. Lost some good men and our bosun to boot. Before we be gettin' to the business at hand, I'd like to recognize some good fortune from our battle. For those of ye that didn't see it first hand, our lad Hawk tasted his first swordplay. Fought like the devil, he did. Smartly killed four Spanish vermin by hisself. 'Cause of his deeds, I hereby declare him no longer a swab, or cabin boy, but a pirate!"

The throng of pirates cheered loudly. There had been whispers and murmurs about Hawk's fighting prowess. In light of losing fourteen good men, and many of the crew aging, that was good news for all. There were no more reservations about Hawk being a man, or pirate, now.

"And if this be me last act as cap'n, I want to put to vote Hawk replacin' Spider as me bosun."

The pirate crew cheered even louder now and several fired pistols into the air. Diablo didn't hide his look of shock. He stared at the captain for a moment, and then at Hawk. Hawk too was surprised.

Bloodstone ignored both. "Those in favor say aye."

The crowd roared aye as one.

"Anyone opposed say nay."

The roar died down as everyone looked around.

Bloodstone looked directly at Diablo. Diablo's face was stone. "Then so be it. Hawk is bosun!"

He gestured to Diablo. "Mr. Diablo, the next vote." Bloodstone stepped back and let Diablo step forward.

"Because of the results of the last battle, Captain Bloodstone has asked that we vote to see if he remains our captain. All of those in favor of him remaining captain?"

The crowd roared aye as loud as they had for Hawk.

"Opposed?"

There was silence.

"Captain Bloodstone remains our captain!"

CHAPTER VII

ANNA

‹❧

$\mathcal{I}$t was some celebration at the Rock that night. The barrels of rum were opened and quickly emptied. The fiddles, penny whistles, and lyres played loudly, and the pirates sang and danced with gusto.

Bloodstone brought a large wooden tankard over to Hawk. "You're a man today, Hawk, and a pirate. It be time ye took your first taste of grog."

Hawk took the mug and looked inside. He swirled the liquid around and then sniffed it. He slowly brought the mug to his lips and let the liquid touch his tongue. The rum was watered down to make grog, but it still burned as he swallowed. Several of the pirates close by witnessed him drinking and cheered and encouraged him to drink more. He held his breath and turned the tankard up, managing not to gag as the liquid burned its way down his throat and into his stomach. Bloodstone laughed and cheered loudly.

Very soon, Hawk's head was spinning, but he found himself uncontrollably happy. He danced and sang, laughed, yelled and shouted, listened to the tales of debauchery that he had never been privy too, and drank. Everyone stayed outside that night, even Bloodstone and Wesley, and celebrated beneath the stars. Diablo was even seen dancing and laughing a time or two. The recent battle and fallen men were quickly forgotten. For that night, Bloodstone and his crew ruled the world, and all was right.

Hawk woke up the next morning face down on the ground beside the burned-out fire. He slowly pushed up to his elbows and forearms and looked around, trying to remember the events of the night before. Many other pirate bodies lay strewn about the ground inside the fort. The sun was already up and blazing hot. Hawk's head pounded, and he was nauseated. He slowly stood, nearly falling back down. He stumbled to his new cabin, Spider's old one, and collapsed into the hammock. Chores could wait. *Cursed grog!*

The next day, just after lunch, half the crew started getting ready for a trip to New Orleans—the first since the war had ended. Most bathed in one of the fresh water ponds on the island and changed into their city clothes. These were normally the clothing taken from plundered ships that weren't sold or worn aboard the *Bloody Seas*. The pirates reveled in dressing and acting like the upper class when in towns. The other half of the crew would go the next day. There was a lot of excitement over returning to their favorite haunt.

Bloodstone strolled into Hawk's cabin without knocking. "So, ye goin' or sittin' here playin' in the dirt?"

"I get to go?" Hawk asked, his voice loud with excitement.

"Aye, s'ppose it's time. After all, I reckon if you're old enough to kill a man and drink grog, you're old enough for a woman."

"A woman?" Hawk had never been around women. He barely remembered his mother.

Bloodstone laughed. "Get cleaned up and meet us at the beach."

Hawk joined his companions a half an hour later. He was dressed in black leather pants and boots, a loose-sleeved white shirt, a red sash around the waist, and a black waistcoat. He wore no head covering, as usual. He and most of the other pirates had not only bathed but also used the perfume they'd taken from some of their prey. Most of the pirates looked like respectable sailors or navy officers. Bloodstone had undergone the most shocking change. He wore tall black boots, white breeches, a white ruffled shirt, blue waistcoat, a gold scarf around his waist, blue doublet with gold trim and buttons, and a blue tricorne with gold trim. His hair and beard were neatly trimmed and combed.

It took several trips in the longboat to get them all onboard the *Gator*, the schooner named in honor of Razortooth. They were soon under sail. Hawk was almost as nervous as he had been going into his recent first swordfight, though this nervousness was also mixed with excitement. He wasn't sure exactly what took place in New Orleans, but he'd heard enough to know it was an adventure in its own right.

The ship sailed west, with the mainland in the distance on their starboard side. With the good wind, it was just a few hours before they turned, and Hobbs headed straight for the landmass.

Soon the mouth of a huge river opened up before them. "The mighty Mississippi," Mr. Bones said, coming up to stand on the bow beside Hawk.

The *Gator* continued sailing up the river, around several large bends, for over an hour. Finally, they came to a long row of docks on the starboard side. There were over a hundred ships, of all sizes and shapes, docked on the riverside. Hobbs steered them to an open berth, and a few pirates quickly leapt onto the dock and moored the ship to large wooden posts with thick hawsers.

"All right, ye bunch of heathens!" Bloodstone roared from the gangplank. "Be back here by noon tomorrow, or ye'll be left behind. No gettin' into somethin' ye can't get out of. Ye know where to find me 'tween now and then."

The forty pirates quickly crossed the gangplank to the dock and then dispersed into the city. Hawk stayed with Bones. They made the short walk from the docks to a large open square surrounded by buildings. "Jackson Square," Bones said, holding his arms open wide. The ground of the square was covered with colored brick, cobblestones, and wooden boardwalks. Smells assaulted Hawk's nose, but unlike those on the pirate ship, these smells were wonderful—sugarcane, peanuts, fruits, and vegetables. Open tables were scattered about selling the sources of the smells, along with clothing, jewelry, trinkets, and dozens of other items. Buildings, many two and three stories tall, lined the edges of the square. Some had sunken arcades and recessed courtyards in front. Iron poles were scattered about. Oil lanterns sat on top to be lit at dusk.

Bones guided him past the many restaurants, coffee houses, taverns, gaming houses, stores, and warehouses. Some of the restaurants had tables outside in their courtyards where people were busy eating supper. The square was crowded with people. There were some that were clearly sailors—a mixture of navy, merchant, and pirate. There were also a lot of finely dressed men and women. The women wore long colorful dresses and smelled of sweet perfume, and the men wore fancy suits.

There were also some horse-drawn coaches. A man seated on a bench in front of the cart guided the horses, and people sat inside the enclosed cart behind. Hawk had never seen horses before but realized what they were from some of the books he'd read. He was mostly silent as he absorbed the sights and smells. His world had been so limited all of his life. New Orleans was totally foreign to him—and exciting.

They made their way toward three huge buildings on the north side of the plaza. The one in the middle had ten large columns in front supporting the high roof. "St. Louis Cathedral," Bones said, before Hawk could ask. "The building on the left is the Cabildo—the old city hall. On the right, the Presbytere—the new city hall."

Bones led him onto a street beside the cathedral. "Pirate's Alley," he called out. Both sides of the street were lined with tall buildings, mostly alehouses and restaurants. A few booths and tables were scattered about selling wares. Halfway down, Bones stopped at a three-story building. A sign hanging over the door read "The Treasure Cove." "Bloodstone and most of the pirates will be in here. This can be a rough place. You would be best to lay low and just listen. There are women and rooms here, so most of us will stay here for the night. You'll be expected to do the same. Enjoy."

The inside of the building wasn't too full of people, since it wasn't even dark outside yet. It was easy to find their crewmembers. The rum was already flowing, and they were talking and laughing loudly. Round tables filled the large open room. A long counter stood in front of the left wall, with a doorway in the wall behind it. Bloodstone and about two dozen of the crew sat at a group of tables that had been slid close together. Women servers walked around to the tables in colorful dresses that billowed out from the waist to the floor and were cut low in the front. Hawk and Bones sat down in two empty chairs at one of the tables.

"Well, lookey here! Me new bosun! Hey, Madame Cynthia, get the Hawk some rum! And some hot grub."

"Make it ale," Hawk said. After seeing the alehouses, he wanted to try it. Plus, he didn't want a repeat of the night before.

Madame Cynthia walked over to Hawk a few minutes later and set a tankard of ale down in front of him. She was an older but attractive lady. Her red hair was put up into a bun on the top, and she wore a blue, white-trimmed dress. "What have we here, Captain? Where have you been hiding, Mr. Hawk?"

Hawk instantly felt his cheeks warm. "Uh...just on the ship...and island," he stammered. The nearby pirates burst into loud laughter and gave some catcalls.

"Hmmm. I might take this one for myself tonight," Cynthia said, looking from Hawk to Bloodstone."

"Ye'd kill the poor boy," Bloodstone said to even louder laughter. "Better stick with a man that can handle ye."

"Yeah. I suppose you're right, Captain. But I do have a good companion for Mr. Hawk. She's not too much older than him and very gentle." She looked back at Hawk and brushed his cheek with the back of her hand. His cheeks burned even hotter. "Maybe one day...when you can handle me." She turned and walked off, swinging her hips side-to-side.

Hawk quickly took a swig of ale, which he liked much better than the rum, and waited for the pirates to grow tired of teasing him. Soon they did, and all listened to Bloodstone tell stories. He told them about a privateer, which most had heard of, named Jean Lafitte. Lafitte used to have a base on nearby Grande Terre. He had up to fifty ships and a thousand men. He stole from the Spanish ships and brought the goods to New Orleans. His brother, Pierre, ran a nearby warehouse that actually sold the goods.

A couple of years earlier, Lafitte had fallen out of favor with the local merchants trying to make an honest living. The US Navy overran his base and forced him and his crew to leave. When the war with the British started, Andrew Jackson, the US general in charge of fighting the British, sought out Lafitte's aid. With the help and skill of his men, the United States repelled the British attack and ended the war. Lafitte then moved his fleet to Galveston Island, off the coast of New Spain. So now Bloodstone and his crew had to pretend to be merchant sailors and fishermen so as not to be mistaken for some of Lafitte's crew. Hawk realized that was why Bloodstone had dressed up like a naval officer and referred to himself as Captain Blackburn.

As the night wore on, the pirates consumed more and more rum and ale. They were also served hot, fresh food. There were slabs of beef, pork ribs, and pieces of chicken. There were also cooked vegetables and pieces of bread that were actually soft. Wesley could cook well, but didn't usually have the option of serving food this fresh. There were a lot of women serving drinks and some that just came by and talked with the men. Occasionally, one of the pirates would get up and follow a woman up the spiral staircase in the corner of the room. Soon, there was just a handful of pirates left. Hawk was feeling good from the ale but not out of control like he had been with the grog.

Madame Cynthia finally returned to the table with a young woman. Her companion had long reddish-brown hair, pale skin, and green eyes. She wore a low-cut green dress, similar in style to Cynthia's, with gold lace trim. She was the most beautiful woman Hawk had ever seen, although before tonight, that was none. She glanced at Hawk briefly and then looked down shyly at the floor.

"Mr. Hawk, this is Anna. She'll be your...companion for the night. Now, Cap'n, are you ready for your companion?"

"Thought ye'd never ask," Bloodstone said as he laughed. He slammed his mug down on the table. "Well, Hawk, this week ye became a bosun. Tonight, ye become a man!" Bloodstone stood up grinning and followed Madame Cynthia, slapping her on the rear more than once. She led him up the spiral staircase.

"Are you ready to go upstairs?" Anna asked, smiling shyly. Her voice was sweet and pure.

Hawk's heart started pounding as hard as it did at the start of a battle. He nodded, smiled nervously, and got up to follow her across the room and up the stairs. He really didn't know what was to happen next. He just knew everyone else was going up the stairs with women. At the top of the stairs, she turned left. The hallway ran in both directions. Doors were spaced closely together on both sides. She opened the last door on the right and disappeared into the room. Hawk followed quickly after.

The room was small and sparsely furnished. There was a small round table and two chairs close to the door, a small bed in the corner, and a washbasin with a mirror above it in the other corner. A pail of water sat on the floor beside the basin. There was a burning oil lamp on a small square table beside the bed. The window in the wall opposite the door was covered with old, torn curtains. The room was dusty and smelled of must.

Anna shut and locked the door once Hawk entered. She walked to the bed and sat on its edge. Then she patted the bed beside her, and Hawk slowly walked over and sat down. He stared down at his boots and the dusty floor. Her sweet, flowery, perfume quickly found his nose. She smelled wonderful.

"So, how old are you, Mr. Hawk?" She asked sweetly, staring at the side of his face.

He thought briefly about lying, but he was sure his behavior would betray him. "Sixteen."

"Wow, so young!"

"How old are you?" he said, a little defensively.

"A woman does not tell her age, silly boy! But several years older than you." Her laugh was musical. "I assume this is your first time?"

Hawk finally looked up and turned to gaze upon the beautiful creature beside him. Her skin was soft and smooth. It was such a contrast to the tough, leathered faces of pirates and sailors. Her large green eyes flickered in the lantern light. Her lips were full and pink, glistening slightly with moisture. He glanced briefly at her ample cleavage and the exposed tops of her shapely breasts. He quickly looked back up at her face. She smiled, showing perfect white teeth, also rarely seen on a ship.

Anna laughed, a little louder than before. "Am I that hideous, Mr. Hawk? You look at me like I am a sea monster!"

Hawk's cheeks burned even hotter than they had downstairs. "Uh… no! You're…you're the most beautiful thing I've ever seen!"

"Hmmm…thing?" She quickly spoke again before Hawk suffered even longer. "Thank you very much. You are a very handsome young man and certainly not like your sailor companions."

"Uh, thank you." Hawk looked away, not able to keep looking at her beautiful face.

"So, Mr. Hawk, should we get started?" Anna reached out and laid her left hand on top of his right, her fingers wrapping around the edge of the palm and rubbing softly.

Her hand was so warm and smooth on Hawk's rough, calloused skin. Tingles raced up from his hand to his arm and quickly spread throughout the rest of his body. He felt the hair stand up on his arms and the back of his neck, as if it were cold in the room. He wondered for a moment if she was a siren or some other magical creature—like he'd read about with Wesley—casting a spell over him. He slowly turned his hand over, allowing their palms to touch and his fingers to squeeze her hand too. He looked up to stare into her mesmerizing eyes. "Can we just talk for a while first?" he whispered.

The sweet, young, attractive sailor in front of her intrigued Anna. She had been forced into prostitution when she was not much older than Hawk. She had sold her body to more sailors and pirates than she cared to count. None of her encounters had ever gone like this. None of her patrons wanted to hold hands or talk. They were mostly animals. She was also a little concerned. She felt something with the touch of Hawk's young yet strong hand. Chills ran up her arm, and her heart fluttered quickly. "The night is yours. What would you like to talk about, Mr. Hawk?"

"Well, first, I'm just Hawk, not Mr. Hawk." He grinned at her. He was slowly gaining his composure and feeling a little more at ease. He continued holding her hand and lightly stroked it with his fingertips. "How does someone as beautiful and kind as you end up doing this… working here?"

It was Anna's turn to look away from him and down at the floor. "That is a long story that you do not wish to hear."

"Yes, I really do want to hear. Please tell me."

She had never told her story to anyone other than Madame Cynthia, but for some reason she felt at ease with Hawk. She found herself talking before she could reconsider. "My father was a wealthy fur trader. He traveled around a large area, trapping and hunting animals, and sold their pelts back here. My mother went with him on one long trip, and my uncle watched over me. We received word that they were attacked and killed by Indians. My uncle sold everything my father had, took the money, and disappeared. I had no money or food. I lived on the streets begging for a couple of months until Madame Cynthia found me. She gave me clothes, food, and a place to stay. She taught me how to talk and act like a lady. She told me that even though our patrons were rude and crude, they did not want the same in a woman. In exchange, I had to work for her and take care of men."

Hawk thought he saw tears in Anna's eyes as she turned away to look toward the lantern. By her speech and mannerisms, he would have never guessed she hadn't come from royalty. "That's a terrible story. I'm sorry about your family." Without thinking, he removed his hand from hers and placed it on her back. He rubbed her through her dress.

The tingling sensation on her back snapped Anna back into the present. She quickly wiped the corners of her eyes and turned back to face Hawk. The tingling was turning to heat, spreading all over. "Now your story, Hawk."

He told her his story, except he carefully skirted around the pirating part, since he'd heard about the price on Lafitte's head. He told her that he worked aboard a merchant ship. Everything else he told was the truth, but he was vague when it came to the Rock and how they obtained their merchandise. "So, it sounds like we have a lot in common," he said.

"Yes, I suppose we do. But I believe you have more freedoms and get to have adventures. And you are not just a plaything for nasty sailors."

"Nasty sailors like me?" Hawk asked, flashing his smile.

"You know what I mean," Anna responded, playfully slapping his leg.

"I'm not sure if I would consider my life freedom. I'm pretty much confined to the ship most of the time. And life on a ship is not as fun as it sounds. The work is hard, the food terrible, and the smells unbearable. You're at the mercy of the weather and winds. Sometimes the wind won't blow for days or even weeks. Disease is a constant worry. The Rock is nice, but we're not able to stay there often. We always have to find more goods to sell for money."

"I guess we both got dealt a bad hand," she replied softly.

"It also just struck me for the first time today, as we entered the city, that there is so much I haven't seen or done. I saw my first horse today, and a horse-drawn carriage. I saw my first town, with stone streets and markets and restaurants. And I just saw my first woman today!"

Anna laughed. "And you are getting ready to experience something else new." Anna slowly leaned toward Hawk.

Hawk didn't move as Anna leaned toward him. He wasn't sure exactly what was going to happen next. He was scared, but he knew he wanted to experience more with that young woman beside him. Instinctively, at the last moment, he leaned in to meet her. Her soft, warm, moist lips touched his. The sensation was incredible. The tingles he felt at the touch of her hand were nothing compared to now. It felt like even the hair on his head stood. He closed his eyes and enjoyed her lips moving across his. She was soft and gentle at first and then began to move her lips faster and press them more firmly against his. He didn't know what he was doing, but he tried to move his together with hers. Soon he felt an incredible desire stirring. The rush of sensations and emotions was almost overwhelming.

Anna didn't know what possessed her to kiss the young sailor. Madame Cynthia had taught her early on not to kiss any of the men she entertained. She said kissing led to feelings, and she didn't want or need any feelings for sailors. Maybe it was just his naïvety and innocence, but she was drawn to Hawk. There was no hiding his inexperience at kissing, but the touch of his lips still excited her. She felt a warm flush spread over her body. As she kissed him more passionately, Hawk seemed to catch on, and he began to kiss her back. For the first time ever, she actually wanted to make love to someone, not just do her duty.

Anna finally broke off the kiss and stood up. Hawk opened his eyes and looked up at her, silhouetted in the lantern light. She reached up and started to pull the top of her dress down.

"Whoa! What are you doing?" he said.

She laughed. "Why, disrobing of course."

"Why?"

"You really are a naïve one! That is what comes next."

"Sit back down. Please," he said, patting the bed beside him.

She slowly sat back down on the bed. "What would you have me do, Hawk?"

"Let's lie down together and talk and hold hands and press our lips together some more," Hawk said with a big grin. He crawled behind her and lay down on the bed, his head on the old, lumpy pillow and his right arm underneath it.

Anna laughed and joined him. "So, what should we talk about now?"

Hawk experimentally reached his left arm around her and pulled her close. He ran his hand through her long, thick hair and stroked the soft skin of her neck and shoulders. She reached her arm around him and rubbed his muscled back through his shirt and waistcoat.

"What are your plans in life?" he said.

"Plans? I do not understand."

"You're not going to do…work here forever, are you?" Hawk's left hand continued to roam over her body from her shoulder down her arm to her side and hip.

"I have not really thought about it. I save what money I can, but Madame Cynthia takes a large portion for my room, food, and clothing. I am nowhere near being able to leave. There are very few jobs for women too. Unless of course I find a rich man to steal me away." She laughed. She brought her hand up to run it through Hawk's wavy blond hair and touch his cheek.

"And where would this rich man whisk you away to?" Hawk found it occasionally hard to concentrate with Anna's caresses. His skin prickled at almost every touch.

"Hmmm. I would not be very hard to please. Maybe to a big farm in the country. He would build me a brand new log cabin in the middle." Anna's voice quickened with excitement as she momentarily allowed her mind to escape her life. "We would own horses that we would ride almost every day across our land. There would be a forest and a river. We would sleep out under the stars on occasion and spend hours on the riverbank. We would have lots of farm animals and crops for food and to sell, and we would help each other with the chores. It would be our own private paradise. Then of course we would have to raise children to enjoy it with us and help with the farm."

"Wow! That's a good plan," Hawk exclaimed, laughing at her enthusiasm.

Anna's smile slowly disappeared. "No. Not a plan. Just a foolish girl's dream. Now, what is your plan for your future?" Anna enjoyed talking to Hawk, but his hand touching her body had her mind on other things. He was so close, yet so far away.

"I'd never thought about anything except pir...being a sailor." He silently cursed himself for his slip of the tongue. "Until this trip. Now I just wonder how much more is out there that I've never seen. I've saved up some money too, but like you, I doubt I have enough to leave the ship. And if I did leave, I wouldn't even know how to survive in this city or anywhere else. But I do like the sound of your dream. The only thing I would add is occasionally leaving the farm to go on trips, exploring the world."

"I guess we are both just foolish dreamers," Anna whispered.

"No. Dreams can come true. Maybe one day I'll become rich and be the man to steal you away to that farm!"

Anna laughed loudly. "Should I pack a bag and be ready for you?"

Hawk playfully slapped her hip. "No. It will take a while. Just don't let go of that dream." He leaned forward and gently kissed her. He wasn't sure if he had figured it out yet, but it definitely felt right. Anna moaned softly as she kissed him back. Their wet lips slid back in forth, moving in perfect unison now. They continued to caress each other through their clothing. They kissed, touched, talked, and finally slept—clothed—for a few hours. Anna faced away from Hawk, holding the hand on the arm he kept wrapped tightly around her. She felt safe and secure for one of the first nights ever—although it was a restless night, as both of their minds were occupied with much more than sleep.

The last couple of hours of sleep were finally deep. It was rare for Hawk to get to sleep in a warm bed and one that was not moving with the waves. When Hawk finally awoke the next morning, he was alone. There was no sign of Anna. He quickly pulled on his boots and headed downstairs. Madame Cynthia met him at the bar. "So, did you have a good time, Mr. Hawk?"

"Uh, yes, the best, ma'am!" He looked around the room, but it was nearly empty. "Where is Anna?"

"I'm glad. You'll have to come back soon. I'm sure Anna would like to see you again. I had to send her out to run some errands. Captain Blackburn has already paid. He and the rest of your crew have already headed back to your ship."

Hawk couldn't conceal his disappointment. He nodded to Madame Cynthia and quickly made his way back to the ship. As he walked back through the square, he wished he could stay for the entire day. The square was much less busy in the early morning hours, and the shops were just opening up. The smells of the evening before were just starting to waft through the warm, thick air.

His thoughts then shifted to Anna. He wondered where she might be and how she felt about him and the night they spent together. He could still feel her soft skin, taste her warm luscious lips, and smell her sweet perfume. He would be counting down the days until he got to see her again. He was also going to work hard at saving his money. He now received a share and half of plunder, since he was a boatswain, or bosun as the crew called him. Somehow, someway, he would become rich and be the man who rescued Anna from her current existence.

CHAPTER VIII

RESCUE

*I*t seemed a long voyage back to the Rock, with all of the teasing and questions Hawk received from the rest of the crew. He was sure his cheeks glowed red the entire trip. Even Bloodstone threw in his fair share of comments. "Did she let ye swab 'er decks, lad?" The pirates roared with laughter.

"Hawk, is it true your flintlock went off before it cleared your breeches?" asked Lucky, the pirate sporting a hook for his left hand. Another roar of laughter erupted from his mates.

"Now, mates, we are being a little hard on Mr. Hawk. I am sure he mastered the fair young maiden the same way he mastered firing a musket," Mr. Bones said.

Hawk stood up straight and puffed his chest out. "Thank you, Mr. Bones."

"Aye," said Bones. "Grabbed hold tightly with both hands, closed his eyes, and prayed she would not kill him."

Laughter erupted again. Some of the pirates actually fell to the deck. Even Bloodstone doubled over and slapped his knee. Hawk quickly scurried up a ratline to check the sails and rigging. He stayed at the mast tops until they reached the Rock.

"Wesley!" Hawk shouted, running into Wesley's cabin.

The old man looked up from his desk and the book he read, peering over his glasses. "Ah, yes, fresh back from your first night in town."

"I had the best night of my life!" Hawk ran and leapt onto the bed, similar to the way he had so many years before. Only this time his emotions were much different.

Wesley chuckled. "The first fresh-faced lass usually does that to you."

"No. I met the best girl in the world! We talked and held hands and pressed our lips together!"

"Kissed?"

"I guess that's it! But I felt all tingly, and had chills, and the hairs on my arm stood up when she just touched me! I can't even describe all of the feelings I have for her. My stomach's churning like a whirlpool, and my head spins like I've drank too much rum again." The words left Hawk's mouth almost at the same speed that he thought them.

"Whoa. Heave to there, lad!" Wesley's smile disappeared, and he shook his head.

"What's wrong? Is something wrong with me? Am I sick?"

"Aye, I reckon you have a touch of somethin', all right. I'm afraid you've fallen head over tail in love."

"Love?" Hawk asked, his smile also disappearing.

"Aye. What your feelin' is love, I reckon," Wesley said somberly.

"Is love bad?"

"Oh, it's fine while it lasts. Never does though. And love messes with people's heads. It's caused more murders, wars, and heartaches than anything 'cept religion, I'd wager."

Hawk was silent as he mulled over Wesley's words. For a moment his emotions were dampened. "Have you ever been in love?"

Wesley stared at him for a moment, as if deciding whether to tell his story. "Aye, that I have. A sad tale too."

"Please tell it to me!" Hawk pleaded.

"All right, sit back and listen, then. When I was a lad, 'bout your age, I was a sailor on an English privateer ship. We had a charter from the king to attack Spanish ships and take the loot they brought back from the New World. I lost my leg a couple of years into it, and they made me the cook. The gold and silver was plentiful back then and the fat galleons ripe for the pickin'. I saved up a good sum of money to leave that life one day while I was still a young man.

"In London between voyages, I met the prettiest young lass you've ever seen. Her name was Emily. Ah, her voice was like a siren's, and she smelled as sweet as a field of honeysuckle. Her skin was like silk. I felt just like what you described. We got married and bought a little house. I was determined more than ever to save enough money so that I could leave the sailor life behind and be with her every day and night.

"We sailed all the way to Havana on one trip, gone for several months. I thought about my sweet Emily every night, even dreamed 'bout her on most. When we finally returned to England, I rushed home to my little cottage. I found it empty. All of my loot and possessions were gone, as well as sweet little Emily. I never saw her again. After that, I gave up my dreams of leavin' this life and of love and women. Sure, I've had my share of women over the years, but a night here and a night there. Nothing but trouble they are." Wesley spat on the floor beside his chair.

"That certainly is a sad tale. But surely all women aren't like that. You might have found another one that would have loved you as much as you loved her," Hawk said.

"My heart was in pieces for nearly a year after that. Don't know that it ever totally healed, or at least it healed a little blacker and colder. I'll never risk it again. If it gets broke again, it'll be from a musket ball or cutlass."

They were both silent for a few minutes.

"Well, my Anna wouldn't do that to me," Hawk finally said. "I can't help how I feel, no matter how bad your being in love turned out. I'm going to save up my money too, and when I have enough, we're going to run away and live happily ever after on a little farm." Hawk's excitement was suddenly rekindled.

Wesley chucked again. "All this from one night together, huh?"

"I have given my word and made up my mind." Hawk climbed off the bed and headed to the door. He didn't want Wesley to damage his mood any further.

"Just keep your wits about you, boy. If it happens, it happens, but until then you're a pirate with duties to perform."

Hawk walked out, closing the door firmly behind him.

"Lover boy," a voice called out.

Hawk looked up to see Diablo emerging from his cabin. He was dressed in a blue and red military outfit. He was leading the men that didn't go to New Orleans the night before into town that night. Hawk ignored him and headed toward his cabin.

"Hawk, what was your lass's name? I might have to show her what a real man can do tonight."

Hawk suddenly whirled around, his hand on the hilt of his cutlass. "Stay away from her!"

Diablo laughed. "You're a little on edge, my boy. And I'll tip her well. Oh, and don't pull that blade out unless you intend to use it."

"If I pull it out, it will be used. And if you lay a hand on her, it will come out."

The two men stared at each other for what seemed like minutes. Finally, Diablo grinned, tipped his hat, and headed toward the gate. Hawk stormed into his cabin, overwhelmed by his many conflicting emotions.

In the months that followed, Hawk's fighting skills and prowess only improved with experience. Diablo usually led the pirates into battle, but Hawk was close behind. Many of the pirates even deferred to Hawk as their leader and not Diablo. There was a split between the younger pirates and older ones, with the younger gravitating to Hawk. Hawk and Diablo had their frequent run-ins, but they knew Bloodstone wouldn't tolerate fighting among pirates on his ship. They would either be marooned or forced to duel to the death. Neither was quite confident enough for a duel. So they poked and prodded but avoided coming to blows.

Hawk continued to think about Anna at least every night in his hammock. They did visit the Rock a time or two over the next couple of years. But they didn't go back to New Orleans during that time. It was a little risky after the ouster of Lafitte and with the new attitudes against pirates. Also, the New Orleans Squadron had been assigned to hunt pirates after the end of the war with England. Bloodstone expanded his area of operations to be harder for the navy to find. He also started visiting different cities to sell their merchandise and spend their coin—Tortuga, Havana, Port-au-Prince, Santo Domingo, and Kingston. They used extra caution and took more time with their disguises in the Spanish towns. Kingston was British owned, so they spent most of their time there.

Officially, Kingston was against piracy. Any pirates that were caught were hung at Gallows Point on the island of Port Royal, which had been a pirate haven many years before. Unofficially, pirates brought in cheap goods for the merchants. Even better, most of the goods came from Spanish galleons and merchant ships. So the Kingston officials and soldiers didn't look for pirates, but had to deal with them if they found them. Kingston had enough taverns, gambling houses, and brothels to keep the pirates happy. Hawk partook in the drink and some occasional gambling, but never the women. He couldn't do that to Anna, even though he knew she was with many other men.

Hawk's body and confidence continued to develop. He continued to push himself to be the best in all forms of combat. When at one of their island retreats, he practiced shooting every type of weapon. Soon, he was even better than Andre. In battles, he looked for new and inventive ways to defeat his opponents: shooting them in different body parts, using different cutlass strokes, kicking and punching, etc.

Bloodstone also stopped the cutlass lessons. He would make up excuses why, but he and Hawk both knew the real reason. As Hawk entered his eighteenth year, he was at the prime of his life. Bloodstone was well on the backside of his. He might still be able to defeat Hawk through cunning and trickery but couldn't risk Hawk defeating him. The crew already looked to Hawk more and more for leadership. It wouldn't take much to have Hawk officially voted in as captain.

Hawk continued to amass a small fortune in gold and silver. Most of his comrades spent all of their loot on alcohol, gambling, and women. That's why most pirates could never leave the trade. The more they made, the more they spent, and the more they had to make. Hawk had to spend a little on food and drink and clothing, but the rest he stashed away. Although the visions of Anna faded somewhat, he still thought of her almost daily. He still enjoyed the battles and the admiration of the crew, but his mind was with Anna, and dry land, during the quiet moments.

Captain Bloodstone didn't make many mistakes, or else he wouldn't have lived so long in the pirate business. His greatest occurred during this time period away from New Orleans and the Rock. During their long voyage, they used several different uninhabited Caribbean islands for their bases of operation. Most of the infamous pirate hideouts, like New Providence, Tortuga, and Port Royal, had been cleared out. The US Navy had also started searching unpopulated islands. Setting up a long-term base was not going to be a good option for survival, and the voyage to the Rock was too long to make on a regular basis. So, they just searched for a safe-looking harbor to use long enough to careen the *Bloody Seas* and make repairs.

Many of these islands had shallow harbors, and the *Bloody Seas* had a deep draft. That made it difficult to careen her and to transfer items from ship to shore. Bloodstone wanted a smaller, faster ship that could better navigate the small islands and escape the British naval ships if necessary. He happened to spot the perfect twenty-gun, two-masted Bermuda sloop on one trip while searching for Spanish prey. Bloodstone fell in love with the vessel and had to have it.

The only problem was that the sloop belonged to the Royal Navy. Bloodstone put taking the ship to a crew vote. The crew, always up for a new challenge, voted in favor of taking it. Hawk disagreed. The Spanish were their prey and the ones they could justify attacking. Hawk had no issues with British, especially since his family was from England. But he didn't want to vote against the crew. He did ask Bloodstone to show mercy on the sailors.

Bloodstone used his tactic of flying the same flag as the prey, in this case a Union Jack they found aboard the a Spanish merchantman some time back. They hailed the sloop, easily sailed close, and put the *Bloody Seas* broadside. By the time Bloodstone revealed their true intentions, the sloop captain knew he couldn't match the firepower of the pirates or escape. In return for not resisting, not risking damaging his new ship, and to appease Hawk, Bloodstone offered to maroon them on a nearby island. The area was a busy sailing lane, so marooning would not be the death sentence that it normally was.

Bloodstone sailed the *Bloody Seas* and his new prize, the *Cobra*, named for its speed, to a nearby haunt. Bones and a select crew stayed behind on the island to customize the *Cobra*. They ripped out cabins and upper decks and took out as much weight as possible. Bloodstone also instructed Bones to mount oars inside the cannon ports so the cannons could be rolled back and the ship rowed if the winds were not in their favor. Hawk decided to stay with Bones and assist, as Bloodstone and his crew returned to the sea to hunt Spanish. Another trip to Kingston was also in their near future.

Two weeks later, work on the *Cobra* was complete.

"There they be!" a young pirate, Benjamin, called out from the top of a palm tree.

The *Bloody Seas* had been gone the entire time that work on the *Cobra* had proceeded. That was a little long for a typical treasure and carousing run. Hawk had been close to taking out the *Cobra* to search for them. Pirates gathered on the beach from various makeshift huts and shelters and from performing various tasks about the new ship and island to greet their captain and crewmates.

The *Bloody Seas* dropped anchor, and a longboat was lowered into the water. A group of pirates quickly filled it and rowed to shore.

Hawk stood in front of the crowd to greet them. "Where's the Captain? And Diablo?"

Wesley and Andre limped onto shore, followed by a half dozen other pirates. "Let's go to your hut and talk," Wesley said. Hawk had never seen that look on his face before. Andre was also unusually quiet. The three quickly headed to the makeshift, thatch-roofed hut Hawk was using as a cabin. The rest of the pirates gathered around the other six to find out what information they could.

"It's bad, Hawk, real bad," Wesley said, breathing slightly hard from the short but brisk walk.

"What happened?"

"We took a nice Spanish prize nigh a week ago. Course, the boys all wanted to head to Kingston to celebrate. One night of celebratin' led to two. The second night, Diablo, Bloodstone, Billy, and a couple of mates left us to seek out a new tavern. Little did they know it was a favorite haunt of the Royal Navy and city garrison. By the powers, who do you suppose was in there that very night? The crew of that sloop out there! Apparently, they had already been rescued from their maroonin' and returned to Kingston. That cursed captain made Bloodstone and Diablo right away. All 'cept Billy was immediately taken off in chains to the prison.

"Billy managed to slip off without bein' caught and found us before the garrison did. We made haste to the *Bloody Seas* and set sail before they found us. From what we heard, they was to be tried the next day and hung at Gallows Point a week later if convicted." Wesley's face was pale and sweat-covered by the time he finished the story.

Hawk collapsed into a chair beside the small table in the middle of the room. He was stunned by the news that Bloodstone, Diablo, and two other pirates were going to be hung. He was distraught over the fact that he'd helped talk Bloodstone into showing mercy on the British sloop crew instead of dealing with them the same as they did the Spanish.

He nodded to the other chairs around the table. Andre and Wesley gladly sat down.

"So, when do you think the hanging will be?" said Hawk.

Wesley scratched his beard. "It took us four days to sail back here. I s'ppose that'd make it three days."

"Blast! Can we sail back there in three days?" Hawk stared at the table and rubbed his hand through his thick hair.

"Not in the *Bloody Seas*. The winds won't be any better going back. Wouldn't do no good anyway, unless you just want to watch Bloodstone and the others swing."

Hawk stood up and quickly walked over to the canvas sheet that served as a door and flung it open. "Bones! Get in here!" His voice carried across the entire beach.

He returned to his seat and waited a few minutes until the man arrived. "Mr. Bones, can we sail from here to Port Royal in three days on the *Cobra*?"

Bones looked briefly at the stern faces of Wesley and Andre and then back to Hawk. "It would be tight, and it might require some rowing, but I would say with a good crew it could be done."

"What are you thinking, Hawk?" Andre said.

"We're going to rescue them. It's my fault that we let that British crew live. I can't let Bloodstone and the rest, even Diablo, swing for that."

"Your mad, Hawk!" Wesley exclaimed in a tone that surprised Hawk. "And what would your plan be?"

"That's what we're going to figure out. Who knows Port Royal and Jamaica the best?"

Wesley thought for a moment. "I s'ppose that would be Billy. I believe he lived most of his life in Jamaica before goin' on account."

"Bones, get Billy in here. Gentlemen, we're going to stay in this cabin until we have a plan. Then we'll have the entire crew vote on it. But either way, with a crew or not, I'm leaving before sunset for Port Royal."

The *Cobra* set sail shortly before sunset, just as Hawk had promised. He had put his plan to the pirate crew, and they unanimously voted in favor of it. None questioned Hawk's assumption of leadership, with the captain and quartermaster not present for duty. He didn't put being temporary captain to a vote. He just took charge. Bones, Andre, and Billy—Hawk's officers for the voyage—and Wesley and forty pirates joined Hawk. Fourteen of the pirates manned the oars when the wind wasn't behind them. The remainder worked the sails. Hawk spent much of his time with his officers finalizing the plan. They sailed hard for three days and nights.

The air already hung hot and thick above Port Royal as the sun climbed above the haze over the eastern horizon. The crowd was filing into Gallows Point to see the hanging of the most famous pirate since Calico Jack Rackham almost a hundred years prior. The common people walked, while the well-to-do arrived in horse-drawn carriages. There was a large contingent of garrison soldiers scattered among the crowd. Most were more interested in watching the hanging than ensuring the other spectators were orderly.

Port Royal was a shell of its former self, since the earthquake had destroyed it many years before. But today, the large crowd and buzz in the air made it feel as important as it had ever been. Many boats crowded the docks and filled the channel between Port Royal and Kingston. The berth closest to the shore remained open, waiting for the ship from Kingston that would soon arrive with the governor, executioner, and prisoners.

The gallows consisted of a large, elevated wooden platform, with a long beam running nearly the entire length ten feet above. Five nooses hung down from the beam. A lever at the end of one of the side support beams would cause the portion of the platform beneath the nooses to drop away, allowing the victims to fall through the platform, breaking their necks.

Garrison soldiers formed a hundred foot perimeter around the platform and kept the area clear of spectators. They also kept a wide pathway open from the circle to the docks. Two horse-drawn carts, with a man sitting on each horse, sat at the eastern edge of the circle just behind the soldiers waiting to haul the bodies off after the ceremony had been completed.

"Good day for a hangin'," a man in the crowd said to one of the soldiers surrounding the scaffold.

"It is always a good day when a cowardly villain is brought to justice," the soldier said, hardly glancing at the armed sailor behind him.

"Aye, 'twill be a day to remember for sure," said the man.

A cheer erupted through the now large crowd. All eyes turned toward a beautiful schooner that approached the docks from the direction of Kingston. The ship was in pristine condition, its rails and gunport trim painted gold and the boards of the brown hull polished until the sun reflected off of them. The sails were new and glowed a brilliant white in the sunlight. Ten polished bronze cannons could be seen through the open ports. It sailed effortlessly across the glassy water and soon glided to the open berth at the dock. A gangplank was quickly extended, and a small party crossed from the deck to the dock.

At the edge of the docks, two drummers began to tap their drums. The garrison captain led the small column, dressed in his finest bright red military uniform. Behind him walked the governor, dressed in white silk stockings, maroon velvet breeches, a white silk and lace-trimmed ruffled shirt, a maroon waistcoat, and a long maroon velvet coat with polished brass buttons and gold trim. A golden sash circled his waist. His face was red and puffy, already gleaming with sweat, and his head was adorned with a powdered wig. The executioner was next—a burly, bearded man that bore a slight resemblance to Bloodstone. Two garrison soldiers followed, with the four convicted pirates next, their hands chained behind their backs. Two more soldiers brought up the rear.

Captain Bloodstone was the first prisoner. He'd been stripped of his fine town clothes and was dressed in a plain gray linen shirt and pants. His head was bare and his hair tossed wildly about his head and shoulders. Despite not wearing his black pirate clothing, or being armed, he was still an intimidating man. He grinned at the cheering crowd lining the narrow path that led to the gallows. Diablo followed, dressed in similar clothing. His grin was more of a sneer. He spat several times on the ground as they walked. Stephen Martin and Jeremiah Parker stared at their feet, their fear evident to all.

The crowd turned from cheering the governor and soldiers to jeering the pirates as the procession made its way to the platform. The garrison captain led them up the stairs and across the back of the platform. The crowd fell silent as the executioner, governor, and captain stepped forward to the front. All eyes were upon the platform and those gathered upon it.

"Mr. Executioner, what are the crimes that these men have been convicted of?" the governor asked in a loud, but high-pitched voice.

The executioner's baritone voice boomed across the entire square. "Governor Worthington, these men—Captain Bloodstone, his quartermaster, Diablo, Stephen Martin, and Jeremiah Parker—have been convicted of murder, theft, and acts of piracy against the Royal Navy. Their sentence is hanging until deceased."

An excited murmur spread through the crowd. Soon, random shouts and chants erupted. Gallows Point had a long history of pirate hangings, but the frequency had decreased since the golden age of piracy had ended many years before. Captain Bloodstone was a well-known name. The one-eyed Diablo had also earned a reputation for his cruelty and brutality.

As the crowd roared and cheered, no one noticed four sailors climbing onto the backs of the carts, two into each. Two of the men were whole and healthy. Each of the other two had a peg for one leg. Two men stayed in the carts. One of the healthy men and one of the peg-legged men slid onto the backs of the horses. Before the rider's could even turn in surprise, their throats were slit. The thuds of their bodies hitting the ground and the shuffling of the horses went unnoticed by the enthralled crowd.

The soldiers on the platform pushed the four pirates forward to stand before the nooses. "Do the convicted have any last words?" the executioner said in his booming voice. The noise in the crowd quieted to a dull murmur. The other three pirates looked to their captain.

Captain Bloodstone somberly surveyed the exuberant crowd. His eyes fell briefly upon the two carts. A slight grin appeared, and he turned back to the crowd in front of the gallows. "Arrr!" Bloodstone roared loudly, as if he was addressing his crew. "I reckon I do."

The crowd suddenly fell completely silent as the legendary pirate spoke. "I used to only hunt those thievin', blasted Spanish devils and take back their stolen loot. Made a good run of it, I did. Never had anything 'gainst the British." He spat onto the platform in front of him. "I reckon that be changed now. When I get back to me ship and back to the sea, I'll be killin' ye British cowards too."

The crowd erupted with shouts and boos.

The governor's face went pale, or at least paler. "Get this over with," he said to the captain and executioner. The soldiers placed the nooses around the necks of the four pirates and slid the knots down until they were tight. The governor, captain, and soldiers returned to the back of the gallows. The executioner walked over to the lever.

The two carts began to roll forward. The soldiers in front were nudged to the side. They were somewhat surprised, since the drivers normally waited until after the pirates were dead, but they quickly turned their attention back to the gallows. If the driver's were not following the ceremonial protocol, they would have to answer to the governor after. Once the carts cleared the soldiers, the rider's spurred their horses into a near gallop.

The noise of the crowd was so loud that scant attention was paid the body carts and their occupants. The drummers from the dock now stood just inside the perimeter. They began playing a drum roll. The executioner placed his hand on the lever. The sailors in the back of each cart rose up to their knees, each bringing up a musket. Two shots rang out just as the lever was pulled and the platform broke away. The four pirates fell. Bloodstone and Diablo totally disappeared through the gallows, landing on the ground below. The musket balls had severed their ropes. The other two pirate's bodies dropped halfway down, and then their momentum halted as the nooses snapped their necks.

Chaos erupted on the gallows and within the crowd. It took a moment for everyone, including the executioner, governor, and garrison soldiers, to realize what had happened. The two carts were now in front of the gallows. Diablo and Bloodstone ran out from beneath the platform and were quickly helped into the carts by Hawk and Andre. Wesley and Billy, the two drivers, spurred their horses harder and galloped toward the open path to the docks.

As the garrison soldiers began to recover from shock, most drew their weapons. Then commotion erupted from their ranks. Bodies started to fall as daggers were plunged into their backs. Twenty-six of the pirate crew of the *Cobra* had positioned themselves just behind the soldiers along the path. They were some of the same ones who had struck up conversations with them just moments before. The soldiers were torn between stopping the carts and defending themselves from the attackers behind. A couple did get off shots, but none hit the carts or the pirates within. As the carts sped by, many of the pirates leapt onto them. Once onboard, they turned, drew their flintlocks, and began firing at the pursuing soldiers. Other pirates ran behind the carts, shooting and stabbing at any one following. The spectators were frozen in shock.

While the ceremony had been in progress, the *Cobra* had sailed up to the dock, wedged in beside the large schooner that had delivered the prisoners. The two carts sped toward the *Cobra*. The driver's halted the carts on the dock in front of the sloop, and their passengers quickly hopped out. Several muskets fired behind them, the balls sailing harmlessly past. Hawk helped Wesley off of his horse, and Billy helped Andre out of the wagon, and the pirates all crossed the gangplank.

Once aboard, they headed to the loaded muskets that were leaning against the rails. They quickly grabbed them, aimed, and fired into the garrison soldiers chasing the remaining pirates. The last pirates ran and leapt from the dock to the ship as their mates continued to fire the muskets, blunderbusses, and flintlocks. Bloodstone and Diablo were still shackled, so they, Wesley, and Andre hurried below deck. Andre shouted out orders to the gunners. Hawk assumed command of the ship.

The ten cannons on the port side fired into the side of the governor's schooner. At point blank range, the middle of the beautifully polished hull was shattered. The cannons were quickly rolled back and secured, and twenty pirates took their positions and started rowing. The last group of garrison soldiers reached the dock and stopped to bring up their muskets. The two swivel guns on the bow of the *Cobra* fired canister shot into the group, sending the soldiers either collapsing onto the dock or fleeing back into the crowd. There was no more pursuit or shots as the *Cobra* rowed into open water and then unfurled the sails to catch the strong wind. There were no cannons fired from the many forts spaced around the Jamaican coast. Word could not travel as fast as the sloop. If any other ships followed, they were quickly left behind.

CHAPTER IX

HOMEWARD BOUND

*O*nce the *Cobra* was in open waters and running before the wind, the celebration started. Bloodstone and Diablo had their chains cut, and all of the pirates gathered on deck to celebrate. Although they had lost Stephen and Jeremiah and five other pirates at Gallows Point, Hawk had pulled off something that had never been done—rescuing someone from the gallows, and two people at that.

"Well, blow me down!" Bloodstone roared, a tankard of rum in his hand. "What a bloody fool of a plan, Hawk!"

"Would you rather us go back?" Hawk asked, grinning. The pirates howled and laughed around them.

Bloodstone clapped him hard on the back. "Don't reckon me neck is ready for that yet. Foolish, but the bravest plan I've ever seen, no doubt. Drink one to the Hawk, boys!" The pirates all raised their mugs and tankards of rum and shouted in salute. Even Diablo nodded his head toward Hawk and extended his cup before drinking deeply.

With Billy's knowledge of Port Royal, and a quick scouting of Gallows Point by Hawk and his officers, Hawk came up with the exact plan the night before the hanging. Just hours before the execution, Billy had contacted some old friends in Kingston. One had a connection in the prison and got word of the plan to Bloodstone and Diablo. Although some good men were lost, it went as well as it possibly could have. There were a hundred ways the plan could have ended with most, or all, of their deaths. There was only one way it could have succeeded.

"Where did ye learn how to shoot a flintlock like that?" Bloodstone asked a few minutes later.

"From the other shooter of course," Hawk replied, nodding at Andre.

"And could ye make that shot again?"

"One out of four." Hawk laughed.

Bloodstone shook his head and chuckled. "And Wesley, how in the blazes do ye ride a horse with one leg?"

"Very carefully, Cap'n. Very carefully," Wesley said as he laughed. He had been a very good rider in England before going on account with Bloodstone. It had been difficult to balance, but the ride wasn't long. A longer ride might have been problematic.

There wasn't time for a proper celebration once they reached their current hideout. Bloodstone knew the Royal Navy would be scouring the islands in full force. The exploits of Hawk and his crew would quickly spread across all of the Caribbean. It was a huge embarrassment for Jamaica and, by association, England and their King. It was now time to see how the atmosphere in New Orleans was.

"Hawk, me boy, I need someone to cap'n the *Cobra* back to the Rock," Bloodstone said when the men began boarding the ships. "I reckon ye've earned it. Take a hand to be your quartermaster and ye can keep most of the men ye took to the gallows with you. I'll be takin' Diablo, Wesley, and Andre with me, of course."

"I'll race you back," Hawk said.

Hawk quickly walked away and sought out Billy among the throng of pirates on the beach. "Ho, Billy," he called out when he spotted him.

Billy quickly made his way over to Hawk. Billy wasn't much older than Hawk, but he was a skilled and experienced pirate. Had it not been for Hawk, he might have replaced Spider as bosun. Hawk had been impressed with Billy during the rescue. He had a quick mind and was absolutely fearless. His job before pirating was an apprentice blacksmith. As a result, he was very knowledgeable about weapons and was skilled with a dagger and cutlass. He was also skilled with a horse, as he had shown.

"Yes, sir," Billy said. He was a few inches shorter than Hawk and clean-shaven with short black hair and big blue eyes. He was slight of frame but wiry and strong.

"I need a quartermaster for the trip back to the Rock. I'd like that to be you," Hawk said.

Billy's eyed widened in shock. "Me, sir?"

"If you would. You proved yourself back at the gallows. I need some-one I can trust."

"Uh…OK…I guess," Billy stammered.

"Good! You'll be a fine mate." Hawk grinned and clapped Billy firmly on the shoulder. "Now, let's get these bilge rats rounded up and on the sloop."

After many months of absence, the *Bloody Seas* and *Cobra* sailed un-eventfully back to the Rock. Both vessels were abuzz with the leader-ship, cunning, and bravery of Hawk. The men were also happy that their captain and quartermaster were rescued. But Hawk was greatly elevated in their eyes, even with most of the older pirates that had fa-vored Diablo. The young pirate had the clear support of almost the entire crew now.

Hawk arrived at the inlet first. He sounded the horn to let the pirates ashore know to raise the trees. There was no response. After a few more tries, he fired his flintlock into the air. Still nothing. He cursed and had his men row the *Cobra* to the starboard shore. Three quickly hopped off to man the wench. The ship was then rowed to the main part of the is-land on the port side. Three more men rushed into the thick vegetation to operate that wench.

Slowly the trees rose out of the water, and the *Cobra* sailed into the harbor. Hawk knew immediately that something was amiss. The *Gator* was nowhere to be seen, nor was the sloop. No pirates were there to greet them. There were always lookouts stationed either near the wench-es on the outer part of the inlet or on the beach area. He sailed the Cobra almost to the shore. Its shallow draft allowed it to go much closer than the schooner and frigate.

He and his men quickly leapt or climbed down to the water and waded onto the beach. Although he knew the *Bloody Seas* was close behind, Hawk didn't wait. He drew another flintlock and led the way to the jungle path. "Be ready men!" he shouted. His crew followed single file behind.

The trail was much more grown up than usual, and Hawk had to use his cutlass to clear the way. He felt sick to his stomach. They had been gone for a long time, longer than any other voyage before. Pirates didn't do well with idle time, especially with no leadership. Lewis Walker had been left in charge. He had been a captain on a merchant ship they captured a couple of years prior. He seemed a capable sailor and leader, and Bloodstone was grooming him for bigger things.

The party hurried up the trail and soon arrived at the fort. The gate was closed, and no one stirred upon the walls. Hawk strode up to the thick wooden door and rapped hard with the butt of his pistol. There was no response. He repeated, even harder. "Open the blasted gate! It's Hawk."

Finally, some noise was heard on the other side. There was a muffled whispering, and then the heavy wooden post that held the door shut was removed. The gate slowly swung open.

Hawk quickly strode in and surveyed the scene. "What's going on here?" he demanded of the first two pirates he came to. The men before him were pale and skinny and didn't look well.

"Thank the gods. It's you, Hawk!" the first one said excitedly, his eyes wild and darting.

"Aye, ye came back to save us!" the other said, looking similarly crazed.

Hawk knew getting answers from these two would be tough. "Where's Walker?"

"He be in his cabin, Hawk. Ye want me to go fetch him?" the first pirate asked.

"With all haste," Hawk replied impatiently. By now, several more pirates had come out of various huts. They all looked ragged and emaciated.

They weakly shuffled down to meet Hawk and his crew that had filed in behind him.

By the time Walker emerged from his cabin and walked quickly down to meet Hawk, Bloodstone and Diablo had made it inside the palisade, followed by the crew of the *Bloody Seas*. The two crews fanned out into a large circle around Walker and the dozen or so pirates.

"By the blazes, Walker, what be goin' on?" Bloodstone roared. Like Hawk, he had a flintlock in his hand.

"So good to see you, Cap'n and Hawk and Diablo. A sight for sore, sick eyes to be sure."

"Where be the *Gator* and the rest of me men?" Bloodstone demanded.

"Sir, it's a terrible tale. The *Gator*, she was sank by a US Navy frigate and—"

"Why was she away from the Rock?" Diablo said.

"Well, Mr. Diablo, we were dangerously short of supplies. And I feared somethin' bad had befallen you. So I took a crew and sailed to New Orleans. We traded for supplies and were headin' back home. That's when the USS *Enterprise*, led by a Captain Nathaniel Cord, attacked us. They destroyed the ship, but for some merciful reason they let me and three lads escape in the longboat. We rowed for a hard week back here, nearly dying of thirst in the process." Walker shifted from foot to foot while he talked, his eyes darting between the three men before him. He wiped sweat from his forehead with the back of his hand.

"Were you flying colors, or why would the *Enterprise* attack a merchant ship?" Hawk asked, before Bloodstone or Diablo could speak.

"They just came up with guns a blazin', Hawk."

"And which three of these lads were with ye?" Bloodstone asked, squinting at the nervous pirate.

"Uh, Jimmy there was one of them."

Jimmy was the pirate that had opened the gate. Bloodstone turned to face Jimmy, who stared at the ground, digging his toes into the dirt. Bloodstone raised his flintlock, cocked the hammer, and pointed it at Jimmy, inches from his face. "Jim, I need the next words out of your mouth to be the truth. Or they'll be your last words, I swear to ye."

Jimmy looked up to stare into the barrel of the Bloodstone's pistol. He swallowed hard. At this point, it was hard to say which one would result in him dying sooner, the truth or a lie. He finally decided the truth was his best option. "Uh, Cap'n, sir, Mr. Walker's not exactly tellin' the story like it happened."

"Jimmy!" Walker roared, reaching a hand for his pistol. Diablo was quicker, and in a flash, his flintlock barrel was pressed to the side of Walker's head.

"Do go on," Bloodstone said to Jimmy, not even looking at Walker or Diablo.

"Well, sir, we did go to New Orleans and get supplies, that's for true. But on the trip back, Mr. Walker spied a small merchantman headin' to the city. Without even puttin' it to a vote, he ordered us to attack. We were barely out of site of New Orleans. A large US Navy frigate, one of them new ones with all the guns, spotted us on their way out. They swooped in with guns a blazin' before we even boarded the merchant. They killed us all 'cept four. They told us to get into the rowboat and proceeded to sink the *Gator*. The captain, a man named Cord, and his lieutenant, who he called James, told us to tell all of the pirates that their time be over. Now that they had defeated the British, they were declarin' war on pirates. Mentioned you and Kragg, they did."

"By the powers!" Bloodstone roared, his face quickly glowing red. "Did ye have me colors raised?"

"Certainly not, sir," Walker jumped in.

"And did any of ye tell them ye were part of me crew?"

"No, sir. We would have never betrayed you like that," Walker replied.

"But takin' me ship and attackin' another ship within sight of New Orleans wasn't betrayin' me?" Bloodstone turned to squarely face Walker and moved his flintlock from Jimmy to him.

"Uh, no sir. I was just—"

Bloodstone squeezed the trigger. The shot hit Walker in the face and exited the back of his skull, sending blood and brains spraying toward the pirates behind him. He was dead well before he hit the ground.

"Now then, Jimmy, what happened to the men that stayed behind?"

Jimmy glanced briefly at Walker's body and then turned back to the captain. He was shaking and close to tears. "We came back and told 'em the story. They was upset. They feared you were lost, and now the *Gator* was lost. One morning we woke up and found that all of the crew, except ten of us, was gone. They'd taken all of the loot, weapons, and food they could carry, took the sloop, and sailed away. We think that Elijah Wright was the leader. We ran out of ammo soon after and have been trying to survive on fruits and plants. But the fruit ran out last week, and as you can see, we're not far from death, and most of us have the scurvy."

"Curse that English devil to hades!" Bloodstone roared. He dropped his empty flintlock, letting it swing by his side, and grabbed another one. He pressed it to Jimmy's nose. Jimmy looked down at the ground and waited for his fate. "Arrr!" Bloodstone roared. He turned the gun away and fired a shot into Walker's stomach.

"Diablo, secure the fort and take some men out to get some meat. Bones, tend to the sick and see what ye can do for 'em," Bloodstone ordered, and he stormed off to his hut. The pirates set about restoring order to the fort and most went out to hunt and fish.

Hawk gave Bloodstone a couple of hours to cool off before finally going to his cabin. He knocked softly on the door.

"Come in," a voice grumbled from within.

Hawk entered and found Bloodstone sitting at his table, a tankard of rum in his hand. He could tell it wasn't the captain's first cup. Hawk sat down in a chair on the other side. Bloodstone slid the tankard over to him and got up and grabbed another off the top of the cask of rum. He quickly filled it and sat back down.

They drank in silence for several minutes. Hawk waited for Bloodstone to speak first.

"I pity ye, Hawk," the captain finally said.

"Pity me? Why?"

"Ye come along too late. The time of pirates be comin' to an end, I'm afraid." Bloodstone took another swig of rum.

"This is just a setback. We'll get more men, ships, and loot."

Bloodstone shook his head. "The *Enterprise* be just one of the United States' new frigates—part of that cursed New Orleans Squadron. Their job be to hunt us down, Hawk. Already searchin' the islands, they are. And the Royal Navy will be trackin' us like dogs. There's nary a safe port or harbor left for an honest pirate, Hawk. Our world is shrinking by the day."

Hawk looked at Bloodstone, who was staring into his tankard. For the first time, his captain looked old and defeated. "You're the craftiest pirate ever. We'll figure out something."

"Ah, to have lived a hundred years ago! Back when pirates ruled the Caribbean. Almost every port welcomed 'em with open arms. As long as they preyed on the Spaniards and French, no nation would touch 'em. The golden age they call it. We could have ruled the world, me boy!" Bloodstone downed the remainder of his drink and quickly refilled it.

"We can make this the new golden age, Captain."

"By thee powers, we can't even be seen in New Orleans now, thanks to that scurvy dog Walker!" Bloodstone slammed his tankard on the table; the contents sloshed out over the sides. "And even if it's not totally over, it's close for me, me boy. I'm old. Look around ye, Hawk. Piratin' is a young man's game. I've lived much longer than most, and much longer than I deserve. And with me 'bout gettin' hanged, and now that cursed Walker, me crew's probably 'bout ready to depose me anyway. It'll be your crew soon me boy, mark me words."

"It's your crew, sir. I would never betray you and try to take your place." Hawk leaned forward in his seat to stare into the captain's blood-shot eyes.

Bloodstone chuckled softy, his rum breath strong. "Ye won't have to do a thing, me lad. They'll pick ye. But I'm afraid it'll be a short run for ye, no matter how good ye are. The navy will get stronger. And they'll keep comin', they will. Huntin' pirates and escortin' merchants. And soon they'll search all the islands, mark me words. There'll be nowhere left to hide. A hundred years too late, blast it!"

Hawk was thoughtful for a moment. "We just need a plan. We need a way to get back on our feet and turn the tide against the US."

"What ye got in mind?"

"Maybe it's time to hunt the hunter," Hawk said, taking a swig of his drink.

Bloodstone looked up from wiping rum from the table and stared at Hawk. "Ye are a crazy one, that be for sure. Those new frigates carry fifty or more guns and a crew of three hundred. We'd need many more ships and men."

"Or perhaps not," Hawk said, flashing a grin.

"What be ye thinkin', Hawk?"

"I'll leave that plan to you. You taught me everything I know. But while you're thinking, I have a request."

"S'ppose you're right. Maybe we ain't dead yet. What be your request?" Bloodstone was beginning to rock in his chair. The rum was having its affect on him.

"Let me take the *Cobra* and a small crew and go to New Orleans. We're in desperate need of supplies. And we need news of what's happened since we've been gone and of what impact Walker's blunder has had." Hawk knew he had to ask quickly before Bloodstone passed out.

"I don't know, me boy. Might be too dangerous."

"No one will recognize me. I'll take Billy and some of the younger crew too. Besides, our ship is obviously not a ship of war or pirate vessel. I'll leave in the morning and be back in three days. You can tell me the plan then," Hawk pleaded, sitting on the edge of his chair.

"I s'ppose that sweet young lass at the Cove has nothin' to do with your visit?" Bloodstone asked.

"Well, they do have excellent food and drink there. And I'll need a place to lay my head after all, and—"

"Ye old dog! Ye saved me neck. I reckon I can trust ye on a mission such as this. Three days, Hawk."

Hawk floated back to his hut. He couldn't have stopped grinning if he wanted to. Despite the events he had learned of today and Bloodstone's words, he was going to get to see his sweet Anna again. Right then, nothing else mattered.

CHAPTER X

PIRATE WAR

"Bloodstone?" Captain Cord asked. The *Enterprise* had been a terror to pirates since being assigned as the flagship of the New Orleans Squadron. They were fresh from attacking Galveston Island and driving Lafitte and his pirates out.

"Unfortunately not. Looks like it might be one of Kragg's though." James responded, squinting into the spyglass.

With Lafitte on the run, Bloodstone and Bartholomew Kragg were the two most powerful pirate captains left in the Caribbean. Cord and James knew if they could take them out, most of the remaining pirates would disappear. "Your plan?" Cord decided to let James plan the battle again, since it had been a while since his last.

"Let's show our colors—the Jolly Roger. Load the canister shot and ready the granadoes. Have all of the men get down out of sight with a granado in hand and a blunderbuss close-by. I'll take care of the rest." James walked off to prepare his weapons.

Cord acted as first mate and rushed off to carry out James's orders. This was a risky plan, but that was nothing unusual for James. Cord just hoped the man didn't learn humility the hard way someday.

The *Enterprise* had the wind behind it, and it headed on a perpendicular course toward the black schooner. The pirate ship flew a black flag with a red devil holding a pitchfork in his hand. It was one of Bartholomew Kragg's ships. It was too small to be his flagship, so was most likely just one of his captains. Kragg had more ships and men than Bloodstone and was nearly as feared but not nearly as clever. With Kragg, it was just a matter of sheer numbers and brutality. With Bloodstone, it was intelligence, cunning, and pure evil.

The danger with James's plan was that the pirate ship was already broadside to the *Enterprise*. The enemy vessel could fire first, with all of its cannons. However, that wasn't the norm for pirate encounters. Normally, the two pirate captains would parley with each other. Although there were rivalries, they usually realized they had a bigger, much more powerful common enemy. If there were a dispute, the two captains would normally face off and have a duel. This pirate captain would have no such opportunity.

As the *Enterprise* quickly closed the distance, the schooner didn't fire its guns. There was a lot of activity on the decks though, and most of the pirates lined the port railing. James knew they were leery but probably not expecting what he had planned. He took a flintlock in each hand and crossed them behind his back. As the navigator brought the ship about hard to port, they were soon broadside to the pirate ship. James walked over to the gangway. Fifty of his men crouched to either side of him, behind the gunwale. A pirate stepped forward out of the throng on the schooner and stood directly across from him. The ships continued to drift together. Now only twenty feet of water separated them.

"Ho, pirate, what means ye overtakin' me in such a hurry?" the other captain called out. "And where be your crew?" The pirate captain wore a red doublet, customary of Kragg and his captains, with black breeches and boots. An old, worn black tricorne was on his head.

Although James wore a navy uniform, it wasn't that unusual for pirates to wear the uniforms of their victims. "Arrr! This be the first wind to blow in weeks. Been dead in the water by the blazes. Lost most of me men to the fever and thirst. The livin' ones be dyin' below deck. Been livin' on bilge rats, maggots, and fouled water, I have. I hailed ye to see if ye can help a pirate mate and his dyin' crew."

The pirate captain scanned the ship in more detail and then looked back at the other captain. "Your ship 'pears to be shipshape, as do ye. What be your name, Cap'n?"

A slightly different plan just came to James's mind. He almost grinned. "Ye should know me. I be the fiercest pirate of all, Cap'n Bloodstone. I see ye fly Kragg's colors. What be your name, Cap'n?"

The pirate captain put his hand above his eyes and squinted. "Ye don't look much like Bloodstone. I be Captain Grant."

"And have ye ever seen him before?" James roared in his best pirate voice.

"Don't reckon I have. Heard about him though. Big beast of man with black hair and black beard and dressed in black. Ye look more like a swab without a hair on your chin." The pirate crew behind him laughed loudly at the insult.

"And what do ye reckon Bloodstone would do if he were insulted by a cowardly servin' wench of a captain of Kragg's?"

Captain Grant's hands dropped down to the hilts of two of the pistols that were tied to his belt. His crew likewise tensed and put their hands near their weapons. "I be in a generous mood today. Seein' you're by yourself on that ship, I suggest ye sail away. Else I decide to brave the disease and take your ship for Kragg."

"That be a right kind offer, it is. If I were not Cap'n Bloodstone, I'd take ye up on it. But I'm afraid I have only one word in response."

"And what word be that?"

"Fire!" James brought both cocked pistols forward and fired, one at Captain Grant and one at the closest pirate that appeared to be an officer. Both pirates fell to the deck, either dead or dying. Before the other pirates could draw their weapons, the *Enterprise* crew stood up and launched the granadoes. They had lit the fuses as soon as they realized the conversation was over. The granadoes hit the pirate ship deck and exploded, sending fire and scraps of metal in all directions. The pirates were so close together that the damage was devastating. Then the cannons roared from the deck below. The canister shot spewed its deadly content into the pirates that were screaming and running about to avoid the granadoes.

The sailors then grabbed the blunderbusses and tried to find targets to aim at.

"Hold!" James shouted.

There were only a handful of pirates left on the deck of the schooner, and they were desperately seeking cover. Captain Cord appeared beside James, curious as to why he halted the slaughter.

"Yo, pirate crew, who be in charge now?" said James.

The flapping of sails and the slapping water against hulls were the only sounds heard. "Don't make me board ye to figure it out!"

A timid pirate poked his head over the railing next to the forecastle. "I think that would be me. I'm the bosun. You killed the captain and quartermaster."

"I be in a generous mood today too, just like your cap'n was. If ye throw all of your weapons in the sea, including your shot, I'll let ye live."

The remaining pirates appeared from different hiding places about the deck. They huddled together for only a moment and then began tossing cutlasses, daggers, pistols, muskets, and blunderbusses into the water. Down below, the cannons were rolled back out of the gunports, and cannon balls soon started splashing into the ocean. After ten minutes, the splashing stopped.

"That's all, Cap'n," the bosun called out.

"Thank ye. Now, never let it be said that Captain Bloodstone doesn't have a heart. Ye sail back to Cap'n Kragg and tell him the Spanish Main not be big enough for the both of us. Now get ye gone before I change my mind."

The few remaining pirates scurried about the deck, and the two ships disengaged.

James turned to look at Captain Cord. "Well? What do ye think?"

"Do you think they believe you are Captain Bloodstone?"

"No. Those fellows over there don't. But by the time they get back to Kragg and have to explain how they lost their captain, quartermaster, two thirds of their crew, and all of their weapons without having fired a single cannon, I'll have been Bloodstone and on the *Bloody Seas* no less. Kragg wouldn't accept them losing to an anonymous pirate."

Cord clapped James on the shoulder. "Bloody genius! Now you'll have Kragg and Bloodstone in an all-out pirate war."

"And we'll be there to congratulate the victors. Now, let's do some more hunting."

CHAPTER XI

RETURN TO NEW ORLEANS

❧

The short trip to New Orleans seemed to take forever. Hawk impatiently paced the deck as if they were going into the battle of their lives. Actually, the trip was much quicker, with the lighter, faster sloop and the ability to row in weak wind. Hawk had Billy and twenty men with him. As he told Bloodstone he would, he took many of the newer, younger pirates. They wouldn't draw attention in New Orleans, plus they naturally gravitated to Hawk. After his exploits at Port Royal, he was a living legend to them.

Hawk noticed a difference in the type of ships anchored at the New Orleans docks. In the past, pirates did nothing to disguise their heavily armed pirate ships other than not flying their colors. Now, most ships were clearly either merchant or navy. Their sloop wouldn't attract any attention, nor would the young sailors that disembarked.

"Billy, take half the men and take what goods we have and trade for food and supplies. Buy the rest," Hawk said, handing Billy a leather pouch of coins. "Spread out and gather information tonight. Make time for a little fun after."

Billy took the pouch and quickly rounded up ten men. They set about bringing up boxes and crates out of the hold and headed off with

Billy to visit some of their regular merchants. The sun hung low in the sky, and the merchants would close soon.

"All right ye lot o' scalliwags," Hawk liked to mock-chide the pirates. They all knew when he was serious and when he was playing. He could go in and out of pirate talk easily and did a great imitation of Bloodstone. "I want you to spread out to your usual haunts. If you haven't been here before, pick a direction; you'll find a new one soon. But before you get too far into drink and women, listen for any talk of Bloodstone, pirates, or the navy. Our lives could depend on what you hear tonight. I need you all back here by sunrise. I've got a short mission for you then." Hawk strode onto the dock and toward the Treasure Cove without waiting to see the pirates' reactions.

The Treasure Cove hadn't changed much since the last time Hawk was there. It might have been a little more crowded, and the crowd a little better dressed and respectable, but it was the same. He excitedly scanned the room for Anna but didn't see her. His heart skipped a few beats. *What if she's gone?*

He found a small, unoccupied table in the corner. He sat down with his back against the wall and did his best to eavesdrop on the people sitting close by. It wasn't hard, since most were in at least some state of drunkenness and tried to talk above the din. Finally, Madame Cynthia saw the new patron and walked over to his table.

"May I help you, handsome?" she asked sweetly.

Hawk looked up and grinned. "Hello, Miss Cynthia."

"Well, I'll be!" she exclaimed. She quickly leaned down and hugged him. She smelled sweet, despite the odor of food, alcohol, and smoke in the room. "Let's see…Hawk!"

"You're good."

"My, you've grown into quite the strapping man!" She laughed when she saw Hawk's cheeks turn red. "Now, where is that old Captain Blood…Blackburn?"

Hawk was surprised at the slip and that she must know who Bloodstone really was. "He didn't make this trip. It's been a while since we've been here. He wanted me to see how the market was for…honest sailors."

Cynthia flashed a quick grin, followed by a wink. "That was probably wise. It's definitely not as good trading here as it used to be. Despite his saving New Orleans's arse in the war, Lafitte and his crew still aren't welcome here.

"I figured as much," Hawk replied, shaking his head. "I heard one of Captain Bloodstone's ships was sunk near here a month or so back." He talked louder now, so their whispering wouldn't draw attention.

"Blasted fools! They say the ship attacked a merchantman just out of sight of the city—an American merchantman no less. The *Enterprise* took them out in quick fashion."

"What is the *Enterprise*?"

"They say it's the pride of the American navy and the flagship of the New Orleans Squadron. It's sailed by Captain Cord and his Lieutenant, James Wellington. They say they are as ruthless as Bloodstone himself, especially the younger man, James. They'd rather convict and punish the pirates on their ship than wait for a judge and gallows. Now that the war is over, they're focused on hunting down pirates. I heard they just chased Lafitte and his men out of their stronghold on Galveston Island." Cynthia's eyes looked a little glassy just for a moment. "I'll be back with some ale and a plate of food."

Hawk mulled over what she'd told him. That was the first time he'd heard James's last name. Something sounded familiar about *Wellington*. He searched his memories until Cynthia returned with his tankard of ale and a plate with a huge slab of roast beef, boiled potatoes, and some kind of greens.

"Now that the business is out of the way, I suppose you would like to inquire about a certain sweet, young lady?" She reached out and rubbed his thick blond hair as she had two years prior.

Hawk quickly forgot about James Wellington. He grinned. "I think I might like to say hello, if she still works here, that is."

Cynthia laughed loudly. "I bet you would. Finish your meal and get some ale in your belly. I'll have her come by and say hello."

"Oh, Madame Cynthia," Hawk called out as she turned to leave. She quickly turned back around. Hawk reached into his waistcoat and pulled out a gold coin, careful so anyone happening to look that way didn't see. "This is for the food and for Anna tonight and tomorrow. I'd like to take her out for the day. Also pack us some food and drink. Throw in an old blanket too. I'll pick it up in the morning."

Cynthia quickly scooped up the coin and grinned. "For this, you can have her tomorrow night too. The food will be in a basket behind the counter."

Hawk didn't pick up much more news as he ate his dinner and drank his ale. His eyes scanned the room until he finally spotted her. She emerged from the kitchen, behind the bar. She looked almost the same as she had two years ago, only dressed in a blue and white lace dress this time. Her eyes searched the room and then met his. She walked quickly over to his table.

"Hello, Mr. Hawk," she said in her sweet, musical voice. She looked shyly at the ground.

"Hello? I thought you might be more excited."

"It has been a long time," she said unemotionally.

Hawk tried to hide his disappointment. His fantasy had involved her running over, wrapping her arms around him, and kissing him passionately on the lips. He didn't expect this. Apparently, he hadn't been on her mind as much as she was on his. "Can we go upstairs and talk?"

"Madame Cynthia said you had paid. We can do as you wish." She turned and led him up the stairs. She opened a door to a different room this time, although the interior was almost identical. She walked over and sat on the bed, staring straight ahead. Hawk quickly joined her.

Hawk reached over and caressed her smooth, soft cheek with his left hand. He gently turned her head so she looked at him. "Anna, it's me. What's wrong?"

"It's you? Who are you? Oh, you're the young boy that filled my head with crazy dreams two years ago—the one that promised to come back and rescue me from…this. Not only didn't you rescue me, you never even came back to see me." She pulled her head back away from his hand and stared at the floor. Her eyes were glassy.

Hawk was stunned by her honest and cold response. She didn't sound like the sweet, proper young lady from his last visit. He suppressed the frustration that was quickly building. "Anna, I've thought about you every night for the past two years. You don't know how bad I wanted to see you again."

"Then why didn't come see me?"

"We…our ship…we sailed to a different area to find new places to… trade. We just returned yesterday and came to town to find out news of the trading conditions here. Anna, you have to understand, I'm not the captain of the ship. I'm just the bosun. I have to go where the others vote to go." Hawk reached his right hand over and placed it on top of her small, warm left hand.

"That story doesn't make sense. Just what kind of trade do you and your ship engage in?" She now turned to look at him.

Hawk was silent for a moment. Despite her anger and sorrow, she was still a beautiful creature. His heart fluttered as he inhaled her perfume again. "Almost anything really—cloth, weapons, spirits, food…"

Anna quickly wiped a tear from the corner of her left eye. "Are you a pirate? Don't lie to me, Hawk."

"Let me tell you the entire story."

Anna turned, pulled her hand away from his, and placed both of her hands over her face. She sobbed softly.

"Anna, please just listen; then you can judge." Hawk waited a moment for her sobbing to subside. When he judged she was listening, he told her his life story.

They were both silent for a few minutes after he'd finished. "I don't know, Hawk. You're a criminal. You have killed and stolen your entire life," Anna said softly.

"What was I to do, Anna? I was six years old when Bloodstone rescued me. Other than the Rock, I never even set foot on land until I met you last time at sixteen. Was I to subdue or kill one hundred and fifty pirates, take the ship, and sail it blindly, hoping to find land I could escape to? It's the only life I've known. But two years ago, when I finally did realize that there is life outside the ship and the Rock, I did start dreaming of leaving it behind. I've been saving every coin I can so that one day I could keep my promise to you."

Anna finally turned to face him again. Although he was still innocent, he was a grown man now. He was even more handsome and strong than two years ago. She had cursed his name and memory for most of the past year. But now, face-to-face, she struggled to keep the same feelings from two years ago from returning. For some inexplicable reason, she was drawn to him like she had been to no other man. "I don't know, Hawk. I don't know if I can accept how you make a living."

Hawk felt a quick flash of anger. He took a deep breath before he calmly spoke. "Anna, you questioning me being a pirate would be the same as me questioning what you do for a living. I could easily ask you why you haven't run away, why you haven't done something different. I could say I can't accept that you've been with hundreds, if not thousands, of pirate and sailors."

Now anger flashed in Anna's eyes. But Hawk continued before she spoke. "But I don't. You told me your story last time. I accepted it. As long as you are with me, there are no other men. We can't influence each other's pasts. We can't change each other's or our own. All we can do is live in the present and try to change each of our futures. We both want out of our current lives. We want to start over fresh and lead new lives. I *will* leave this life behind and start a new one. But I want you to be a part of the new one. Yes, two years have passed. And two or more might pass again before I can leave it behind. But we are young. We will still be young in two years. We have our entire lives ahead of us. Please, just judge the man sitting here beside you. Judge what you're feeling right now. Don't judge the pirate that you've never met."

Anna's face and eyes softened. This time it was she who reached out and placed a hand on one of his. "I want to trust you, Hawk. I want to believe in you." She squeezed his hand gently.

"Then just do it." Hawk placed his right hand behind her head and gently pulled her close. He leaned forward until their lips met. They were even softer and warmer than he remembered. Tingling instantly spread from his lips to his entire body, leaving chill bumps in its wake.

They were both hesitant and tentative for a moment. Then slowly their fears and concerns melted away. Hawk reached his other hand around to softly stroke her right cheek. Their kisses became firmer and more intense. Hawk felt his face and skin transition from warm to hot despite the chills. If anything, kissing Anna was even better this time than it had been the first time.

Hawk's kiss and touch had the same effect on Anna as it had the first time—her heard raced; a thin layer of perspiration coated her skin; her body trembled as her skin prickled. She still had never experienced any feelings of desire with any of the men she had to sleep with. Sex was a job. Now she was being swept away by a man who was still a virgin. All of her pain and anger at him not coming back sooner was gone. He was right. He was here now, and that was the only moment she could control.

They continued to kiss as Hawk lay down on the bed, pulling her down beside him. Their hands began to explore each other's body through their clothing. Soon, both were panting—their hearts beating wildly together. Anna moved Hawk's hand from her side to her breast. He started to resist, but she kept her hand on his, guiding him.

Finally, it was Anna's turn to break off the kissing. She stood up and looked down at Hawk. "Do not say a word," she said, stopping Hawk's protests in his throat. She reached behind her neck and untied her dress. She then pulled the silk material off of her shoulders, allowing it to drop to the floor around her ankles.

Hawk couldn't have spoken even if he'd wanted to. The light from the lamp flickered across her perfect body. The flickering made it seem as if her skin pulsed and moved. He'd never seen a naked woman before, but he knew she had to be a perfect one. Her pale, smooth skin was flawless. Her breasts were firm and round, her stomach flat, and her curvy hips eventually gave way to long, lean legs. His body's reaction was overpowering. Any fear or doubt was replaced by lust and desire. He wasn't sure exactly what came next, but he would enjoy figuring it out.

Anna smiled at Hawk's stunned expression and open mouth. The hunger in his eyes only further fueled her own. She almost felt like she was the virgin. She leaned over, placed her hands on his shoulders, and kissed him passionately. Now he wouldn't need to try to speak. She pulled his waistcoat off and then unbuttoned his silk shirt. She then pushed him back onto the pillows and untied the sash around his waist. Hawk didn't protest as she next removed his breeches and boots and threw them on the floor.

Anna straightened up and admired Hawk's body in the dim lamplight. His body could have been chiseled out of stone. He was tan, lean, and muscular. The scars scattered about only made him that much more manly. He was so strong, yet his touch so soft and gentle. His thick blond hair was ruffled from their touching and kissing. His blue eyes stared at her with desire. His lips were full and glistening from her kisses. She'd been with hundreds of men, but never a perfect one.

Anna slowly climbed onto the bed and lay down beside him. "Do not worry, Mr. Hawk. I will teach you." Anna whispered softly into his ear. Now she sounded like she had when he first met her. They just kissed at first, enjoying the feeling of their hot naked bodies pressing and moving together and letting their hands discover areas previously untouched. But soon the desire was too much and kissing and touching weren't enough.

Anna quickly realized the difference between having sex and making love. With her gentle guidance, Hawk quickly learned how to touch her in ways she had never been touched. The rush of emotions was almost too much as they made love that night. It was as if their minds and bodies merged into one. She was pleased in ways she had never dreamed of. Hawk was young and very virile, and they made love several times until late into the night. Finally exhausted, they collapsed into each other's arms. The last thing Hawk told her was that she was spending tomorrow with him, and they were doing something wonderful. As tired as she was, she hardly slept in Hawk's strong arms, waiting on the sun to rise.

CHAPTER XII

A Picnic

When Hawk awoke, it took him a second to realize where he was. Then he quickly rolled over and was relieved to see Anna still lying beside him, sleeping soundly. The events of the night before replayed in his mind as he stared at the beautiful woman beside him. He was still overwhelmed with emotion. First, there was the physical pleasure, which was better than he'd ever imagined. Second, there were the other feelings that came from touching her, and now, just gazing upon her—the butterflies in his stomach, his swimming head, and his racing heart. He had been a little worried over the past two years that maybe he'd built up Anna—and his feelings for her—too much based on just one short night together. But after a second night, he realized she was even better than he'd dreamed.

He reached over and lightly touched her long, soft hair. Then he stroked her cheek and lightly brushed her slightly parted lips. She stirred then and in a moment opened her eyes. She slowly turned her head to look at him. As soon as her eyes focused, she smiled.

"Good morning, beautiful," Hawk said, and he leaned over to kiss her. He would have liked to enjoy another session of lovemaking but knew they didn't have time. "It's time for your big day."

"What do you have in mind, Mr. Hawk?" she asked, rising up on her elbows.

"It's a surprise. Now, we need to make haste."

They kissed again, and Anna quickly hurried off to her room to freshen up. Hawk poured water from the nearby bucket into the basin and quickly washed as well as he could while standing. Then he dressed and headed downstairs. The room was quite. He went behind the counter and found a basket of food and drink. He set it on the counter and waited for Anna. She came down the stairs a few minutes later wearing a tight beige dress and a low-cut pair of boots. She wore a white, wide-brimmed hat.

They walked quickly through the square. Hawk took the basket in his right hand and held Anna's hand in his left. There weren't many people stirring yet, as the sun was still a few minutes from rising. Hawk was pleased that Anna seemed so excited. They made their way quickly to the docks. The last couple of pirates stumbled sleepily onboard just before Hawk and Anna crossed the gangway.

"We are going sailing!" Anna said.

"Just for the morning. Then we have other plans after that."

The ten members of his crew milled about the main deck, staring at Hawk and Anna in surprise. There were several grins, elbows, and whispers among them. Their hangovers seemed to ease at this bit of excitement.

"All right, you bunch of bilge rats! Act like you've sailed before! Haul in those mooring lines and make ready to sail. Then you six get below deck and man the oars; you other four stay up top and man the sails. I'll man the helm." The pirates slowly began setting about their tasks. Hawk winked at Anna and led her to the quarterdeck.

By the time Hawk grasped the large wheel, the ship was moving. A little wind caught the sails, and the oarsmen rowed hard. Hawk steered around the bends of the river and toward the open sea. The sun had risen now, making the water of the river, and the nearby marshes, glow orange.

"Oh my, this is wonderful!" Anna exclaimed. She walked around the entire deck, taking in the view from each side and the stern. She finally returned to stand beside Hawk.

"First time on a ship, I take it?"

"Oh yes! I love it though! My stomach feels a little strange, but it is great. The men obey you like you are their captain," Anna said. She placed her right arm though the bend in his left.

Hawk looked at her and smiled. "I am, for this voyage at least. Here, would you like to steer a pirate ship?" Hawk took her hands and placed them on the helm.

Anna looked concerned for a moment, then once she started turning the big wheel she laughed. "Arrr! I am Anna, the Pirate Queen!"

Hawk laughed loudly. Now that she was away from the tavern and her job, her personality started to show. He stood beside her and wrapped his right arm around her waist. "And I'm Hawk, your Pirate King! Now, my dear, as pirate queen you may act as such. You can talk and act however you'd like today…and every day with me."

Anna grinned at Hawk and then turned her attention back to steering the ship.

The sloop made its way down the river and out into the open water. Anna was amazed at her first sight of the sea.

Hawk shouted for Jimmy, who was close by on the main deck, to come over and man the helm. Hawk had been impressed with Jimmy's honesty and bravery at the Rock and wanted to see how he handled himself on the ship. Hawk then led Anna to the bow. They stood against the front rail, at the base of the bowsprit. They talked and laughed and enjoyed the thick, salty air.

"It's funny," Hawk said. "You've never been on the sea, and I've hardly ever been on the land. And we both are fascinated with what has become boring for the other."

"This is wonderful. But I think I'd be happy on land or sea as long as you were by my side." She leaned back against him and turned her head to look up. He leaned down and kissed her.

After a couple of hours, a small island came into view. It was toward this island that Jimmy steered the *Cobra*. Hawk had taken a break from Anna along the way and told Jimmy and several of the crew what the plan was. The speck of land was one of a number of small islands not far from New Orleans. Actually, it wasn't too far from the Rock. Hawk had explored all of the islands between the Rock and New Orleans over the years. This one was similar to their stronghold, with its hardwood forest and lagoons. But it was much smaller and surrounded by water that was too shallow for a ship like the *Bloody Seas* to get close. The *Cobra* could sail almost to the beach.

Hawk disappeared into his cabin and changed into his normal pirate garb. Now he wore a baldric, stretching from his shoulder to his waist, over the top of his white linen shirt. In it were two flintlocks, his dagger, and a cutlass.

When he reappeared on the main deck, Anna looked him over from head to toe and grinned. "So, this is pirate Hawk?"

He laughed. "Do I look brave and dashing?"

"Yes...and a little scary. Do you need all of those weapons?" Her mirth gave way to concern.

"Hopefully not today. But you never know. These are dangerous times. Especially for honest pirates."

He turned to the helm. "Ho, Jimmy!"

"Yes, sir," Jimmy called back.

"I need for you to be back here by sundown today."

"Aye, Captain," Jimmy said heartily.

"I'm not your captain. And, Jimmy, I'm counting on you. Sundown."

"You can count on me, sir."

The ship sailed as close to the white, sandy beach as it could safely go. There was still a wide strip of water between it and dry land. Hawk shouted commands to the pirates nearby, and soon a longboat was lowered over the side and into the water.

Hawk dropped a rope ladder over the rail. "I'll go down first," he said to Anna. "Jimmy will drop the basket down to me, then you can come down, and I'll help you into the boat." He swung his legs over the rail.

Anna watched Hawk scramble down the ladder. He stood in the boat as Jimmy dropped the basket over the side. Hawk caught it effortlessly and placed it in the front of the boat. He then nodded to Anna. She frowned. She didn't want to climb down the unsteady ladder. Hawk stared up at her, smiling. "Come down, my lovely pirate queen!"

Anna finally shook her head and showed the smallest of grins. Jimmy held onto her as she tentatively swung a leg over. After a moment, her foot found one of the rope rungs. Grabbing firmly onto Jimmy's shoulder and the rail, she swung the other leg over. It found the rung too. The ladder swayed some, side-to-side and forward and back. She inched her way down, glad that Hawk and the boat were below her.

"Hmmm. I like the view," Hawk said as her feet reached the rung just above his head.

"You'll see the view of the bottom of my boot in just a moment," she said, not entirely joking.

Hawk laughed.

When her feet were almost to the boat, Hawk reached up and put both hands on her waist. He gently lowered her down to stand in front of him on the rocking vessel. "Ho there, Miss Anna," he said, smiling at her until she finally smiled back. "It will get better, don't worry."

"It had better!" Anna was actually very happy and excited now that she'd made it down the rope.

Hawk motioned for her to sit on the board closest to the back of the boat. He sat down in the middle and grabbed the two oars. He began rowing with long, powerful strokes. Anna liked watching his muscles strain beneath his thin white shirt. It was unbuttoned halfway, exposing his bare, muscular chest.

Her gaze darted away when he caught her staring. The sea was a beautiful, nearly clear blue. The sky above was close to the same color, with a few large billowy clouds floating past on the gentle warm wind. Her heart raced as she accepted the reality that she was going to spend the day away from the tavern, Madame Cynthia, and dirty sailors. And she got to spend it on a beautiful island with her handsome pirate.

Gentle waves soon caught the boat and sped it along toward the white-sand beach.

When the boat hit ground, Hawk leapt out, grabbed the bow, and pulled it further up the beach. He reached out for Anna's hand and helped her out to stand on the warm sand. He gave her a big hug and a long, slow kiss.

"What is this place?" she finally said.

"I'm not sure if it has a name. It's not far from the Rock. I've only been here a couple of times, usually hunting and gathering fruit. I love it though. It's too small and the waters are too shallow for it to be used by big ships."

"And what are we going to do?"

"Whatever you like. I had the madame pack us a meal in this basket. There's a small pond in the woods near the center of the island. I thought we could eat there. And then maybe we can enjoy some swimming."

"Oh, that sounds perfect!" She kissed Hawk again.

He grabbed the basket out of the boat and led her up the beach. An old animal trail led into a stand of palm trees. Anna's head constantly swiveled. She had never seen anything except New Orleans. She soaked in all of the new sensations like a sponge—the smell of the ocean and lush vegetation, the feel of the leaves and trunks of the trees, the warm breeze, the sounds of birds singing and animals scurrying out of their way.

She reached a hand inside the bend in one of Hawk's arms. "I've never felt like this!"

Hawk turned to look at her beaming face. "Like what?"

"I don't know—just so...so excited...so happy! I never knew a person could feel this way."

"And to think you were so rude to me last night," Hawk said, laughing.

Anna pinched his bicep. "You didn't tell me we were going to a beautiful island." She laughed too.

The palms gave way to a thicker patch of oak trees. It was shady and cooler here, with only occasional shafts of sunlight penetrating the thick foliage. Anna loved the earthy smell. Green grass and short clumps of plants covered the ground. Finally, they came to a large oval pond. The water was a dark, murky, blue-green color. The far side of the water was covered with a thick patch of reeds. Several clumps of white flowers dotted the banks. A bed of ferns surrounded the water and the flowers.

"Wow, this is lovely!" Anna exclaimed. She gave him a quick peck on the lips.

Hawk walked to a thick, semishaded patch of ferns on the near side of the water and set the basket down. He opened it up, took out an old stained cotton blanket, and spread it out over the ferns. He then set the basket on the edge of the blanket and placed its contents around him. There was a loaf of soft bread, a block of cheese, hunks of roast beef, a couple of apples, two onion bottles of red wine, and two silver goblets. The madame had done well, although for a doubloon, she still came out much ahead.

"Are you hungry, my dear?" Hawk asked, motioning for her to come over to the blanket.

Anna ran over and kneeled beside Hawk. She couldn't stop grinning. Every moment they were together, things only got better. She watched as he removed his dagger and placed it beside him. He took off his baldric and laid it on one corner of the blanket. He then took off his boots. Only eighteen, he was full of confidence. She quickly took off her boots too and sat down beside him.

Hawk wrapped his right arm around her, and she laid her head on his shoulder. A warm shaft of sunlight shone down on them. It was a warm day but comfortable since they were in the forest. They stared at the pond without speaking. Bullfrogs croaked from the direction of the patch of reeds. Birds called out from the tree limbs somewhere overhead. An occasional rustling in the leaves indicated some kind of forest creature scurrying about.

"You're quiet. Is everything OK?" Hawk asked, turning to look at her. Her cheek and hair glowed in the ray of sunlight.

"Oh, Hawk, I cannot even speak! I have so many emotions flowing through me. I want to cry; I want to scream; I want to laugh; I want to run and jump around like a little girl. I've never felt this before." She looked at him, tears welling up in her eyes.

"But it's a good feeling, right?" Hawk was a little perplexed at her reaction.

"Very, very good! Just a little overwhelming."

Hawk leaned over and kissed her gently. It very quickly turned passionate. Hawk felt the blood rush to his face and to other parts of his body. He had planned on them eating first, but he was quickly swept away in desire. He slowly lay her down onto the blanket while continuing to kiss her. Soon they were panting as they stopped only long enough to remove each other's clothing. In moments, they were making love. Now that the nervousness was gone, it was even better than the night before. There was also something special about being in nature and their bodies being caressed by the rays of sun and kissed by the soft breeze.

When they had finished, they lay on their backs, Hawk's arm beneath Anna's head, and stared up at the patterns of leaves on the limbs above. The gentle breeze cooled them off and quickly dried their sweat. After several minutes, Hawk rolled over, kissed her, and then sat up. "I bet you're hungry."

Anna sat up too. She grabbed her dress and placed it over her lap. "Famished."

Hawk placed his shirt over his lap too and began making them sandwiches, using his dagger to slice the beef and cheese, which he placed between hunks of bread. He then removed the cork in one of the onion bottles and poured them each a goblet full of sweet red wine. They both quickly drank most of their goblets. Hawk refilled them, and then they started on their sandwiches. They hadn't eaten since the evening before and had definitely worked up a good appetite. Once the sandwiches were finished, Hawk sliced the apples and they ate those. After the feast was done, they both lay back down on the blanket to let it settle.

"This is so amazing," Anna said softly.

"This place is nice," Hawk replied, his eyes closed.

"No. Not just this place. I guess it is the…the freedom. I don't remember what it is like to not have chores to do. For this moment, we're totally free. We can do whatever we want. I don't have to pretend to be someone I'm not. Of course I guess you're used to having freedom."

Hawk was silent for a moment. "Not really. Whether on the ship or on land, pirates all have chores and jobs too. While you do have some free time at night on the ship and when you're at a hideout, you're still not free to come and go as you please. You also never have privacy. There are always mates nearby, except when you're sleeping in your cabin or hut. This kind of freedom is much better." He paused for another moment. "Really, Anna, our lives aren't that different."

"I think that's one reason I'm so attracted to you. It does sound like in many ways we're both slaves to our lives—forced into them not by our choosing and not able to break free. Now we're both old enough to realize there are other options and other lives we could lead." She turned her head to gaze at him.

Hawk rolled his head over and grinned. "You're very right, my dear." He gave her a quick kiss. "So, is your dream still the same one you told me about last time?"

"Yes! And this day has just made me realize that reality could be even better than my dreams. Now I'll add a pond to my dream though." She laughed. "Can you imagine having our own piece of land? Having privacy like this? To do what we wanted, when we wanted? Sure we would have chores to do, but chores we wanted to do."

Hawk laughed at her excitement. "Yeah, I've been doing a lot of thinking about your dream. With each voyage, I grow more tired of the pirate life. It's no longer exciting, even after a great battle or big haul. Well, it's only exciting because the more loot I receive, the sooner I can leave the life behind. I'm just so ready to do something different, to sleep in a bed that doesn't move during the night, to breath air that's not heavy with salt or tainted with foul odors, to not have to wonder every day if that day will be my last."

"You wouldn't get bored, leaving all of the adventure and fighting behind to be stuck on land with me?" Anna asked, her lower lip pushed out a little.

"Tired of this? Spending every moment in paradise with the sweetest, most beautiful woman ever? Not on your life! It would be Heaven on earth."

"Oh, Hawk!" She rolled over on top of him and kissed him forcefully.

"And would you not miss all of the excitement of the tavern and meeting and entertaining of all of those handsome sailors?" Hawk asked when they finally ended the kiss.

Anna lightly smacked his cheek. "You would be all the excitement I needed. And you're handsome enough. You'd do." She laughed. Suddenly she leapt to her feet, dropped her dress, and ran down to the pond, diving in headfirst.

In a moment she reappeared, shaking the water from her long hair. She smiled and motioned for Hawk to join her. Hawk laughed and quickly obeyed. He dove in and swam beneath the surface until he could see her white legs in the murky water. He bit her thigh playfully, almost receiving a surprised knee in the face. He then kissed her leg and slowly kissed his way up her body until he eventually stood in front of her in the chest-deep water. Her naked body was warm against his, despite the cold water surrounding them. They kissed each other passionately for several minutes, their wet lips sliding together effortlessly.

"Want me to teach you how to swim?" Hawk asked when they finally paused to catch their breaths.

"I had heard that pirates cannot swim," she said playfully.

"I'm not your ordinary pirate." Hawk pinched her hip beneath the water.

"So, are you now the Seahawk?"

Hawk turned and swam to the edge of the pond. He reached it quickly with long, powerful strokes. It was true that most pirates and sailors couldn't swim, and falling off of a ship in a storm or battle was usually a death sentence. But Hawk had mastered the skill, as well as most other skills. He might die in a battle, but not from the water. He turned and swam back to her. "Now, your turn."

Hawk held his strong arms beneath her stomach and told her how to move her arms and legs. He walked with her, supporting most of her weight, as she kicked and paddled. There was a lot of playful splashing, laughing, touching, and kissing, but she soon learned the basics.

As she practiced swimming on her own, Hawk waded out to the blanket and sat down to drink some wine. He smiled as he watched her splash about. He loved the carefree Anna—so much different from the one at the Treasure Cove. Suddenly, another movement caught Hawk's eye. It came from within the patch of reeds. When he scanned the patch, he only saw some ripples and bubbles. He almost dismissed it, and then he thought about Razortooth.

"Anna! Swim this way as fast as you can!"

Anna stopped swimming and let her feet hit the sand below. "What's the matter?"

Hawk knew she would never make it. He grabbed his dagger from the blanket and ran full speed to the edge of the pond. "Swim!" he yelled as he leapt as high and far as his powerful legs would carry him. He disappeared headfirst into the water almost at Anna.

Just as Hawk dove into the water, Anna felt something big strike her left thigh. The blunt forced was quickly followed by several sharp pains. She screamed and tried to run. There was great commotion in the water just behind her.

Suddenly, Hawk reappeared. In his arms was a massive grayish-green scaled head. Its mouth was open, filled with razor sharp white teeth. Hawk's left arm was bleeding in several spots.

Anna knew from hearing sailor's tales that it was an alligator. "Hawk!"

"Get to shore!" Hawk shouted. The alligator started rolling its body, and soon both of them disappeared beneath the surface. A small red stain appeared in the water, a mixture his and Anna's blood.

Anna ran out of the water and onto the shore. She realized her leg had been punctured in several places by the beast's teeth. Blood streamed down her leg and dripped onto the ferns. Hawk must have reached the alligator just before it completed the bite on her leg. His arm had paid the price. The pair continued to roll and thrash beneath the water and moved back and forth across the pond. Occasionally, Hawk broke the surface, gasped for air, and then disappeared again. Other times, the alligator's tail or back would momentarily appear and quickly disappear again.

The red stain in the water began to spread at a much faster rate in the middle of the pond. Neither combatant had broken the surface in over a minute. The churning and splashing in the water slowed until there was soon no movement at all.

"Hawk!" Anna screamed, tears flowing down her face.

Still nothing. Then she saw the alligator's body appear at the surface—without Hawk attached to it. "No!" she screamed.

She sobbed as she stared at the still surface of the water for what seemed like minutes. Then, there was movement in the water just in front of her. Hawk's head appeared first, and then the rest of his body, as he crawled up onto the bank, turned and collapsed onto his back just beside her. He still held his bloodied dagger in his outstretched right arm. Anna realized that the alligator wasn't swimming but floating. Blood was spreading from its neck. Hawk's arm still bled profusely. There were also gashes in his side and on one of his legs. He lay there panting hard, his eyes closed.

Anna knelt over him. "Hawk! Are you OK?"

Hawk slowly opened his eyes, blinked hard a few times, and focused on her. "I've been better," he whispered, grinning weakly.

"Oh, Hawk! You saved my life! You're so brave and strong!" She leaned down farther and kissed him.

"If I'd known I'd ended up like this, I might have changed my mind," Hawk chuckled softly.

Anna slapped him playfully on his unharmed arm.

"How is your leg?" he asked, suddenly remembering her being struck first.

"It has a few holes in it and hurts, but I think I will be OK."

Hawk slowly sat up. He surveyed his wounds and then Anna's. "Let's patch ourselves up, get dressed, and head back to the beach. The ship will be here soon. I can clean our wounds and stitch them up on the way back to New Orleans. I've had lots of training with Mr. Bones."

They moved up to the blanket, and Hawk quickly cut his shirt into different sized strips. He tied one around Anna's leg. The wounds were deep, but had almost quit bleeding. Anna helped him tie another one around his arm. His leg and side weren't too bad. They put their clothes back on, packed up the basket, and limped back down the trail to the beach.

It was later than they realized, and Jimmy and Benjamin had just swum to the beach in preparations to go find them.

"Hawk! What happened to you?" Jimmy looked at Hawk and Anna and then quickly scanned the trees behind them in case their attackers were following.

"I think I found Razortooth's brother," Hawk said with a laugh. He told his story to Jimmy and Benjamin.

"Wow! You killed an alligator with your bare hands?"

"Well, I had help from a dagger. I'm glad you two came to shore. You can row us back to the *Cobra*."

The four climbed into the boat, and Jimmy and Benjamin rowed them back to the ship and helped them board. Onboard, the story quickly spread until every man had heard it. Hawk's legend continued to grow. The crew almost fell over themselves trying either to be of assistance or to get out of his and Anna's way. Hawk took Anna to his cabin and grabbed the alcohol, needle, catgut, and bandages. A painful half hour later, their wounds were cleaned, stitched, and bandaged. Hawk changed back into his city clothes.

Hawk let Jimmy handle most of the duties for their short voyage back. Hawk and Anna sat on the bow of the ship, arms around each other, and watched the sun set, its orange rays reflecting off the calm water. Despite their pain and discomfort, it was a perfect end to a nearly perfect day.

"So, other than being bit by an alligator, did you have a good night and day?" Hawk asked.

Anna's head lay against his shoulder.

"Oh, yes, Hawk. It was the most wonderful night and day of my life!" She squeezed his arm, the uninjured one, tightly.

"Good. Once we get back to New Orleans, I'm going to walk you to the Cove, and then me and my crew are going to have to sail back to the Rock."

Anna was silent for a moment. "When will I see you again?" she asked softly, and she lifted her head to look at him.

"I'm not sure. I have a feeling Bloodstone has something big planned for us. I told you about our current situation. I don't have enough money stashed away yet for me to leave. Just know this, Anna. I swear that I will come back for you. One way or the other, I will come back rich enough for us to disappear into our dream. It might be a year...it might be five years, but I will be back." He leaned forward and kissed her. He felt her tears run down her cheeks onto his. He was pretty sure some of his tears joined them.

"Please hurry," she whispered.

"I will. But now you've at least had a taste of what it will be like together. It's no longer a dream. You've touched it—held it in your hands. Now you have memories to live on, not just dreams. And one day, all this time we've waited will be long forgotten."

"And you know what is waiting for you too."

CHAPTER XIII

A Desperate Plan

༰

*D*iablo watched from a distance as Hawk and his crew returned from New Orleans. He grinned when he saw Hawk's bandaged arm and noticed him limping. Then the story of his alligator battle quickly made its way throughout the fort. Even Bloodstone rushed out of his cabin to greet the Hawk. That's all he needed—for Hawk to become even more of a legend with the crew. First the rescue, now this. Diablo had always been the assumed successor to Bloodstone. Bloodstone had outlived all other pirate captains, but Diablo bided his time. Now Hawk was a strong threat to his plans.

Most of Diablo's loyal supporters—the older crew—had been killed, had died of disease or old age, or had left the profession. The younger crewmembers only knew of Hawk's exploits, not all of the deeds Diablo had done over the years. He had to do something soon, or he would lose all of the crew to Hawk. Even if it meant disposing of Bloodstone and Hawk himself, he had to change things.

That night, Hawk, Diablo, Bones, Andre, Hobbs, and Bloodstone gathered around the large table in Bloodstone's cabin. They had spent the first hour drinking rum, talking of Hawk's recent fight, and swapping stories of the sea. Finally, Bloodstone called the meeting to order.

"Arrr! It be time for business, me mates. As ye know, we be short of men and money. The times, they also be a changin'. The New Orleans Squadron, led by that devil Cord and the *Enterprise*, be a scourge to pirates. They have at least a dozen ships now and be addin' more all the time. Prizes be harder to find and take. They also be searchin' all the islands. Ain't no hideouts safe now." He paused and took a large swig of rum. "The way I reckon it, we have two choices to ponder. One be to leave the trade and become honest men."

"That ain't no option," Diablo said.

"Aye, I reckon it ain't, for sure. The second be to do somethin' big— to even the odds, or least buy some time." Bloodstone sat back in his chair and puffed sweet smelling tobacco smoke from his long pipe.

"And what do you propose?" Andre asked.

"There be three parts to me plan. First, we need men and loot. As ye know, slave ships be more common than treasure ships. In the past, we set free those that we didn't kill. As bad as it pains me, I propose we offer quarter to all ships we attack, slave or merchant, if they'll join us. If they think they won't die, I reckon most won't fight. The blacks will join without pause. We take 'em all, sailors and slaves, and their loot. We train 'em how to shoot, and we buy more weapons. That be the first part."

The officers exchanged glances and nods. Other than Diablo, they all secretly disagreed with Bloodstone killing the innocent sailors.

"And the second part?" Bones asked.

"The second part ye won't like as much. We need to make an alliance…with Kragg."

That statement brought an eruption of exclamations and chatter from the officers. Diablo's voice rose above the rest. "We can't trust that devil! He's as much our enemy as Cord!"

"Why would you suggest that?" said Andre. "The crew will vote you out in a heartbeat."

"Let's hear him out," Hawk said, staring coldly at the others. He guessed Bloodstone's plan before he even explained it.

"It do leave a bad taste to even utter such, that be for sure. But I suggest it, because of the third part of me plan. I want to kill Cord and sink the

Enterprise. We can't do that with just the *Bloody Seas*, and we don't have time to capture and man an extra frigate. We join up with Kragg for one battle. If we take out the flagship of the squadron, that'll set the entire fleet back. Plus it will give pause to the navy officers and hope to all pirates. It'll at least buy us some years. If we do nothin', we'll all be hangin' in a years' time."

The officers sat in silence, mulling over Bloodstone's plan. As bad as they wanted to object, they realized they were in desperate straits. Bloodstone's last statement rang all too true. If something didn't slow down the navy, the noose would quickly tighten around their necks.

"Let's hear the rest of the plan," Diablo said. He wasn't sure if the plan would work, but a battle like that could take care of his problems. It would be easy for Hawk and Bloodstone not to survive. Even if the future was clouded, he would rather be a captain for a short time than remain a quartermaster forever.

Hawk and Diablo were the last two to leave Bloodstone's cabin. As Hawk turned to walk to his, Diablo firmly grabbed his arm.

Hawk spun around, pulling his arm free of the strong grip. "What?" Hawk barked.

"You're becoming quite the hero, aren't you?" Diablo hissed, keeping his voice low enough that Bloodstone wouldn't overhear.

"I just do my job and look out for my crew."

"Your crew? *Your* crew? This will never be your crew, swab! The old man is going to get himself killed—probably very soon. When he is gone, I will be captain." Diablo flashed his evil grin.

"That will be for the men to decide." Hawk was tired and not in the mood to deal with Diablo.

Diablo ignored Hawk's words and continued, "I will be a fair captain to you though. You will have the choice of me killing you or marooning you on a deserted island. Well, actually, I think I'll stick with killing. You'd find some way to escape the deserted island and become even more of a legend."

Hawk leaned close, his face inches from Diablo's. "Look, if you want to fight like a man, then let's go right here. If not, then turn and walk away. I don't have time for your drivel."

Diablo's smug grin shifted into a fierce scowl. His hand dropped to the hilt of his cutlass. He wanted so bad to kill the cocky upstart. But he knew they couldn't fight here. Even if he killed Hawk, the crew would be too angry to make him captain. He would be killed or marooned himself. He would wait and see if Cord did it for him. If not, he would see to it soon enough. "Watch your back, swab. It's going to be a dangerous battle." Diablo turned and walked toward his cabin. Hawk shook his head and limped to his.

The next morning, Bloodstone and his officers presented the plan to the entire crew in the middle of the fort. The men were likewise skeptical of making a deal with Kragg, but once they heard the entire plan and understood the alternative, they voted in favor of it.

Bloodstone and his crew thrived over the next two years. They did have to be vigilant to avoid contact with the *Enterprise* and the other frigates. The West Indies Squadron replaced the New Orleans Squadron. The *Enterprise* was still the flagship. The larger squadron included new ships, such as: USS *John Adams*, USS *Congress*, USS *Lynx*, and USS *Nonsuch*. They heard the tales of many other pirate ships being taken and their crew's hanged.

The slave ships were easy targets though. They were lightly defended and rarely escorted. Once word got out that Bloodstone was offering quarter, many sailors and slaves eagerly went on account. Soon Bloodstone's crew swelled to nearly 180 men. Thirty stayed at the Rock and 150 manned the *Bloody Seas*.

The new hands received training, and Bloodstone amassed enough wealth to repair and replace weapons and supplies. The captain resisted the urge to add more ships to his fleet. The more ships he had sailing, the more risk of one being caught. That was another reason teaming up with Kragg was a good plan—he could share the risk.

Hawk thought of Anna every day and especially every night. And his personal stash was growing very quickly. If he managed to survive the coming battle, he could see being able to leave pirating behind in the next year or so. They would still have most of their lives to spend together. He just had to stay alive long enough to get that opportunity.

CHAPTER XIV

DECEIT AND BETRAYAL

"**I** don't have a good feeling about this," James said.

"You should be ecstatic, my boy. This is your chance to finally face Bloodstone and exact your revenge," Cord said, scanning the horizon for sails.

"I don't trust that Vasquez."

Two days prior, a small Spanish sloop had hailed them just off of the coast of Cuba. One of the sailors, Vasquez, came aboard to speak to Captain Cord. With a patch over his left eye, he looked more like a pirate than a sailor. He told them that he was the first mate aboard a Spanish merchantman. They had a cargo full of gold and silver and were headed back to Spain. His captain had heard that Captain Bloodstone's *Bloody Seas* was praying on ships around the Bahamas. There were no Spanish warships in the area to escort them, and he didn't trust the British navy after they'd failed at hanging Bloodstone and his quartermaster. They had heard of the powerful US Navy ships hunting pirates in the area, so he was requesting an escort. They would be passing through in two days. He offered gold for the escort, whether or not they encountered pirates.

Cord asked where his ship was, and Vasquez explained that it was in Havana getting prepared for the voyage. That's when they learned there were no escort ships available. The relationship between Spain and the

United States wasn't strong enough for Cord to risk going to Havana to investigate. After thinking it over, he offered not to escort the ship, which would scare Bloodstone away, but to sail around the western-most tip of Grand Bahama Island. If Bloodstone attacked, the *Enterprise* would swoop in from behind. A day and time were agreed upon for when the merchantman would be passing the island.

"No matter," he said to James now. "Even if it is a trap, the *Bloody Seas* is no match for the *Enterprise*. We'll be ready. Very soon, Captain Bloodstone, Diablo, and his Hawk will be dead. After Bloodstone is gone, we'll hunt down Kragg. The end of the pirates is near, James, very near." Cord clapped his lieutenant on the shoulder.

James stared out over the water thoughtfully. The legend of Bloodstone's bosun, the Hawk, had spread all over the country through word of mouth and newspapers. The Hawk had rescued Bloodstone and Diablo from hanging at Port Royal. His shooting and fighting prowess were also legendary, based on reports from the few sailors that survived Bloodstone's attacks. Diablo had been the most feared of Bloodstone's crew, but he was all but forgotten since the appearance of Hawk. James remembered Diablo's role in the attack on his ship so many years ago. He hated him almost as much as Bloodstone. He didn't know this Hawk, but the bosun would face his wrath too, as would all of Bloodstone's crew.

The *Enterprise* had passed the town of Freeport and continued to-ward the western end of the island. If the attack were going to happen, it would happen just around the western tip. If not, the merchantman would hit open water and escape the pirate's normal hunting range.

Suddenly, Cord and James heard the unmistakable distant booms of cannon fire. "Unfurl the sails!" Cord cried out. They had only been running at half-mast so as not arrive in the channel too soon. Now the sails were fully raised, and they caught more wind, speeding them northwestward.

"All hands prepare for battle!" yelled James. Sailors began rush-ing about the deck loading and preparing the muskets, blunderbusses, flintlocks, and cannons. Others climbed quickly down through the hatches to the gun deck to prepare the remainder of the cannons.

"This is it, James! The moment you have waited for all your life," Cord said, grinning at his lieutenant.

James couldn't help but to grin back, despite his still lingering concerns. Both men checked their flintlocks and other weapons and prepared for the battle of their lives.

As the tip of the long island neared, they spotted the stern of a large frigate, painted black. Soon the sails and flag came into view. The flag was the legendary white skull with red eyes on a black background. The ship was broadside to them. Behind that ship, the front half of another frigate was visible, turned broadside to the *Bloody Seas*. The two were locked into a cannon battle. Smoke hung heavy in the air, obscuring what kind of damage either ship was giving or receiving.

"The *Bloody Seas!*" Cord exclaimed. He looked at James's face, which was no longer grinning. "What is wrong my boy? You should be jubilant."

"Something isn't right. That other frigate doesn't look like a Spanish merchantman."

"No matter if it is a merchant or a pirate. Bloodstone and his men are fully engaged in a battle. We will sail up beside the *Bloody Seas* unnoticed and give them a full broadside. Once she sinks, we will deal with the other ship if necessary. Today will go down in history, James."

James still felt uneasy, but the *Enterprise* was a formidable ship. And they had finally found Bloodstone and the *Bloody Seas*. Soon he felt his usual excitement over an impending battle building. His heart raced as the adrenaline coursed through his body. He clutched the railing and waited impatiently for the wind to carry them into the battle.

As they closed the distance, they could make out the crew of the pirate ship. They all seemed to be facing the starboard side of their ship and the foe they engaged. There was no sign that they saw the approaching *Enterprise*. Their ship looked in surprisingly good shape to be locked into a long cannon battle. The other ship was of similar size. It was too far away and too smoke-obscured to make out its crew or condition.

Cord shouted orders across the deck. "Ready the guns! Helmsman, bring us alongside. Reef and trim the sails." The ship slowed greatly as the sails were lowered and turned. They silently drifted behind the *Bloody Seas* and turned into a broadside position. There was still no indication of being spotted by the pirates, despite their proximity.

Just before Cord could shout the order to fire, the fourteen cannons on the port side of the pirate ship fired into the *Enterprise*. The six from the main deck fired canister shot, spraying the main deck of the *Enterprise* with flying pieces of metal. Booms from below deck indicated explosive shot was fired from the eight cannons on the gun deck. Screams rang out from all around James and Cord, and more were heard from below deck. Before their shock wore off, eight cannons from the front half of the other ship fired at the *Enterprise*. It was farther away, but at least five balls hit the bow of their ship.

Cord realized now that it was indeed a trap. Pirates had been crouching below the gunwale on the main deck and manning the cannons on the gun deck. They had probably just been manning a few cannons on the starboard side to shoot harmlessly over the other ship. Now the other ship hoisted its topsails, catching enough wind to pull it out from behind the *Bloody Seas*. Cord could also now see its colors—a red devil with a pitchfork. It was *Hell's Fury*, Kragg's flagship. "Kragg!" he yelled. He was now facing the two greatest pirate captains of the era.

"Fire!" Cord yelled, hoping he had enough men and undamaged cannons left. Twenty of the twenty-six cannons on the port side of the ship fired into the *Bloody Seas*. The damage inflicted was great, with most of the *Bloody Seas's* gun deck and cannons destroyed. Explosive shot set fire to large parts of the main deck and sails. Having a crew of three hundred was a huge advantage to the navy frigate. There were plenty of sailors to step up and replace the fallen. The cannons on both decks were quickly reloaded. Damaged ones were rolled out of place and replaced with ones from the starboard side of the ship.

Captain Bloodstone, Hawk, and Diablo stood together on the flaming deck. The trap had worked perfectly so far, but the *Enterprise* was a formidable ship and had twice as many men as theirs. Bloodstone shouted orders that were relayed below decks to pump the water from the hold up to the upper deck to help fight the fires. Other men rushed about with sand and buckets of water. The main deck cannons were pretty much ruined and the death toll high. He ordered the gun deck cannons to be reloaded with explosive shot, and the remainder of the men opened fire with muskets and blunderbusses. The two ships were slowly drifting together and would soon be within grappling range.

The remainder of *Hell's Fury's* cannons fired at the *Enterprise*. Only about half the shot hit the upper deck, doing minimal damage to the structure and sailors, but damaging the foremast and its sails. Cord ordered as many cannons as could be turned toward *Hell's Fury* to return fire. The *Bloody Seas* was mostly neutralized now, other than the small guns.

Fourteen of the *Enterprise's* cannons fired at *Hell's Fury*. Despite the distance, the crew was well trained and most made contact. They fired a combination of canister and explosive shot. The loss of life and damage was great. The main mast was hit, the deck set on fire, and holes ripped open in the hull. Six more cannons fired into the hull of the *Bloody Seas*, opening more huge gashes in the side, some low enough to take on more water.

The pirate crew shot at the gun crews on the *Enterprise*, trying to prevent more cannon fire. They were accurate and dropped men, but more stepped up to take their places. There were now less than fifty pirates on the deck of the *Bloody Seas* and hundreds on the *Enterprise*. The pirates then tossed all of the granadoes and stinkpots they had onto the *Enterprise's* main deck. That finally disrupted the sailors enough to halt them from reloading the cannons.

"What do we do?" Hawk shouted to Bloodstone. Normally, they would board the other ship at this point. But no matter how skilled they were as fighters, they could not overcome those odds.

"Hang me!" Bloodstone shouted, spitting onto the deck. "Where in the blazes is Kragg?" He rushed over to the starboard side of the ship, Hawk and Diablo following.

"Kragg!" Bloodstone shouted to the *Hell's Fury*.

The large redheaded pirate, dressed in white breeches, a red shirt, long blue coat, and a black tricorne hat, made his way through the throng of pirates putting out flames and loading cannons. "Aye?" he shouted back.

"Get your bloody ship into place and attack those navy dogs!"

Kragg laughed loudly. "I think me men tire of fightin' today. Ye can take the glory, Bloodstone."

"Ye can fight, or by the gods I'll pull your cowardly heart from your chest and feed it to ye!" Bloodstone yelled, his face glowing red.

Suddenly, the remaining sails on *Hell's Fury* were hoisted. The breeze quickly filled them, and the ship began to move away. "Save me a spot in hell, ye scurvy dog," said Kragg. "This is for attacking me schooner and killing Captain Grant. Did ye think I'd forget?"

Before Bloodstone could reply, half a dozen cannons fired from the other pirate ship. Ball and chain shot tore through the sails and rigging, doing great damage. Kragg laughed loudly again and turned and walked toward the helm of his ship. It moved faster now, turning to the northwest and away from the battle. "Curse his hide! If I die today, lads, someone has to kill that mangy coward for me!" The three rushed back to the battle with the *Enterprise*.

By the time they rejoined the battle, the navy sailors had thrown grappling hooks over their rail and pulled the two ships together. James followed the surge of sailors leaping over the railing onto the *Bloody Sea's* deck. The pirates that had flintlocks fired them into the charging sailors and then dropped them and drew their cutlasses. Diablo, Bloodstone, and Hawk became separated. Hawk tried to keep the sailors from surrounding the pirates to the stern. Diablo did the same toward the bow. Bloodstone tried to keep the middle of the ranks from collapsing.

The badly outnumbered pirates fought bravely. They were more experienced and better trained with the cutlasses. The deck quickly became slick with the mixture of blood, water, and sand. The pirates even started pushing the onslaught back toward the *Enterprise*. Then more sailors swung and leapt aboard. The gun crews from below deck were now all on the main deck. The ones who couldn't find room to board the *Bloody Seas* stayed on the main deck and shot at any pirate they had a clean shot at.

James purposely stayed back behind his men. He wanted a shot at Bloodstone but knew the pirate captain would be surrounded by his men. After the navy crew withstood the pirate counter surge, James began to push his way through the ranks until he reached the main group of pirates. Bloodstone was easy to spot, towering above his crew. The pirates were skilled, James gave them that. But he was fresh, and fueled by fourteen years of pent of hatred and hostility. His blade was a blur, dealing death on all sides.

The pirates had another surge as the remaining men that were alive below deck abandoned the pumps and cannons and made their way up through the hatches. The mass of bodies moved back and forth, almost like water sloshing in the hold. But inevitably the pirates were driven toward the starboard rail. Once they were cornered and pinned, the battle would soon be over.

Hawk fought like a mad man, leaving a pile of bodies surrounding him. He would have lost count of the sailors he killed had he been counting. In a brief break in the fighting, as more sailors surged aboard to replace the ones he had killed, he surveyed the scene on both ships. There were less than four-dozen pirates alive on the main deck. There were almost twice as many sailors, plus the *Enterprise's* deck was still full of more waiting their turn.

For the first time in his life, Hawk contemplated his own death. He had never been truly pushed before or in a no-win situation. The alligator had been a little frightening, but he was more worried about losing a limb than dying. He had fought plenty of battles with sword and gun, but his confidence never let him think about dying, not since his very first battle.

Then a vision of Anna came into his mind. They were together again on the blanket by the pond, holding each other after just making love. She smiled her sweet smile and stared into his eyes. He wondered what she would do when she found out he broke his promise and died before returning to her. He imagined her crying. She might not have another way out of her life of prostitution. He might be her only hope for a better, and happy, future.

He had to do something to turn the tide, or it would soon be too late. He recalled every battle he had been in and all of the cunning and trickery Bloodstone had used. Then an idea hit him. It was foolish and had a slim chance of succeeding, but it was at least something. He turned and bolted toward the quarterdeck before the next wave of sailors could reach him. He scampered up the ladder, ran across the deck, and with several long strides, he dove over the rail and disappeared headfirst into the sea below.

The pirates that had been fighting with Hawk were stunned, as their fiercest fighter, and possibly best leader, ran from the battle and abandoned ship. They suddenly realized that they were going to lose this battle, something that had never happened to any of them in Bloodstone's crew. The constant press of sailors steadily drove them back. They fought, but with little conviction. They waited their turns to die and contemplated surrender.

James finally found himself standing before the mighty Captain Bloodstone. He was even more imposing and intimidating up close. He stood several inches taller than James and was much broader. But he panted hard and was covered in blood—some of it is his own. For a moment, neither man attacked.

"You devil!" said James. "You killed my father and brother and many good men on our ship. I've hunted you for fourteen long years so I could finally avenge my family!" The fighting around them slowed and the din quieted somewhat. The sailors and pirates each knew that their leaders were about to engage in a battle to the death.

"Arrr! I don't doubt I killed 'em, but they like as not deserved it," Bloodstone replied, flashing an evil grin.

"They were unarmed! We were just sailing to the New World on a merchant ship. My brother was six years old!"

The shouting had now halted all of the fighting. The pirates were in desperate need of a rest, and the sailors all knew that this was the man that James had devoted his entire life to finding. The two crews moved back, forming a circle with pirates on one side and sailors on the other. The men on the *Enterprise*, with Cord in front, also gathered against the railing, watching the impending duel.

"I've never killed any six-year-old boys. But if ye be set on killin' me, then I s'ppose we best get to it."

James wondered momentarily why Bloodstone would lie about killing Henry. But Bloodstone swung an overhand blow at him, and he had to quickly raise his cutlass to block it. Instantly, all the years of pent-up rage and hostility surged through his body and into his sword arm. He knew Bloodstone was tired and wounded. James had fought some, but was much fresher than his opponent. He went on the offensive, raining blows down on Bloodstone from every side and angle. The crowd surrounding them erupted into yells and cheers.

Bloodstone was able to keep up with James and block all of his attacks. But he was forced to give some ground, despite his size advantage. He was exhausted from the battle thus far. Over the past few years, with all of his cunning plans and traps, he actually hadn't had much hand-to-hand combat. He usually came aboard just for mop-up and to dispatch the other ship's captain. His opponent was as skilled as him, plus much fresher and younger. He would have to resort to some of the tricks he used to defeat Hawk in sparring.

James swung a hard overhand blow at Bloodstone's head. Bloodstone blocked it just in time, and their swords locked together. James pressed down hard with his cutlass, using both hands and all of his strength. Bloodstone's blade slowly lowered toward his head, now bare since his hat had long since fallen off. Suddenly, Bloodstone leaned backward, removed one hand from his blade, and reached for a dagger on his baldric. He had the blade drawn and swinging toward James before the lieutenant could react.

Just before the blade struck James's exposed side, Bloodstone's right foot slipped in a puddle of blood on the already slick deck. The pirate captain collapsed onto his right knee and nearly fell from the force of the dagger swing and James's sword pushing his down in front of his chest. The slip gave James just enough time to leap back, and the blade only slashed his shirt. James landed and quickly jabbed his sword into Bloodstone's left knee. Bloodstone howled in pain. James quickly pulled his blade free and landed a short, quick blow into Bloodstone's left shoulder, which was still extended from the dagger swing.

The big pirate stumbled backward, nearly falling on his back. He managed to regain his feet and held both blades in front of him. His left knee was damaged badly, and he had to shift most of his weight to his right leg. He knew he was losing this fight, something he had never done before. His opponent strode confidently forward. Bloodstone flung his dagger underhanded at the sailor's midsection. James effortlessly swung his blade down and sent the dagger flying to the deck.

The sailors on both ships now cheered and yelled loudly. The pirates were mostly silent, watching in horror and shock. James swung a series of blows at Bloodstone's right side. The pirate shifted more weight to his right leg and managed to block all of the blows. Then James suddenly kicked his right leg out and struck Bloodstone hard on the left knee. The leg instantly buckled.

Bloodstone saw the kick, a favorite trick of his, but was powerless to stop it. His knee exploded in pain as he collapsed onto it. He tried to rise, but knew he couldn't. He fell to both knees. He struck at James's legs a couple of times, but the sailor was too quick. His opponent grinned, and his blade became a silver blur. Bloodstone heard the roar from the sailors behind James. He was late on a block and felt the cutlass dig deep into his right shoulder. He quickly reached for a flintlock in his baldric, only to have the cutlass nearly sever his left arm just above the wrist. Another blow hit his right arm and sent his cutlass flying.

For James, it seemed that time had nearly stopped as he rained the last few blows onto the man who'd destroyed his life and killed his family. For a second, he almost felt pity for him. Bloodstone was on both knees, bleeding from numerous cuts and slashes. He was defenseless. His eyes almost looked sad, not angry. Then James replayed the image of Bloodstone coldly shooting his father. He imagined what torture Henry probably endured before his death. He raised his sword over his head, holding the hilt with both hands.

"I'm James. James Wellington. This is for my father, Peter Wellington!" His blade dropped and cut deeply into the side of Bloodstone's neck. Still Bloodstone remained on his knees, blood pouring down his shirt and onto his breeches. "And for my brother, Henry." James was puzzled at the look of surprise on Bloodstone's pale and bloody face.

The pirate opened his mouth. "Haw—"

James's cutlass dropped one more time, hitting the same deep gash. Bloodstone's huge head stayed on his shoulders for a couple of seconds. Then as the pirate captain's body tumbled backward, his head rolled forward. It landed at James's feet, its mouth still open trying to finish his last word.

Both crews had fallen silent during the last exchange. The sailors now waited on some word from James or Cord. The pirates looked to Diablo since their captain was dead, and Hawk had deserted them. At this point, the choice was death by sword now or hanging in the very near future.

James wanted to collapse onto the deck too. He was exhausted—physically and mentally. Most of his life he had dreamed of this day. He now had avenged his father and brother and all of the innocent people on that ship so long ago. He was elated and relieved but also felt strange. He somehow felt empty. He turned, sheathed his sword, and walked back through the sailors, who parted to give him a wide path. "Finish them," he said, breaking the silence.

The men resumed the fight. The action started slow and then built into the loud roar of battle. James didn't look back as the sailors rushed past him to get at the remaining pirates. As James reached the rail, a huge explosion erupted from deep within the stern of the *Enterprise*. A gaping hole ripped open from the inside and flames rolled out. Many of the men on the *Enterprise* were knocked off their feet. James realized the explosion was in the magazine. More explosions followed, tearing out more of the hull and the deck above. The battle aboard the *Bloody Seas* halted once more, and all eyes turned to the *Enterprise*.

James quickly leapt over the railing back onto the deck of his ship and followed Cord and the other sailors down through the hatches to the hold. He knew they had to act quickly if they were to save the ship. More sailors followed them, returning from the *Bloody Seas*, all forgetting about the remaining pirates.

At first, no one noticed the man who emerged from the hatch closest to the bow of the *Enterprise*. The shirtless man in blue breeches shoved two flintlocks into the red sash around his waist, placed a dagger in his teeth, and scampered up the closest ratline to the main mast. He paused to cut the rigging all the way up to the crow's nest.

Billy was the first pirate to notice. He instantly recognized the man. "The Hawk!" he screamed. The remaining, startled, sailors on the *Bloody Seas* turned to look at the *Enterprise*. Most started running back toward their ship, not knowing how many pirates might be aboard. The other pirates started yelling and cheering.

Diablo saw Hawk too. And despite his disappointment at him still being alive, he was actually glad to see him. "The guns!" he shouted, running to the starboard rail. The gun racks on that side of the ship were still full of loaded blunderbusses and muskets. The pirates never had a chance to use them before the assault began. The other pirates followed suit and within moments fired guns into the sailors still staring at the *Enterprise* and the ones running back onto it. The volley was devastating from that close range.

Hawk was relieved to see that Billy, Diablo, and some of his crew were still alive. He had slashed all the lines he could reach, devastating the rigging. He then dove into the air with his dagger held tightly in both hands. The dagger stabbed into the mainsail, and he slid all the way down it, splitting it in half as he did. He let go of the dagger as it reached the spar and dropped lightly to his feet on the deck below. He snatched up a cutlass from among the dead sailor's bodies. Then he ran and jumped onto the *Enterprise's* rail, pausing momentarily, and then leapt onto the deck of the *Bloody Seas*, crashing into the few remaining sailors.

He went to work, dispatching them with his blade. The pirates rushed forward and soon the deck was clear of sailors. Hawk and the other pirates quickly began cutting the grappling lines.

"Some of you grab the pikes and push us free," said Hawk. "You four get down below and man the pumps. Tell Bones to get to work patching holes. Billy, hoist the sails and tell Hobbs to steer us leeward!"

Diablo helped Hawk get the men rushing about to set sail. Soon their ship started drifting away from the *Enterprise*. Its crew was still below deck trying to extinguish the flames and patch the holes. Hawk stood at the port rail and stared at the damaged frigate. He wasn't sure the sailors and ship would survive. The fire was still raging, and an occasional explosion was still heard. It would be a tough voyage to safety if they did survive. Then he saw two people climb up through one of the hatches. He recognized them as the Captain Cord and his lieutenant, James. They rushed to the rail in disbelief.

James saw the shirtless pirate standing against the rail of the *Bloody Seas*. He surmised he was the one that had blown up the magazine and destroyed the mainsail and rigging. As he studied his blond hair and face, he noticed the birthmark on his left breast. They were still close enough for him to see that it resembled a bird. His mind instantly raced back to his childhood and his little brother Henry. *Henry had a birthmark...just like...that.*

His conversation with Bloodstone came rushing back to him. Bloodstone had said he never killed any six-year-old boys. Then he remembered the last word that Bloodstone had tried to speak when he had mentioned Henry's name: "Haw—" *Hawk? Henry?* "Noooo!" he shouted.

CHAPTER XV

CAPTAIN HAWK

ᘓᘿ

*D*iablo approached Hawk on the center of the main deck once they were under sail. Hawk tensed and placed his hand on his cutlass. This was not the time for a confrontation. Diablo actually flashed a grin that wasn't a sneer. "As bad as it pains me, I will give you credit for saving all of us."

"You're welcome. Look, let's just get this wreck back to the Rock, regroup, and then we can get a plan together."

Diablo nodded and walked off to see to the many tasks taking place. Hawk climbed down to the lower decks to inspect the damage. Luckily, Bones had been working on patching the holes on the lower decks while the battle raged. Water was still several feet deep in the hold and more was coming in from holes that Bones and some pirates were still working on closing. Most of the powder and stores were ruined. Several men rotated on working the pumps, trying to keep the water level from rising until the holes were patched.

Hawk's heart leapt into this throat when he saw the body of Andre. He was apparently killed in the first broadside. Most of the cannons were heavily damaged and many of the ports and surrounding hull and deck destroyed. They would be basically defenseless if they encountered another navy ship or Kragg. Hawk then made his way to Wesley's cabin. He slowly opened the door, praying that the old sailor had survived.

Wesley sat at his table pointing a flintlock at the door, a dagger on the table in front of him. When he saw Hawk, he set the flintlock down beside the dagger. "Thank the gods! I haven't fought in many years, but I wasn't lettin' 'em bilge rats hang me. You're a sight for sore eyes to be sure. How bad is it?"

Hawk dropped wearily into another chair. "Bad. Bloodstone is dead."

Wesley dropped his eyes to the table and shook his head. "Poor ol' devil. I s'ppose it was well past his turn. Can't live forever, that's for sure."

"And Andre. Looks like there are just fifty or so of us left, counting the wounded."

"Blast! And the *Enterprise?*"

Hawk told Wesley of the battle and Kragg's betrayal. Wesley cursed and spit on the floor at that news. Then Hawk told of his diving into the water and swimming underneath the *Enterprise* to the other side. The ship was listing enough that he was able to grab the edge of a gunport and climb inside onto the gun deck. The only sailors there were dead or dying, so he grabbed a linstock and made his way down to the hold and to the magazine. He cut a hole in a powder keg and ran out a long line of black powder halfway across the deck. He lit the powder, scurried back up to bow of the gun deck, and hid behind a cannon until the explosions started. Soon after, the sailors, along with Cord and James, climbed down the ladders at the far hatches and made their way below, not one looked toward his hiding place. When they were all below, he made his way to the main deck and began destroying the sails.

Wesley grinned and shook his head. "I knew you were special, but you keep outdoin' yourself, my boy. A smarter and braver act I've never heard, for the likes of me."

"I just wasn't ready to die yet. That's the only chance I could think of. Luckily it somehow worked. So much death though."

"Aye. Our luck has definitely been bad lately," Wesley said, still thinking about Hawk's deeds.

"You know, the night we got back from Port Royal, I spent some time with Bloodstone in his cabin," said Hawk. "He kept talking about pirating coming to an end. He spoke of the golden age a hundred years ago. But he said now the US Navy will only grow larger, and soon we'd have nowhere left to hide. I think he knew his time was short too."

Wesley scratched his scruffy beard. "The old devil had his faults, to be sure, but he was a wise man. Had an uncanny ability to predict the future."

"Our working with Kragg to try to sink the *Enterprise* was our best plan for trying to extend the pirate age," said Hawk. "We figured we could set the navy back a few years and make sailors think twice about coming after us."

"'Bout the only chance we had, I reckon."

"We might have sunk it or pretty much destroyed it anyway. But you know, I don't think it will make a difference. There are at least four more frigates just like it. I'm sure more are being built. Like Bloodstone said, there's not a safe harbor left for pirates. Sure, we might could regroup and sail around a couple of more years, but it's over." Hawk leaned back with his hands behind his head, staring at the ceiling.

"Aye. I'd like to say something reassurin' to you. But I'd say you and Bloodstone are right. Not much of a livin' to be had for honest pirates, huh?" Wesley chucked softly. He got up and poured them both a tankard of rum from a small cask he kept. He sat back down and placed one in front of Hawk. They drank in silence for a few minutes.

"So, what's your plan? Just callin' it quits now?" Wesley finally asked.

Hawk stared at Wesley for a moment and took a large swig of rum. "Not quite yet. Bloodstone told us that if he was killed we should go after Kragg and make him pay for his treachery."

"We don't have the ship or men for that!" Wesley exclaimed.

"No. He'd win in an all-out battle. Yet he has to die. I'm working on a plan."

Wesley laughed and finished his rum. "You and your bloody plans!"

Hawk helped to tend to the wounded pirates in the infirmary as Bones was occupied mending the ship. That night, with the *Bloody Seas* limping back to the Rock, the crew gathered on the main deck. All of the dead pirates were laid in rows across the deck, nearly one hundred bodies. They placed Bloodstone's body in the center of the first row. Chain shot was wrapped around their legs, as was the crew's custom. It took nearly all of their remaining shot. The officers were in front of the bodies, against the starboard rail. Wesley read a few verses from the Bible.

Hawk stepped forward when Wesley was done. "These men fought hard and died like men. Let's remember and honor their bravery and deeds. Captain Bloodstone was the fiercest pirate captain ever to sail the seas. For twenty years he reigned supreme, causing men to fear the very mention of his name. If not for an unfortunate slip, he'd be standing here tonight. When we get back to the Rock, we will elect a new captain to lead us. But none can replace Captain Bloodstone. May God watch over these men in their next journey."

Hawk stepped back and nodded to Diablo. Diablo frowned and then stepped forward. "They lived hard, fought hard, and died brave. I hope hell knows what's coming."

There was some chuckling and laughing to break the somber moment. Then the pirates began grabbing up their dead mates and tossing them into the ocean. Bloodstone was saved until last, and Diablo and Hawk did the honors. His head had been placed inside a canvas bag and tied to the chain at his feet.

The wind was generous, and they made decent speed back to the Rock, arriving several days later. Once the ship was out of danger, word spread of how Hawk saved them. The excitement over his deeds took the crew's mind off of the loss of so much life and their current situation. Soon the whispers started that Hawk couldn't die. As Bloodstone had stated so long ago, he was marked by the gods.

A celebration quickly died out at the Rock as the pirates there realized the *Bloody Seas* wasn't exactly returning in victory. When only fifty men made their way to the beach, Captain Bloodstone and Andre not among them, a heavy silence fell over the welcoming party. The pirates all made their way up the trail to the fort. Hawk instructed everyone to eat and then meet around the bonfire after. He asked the officers, along with Billy and Jimmy, to join him in Bloodstone's cabin.

Once they were all seated around the table, Hawk poured them all tankards of rum, sat down, and then spoke. "I don't need to state the obvious. I have several proposals to make here, and then we can have the entire crew vote."

Diablo stared at him, unblinking. His scowl was fierce.

"First, I propose that Jimmy take Andre's place as gunner." Jimmy had continued to prove himself as a solid and dependable pirate and had gained the favor of Bloodstone and Hawk. "Next, I propose that Billy be the new bosun."

"Bosun?" Diablo roared. "So I s'ppose I know what's coming next?"

"I propose that I be elected the new captain," Hawk said flatly, staring at Diablo.

"Over my dead body! I should be the captain. I've been a pirate since before you were born, swab. Not to mention I've always been Bloodstone's right-hand man," Diablo stood up and placed both fists on the table.

"Let us hear him out," Bones said, looking from Diablo to Hawk. Diablo glared at Bones for a moment and slowly took his seat again.

"There's a reason I want to be captain, Diablo. If I'm elected, I will then have the men vote on going after Kragg. He must pay for his cowardice."

"I can do that as well as you," Diablo shot back.

Wesley shook his head. "I don't know how either of you fools can propose to do that with a handful of wounded men and a broken ship."

There was a murmur of agreement from Bones and Hobbs. Jimmy and Billy were silent, taking in the exchange with wide eyes.

"*We* are not going to fight him," Hawk said.

"Then what are you proposin', lad?"

"I am going to challenge Kragg to a duel to the death. His crew can't be happy with his treachery. They know that their only hope, as well as ours, is to join together against the United States. Kragg will have no choice but to accept my challenge. I will further propose that the survivor become the captain of both crews. Now, Diablo, would you rather do that in my place?"

Diablo muttered something under his breath and finally shook his head. He had heard about Kragg's prowess with a blade. He would fight him if he had to, but he wouldn't voluntarily do it. Hawk was much younger than he and, as badly as he hated to admit it, stronger and a better fighter. Besides, there was a good chance Kragg would kill Hawk. Then he would just have to organize a mutiny against the new captain. As Hawk said, his crew couldn't be happy with his treachery and helping the US Navy. If Hawk won…well he would come up with a plan for that too.

"I don't know, Hawk. Heaven forbid, but what if Kragg kills you?" Wesley asked.

"I will do my best to see that doesn't happen. But if it does, join his crew. Then organize a mutiny as soon as you can. His crew will be ready to turn on him. Diablo, you could have your long awaited captaincy then."

Diablo grinned at Hawk. *Either way*, he thought.

The men around the table voted unanimously for all of Hawk's suggestions. They then proceeded to the bonfire and the congregation of pirates. Hawk presented the proposals to the assembly, to which they all enthusiastically voted in favor. If there were some in favor of Diablo's becoming captain, they didn't openly express it. The chant of "Hawk, Hawk, Hawk" filled the air. Soon some pirates fetched casks of rum, and the celebration started. The musicians played and the pirates danced and drank late into the night. Hawk let them have their night.

The next day, he put every available hand to helping him and Bones repair the *Bloody Seas*. He wanted to set sail the next morning by sunrise. He figured that Kragg would be at his hideout for several days. Kragg wouldn't have known the outcome of the battle, and if the *Enterprise* had sunk the *Bloody Seas*, he would be their next target. *Hell's Fury* also needed repairs. It was doubtful Kragg would be in any hurry to get back on the water. His men were likely near mutiny, and letting them be drunk and happy on land was better than the options at sea.

The *Bloody Seas* left the cove and unfurled its sails just as the sun rose in the east the next morning. All eighty of the remaining pirates were onboard—healthy, injured, old, and sick. Hawk knew that the coming events would forever change the fates of his crew, Kragg's, and probably the fate of all pirates. All needed to be present, for better or worse.

Hawk had learned the location of Kragg's home base during the parleying before the attack on the *Enterprise*. Kragg used one of the many islands in the Turks and Caicos, north of Hispaniola. It was a several-day voyage to the islands. They didn't show their colors and generally skirted ships of any type. The *Bloody Seas* was sailable, but definitely not battle ready. Only half the cannons were operational, and they hadn't had time to replace most of their powder and shot. The crew was unusually subdued. They all knew what was at stake.

It was late evening of the fourth day when Billy spotted the island Kragg had named "Devil Island." The two rock peaks rising from the center did resemble horns. The water on the approach to the island was shallow and filled with small rocky islands and submerged coral. It took all of Hobbs's years of experience to navigate the frigate through the maze. Billy helped spot from the crow's nest. Had their ship been fully armed and the hold full of booty, they would have had trouble approaching the protected harbor.

As they squeezed between two fairly large rock islands, they spotted the deep, clear harbor just ahead. *Hell's Fury* lay on its side on the left side of the harbor, repairs and careening in full swing. Two schooners and a sloop were anchored at other points in the large bay. There were no walls or fort, but the wide, deep beach did have a number of huts and wooden structures on it similar to those inside the fort at the Rock. Most of Kragg's men appeared to be working on the *Fury*.

Horns suddenly sounded on rocky outcrops on each side of the harbor. The pirates on the beach began scurrying about, and more joined them from the huts and buildings. Most held muskets, pistols, or cutlasses. Some filled the two longboats and began rowing out to the schooners. They would be too late and of little consequence if the *Bloody Seas* was bent on attacking.

The *Bloody Seas* sailed in as close as was safe and then came about hard to port until it was broadside to the beach. The sails were furled and the anchor dropped. By this time, it looked like Kragg's entire crew was on the shore. Kragg himself, in the same clothes he had worn in the battle, pushed his way to the front of the throng. Hawk stood against the starboard rail, along with his officers. Most of his crew formed a semicircle behind him.

For a moment, Hawk was tempted to change his plans and fire a broadside of explosive shot at Kragg and his crew. The damage would be devastating. Follow it up with a musket volley, and there would be few left standing. He was surprised at the laxness of Kragg's defenses. Obviously he didn't expect anyone to navigate their way to his harbor. But destroying Kragg's crew wouldn't help him at all. That would just make the US Navy's job easier. He had to try his plan.

"Captain Bloodstone and crew, so glad ye survived that battle," Kragg called out. "I hope ye sent those navy dogs to the bottom of the sea!"

Hawk waited for the hisses and mumbling from the pirates around him to die down before he spoke. "Thanks to your treachery, Captain Bloodstone and a great many of his crew are dead. I am Hawk, the new captain of the *Bloody Seas*."

Kragg replied with feigned shock at the accusation. "Treachery? Me cannons must have misfired. They were pointed o'er your bow at the *Enterprise*. We had to sail because we were taking on water."

"Spare me and our crews your lies. You did two things no decent pirate would ever do—double-cross a fellow pirate and help out the navy. I have no idea why your crew has let you remain their captain or even continue living. You are the biggest coward I have ever encountered." The crew behind Hawk erupted in cheers and laughter. Kragg's crew was strangely quiet.

"Double-cross? Need I remind ye about your captain's cowardly attack on me ship a few years back? Ye killed a lot good men for no reason." Kragg gave up any pretense of being nice.

"You're mad. We have never attacked any of your ships or any other pirate. The only treachery was from you, you lice-ridden, mangy dog. And today you will pay for it."

"So you're just going to slaughter me and all of these good men? Looks like ye would be the coward."

"No. I have no quarrel with your men," Hawk replied, calmly. "Just you. Both of our crews have suffered enough. The only hope for all pirates is for our two crews to join together. Then we might have enough men and ships to hurt the navy, or at least stay alive a little longer." He scanned the faces of Kragg's pirates.

"And who would captain this crew?" Kragg retorted, not sure what the young captain was suggesting.

"The winner of our duel. The fight is between us, not our crews. I challenge you to a duel to death or surrender. The winner becomes the captain of both crews. My crew has already voted and accepted my proposal. I suggest you put it to a vote with yours."

Kragg growled and spat into the sand at his feet. He started to object, but it was actually a very good plan, for him at least. If Hawk had wanted, he could have slaughtered him and all of his crew while sitting back and safely firing the guns. He also knew his men weren't happy with his treachery on Bloodstone, even with Bloodstone's attack on Captain Grant. If he defeated Hawk in a duel, both crews would be reasonably satisfied. Plus, he had many years of fighting experience and, despite his being much older than Hawk, was unrivaled with a blade.

Before he even turned to his crew, one of his men shouted, "Aye." The verbal assent quickly spread through his entire crew.

Kragg knew that was their vote. Half or more probably hoped Hawk would kill him, but it was no matter. Soon, the young captain would be dead, and he would be the last and greatest pirate captain. Having the *Bloody Seas* and *Hell's Fury* both in his fleet would be deadly for the US Navy or any other.

"You and your men row ashore, and me and you will have this duel."

"No. I will come alone. Then if you try treachery again, my crew will kill everyone on this beach." Hawk didn't wait for a reply. He had the longboat lowered and hastily climbed down into it. He rowed ashore alone. When he reached the beach and exited the boat, Kragg's crew had moved back to leave a large clear area for the two combatants. Kragg already had his cutlass, a much heavier and bigger blade than Hawk's, in his hand.

"I want this to be a fair fight," Hawk said. "We both discard all of our weapons except our cutlasses." He removed his cutlass and tossed his baldric into the boat.

Kragg cursed under his breath, but he too removed his baldric. He tossed it up the beach to the feet of his crew. He liked to have a full range of options at his disposal in a battle. But no matter, he could still defeat the brash young Hawk.

The two men circled each other in the sand, wet and hard-packed from the tide recently having covered it. They held their cutlasses in front of them. Hawk was barefoot, having known not to wear his boots in the sand. Kragg still wore his knee high black leather boots. Hawk hoped that would give him an advantage before the battle was over.

Suddenly, Kragg leapt forward and jabbed his cutlass at Hawk. The speed of the attack, and the surprising quickness of the big pirate, caught Hawk off guard. He stepped back, but slightly too late. The cutlass penetrated his shirt and bit into his side. He didn't think it was serious, but he felt the warm blood running out of the wound and soaking into his white shirt.

Kragg continued the attack, knowing he had an immediate advantage. He steadily drove Hawk back toward the water with his flurry of blows. Another quick jab, amid a flurry of slashes, penetrated Hawk's biceps on his left arm. A trail of blood soon appeared on his sleeve. Kragg laughed a booming, terrifying laugh. This fight was turning out much easier than he thought. Hawk's crew had fallen silent aboard his ship. Surprisingly, only a handful of Kragg's men were cheering for him.

Hawk was becoming concerned. He felt like he had during so many sparing sessions with Bloodstone. He had thought he was a much better fighter now, if not one of the best. But Kragg kept him on the defensive. Hawk was accustomed to using his aggression to keep his opponents off balance. Unless Kragg tired and slowed on his own, Hawk had to think of something quick to turn the tide. One slip or mistake on his part and the fight, and his life, could be over.

Slipping. The thought suddenly gave Hawk an idea. The water was washing over his bare feet as Kragg continued his onslaught. He parried his blows and waited for the next overhand one. When Kragg swung a hard blow down at his head, Hawk reached up and blocked it with his sword. Instead of trying to knock the blade away, he let Kragg's blade stay on top of his.

Kragg had been trying to weaken Hawk with his greater strength and heavier weapon. Although he was tiring some, he knew his attack was also weakening Hawk. He felt Hawk's strength giving way now beneath his blade. He leaned forward and pressed down with both hands on the hilt of his cutlass. Hawk's blade continued to lower toward his bare head. Kragg knew that at any moment Hawk's strength could give out, and both of their blades could sink deep into his skull. He grinned despite the exertion.

Suddenly, all of the resistance against Kragg's blade gave way, although neither blade struck Hawk's skull. Hawk had spun to the left, causing Kragg's blade to slide off of his. Kragg was leaning forward, and pressing down so hard, that his momentum caused him to lurch forward. His boots sank into the wet sand, and he lost his balance. His arms flapped as he fought against falling face down in the waves. Then pain exploded in his back. Hawk had completed his spin and struck Kragg on his broad back with his blade. It bit deeply all of the way across.

The crew on the *Bloody Seas* erupted in yells and cheers. Had Hawk been able to stab, the fight would be over. As it was, his blow was deep, and painful, but not debilitating. Kragg managed to avoid falling and turned around to face Hawk before the younger man could strike him again. But now Hawk was able to go on the offensive. And Kragg's boots continued to sink in the watery sand. Hawk danced nimbly in front of him, jabbing and flicking his sword in all directions. Soon Kragg's shirt and pants were cut in several places, along with the skin beneath.

A moment later, Hawk landed an overhand blow onto Kragg's extended blade. They both realized they were in the same situation they had been in a few minutes before. Kragg's only hope was to do a similar move with Hawk and regain the offensive. Hawk began leaning forward and bearing down on Kragg's blade, just as Kragg had done. Kragg was surprised that Hawk would try the same tactic that had nearly cost him his life. But Hawk wouldn't survive making the same mistake.

Kragg let his sword drop slightly, encouraging Hawk to commit further. As he waited for the exact moment to spin away, Hawk suddenly leaned forward even further. Then, in a move too quick to react to, Hawk raised his knee and drove it hard into Kragg's stomach. Kragg was driven backward and almost doubled over. Their blades separated, and once again Kragg fought for his balance.

Kragg realized his fate a second too late. He looked up just in time to see a flash of silver heading toward him. His blade was much too slow and pain exploded in his chest as Hawk's blade drove through it, all the way to the hilt. Hawk's face was inches from Kragg's when the blade finally stopped. Kragg looked down in shock at his chest and then back up at Hawk.

"I'd stay away from Bloodstone in hell!" Hawk whispered.

The blood gurgling up into his throat and mouth drowned Kragg's last words. Hawk let go of his sword and the large pirate fell back into the surf. The young captain turned and walked a few steps out of the water onto the hard sand and collapsed wearily onto his knees. He was tired from the battle, but also nearly overwhelmed by the events of the past couple of weeks. Cheers erupted from both crews, and soon shouts of "Hawk, Hawk, Hawk" could be heard on the beach and ship.

Hawk closed his eyes and tried to come to grips with the moment. Then gunfire erupted behind him on the *Bloody Seas*. The shouts and cheering stopped on the ship and the beach. Slowly, Hawk stood and turned to face his ship. There was a scuffle on the main deck. He couldn't tell exactly what was happening, but after several more shots, the scuffle and movement stopped.

The majority of the crew had been pushed back to the middle of the main deck. A dozen or so pirates formed a semicircle between them and the railing, flintlocks leveled at them. Diablo strode over to the rail and stared at Hawk, his evil grin visible even from that distance. He held a musket in his hands.

"Splendid battle, Hawk! Once again you've added to your legend. I'm afraid, though, that I get to add the final chapter to your story."

"What are you doing, Diablo?" Hawk wearily called out.

"Doing what should have been done long ago. I am now the captain of the *Bloody Seas* and of *Hell's Fury* and the men behind you. Any that don't agree will meet your fate." Diablo rested the musket on the rail and took aim on the defenseless Hawk.

"You're a madman and a fool! These men will never follow you." Hawk prepared himself for the death that he had so long eluded. Once again, his mind traveled to Anna. The vision of her he could always conjure was as strong as reality. He held her head and kissed her lips. His life was of no consequence. It was just the thoughts of what would happen with her life and of never being able to see her again that made him sad.

"They have no choice. And that will be no concern of yours. Oh, Hawk, I need to tell you something before you die. Bloodstone didn't rescue you from your ship." Diablo smiled.

"What are you talking about?"

"So naïve. He attacked your family's ship. You and your cowardly family were hiding in the captain's cabin. You rushed out, brandishing that confounded wooden sword of yours, and confronted Bloodstone. I wanted to kill you of course, but that cursed Bloodstone wouldn't let me. Your father came rushing out of the cabin, trying to save his sweet, brave son." Diablo paused for a moment, enjoying the emotion on Hawk's face. "Bloodstone had you whisked away to the *Bloody Seas* and then proceeded to kill your unarmed father in cold blood, even while he was restrained by another pirate. He would have killed your cowardly brother too, if a navy frigate hadn't sailed into view."

Hawk fell to his knees again. "You're lying!" he shouted, even though he knew Diablo wasn't. That story made more sense than the one he had been told all of his life. He had spent his life serving, and trying to please, the man that had killed his father and brother.

"I couldn't make it up, Hawk. Oh, and you know the funny part? That Lieutenant on the *Enterprise*, the one that killed Bloodstone, said his name is James Wellington. He said Bloodstone killed his brother and father fourteen years ago. You have to love the sense of humor of the gods. Hawk, James is your brother. Apparently, Cord rescued him before the ship we took you from sank."

"No!" Hawk placed his head into his hands. He was overwhelmed by everything Diablo had just told him. It was too much. He almost looked forward to the musket ball that would end his life. He closed his eyes and waited.

Diablo laughed loudly. "Yes, it would have been even more humorous had you two faced each other and one killed the other, only to find out it was his own brother he had slain. Alas, that won't happen. But don't worry Hawk; James is my next victim. I want to be the one to finish killing your family." Diablo cocked the hammer on the musket and took aim at the easy target on the beach. He had another musket close by if somehow he missed.

Hawk didn't see the commotion behind Diablo. A man pushed his way out of the throng in the middle of the ship and charged him. Diablo turned just as two flintlocks fired. The man collapsed to his knees just behind him. Diablo laughed and turned back around. "Oh, Hawk, Wesley is dead."

Hawk opened his eyes. Diablo was aiming the musket again. He couldn't tell which two of Diablo's supporters had shot Wesley. Hawk hadn't even thought about Wesley, Bones, Jimmy, and Billy and all of the other pirates loyal to him. He guessed many would die that day, or already had in the initial struggle. A tear ran down his cheek. He prayed the bullet would end his life quickly, before more tears fell. The musket fired, flame and smoke issuing from the barrel, but the shot flew somewhere high overhead. Diablo suddenly straightened up. His mouth opened, but no words came forth. He looked down at the dagger blade that had just appeared out of his bare chest. Blood trickled out of both sides of his mouth, and his eyes were wide with shock and rage. The dagger disappeared and he collapsed, vanishing behind the rail.

Another man stood behind where Diablo had just been standing. It was Wesley, holding a bloody dagger in his blood-covered hand. There was blood soaking his white shirt on his left side and right side of his chest. He pointed the dagger toward Hawk, smiled weakly, and fell down behind the rail.

Another commotion ensued on the deck. Diablo's conspirators stood in shock, having watched their leader die before them. They offered little resistance as the pirate crew charged and subdued them. Very soon, the mutiny was over. Billy came over to the rail and shouted, "Hawk." The chant was quickly echoed by the pirates behind him and then spread to Kragg's crew on the beach. Hawk stayed on his knees, staring numbly at the sand in front of him.

CHAPTER XVI

EXIT PLAN

ॐ

"Good morning, handsome," a sweet voice whispered in Hawk's ear.

He opened his eyes and slowly turned his head toward the source. Anna lay beside him, raised up on her elbow. They were lying in a bed in a room he didn't recognize. She was as beautiful as he had ever seen her. A ray of sun danced on her face and hair through an open window, making her glow.

"Where am I?"

"You're in bed with me, silly." She laughed her sweet laugh.

"I can't remember how I got here. The last thing I remember is being on Devil's Island. How did I get here? What has happened to my crew?" Hawk looked around the room and searched his memory for some clue as to how he got there.

"They are close. Much closer than you realize."

Suddenly, Anna's right arm swung into view. Hawk saw the flash of silver but was too slow to stop it from descending and plunging into him. He looked down in horror at the dagger hilt protruding from his chest, Anna's small hand still holding it. He looked back up at her. "Why?" he managed to whisper.

"I want you to join me in hell!" Suddenly Anna's face began to transform. It was now Diablo lying beside him, his cruel smile present again.

Hawk awoke screaming and sat straight up in bed. The door of the hut swung open, and a man he didn't recognize rushed in.

"Are you OK, Mr. Hawk?"

Hawk blinked several times and then looked down at his chest. There was no blade. He breathed deeply a few times as his racing heart began to slow. He realized his head was pounding with a headache, and he felt a little dizzy. He recognized that feeling. He surveyed the large thatched hut he was in. There was a table surrounded by chairs to his right and two huge chests on the floor to his left. The sun was shining behind the pirate greeting him, outlining his body in gold. The pirate had a rough, weathered, but friendly face. He had a short-cropped white beard, and white hair poked out from beneath the black scarf on his head. He was barefoot and wore baggy blue breeches, a white sash for a belt, a white shirt, and a faded blue waistcoat. He wasn't a large man, but Hawk had no doubt he had been in a scrap or two. "Who are you?"

"Beggin' your pardon, sir. I'm Jack—Jack Roberts. I was Mr. Kragg's quartermaster. Don't guess ye 'member too much 'bout last night?"

Hawk searched his memory, just as he had in his dream. He only remembered being helped to his feet by a mob of pirates. Barrels of rum quickly made their way to the beach, and he drank and drank as his crew joined Kragg's and the celebration began. He vaguely remembered staggering to Kragg's old hut, and there the memories ended.

"Not much," Hawk croaked. His mouth and throat were dry. "What officers are left from my crew?"

"Let's see. There's Billy, a right quick lad, Bones, not a bad man for a Brit. I believe that be all. Oh, and I believe a Jimmy."

"Wesley? Hobbs?"

"I'm afraid Wesley just had enough strength left to kill that Diablo. Fittin' name if there ever be one. Was Hobbs your navigator? If so, he was killed in the mutiny. Luckily, Bones was below deck and survived."

Hawk's stomach turned. He had hoped more of his memories had been nightmares. Wesley had saved his life and probably the lives of most of the other pirates. Poor Hobbs—hadn't fought a day in his life and was killed. Jimmy and Billy were young and still inexperienced as officers. That just left Bones as the only real tie to his past. Then he remembered Diablo's words about Bloodstone slaying his father and his brother, James, being alive still. He recalled seeing James on the deck of the *Enterprise* as they sailed away. Did James know he was his brother?

"How about the mutineers?"

"They joined Diablo, Bloodstone, and Kragg. Your crew didn't exactly follow their articles, but I'd say it was a just enough endin'," Jack said, and he added a wink.

"How many men do you have? And supplies, treasure, and all of that?"

"Round one hundred and fifty, give er take a few. The navy's been hittin' us hard, even before the last battle. Now treasure be another story. Kragg had it in his articles that a quarter of each haul was kept out; the rest was divided among the men. He said that would give us somethin' to tide us over should we need to lay low for a while. Personally, I think the ol' dog was gonna steal it for himself someday and disappear. Would you like to see?"

"Sure. I need to clear my head anyway."

"Oh, here, take this first." Jack handed Hawk his baldric.

Hawk instantly noticed a new pistol hanging from it. It was a golden, double-barreled flintlock. A double-barreled flintlock was rare, and a golden one legendary. He drew the weapon out and studied it in awe.

"Kragg took it from a rich cap'n aboard an East India Company ship off the coast of Africa. Richest haul we ever had, I'd wager. It was Kragg's prized possession. And now it's yours."

Hawk finally sheathed it and slung the baldric over his shoulder. His prized dagger was still sheathed in it too. He followed Jack out of the hut and onto the beach. It looked like the two crews were working together fairly well. The *Bloody Seas* had been pulled over to the other side of the beach and was laid over for careening and further repair. *Hell's Fury* was still being worked on, but looked close to seaworthy. The pirates they passed grinned and offered some kind of acknowledgement. There was an excitement in both crews that had been absent for some time. By now, Bloodstone's old crew had shared the tales of Hawk's deeds. Of course, they were embellished a little over the actual stories. Hawk was a living legend for them and offered hope. Somehow, someway, Hawk would have a plan.

Jack led them up the beach and onto a small trail that wound through the dense vegetation. Soon they came to the base of a small, rocky mountain. It was reminiscent of the Rock. There was a small round cave entrance that led back into the mountain. Jack grabbed an oil lantern from just inside the entrance, pulled some flint out of a pocket, and struck it against his dagger until he had the lantern lit.

"This was a volcano at one time. There's caves all through it," Jack reported, and he led him back into the smooth tunnel. After a short distance, the tunnel took a hard right turn and ended at a wooden door. There was lock in the door itself and another lock joining two pieces of chain together over the front. Jack pulled two keys out of his shirt. They were attached to a chain around his neck. "Took 'em from Kragg last night," he grinned.

After a moment, he pulled the heavy door open. He handed Hawk the lantern and nodded for him to enter. Hawk walked into the small round room and nearly gasped. There were stacks of gold and silver bars along the back wall. Several large chests sat in the floor, some with the lids open. They were filled with doubloons, pieces of eight, jewelry, and gems. This was probably more treasure than Bloodstone had taken in his entire career, successful though it had been by most standards. There were other crates and barrels stacked around the sides. Hawk figured they were also full of expensive goods.

"The ol' dog had a good run," Jack chuckled.

Hawk realized there was more than enough treasure for him and Anna to live out the rest of their lives comfortably. He could just take his share and disappear, leaving all the pirates, and the pirate life, far behind him. While that idea was perfect for him, what would the nearly two hundred men looking for him to lead them do? There was no one else that he knew of that could lead them, other than to their deaths. Even though he didn't know Kragg's crew, he still felt an obligation. He didn't want to see both crews hanged.

"Jack, can I trust you?"

"Yes, sir, that ye can."

"Of course if I couldn't, I don't suppose you'd tell me?"

"It'd be a dangerous game askin' a lyin' backstabber if he lies or backstabs, Cap'n," Jack replied with a wink.

Hawk had just met this Jack, but he liked him. He would have to rely on his ability to judge people. There was no time to do otherwise. "I need a quartermaster. Billy's a good man and shows a lot of promise, but this isn't the time for training. I need someone who's done it all. Plus, I need the loyalty of both crews. Would you be interested? And I assume you are well liked by your crew?"

"I was hopin' you'd ask. At your service, Cap'n," Jack said with a mock salute. "And of course they love me. How could they not? Now, do we have a plan yet?"

"Not yet. Walk with me to the top of one of the peaks at the corner of the harbor." Jack locked the treasure room door and led Hawk out of the cave.

There was a trail close to the beach that led through the vegetation around the harbor. It gradually climbed the ridge of a rocky hill to the right and ended at a flat rocky outcropping overlooking the harbor, beach, and ocean. Three pirates quickly stood when they saw the two. They had polished horns hanging around their necks.

"Good morning, men," Hawk said. "Would you mind taking a walk for an hour or so? Me and Jack will keep lookout for you."

The men smiled, nodded, and disappeared down the trail. The watch had changed early that morning, so they had been on the beach when Hawk had slain Kragg the day before.

Hawk sat down on the edge of the cliff and let his legs dangle over the side. He stared out onto the calm, shimmering, sapphire water. The sun was up but still low in the sky, its orange rays reflecting off of the water. The air was still cool, but a warm breeze hinted that it would soon be hot. The sky was a deep blue, with only a few white clouds hanging low on the horizon.

"What be on your mind, Hawk," Jack asked, sitting beside him.

Hawk looked at Jack for a moment and then back to the sea. From here he could see all the small rocky islands and the many shallow patches on the approach. It was indeed a tricky harbor to reach. "What I tell you stays with us, or I'll make Kragg seem like a priest."

Jack was a little surprised at Hawk's bluntness but didn't doubt for a moment that he was a man of his word. "It'll die with me, Cap'n."

"Jack, I've been trying to find a way out for several years now."

"A way out?" Jack asked.

"This is all I've done since I was kidnapped by Bloodstone at just six years of age. I never knew there was any other life until I went to New Orleans for the first time. I didn't see much, but enough to know that there's a lot of world out there on the land. And I met a girl."

"Ah, a beautiful young lass," Jack said. "They'll definitely change your way of thinkin', to be sure."

"I promised her once I had made enough money, I would leave this life and take her away somewhere far from the ocean. We would buy a nice plot of land, build a house, make a small farm, start a family, and live happily ever after." Hawk looked up at Jack. The man reminded him a little of Wesley.

"A good dream it is," said Jack.

"But it doesn't have to just be a dream! I could take my share of the treasure, give the rest to you and your men, and make it happen."

"You could, indeed. But, Hawk, you have to realize that ye might be the greatest pirate Cap'n ever. I've sailed ten years with Kragg. I know of all of Bloodstone's deeds. I've even sailed with Lafitte. All of 'em right fine pirates. But, Hawk, you're special. I've heard of all your feats, and you're only twenty years old. You're smarter than the rest—and more cunning. And, apparently, you just won't die." Jack chuckled.

"Bloody lucky, more like it. But it's like Bloodstone said. I'd have been good a hundred years ago. The time of pirates is over. You know it. We might have sunk the *Enterprise*, but there are four more out there just like it. And there'll be more. There are no ports friendly to pirates anymore and no nations are hiring privateers. We can't go back, Jack. The US isn't going back. We're a hundred and eighty against a nation. Sure, we could buy some time, but how long until we're shot or hanged?"

Jack was silent. He grabbed a piece of long grass and chewed absently on the end. "I don't know, Hawk. I guess the times are changin'."

"Have you ever thought about doing anything else?"

Jack nodded. "Actually did. I started off workin' on a merchantman. I was young and wide-eyed and thought the sea was full of adventure. I slaved on a merchantman for nigh ten years, I reckon. I guess there was some adventure, but it was a hard life. If you think a pirate ship is tough, try a merchantman. One voyage, Lafitte attacked us off the coast of New Spain. He was a fair pirate and gave us crewmen a choice of joining him or going free. I thought I'd had my fill of the sea, so I turned down Lafitte, and he let me go in Galveston.

"I got a job as a carpenter, since I had so much experience on the ship. Met a sweet, pretty young lass in town. We bought a little piece of land, and I built our house. I had everything I wanted."

Hawk thought instantly of Wesley and his story of his young bride. "But apparently it didn't work out."

"Turns out it wasn't what I really wanted. As hard as life on a ship was, I missed the freedom, the open sea, drinkin', gamblin', and swappin' stories with my mates. I missed it all. I hooked up with one of Lafitte's ships and went on account. There I found my true freedom and adventure. A couple of years later, I heard of Kragg and joined his crew in New Orleans. I didn't like being tied to the land as much as Lafitte was in Baratavia." Jack had a slight smile as he reminisced his past.

"And the girl?" Hawk asked.

"Oh, she was glad to see me go. No woman wants a man that has his mind somewhere else. You see, Hawk, the key is to figure out what your heart really wants. If you're stuck on the sea, the land sounds good. If you're stuck on land, the sea sounds good. But once you find your place, you'll know it. Mine is piratin'."

Now Jack really reminded him of Wesley. He was a wise old pirate. "And how will I know where my heart wants to be?"

"Oh, you'll probably have to run off with your lass and give the landlubber dream a go. If not, you'll be miserable on the sea and only half a man. Just don't be surprised if one day you hear the sea callin' your name—she's a powerful mistress and never truly releases you. You'll know where your heart lies if one day you grow so tired of your boring, perfect life, that it makes your belly turn, if adventure and glory beckon to you and you can't sleep at night for relivin' your past, or if you do sleep, then the dreams come. And then you'll find yourself resentin' that sweet, pretty, lass for takin' you away from the life you really wanted."

Both men were silent for some time. Hawk looked over his shoulder to watch his crew work on the ships and move about the beach. They reminded him of ants from this distance. Gulls and osprey dove into the surf below, catching their breakfast. The air was warmer now, but it was still a pleasant day.

"So you're saying I should go?" Hawk finally asked.

"No...least not now. Hawk, I know ye don't owe any of us pirates anything. But you've given these men hope for the first time in a long time. They want to follow a legend for a while. They want one last go at it before their time is up. And you've just been a cap'n for a week now. I know you're bound to have dreamed about bein' a cap'n one day. It's all yours now. You're more powerful than Bloodstone or Kragg. If you walk away now, that would just lead even more to you missin' the sea and wonderin' what might have been. Regret is even worse than longin'. I say ye stay with us for a year. Let's go raise some cane, make some noise, and finish writin' the legend of Hawk. At the end of a year, if you're still set on seeing your girl, then you leave us and go off to do as you want."

Hawk mulled over Jack's words. Like Wesley, he made a lot of sense. He had worked his entire life to reach this moment. He was a pirate captain and probably the last great one. If he left now, he knew he would always wonder what it would have been like, what he missed. His captaincy thus far consisted of one short voyage and one duel. With Bloodstone, Kragg, and Diablo gone, it was truly his crew now. He did hate to postpone his dream with Anna, but one more year would pass quickly. They had the rest of their lives to spend together.

Also, if he left now, what would happen to all his men? Most would continue piracy but without a strong leader. They would be easy prey for Cord and James and the rest of the fleet. If he told them ahead of time that he was leaving, they could plan their futures. They could save money if they needed to. And he could split up the treasure from the cave, so all could at least have a fresh start if they wanted it. Maybe he could even work out getting them pardons before he left.

His mind also turned to James. All his life, Bloodstone and the pirates had been his family. Now he knew that it was Bloodstone who had destroyed his family. He had a real family now—a brother he could barely remember—if James had somehow survived, that is. Somehow, he had to get to James. But getting to a lieutenant on a US Navy ship, bent on eradicating pirates, would not be easy. Not without the visit ending at the end of a noose, anyway. He had to figure out how to talk to James before he ran away with Anna. *Why is life so complicated?*

"What do you think the point of all of this is?" said Hawk.

"Point of what, Cap'n?"

"I don't know—life?"

Jack scratched at his beard and thought deeply. "Don't know that I've ever given much thought to it, Cap'n." He stared out over the glimmering sea for a couple of minutes. "I guess if I had to say, it'd be makin' a name for yourself and leavin' your mark on the world—to have people speak your name long after your body's at the bottom of the sea."

Hawk mulled over his words for a few moments but chose not to discuss it further. "Do we have enough men to sail both ships? I'll need you to captain *Hell's Fury*. I can make Billy my temporary quartermaster. I've got Jimmy as gunner and Bones as carpenter and surgeon. I need a navigator and cook, and it wouldn't hurt to have another surgeon. You'll need a full crew."

Jack smiled. "Edward Hill is as fine of a navigator as you've ever met. Charles Miller could stitch up a fly. Ol' Smokey can stir up a pot of lobscouse as good as any, I reckon. I can put me a crew together. We can fully man both. It wouldn't hurt to pick up a few more hands along the way though."

Hawk nodded and stood. He turned to look down upon the beach and ships. "Oh, we need new ship names too. Those names died with their captains."

Jack stood too. He was excited to have Hawk embracing the role of captain. "Any ideas, sir?"

"The *Bloody Seas* will now be the *Seahawk*. You can name the other."

Jack picked at his beard thoughtfully. "How 'bout the *Phoenix*, Cap'n? Us pirates have been reborn and are risin' from the ashes."

Hawk smiled. Apparently Jack also liked to read. "Excellent. Now, no word to the crew of our one-year deal yet. I don't want it to leak out to the navy that they only have to deal with me for a year. When the time comes, I'll tell everyone, and we'll divide up the treasure.

"We need to make some major changes to these ships. Let's go talk to Bones and your carpenter. We'll also need to find some more cannons. Then we need to pack everything up. We won't be coming back here."

"Yes, sir!" Jack said enthusiastically, giving a salute. "Where are we headin', Cap'n?"

"We need to go to the Rock and clear that out too. It's too dangerous now to have permanent bases. While we're doing that, I need to make a quick stop at New Orleans. After, I'm not sure. But I do know this: the men better be ready. It'll be a year like no other."

At sunrise a week later, the *Seahawk*—with the black paint removed— and the *Phoenix* made their way out of the Devil's Island harbor. The upper decks—quarter and forecastle—were removed. The main deck was now flat like on a navy frigate—only the pirate ship's main deck and gun deck were lined cannons. Each ship carried fifty cannons now on those two decks. They didn't have enough men on either ship to man all the cannons, but just the sight of them would strike fear into most. The ships would be much faster, now that the extra weight was removed. They were fully repaired, armed, and stocked with food. Both their crews went about their chores with excitement. Their wounds were mostly healed, and they had eaten and drank their fill for days. They were ready to get back to pirating.

Hawk had moved his cabin to the gun deck. He and Jack had transferred the treasure from the cave into inconspicuous crates and barrels and had it carried to Hawk's cabin. The other officers' cabins were on the orlop deck below. The *Phoenix* was set up in similar fashion, with Jack having a cabin on the gun deck also. Although he was the acting captain on the *Phoenix*, he and both crew's knew Hawk was the leader.

As Hawk stood on the bow, hands on his hips, he couldn't help but feel a little excitement. First, he was going to get to see Anna again. Second, he was a pirate captain. Although he had liked and respected Captain Bloodstone, at least until Diablo's confession, he disagreed with his brutality and some of his tactics. Not having Diablo's aggressive, confrontational, and negative presence also lifted the mood of all. At least at the moment, and before any battles had begun, Hawk was beloved by his pirate crew. The time of pirates might almost be over, and his reign as captain would be short, but for today, and the coming year, it was going to be a new golden age.

CHAPTER XVII

ONE YEAR

❧

"*I*'ve missed you so much!" Anna exclaimed once the door was shut. She reached her hands around Hawk's head and pulled him down until she could kiss him.

Hawk wrapped his arms around her waist and pulled her close. He loved the feeling of her body pressed against his, warm even through their clothing. He also remembered just how much he enjoyed her kisses. It was amazing how they instantly had such a powerful effect on him. Chills crawled up his spine as his heart raced again. "Hmmm. And I missed you too!"

"Are you here to take me away?" she asked once they finally broke the kiss off to breathe.

"Anna, let's sit on the bed."

Anna frowned but followed him to the bed and sat beside him, as he had done the first time they were together. She went from exuberance to fighting back tears. Hawk proceeded to tell her of what had happened since their day on the island, mostly of the events of the past few weeks. He held her hand and looked into her eyes as he spoke.

"So, you should be free now for us to start our new life?" Anna asked, a glimmer of hope returning.

Hawk told her the remainder of his story and his plan. Now she could no longer hold back the tears. "Anna, I swear, one more year, and I'm done!"

"It is always one more year or two more years! You have all the money we need now. You owe those cutthroat savages nothing!" Anna pulled away and put her head in her hands. Her temper was something Hawk did not enjoy seeing.

"I owe it to them and to me. I don't want to be like Jack. If I leave the sea behind, I want it to be forever. I don't want us to end up being torn apart because I'm wondering too hard about what might have been. Yes, we could run away together—tonight, for that matter. But that wouldn't be fair to either of us. I have to leave the right way, with no what-ifs. Does that make any sense?"

Anna wiped her eyes on the top of her red dress. "I don't know, Hawk. Part of me understands. But part of me doesn't know if I can take another year. You've no idea how bad I hate my life now. The hope you give me lasts awhile, but then I have to wonder if you're still alive or are not coming back. It is so hard to get out of bed each morning and face this life of misery. There is never a good day in this job—never anything to look forward to. Most women in this business don't do it all of their lives. They get married or find some way out. You're my way out, Hawk. Or so I hope. But if you're not my way out, then I have to try to find another."

"Well, I don't want you lying with another man until I return," Hawk replied, feeling sick to his stomach watching Anna's pain.

"Then what would you have me do? Beg for crumbs on the street?" Anna looked at him again with her eyes red and glassy.

Hawk reached inside his shirt and pulled out a large leather pouch attached to a leather cord around his neck. He lifted the cord off of his neck and handed the heavy pouch to Anna. "Tonight is your last night working here."

Anna's mouth dropped open as she held the pouch. Her hands shook as she opened it and stretched it wide. It was stuffed full of gold doubloons and pieces of eight—more money than most people would earn in their entire lives. She closed it back and looked at Hawk, unable to speak.

"After I leave in the morning, take this money and find a place to live around here. You can get another job or even start your own business. This will be enough to last you for many years. If I am not back by this time next year, then something has happened to me, and I won't be coming back. Then you are free to do whatever you want with the money and your life. Can you do that for me, Anna? I haven't let you down so far."

Anna leaned over and hugged him tightly. After a moment, Hawk gently pushed her head back with his hand so he could kiss her. They kissed for several minutes. "While I would take you over the money, you've no idea how happy you've made me! I'll wait a year for you Hawk, and longer if you ask. But please, please just try to make it back to me."

"Well, you know the legend of the Hawk wouldn't be complete if I died now, would it? I'll come back for you, Anna. And it will all have been worth it. Just leave word with Madame Cynthia once you get settled so I know where to find you. And please be careful not to let people know about the money. I don't want something to happen to you."

Hawk spent the night with Anna. They made love and held each other most of the night, only drifting off to sleep in the early hours of the next day. After Hawk left, Anna went to pack and to tell Madame Cynthia she was leaving. She could wait one more year now.

It didn't take long for Hawk to make his name as a pirate captain. His two ships became the terror of the Caribbean. Although once word spread that quarter would be given to any that didn't resist, most ships surrendered at first sight of the pirate ships. They allowed the fittest men, or the most skilled, to join the crews. After a few months, both ships had crews of nearly two hundred. The few ships that did resist quickly paid the price. The Hawk was soon known from Boston to New Spain. Stories from survivors of his attacks were printed in the newspapers of every city.

Although Hawk and his crew were thriving, piracy was still declining. A major blow to pirates came early that year. Spanish privateers near Honduras attacked Jean Lafitte. Although it was never confirmed and his body never found, it was rumored that Lafitte was killed in the battle. Others said he escaped and just disappeared. But either way, another one of the greatest pirates of the day was gone.

Hawk spotted US Navy ships more and more frequently, and more ships were steadily added to the West Indies Squadron. But his ships were as fast as or faster than the frigates and larger schooners. The corvettes, sloops, and gunboats wouldn't challenge them, at least not alone. Since they didn't have a regular hideout and usually just anchored somewhere long enough to careen, restock supplies, and sell merchandise, they were hard for the navy to track down. Hawk also expanded their range from North Carolina to Brazil. They took ships of the United States, England, Spain, France, and Portugal.

Hawk always made sure to take the flags from all of his prizes. A favorite tactic, if they spied smaller and faster ships, was to fly flags of whichever country the prey were from. Then they could easily sail up broadside to parley. Once they identified themselves as pirates and made known their intentions, the smaller ships couldn't escape and were too lightly armed to think about resisting.

Six months after the death of Bloodstone, Hawk learned from a group of US sailors that had recently joined his crew that Captain Cord had been promoted to Commodore of the West Indies Squadron, and James was promoted to captain of his own ship, the USS *Avenger*. The *Enterprise* had sunk after her magazine exploded. James, Cord, and a handful of sailors had escaped in a longboat. Hawk began thinking of some way he could contact James without getting himself or his crew hanged.

He quickly amassed a fortune in gold and silver. His men could all have been rich, but as with most pirates, the more they made, the more they spent on women, gambling, and drink. Hawk thought more and more of a way to leave the pirate life and join Anna. He wondered often what she was doing now that she had her freedom. Hopefully she was running her own tavern. At least she no longer had to lie with men for her money. Even if he died before ever seeing her again, he had saved her life.

Early the next year, most of the West Indies Squadron withdrew to the mainland of the United States. They normally were based out of St. Thomas. Disease had run rampant on their ships, and they were forced to return to the mainland. Although disease was always a concern on ships, good fresh food and water helped Hawk's crew avoid it. With the fleet gone, there was very little to slow down Hawk and his crew. Even the Spanish man-o'-wars that escorted some of the treasure ships were no match for Hawk's two ships.

In less than a year's time, Hawk and his crew had captured over a hundred ships. It was hard to imagine growing bored with one of the greatest pirate campaigns of all time, but Hawk was. There was even some grumbling from the crew about the lack of fighting. The treasure was great, and the lifestyle, but so many ships surrendered, and the ones that didn't were subdued so quickly, that there was very little fighting and killing. Hawk refused to be the bloodthirsty killer that Bloodstone and Kragg had been. Once he learned that it was Bloodstone, and not the Spanish, who had killed his father, he no longer hated the Spanish, or any other country. He merely wanted what they carried in their holds. It was never personal.

It was hard for Hawk not to be overconfident. All he heard from his men, those of the ships he captured, and from the cities and ports they visited, was how great the Hawk was. He had never been defeated in a fight or battle. Even in the fight with the *Enterprise*, he had saved the day. He had done things that no one had ever done, living or dead. His legend was already growing greater than the infamous pirates from the golden age—Blackbeard, Avery, Kidd, and Roberts. Only Lafitte's legend was possibly greater than his in the modern era. With Lafitte dead, Hawk was the only one still adding to his story.

One night after taking a big prize, Hawk addressed his crew. He had drunk a little more grog than usual and was feeling particularly good. "Hail to the greatest pirate crew in history!" He raised his tankard to the men around him. The men cheered and raised their goblets, mugs, and tankards. "The only thing that can stop us now is a mistake or God himself." The crew cheered again. "Hawk doesn't make mistakes, and I'm not sure even God wants to tangle with these two ships!"

A couple of months later, when it was closing in on a year since he left Anna, Mother Nature humbled Hawk and his crew. The *Seahawk* was careening on a small island near Devil's Island. They had found a deepwater, protected cove on the north side of the island. Jack sailed the *Phoenix* to Havana to sell some merchandise and buy supplies. They learned by flying a Spanish flag they could come and go in Cuba as they pleased. There were enough men of every nationality in the crew now that could lead the shore parties to whichever port they visited.

It was just before dark on the small island when the southern sky turned black. The clouds rolled and churned, and the wind kicked up through the palm trees behind the beach. It took Hawk only a moment to recognize the impending storm. Hurricanes were not an uncommon sight while sailing the Caribbean. But, as with most other things, Hawk had been lucky and managed to avoid or survive all of the ones he'd encountered in his life. This time, there was nowhere to run.

By the time Hawk found Billy, the rain was already pouring and the wind gusting. "Round up the crew and head into the trees!" said Hawk. "Make sure all are off of the *Seahawk*."

The *Seahawk* was leaned to one side and secured by the anchor and numerous ropes stretching from the railing to nearby trees. The beach was totally open and unprotected. The only hope was to head into the trees and try to find protection and shelter. Hawk waited on the beach, squinting into the sheets of rain, until all of his men had scattered into the trees. Streaks of lightning lit the skies and thunder boomed close by.

Hawk started to flee into the palms, but then thought about his ship. If the ropes broke or the trees they were tied to fell, the boat would probably be washed out to sea. If it didn't sink, it could be dashed on the rocks or lost for good. They only had one longboat on the shore and that wouldn't survive. Being marooned on this island along with half of his crew was not how he was going out.

Billy came rushing out of the trees to see what was keeping Hawk. "Come on, sir! You'll be blown out to sea. We've found some good dunes to hide behind that should provide shelter."

"I'm going onboard the ship," Hawk shouted above the gusting wind. "Those ropes will never hold, and I'm not losing her."

"You can't man that ship by yourself! And it will be a miracle if it's not dashed to pieces on the rocks," Billy screamed back.

"Won't be the first miracle! Go find shelter. I'll see you in the morning!" Hawk turned and sprinted toward the ship. The wind almost knocked him off of his feet a couple of times. It was too dark and raining too hard to tell if Billy had made it back to the trees. Hawk scrambled up a rope ladder that hung over the side. He was slammed into the hull once or twice, but finally made it onto the sloped deck.

The ship was already rocking in the surf and straining against the ropes that held it in place. Hawk realized the ship was too vulnerable laid on its side. The hull would likely be split open and the masts destroyed if it were washed up onto the beach. He also knew he couldn't turn the capstan by himself to get the anchor back in the ship. He grabbed an axe and quickly started chopping at the hawser line attached to the anchor. The wind battered against him, and the rain stung his face and hands. The frequent flashes of lightning provided enough light to see what he was doing.

He finally cut through the rope and the entire ship lurched. The angle of the deck flattened out some as the ship leaned more upright. He then rushed about the deck cutting the remainder of the ropes attached to the distant trees. He was startled to see movement at the side of the ship and then hear muffled voices. A bright flash of lightning showed Billy leading a small group of pirates over the rail.

"What are you doing?" Hawk shouted.

"Apparently sailing in a hurricane!" Billy shouted back.

Hawk saw Jimmy, Edward, Charles, Smokey, and three other pirates behind Billy.

"Bones said he'd be here to 'patch the heap up' when we return," said Billy.

Hawk shook his head and laughed. He was still upset, but he admired the loyalty of his crew. Most pirates were only out for themselves. His crew was more like a large family.

He pointed to three of the pirates. "You men finish cutting these ropes! Edward, man the helm. Sail her just out of the harbor and keep her turned directly leeward. Billy, raise just enough sail to escape the surf."

The pirates quickly set about their chores. The ship was soon upright again and being tossed roughly in the waves. Once the sails were at half-mast, the wind instantly filled them and began to push the ship out of the surf and toward open water. "Find a spot and tie yourself to a mast or rail!" Hawk shouted. Most used the loose pieces of rope still tied to the railing to secure themselves. They left enough slack to move around, but not enough that they could be washed overboard.

The ship felt small, being tossed about in the huge waves of the ocean. Waves crashed over the sides, battering the small men and threatening to break the ropes that bound them to the ship. Anything loose was swept into the sea. It took all of Edward's skill as a navigator to steer into the large waves and keep the ship from being turned broadside to the wind. That would have resulted in a quick death for them all. Hawk stood beside Edward, shouting out commands and helping him turn the wheel. His worst fear was the masts being snapped in half.

After what seemed like hours, the winds and rain suddenly stopped, as did the lightning. Thunder still rumbled around them, but the stillness of the air and sea was eerie.

"Eye of the storm!" Hawk shouted to the crew. "Check the sails and rigging. Then make sure you're secured and ready for the second half."

The calm didn't last long. The winds soon picked up again, and the rain and wind built back up in intensity. The hurricane raged most of the night, but somehow the ship, and the small crew, survived. By the time the sky began to lighten, the storm had passed.

The ship had taken a lot of damage to the rigging and sails, but the masts had held, and the hull was intact. Hawk knew the lower decks would be a disaster, but they and the ship had survived. The island was still in sight far astern, although they had sailed out much further than he thought. He had Edward swing the ship about and head back to the island. He hoped he would find most of his crew alive.

It took several hours to search the entire island. Many trees had fallen, and some were just gone, carried away by the sea. Nearly two-dozen pirates were dead or missing. Falling trees had crushed some. Some had been hit by flying limbs or other objects. Others had apparently been washed away by waves. They quickly buried their fallen comrades without much ceremony, made quick repairs to the sails and rigging, reattached the anchor, and loaded up the *Seahawk*. The lower decks could be repaired and straightened up during the voyage. Hawk was worried about Jack. He was supposed to have left Havana the night before and been back by noon. It was two hours past now, and they had seen no sign of him.

The sky was blue and the sun hot when the *Seahawk* departed from the island and sailed toward Havana. Both ships shared the same charts, so Hawk knew the route Jack would have taken. Once on the open water, there was little evidence that such a massive storm had passed through just twelve hours earlier.

Halfway there, Hawk began seeing debris in the water—here a barrel, there a crate. His heart sank. The debris field left the charted course and headed north, likely the ship was carried that way by the storm. Edward turned the ship to the north, and they followed the trail. More wooden objects floated in the water on both sides, along with some pieces of sails. Then they saw the bodies. They floated face down in the water, rising and falling with the gentle swells. Hawk was stunned as he stood at the base of bowsprit, desperately hoping against fading hope that somehow his ship, and most of his crew, survived.

"Longboat ho, two points starboard," Billy called down from the crow's nest.

Edward steered the boat slightly starboard then straightened it out. Soon, Hawk saw the longboat ahead. It looked like several people were onboard. There were also large pieces of debris floating close to it. Other objects, hopefully live pirates, appeared to cling to them.

The *Seahawk* reached the small boat a half hour later. It slowed and came along side. Hawk was relieved to see Jack with ten other pirates. There were, indeed, other pirates sitting on, and clinging to, pieces of the ship—barrels, crates, and even a long piece of one of the masts. Three dozen pirates total were pulled from the sea onto the safety of the *Seahawk*.

Jack and his quartermaster, Samuel Mortensen—Mort as he was called—were the only officers to have survived. Once he was sure all of his remaining crew were onboard, Jack rushed over to Hawk. "You're a sight for sore eyes, Cap'n. Never seen anything move so fast. We tried to turn this way and that, but couldn't escape it. Once our mainmast broke in two, we were doomed. The rudder snapped next, then we drifted broadside to it. Wasn't long until we were upside down and sinking fast. Those of us who could swim, or float long enough, ended up together in the debris. The longboat somehow broke free during the sinking, and Mort and I climbed aboard, along with everyone else who could fit." Jack was shaking from cold and clearly rattled from the ordeal. He was also nervous about disappointing his new captain.

Hawk looked at Jack. He had never thought he would see his first mate shaken, scared, and nervous. He looked at Mort, who stood behind Jack and had nodded during the tale. Mort was a large and even-tempered pirate. He was one of few words, but solid, steady, and dependable. "Nothing you could have done different?"

Jack looked down and shook his head. "Not this time, Cap'n. Ol' Matthew went down with the ship, still trying to steer that broken rudder. Blasted shame to lose that ship and all of those men. What about you? How'd you escape it?" Jack surveyed the *Seahawk*.

Hawk told the story of the past night and morning. "Yesterday, we had two ships and almost four hundred men. Today, we have one ship and barely over two hundred."

"We'll get it all back, sir. The squadron is still mostly back in the States. We can take another frigate or nice schooner or two. And men are lining up to join the great Hawk. Like you said, not even God can stop the Hawk."

Mort nodded behind him.

"I think God has spoken loud and clear. Let's get what supplies we can out of the water. Get your men fed and into some dry clothes. Then meet me in my cabin. Bring Billy and Mort." Hawk turned and walked toward the helm. Jack shook his head and went to work getting men organized to fish the crates and barrels from the water.

Billy, Jack, and Mort knocked on Hawk's cabin door a few hours later. Hawk invited them in and sat at the far end of the large polished oak table. Oil lamps hung over the table and around the walls making the cabin bright despite it being dusk outside. Hawk looked up from a chart he had been studying and nodded for the three to sit.

"Billy and Mort," Hawk said. "Jack and I had a conversation a year ago, back when I defeated Kragg."

"Hawk! Shouldn't we talk first?" said Jack.

Hawk glared at Jack and then turned back to the quartermasters. "I wanted to leave the trade then. I wanted to run away from the sea and live on the land with my sweet Anna. Jack persuaded me to stay and give my captaincy a good shot. We decided I owed it to both crews. I agreed I'd give it a year. After a year's time, if I still wanted to leave, I would divide all of the loot, and we could all head our separate ways."

Billy and Mort exchanged a glance. Then they both looked at Jack, who was staring down at his hands fidgeting in front of him on the table. "What are you saying, Cap'n?" Billy asked.

"It's time to get out with our lives and health. The West Indies Squadron is starting to return, and they will have more ships and men this time. Bloodstone, Kragg, and now Lafitte are all dead. Captain Cofresi and I are the only other captains of mention. We're being hunted like never before." Hawk leaned back in his chair, placed his hands behind his neck, and stared at the oil lamp overhead.

"But they're still no match for us!" said Jack. "We just need to replace the *Phoenix* and find a crew for it."

"We gave it a good run, boys. We've taken a hundred ships in the past year. We've never been defeated in a battle. But now, even God is telling us it's time to quit. We could take another ship. And we could find some men to sail it. But for what? Six more months? A year? The sea's getting smaller by the day. Sooner or later they'd catch us, and probably sooner. I can't do that to any of you. We need to get out while we can. There's enough treasure to make every one of us wealthy." Hawk closed his eyes and for a moment saw Anna's smile and heard her sweet laugh.

"Even if that be so, how do you s'ppose we just all go free?" Jack asked. "They won't just let the famous Hawk and his crew walk away and take on honest lives."

"You're right. But I will get pardons for all of you," Hawk opened his eyes and looked at Jack.

"And just why would the US be so kind?"

"I have something they want." Hawk grinned weakly.

"And what do you have that they'd let us all go free for?"

"Me."

CHAPTER XVIII

BROTHERS

❦

The *Seahawk* sailed into the harbor as soon as Hawk spotted the schooner. He had been tailing it, the USS *Beagle*, for several days, waiting for an opportunity to take it. The schooner was small and had a shallow draft, so it was perfect for sailing close to all of the small islands and searching for pirates.

Hawk had hoped to simply sail up and send over a boarding party while its' crew was still searching the island. Unfortunately, by the time they got within firing range, the men had returned and the longboat had just been pulled onboard. But it was no matter. The schooner only had thirty sailors or so and three guns. They would be foolish to resist.

The sailors on the schooner grabbed their weapons and waited on the much larger frigate to drift in beside them. A man stood in front of the crew dressed as a naval officer. He had no weapon in his hands, although he had two flintlocks and a cutlass in his belt.

The *Seahawk* lowered its sails and dropped anchor not even ten yards from the navy ship. Billy quickly hoisted Hawk's flag.

Hawk strode to the front of the throng of pirates and up to the railing. "Who is the captain of the *Beagle*?" he called out.

The well-dressed man on the other ship cleared his throat. "Lieutenant Platt. And you must be the famous Hawk."

"I am. I don't want to destroy your ship or kill any of your sailors."

"So then, you are willing to surrender without a fight?"

Hawk's crew erupted in laugher. Hawk turned to look at his crew briefly, smiled, and turned back to Lieutenant Platt. "I have twenty cannons loaded and prepared to fire into your ship. Forty men behind me have loaded blunderbusses aimed at your men. And they have granadoes and flintlocks close at hand. I don't think we will be surrendering."

Lieutenant Platt surveyed the large frigate. It was imposing. And he knew his men didn't have a chance against Hawk and his crew. But he only had to stall. "What is your offer then?"

"I want your ship. You can take what supplies you need, all of your crew, and stay on that island behind you. I'm sure another squadron ship will find you soon," Hawk said, growing a little impatient with the overconfident captain.

"I'm afraid I cannot accept that offer. Perhaps we can give you some food and water, if you need it, and maybe some powder, but not my ship."

Hawk felt the blood rush to his face. One broadside would reduce the *Beagle* to splinters. But he needed a United States ship for his plan. He really didn't want to slaughter the sailors either. They were just doing their jobs, and for now that meant following a foolish captain. "Would you and your crew rather be shot or sliced up? It makes no difference to me, but I will have your ship." The men behind Hawk took aim at the sailors on the schooner. They shared little of Hawk's compassion. They were ready for a fight.

Platt turned to look at the men behind him. Some words were exchanged and several nods. Finally he turned back to Hawk. "I think we'd rather kill your crew face-to-face, if you please."

"Grapple it!" Hawk roared. Within moments, ropes with hooks were tossed onto the Beagle and then pulled tight until the hooks bit into its rail. "If a sailor touches a rope, shoot him in the head!"

Hawk hoped once he sent a few dozen skilled pirates aboard, and killed the lieutenant if necessary, the rest of the crew would surrender. They had to know his reputation for being fair and honest. The pirates hauled hard on the lines until the schooner was pulled up against the taller frigate. Platt and his crew backed up to the middle of the deck and drew their cutlasses and sabers.

Without a word, Hawk ran and vaulted over the rail of the *Seahawk*, flew over the rail of the *Beagle*, and landed lightly on the schooner's deck, cutlass in hand. There was a loud roar behind him as his crew followed. Hawk slowed now, motioning for his men to hold back. He wanted to give Platt one last chance. "Do you wish to reconsider before I kill you?"

"I think you have a problem, Mr. Hawk," Platt said smugly.

"And just what is that?" Hawk asked with no patience remaining.

"You have a battle on two fronts."

"What?"

Suddenly, the roar of cannons erupted from behind the pirates. Hawk turned to see the *Seahawk* rock violently. On the other side was a large navy schooner, much larger than the *Beagle*. While all the pirates had been watching the unfolding confrontation, the other schooner had sailed silently into range and fired a broadside. Instinct caused Hawk to turn around just in time to knock aside a thrust from Platt's cutlass. He hoped that Jack, Jimmy, and Billy knew what to do, because he had to deal with the crew of the Beagle. Platt was a little stunned that Hawk had turned so quickly and blocked his thrust. He had expected his blade to run straight through Hawk's unprotected back. Hawk's vicious rain of blows quickly overcame the lieutenant. When his sword snapped Platt's smaller blade in two, a quick thrust into his chest ended the fight.

The pirates around Hawk charged the sailors with a berserker-type rage. The sailors held their own for a moment, but after seeing their leader slain, they quickly fell back. Half of them managed to leap off of the railing behind them and into the water below. The rest were quickly slain. Hawk instructed a half dozen pirates to stay on the Beagle and led the remainder back onto his ship, just as the *Seahawk's* cannons roared, firing into the other schooner.

By the time Hawk regained the deck of his ship, the pirates on-board were already firing blunderbusses into the sailors on the new frigate. They had only fired a handful of cannons, but they had done great damage to the schooner. Hawk couldn't tell the extent of the damage the *Seahawk* had taken, but it didn't seem to be taking on water. The schooner, the USS *Grampus*, was a thirty-gun ship.

The sailors returned fire, striking many of the pirates around Hawk. They had more men than the *Seahawk*, but they had been surprised by how fast the pirates had reacted, and they thought more were engaged with the *Beagle*. More cannons erupted from the *Seahawk* as the men below deck finished loading the portside cannons. They had placed all of their attention on the starboard cannons before the battle with the *Beagle* began. The shots ranged from the waterline to the railing of the *Grampus*. Splinters of wood flew into the men, scattering them about the deck.

Hawk led his men in throwing granadoes and stinkpots. The sailors took heavy casualties from the fire and debris, and the clouds of toxic smoke interrupted their reloading of the guns. Before Hawk and his crew could take advantage of the confusion on the *Grampus*, its cannons fired again. The *Seahawk* rocked violently. Hawk could tell from the sound below that the damage was great. He drew his flintlock and fired at the closest sailor. His men quickly followed suit. The pistols were much less accurate, but enough found their mark.

The *Grampus* began unfurling its sails and disengaged from the fight. The *Seahawk* managed a couple of more cannon shots into it, right at the waterline. The schooner limped away, clearly taking on water. A man, dressed as its captain, shouted from the railing just before it was out of hearing range, "The end is near, Hawk!"

Hawk realized the *Grampus* only wanted to cripple the *Seahawk*. The search would begin in earnest now for the Squadron. Hawk hurried below deck to inspect the damage. The ship was taking on water in the hold, but just right at the waterline. Bones was already on the repairs. The damage to the hull was extensive, but nothing that couldn't be fixed. A half-dozen pirate bodies were strewn about the gun deck. He made his way back to the main deck. A dozen more pirates had been killed and many more wounded. The wounded were helped to the infirmary for Charles to patch them up.

"Billy, set sail to Devil's Island, and make haste repairing the ship," said Hawk. "The navy has searched that island a time or two, but that's no guarantee they won't be back. We'll try to be back before you're ready to sail again. Jack, get us a small crew and meet me on the *Beagle*. We need to complete my plan. By the way, yet another sign."

The USS *Beagle* glided smoothly into the harbor of St. Thomas. There were a number of the West Indies Squadron vessels currently at the docks. The navy had recovered from the illness that had ravaged their fleet the prior year and were now returning to their pirate hunting missions.

Hawk, dressed in the clothing of Lieutenant Platt, spotted the ship he was looking for. The USS *Avenger* was at the dock. He had Jack sail the *Beagle* right beside the large frigate. The docks had minimal activity at the moment, with only a few sailors coming and going from the ships. The *Avenger* had more activity than most, and it looked like they were preparing to sail.

A couple of pirates, now dressed as sailors, jumped onto the dock and quickly moored the boat. They extended the gangplank so Hawk and Jack could disembark, and then they returned to the schooner. Jack and Hawk scurried from the docks to the busier street beyond. They wanted to disappear into the crowd before anyone realized they'd just come from the *Beagle*. They would mingle near the docks until they saw an opportunity to return unnoticed. A few minutes later, they spotted a large group of sailors walking onto the docks. Once it was determined that they were heading to the *Avenger*, Hawk and Jack fell in behind them.

They followed the sailors onboard the large ship, joining many more already performing their tasks about the ship. A ship as large as the *Avenger* typically carried three hundred sailors, and men came and went a lot on the navy vessels, so the crews were not as close as those on a pirate ship. It wasn't hard to blend in. Hawk looked important in Platt's clothing, and no one looked twice as he and Jack climbed down to the gun deck. The ship was laid out in a manner very similar to the *Seahawk*, so Hawk knew exactly where the captain's cabin was located.

Hawk opened the door and walked inside without knocking. Jack followed and shut the door behind him. The cabin was large, taking up most of the last quarter of the stern end of the deck. A lone man sat at the end of the large polished table in the middle of the room. He wore a white shirt that was open and a navy waistcoat with brass buttons. He looked up absently from the map, which he was marking with a feather quill and ink.

"Lieutenant Platt? Who are you?" The man demanded, quickly standing up from the table. He wore navy linen pants to match his vest.

"Are you James Wellington?" Hawk asked, approaching the near end of the table. Jack stayed back near the door.

"Yes. Now, who are you and what do you want?" James demanded, his hand resting on the handle of his flintlock.

"Hawk. Or Henry Wellington, if you'd rather." Hawk unbuttoned the top few buttons of his shirt and pulled it open to reveal the birthmark on the left side of his chest.

James stared in stunned silence. "My brother..." he said softly.

"I believe so. And we need to talk." Hawk pulled out a chair and calmly sat down.

"You are the most wanted pirate in the Caribbean. I'm a captain in the West Indies Squadron whose mission is to track down and kill or capture pirates. And you killed hundreds of navy sailors, tried to kill me, and destroyed the *Enterprise*. Tell me why I shouldn't kill you right now?"

"We're brothers. And you'd be dead before you cocked your flintlock. We have a lot to talk about, brother. After we talk, you can then decide what course of action to pursue."

James finally sat down in his chair. He was still shaken. He knew after the battle with Bloodstone that his brother was likely alive. But he never expected to be face-to-face with him. Hawk was his brother and only living relative, yet he was also the most infamous pirate of the era, and responsible for the deaths of countless men, the destruction of hundreds of ships, and the stealing of unimaginable loot. James's head swam with the conflicting emotions.

Hawk didn't wait for James to speak. "Tell me what you remember... before we were separated."

James's memory of that fateful day was still vivid. He could still remember every word and every act, despite only being twelve years old at the time. He told the story of the attack and of him, Henry, and their father hiding in the cabin. Then he told of Henry running out of the cabin before their father could catch him and trying to attack Bloodstone with his wooden sword. He recounted their father running after Henry, leaving James hiding in the cabin. Then he watched his brother be picked up and carried over to the *Bloody Seas*. He described Bloodstone shooting their father in the chest and even killing his own man on purpose in the process. Then the pirates spotted the USS *Enterprise* approaching. They set fire to the ship and sailed off before the *Enterprise* could attack. James had finally snapped out of his paralyzing fear and managed to run and dive out of one of the cabin windows before the ship was totally engulfed in flames. The *Enterprise*, and Captain Cord, found him floating near the burning wreckage of the merchant ship. He was the only survivor.

Hawk shook his head and looked down. It was a moment before he could reply. "I never knew that story until after I slew Kragg. That's when Diablo told it to me during his mutiny. And he didn't tell me the details. My first memories were of being on the pirate ship with the cook, Wesley. Everyone told me that a Spanish warship had attacked my family's ship and killed Father and you. Bloodstone and the pirates rescued me.

"Soon, being a pirate was the only way of life I knew. I've always lived on a ship. I learned to hate the Spanish, like Bloodstone and his crew did. Bloodstone told me the Spanish acquired all their gold and silver by stealing it from the natives of the countries they colonized. They worked the people to death in the mines so they could take the treasure back to Spain. They had also killed his father and forced him and his mother to work in the fields of Cuba. His mother was eventually slain, just as they'd killed my brother and father." Hawk fell silent as he relived his past in his mind.

James finally spoke. "I grew up with the hatred of Bloodstone and all pirates. Cord took me as his son, and I've been in the navy ever since.

We hunted pirates for a few years, until the war with England broke out. Then we had to defend the east coast against the Royal Navy and then fight them at New Orleans. After the Battle of New Orleans, we were commissioned to hunt pirates. I guess you know the rest. I was made captain of this ship shortly after the battle with Bloodstone."

"What a cruel irony," said Hawk. "Two brothers separated as children, growing up on opposite sides. The gods have a terrible sense of humor."

"You said you grew up hating the Spanish. But you and Bloodstone attacked and killed more than just the Spaniards."

"In the later years. But you can justify anything. Most of the merchant ships are hauling ill-gotten spoils too. Look at the United States. The English stole that land from the Indians by force. I didn't agree with everything Bloodstone did. But what was I to do? Mutiny? Leave the only life I knew? For what? I never knew what a town looked liked until I was sixteen and went to New Orleans. It was then I met Anna and decided I wanted to leave this life and run away inland with her." Hawk looked at this brother. His hair was brown, and he was six years older, but there was definitely a resemblance.

"Why didn't you leave then?" James asked, carefully evaluating everything his younger brother, the pirate captain, said.

"Money. I promised Anna I would come back for her when I had enough money for us to live comfortably the rest of our lives. I was close before our battle with you and the *Enterprise*. Then of course I had to avenge Bloodstone and confront Kragg. I then felt I had an obligation to lead the combined crew for a while—one last run."

"And now?"

"I'm done. I have enough money, and I've had my fill of being a pirate captain. I want out."

"And that's why you're here?"

"Aye. I want to make a deal."

"There's no way I can let you and your entire crew go, even though you are my brother. With your time serving with Bloodstone, and now on your own, you've taken more ships and killed more people than any pirate in recent history, maybe ever. Even the president mentions you by name. I would be court-martialed, if not hanged, if I were to let you go. Cord would see to it himself. Besides, even if I did, you and your crew would be hunted. You and Anna would never know peace and security."

"Oh, by the way, I took the *Beagle* too. Unfortunately Lieutenant Platt and his men didn't want to let me have the ship. We had to kill a few. The *Grampus* sailed up, though, and tore my ship up pretty good, if it makes you feel any better."

"What?" James roared, leaning forward.

"I had to have a way of coming to talk to you. I tried every way possible to ask nicely for it." Hawk turned to the older pirate. "Jack, do you mind going out and mingling with the nice sailors? I need to talk to my brother in private."

"But, Cap'n! He could shoot you dead as you sit," Jack said.

"As I should," James said.

Hawk laughed. "He's not that quick. It will be fine. I'll join you in a bit."

Jack shook his head but knew that Hawk had made up his mind. He turned and left the cabin, shutting the door hard behind him.

Hawk turned back to face his brother. "Would they take my life in exchange for my crew getting pardoned?"

"What? How can you offer up your life? What of your dream with Anna?"

"You yourself said I could never go free. But there is no one of any fame in my crew. I'm the only one the Unites States wants. And if I'm gone, my crew will walk away. There's no one left to lead them. Jack is a good man, and experienced, but too old to be a captain. My quartermaster, Billy, is still green. I've got enough loot to keep them all happy and out of trouble." Hawk leaned forward and folded his arms on the table.

"So, you'll just turn yourself in, right here, just like that, to be hanged?" James asked, shocked at Hawk's suggestion.

"Well, not right here. And maybe not just like that. I've got a plan… of course." Hawk spent a few minutes describing his plan to his brother.

James shook his head when Hawk had finished. "I don't know, brother. A lot could go wrong."

"Do you have another plan, other than killing me now?"

"No."

"James, you know you're no different than me. If our roles would have been reversed, we'd have ended up on opposite sides of this table. I played the hand I was dealt, as did you."

"I didn't kill innocent people," James said flatly.

"Really? I've heard stories of your time on the *Enterprise*. They say entire pirate crews were killed without so much as one man taken alive. So you knew without a doubt that none of those men had been forced to be aboard those ships? No innocent navigators, cooks, musicians, surgeons, or carpenters taken for their skills? What about the British soldiers you killed in the war? None of them were pressed into service?"

James was silent, staring at the table.

"And for the record," said Hawk. "Since I've been captain, I've offered to let any crew that didn't resist go free. I have never liked killing, James. Sure, I've done my share. And I'm right good at it. But I've never liked it, other than Kragg, that is. The truth is, both of our hands are stained with blood. And some of it was from innocent people. Killing is killing, brother. The difference is only in the justification."

James stood up abruptly. Hawk tensed for a moment, until James turned and walked back to a cabinet behind him. He brought out a large bottle of reddish-brown liquid and two silver goblets. He walked around the table to Hawk and set a goblet in front of him. He took the cork out of the bottle and filled the goblet. Then he returned to his seat and filled his. "I will mull your plan. For now, let's drink and be brothers. That's fine brandy, given to me by the governor of North Carolina. Smoothest you've ever tasted."

Hawk was surprised at the change in James, but pleasantly so. He swirled the liquid around in his cup, smelled it, and then took a sip. "The *only* brandy I've ever tasted. Don't you know we pirates are all about the rum? It is good though. How long do we have before you sail?"

"We sail when I say we sail. I am the captain, after all." James laughed. "You think Jack will be OK?"

"I'd worry more about your crew."

For two hours the two long lost brothers talked and laughed like brothers. They swapped stories about their lives and filled in the missing details. They mostly avoided the tales of their battles and instead talked about the men they knew, humorous stories, likes and dislikes, hopes and dreams. As the brandy flowed, they laughed more. Soon they sat side by side. There was even a rowdy song or two shared.

A knock on the door interrupted their revelry. "Come in," James called out with a slight slur.

A young officer opened the door and stepped in. He was dressed similar to James. His face was pale, and red hair showed from beneath his tricorne hat. "Is everything OK, Captain?"

"It's great, First Mate Smith," James said, eliciting a smile from Hawk. "Just sharing a little brandy with an old friend."

"When will you be ready to sail, sir? The ship is ready." Thomas Smith stared hard at Hawk as he spoke.

"Oh, no real hurry, Thomas. Give us an hour or two."

Thomas frowned and started to speak again. He had never seen his captain drinking like that on duty. He looked at Hawk once more and turned and left the cabin.

"A worrisome lad, huh?" Hawk asked, laughing and taking a large swig of brandy.

"You have no idea."

Despite having been apart for much longer than they had been to-gether, living opposite lives all along, they both felt the bond that only brothers can share. Their minds worked the same and thought the same. For a time, the real world was forgotten. They didn't even notice the red-faced Jack glaring through the window many times during those two hours.

CHAPTER XIX

SURRENDER

ackson Square buzzed with excitement. It was actually the most excitement since the British had been defeated in the Battle of New Orleans. The crowd started at the docks and spread all of the way to the center of the square. Armed soldiers and sailors lined a long clear lane and kept the crowd pushed back. In the middle of the square, in front of the St. Louis Cathedral, a large platform had been erected, similar to a gallows. Governor Hawthorne himself sat behind a table at the back of the platform. A magistrate sat beside him. Commodore Cord stood close behind with several of his captains. They were surrounded by some of the governor's personal attendants and two dozen soldiers and sailors.

The anxious crowd all stared toward the docks, where they could see at least some part of the *Seahawk*. James Wellington and a large contingent of sailors stood at the gangplank, waiting for the pirate crew to depart their ship for the last time.

Finally, the pirates walked single file off the ship. When a pirate reached the dock, he handed his weapons to two sailors flanking James. Another sailor searched him to make sure he had no daggers or small guns hidden on his body. Then the pirate walked down the lane through the excited crowd to the platform. He walked up the wooden steps on the near side and stood before the governor. He signed a piece of paper, affirming that he would never again engage in piracy. Then he received a signed pardon from the magistrate and exited the stage on the far side. The pirate could wait and watch his mates go through the same process or disappear into the city streets. Most chose the latter.

Two weeks prior, word had spread of a deal that the famous pirate captain Hawk had made with captain Wellington of the USS *Avenger*. Hawk would turn himself in for trial and sure hanging, and in exchange his crew would receive a full pardon. The *Seahawk* would become the possession of the navy to be sank or used as they saw fit. James had gone to the commodore, the commodore to the governor, and the governor to the president, and they had all approved the plan. They all knew that defeating Hawk and his crew, even with the events of the past month, would be no easy task, and they would lose many men and ships. There was also no one on Hawk's crew of particular note. Hawk was the last of the great pirate captains. Once he was gone, there would just be some mopping up of a few small, weak pirate crews in the Caribbean.

Hawk's trial wouldn't be today. After all of his men were pardoned, he would be charged with his crimes by the governor and magistrate. He would then be taken away in irons and jailed until a trial date was set. He would probably be tried and hanged within a week or two. That would be an even greater spectacle than today. But today, just seeing the famous Hawk was enough.

Most of the crowd and soldiers and sailors halfway expected the Hawk and his crew to have some kind of attack planned. All had heard of Hawk's daring rescue of Captain Bloodstone at Port Royal. But as the pirates continued to file past, the crowd's apprehension eased. There was really not much Hawk could do and little to be gained by attacking anyone in New Orleans. After an hour or so, all 180 pirates had received their pardons, including Hawk's first mate, Jack, and his quartermaster, Billy. The crowd now breathlessly waited for Captain Hawk to make his walk down the gangplank and turn in his weapons.

After an agonizing several minutes, Hawk finally appeared on the deck of the *Seahawk*. He wore one of his more common outfits—tight black leather pants, knee-high boots, red sash belt, and white silk shirt unbuttoned halfway. His head was bare, his blond hair glowing gold in the sunlight. The baldric across his chest held two pistols and a dagger. A cutlass was at his side.

He walked over to the rail and surveyed the huge crowd stretched from the dock to the square. The crowd suddenly fell silent as they waited for the famous captain to make a move. Some still thought he could somehow fight and defeat all of the soldiers and sailors there. But after a moment, he gracefully strode across the deck to the gangway. He stopped and looked at James and the sailors surrounding him. They all stared up at him, impatiently waiting for the show to be over. His gaze then went past them to the ships on the other side of the dock. Finally, he walked down the gangplank, moving with the grace and ease of a lion.

He reached the bottom of the ramp, where the two sailors extended their hands for his weapons. James stood in front of him, his gaze solemn and unreadable. Hawk handed the first sailor a flintlock and the second one his cutlass. He drew out his golden, double-barreled pistol next. The eyes of the sailors widened as the rays of the sun reflected off the polished barrel. Then, in a blur of motion, he leapt forward, grabbed James, and spun him around. His left arm was wrapped around his neck, and his right hand held the flintlock to his temple. The sailors around him drew their weapons in a near panic. A gasp spread throughout the crowd. Most couldn't see what had happened, but they knew all wasn't going according to plan.

"Make a move and you'll be covered with his brains!" Hawk shouted. James tried to wrestle free, but Hawk's grip was tight. Hawk pressed the tips of the barrels harder into his temple, and James stopped resisting. Hawk quickly turned and walked backward through the sailors, half dragging James with him.

Hawk stopped at the far edge of the dock. "Tell Cord not to follow us, or James will die. If no one follows, I'll free him somewhere along the way." Hawk used his left hand to grab James's flintlock and throw it on the dock. He did the same with his cutlass. He then quickly dragged him down another gangplank onto a small catboat.

The sailors stood frozen on the dock and watched. More soldiers and sailors rushed down the lane and to the crowded docks. The commodore and governor followed close behind. Hawk kept his pistol to his brother's head as James unfurled the sails on the single mast. The two men then walked to the tiller, and Hawk made the navy captain steer the ship out into the river. The wind was blowing steady from the west, aiding the strong current. The catboat quickly passed out of flintlock and musket range. As the boat disappeared around the first bend, the governor and commodore engaged in a heated discussion—the governor blaming the commodore for agreeing to Hawk's plan and for his escape.

"You can probably pull those barrels out of my temple just a bit," James said, once he was sure they were out of sight of the town. "Nice pistol, by the way."

"Maybe just a bit, but I'm still going to keep it in hand. We'll surely pass some ships on the way out. Oh, and it was gift from Kragg." Hawk moved behind James and opened a hatch in the deck.

"Do you think they bought it?" James asked, sailing the catboat smoothly and swiftly down the river.

Hawk now squatted above the deck and peered down the ladder. "Probably—for now anyway."

James turned to see what Hawk was doing. He saw a female's head poke just above the deck. Hawk leaned down and kissed the woman. After some quite conversation, she disappeared back down the ladder. Hawk closed the hatch again and went to check the sails. "It will be your return that will be the test."

"Yes, you are right. You may get me court-martialed or hanged before this is over with. How is Anna?"

"She's good," said Hawk. "Anxious to get into the fresh air of course. You should just come with us, brother. You have no business in the navy now." He turned the boom slightly to keep the wind square into the sails.

"Sounds tempting. I would kind of like to finish up the pirate eradicating though. Cofresi is still out there and a few more scoundrels. I guess I'm in a similar situation as you were last year. I need to leave the right way."

They did pass a couple of ships on their way down the river and out to sea, but none were navy. Their little catboat wouldn't draw much attention either way, and none would be able to confirm if James was or was not a hostage. When they reached the sea, they headed east. Hawk opened the hatch again, and this time Anna climbed out onto the deck. They embraced and exchanged a long kiss.

"I cannot believe it!" Anna exclaimed when they finally ended the kiss. Hawk had snuck into the town the night before and found Anna, running a small tavern several streets away from the Treasure Cove. She had packed a few belongings, and Hawk whisked her away to the small hold of the catboat. He stayed with her until close to sunrise.

"I told you I'd come back for you someday. That someday ended up being a few years late, but I am a man of my word." Hawk laughed and hugged her again.

James cleared his throat from the helm.

"Oh, Anna, meet my brother, James."

Anna quickly walked up and bypassed James's outstretched hand and hugged him. "I'm pleased to meet you, James. And I want to thank you for helping us."

"Probably against my better judgment, ma'am. He forced me to drink brandy and agree to this scheme."

"Well, either way, thank you very much."

"You are very welcome and very sweet, Anna. Why in the world are you running away with this scallywag?"

"Hey, watch it now!" said Hawk. "I'm a retired scallywag." He put his arm around Anna.

They sailed all day and into the night. They took turns steering and working the sails, including Anna. Soon after dark, the stars appeared. It was an unusually clear night. Anna couldn't help but stare up at the sky, fascinated by the millions of twinkling flecks of light. At one point, she and Hawk lay down on the deck on some old wool blankets that Hawk found in the hold. His right arm was beneath her head, providing her a pillow. James manned the helm and used the stars to guide his way around the many islands in their path.

"What was that? That star moved across the sky and disappeared," Anna said excitedly.

"A shooting star," Hawk said. "Some people say they are an omen."

"Good or bad?"

Hawk reached over and found her left hand. "Good. It means we're heading off to a great and happy future."

Anna laughed and leaned over to kiss him. Hawk proceeded to point out some of the constellations that he knew—Orion, his favorite; Cygnus, the Big Dipper, Pisces, and Andromeda among others. She snuggled close and barely listened after the first couple. She just enjoyed the warmth of his body in the cool night and listened to his strong heartbeat.

Hawk eventually got up and disappeared below deck. When he returned, he was dressed in different clothes—nondescript beige canvas trousers, a dirty white cotton shirt, work boots, and a floppy hat. He still wore his baldric, with his dagger and pistol sheathed in it, and a leather satchel over one shoulder hanging under his arm. "Do I look like a famous pirate captain now?"

Anna and James both laughed. "If not for the weapons, I would almost think you were an honest man," James said.

"Almost," Anna added, still laughing.

"Oh, James, my clothes are below, as well as the chicken." Hawk said. James nodded in reply.

Hawk relieved James at the helm, and James went to sit and talk with Anna. They shared their life stories and what they knew about the Hawk, which really wasn't much. But they quickly found they had a bond almost as brother and sister. For the short voyage, all of the uncertainty and danger disappeared. The three all felt light-hearted and free. It almost seemed too soon when, around midnight, Hawk steered the boat toward land and the twinkling lights of a small town.

The few lamps on the docks helped Hawk sail the boat silently to an open berth. There were several larger merchant ships docked there, the kind that transported goods up and down the east and gulf coasts of the United States. Some of the smaller ones even went up and down the larger rivers to trade with the small towns along the way. James quickly jumped out and tied the boat to a post on the dock. The docks were quiet, as was the town. Hawk extended the gangplank, and he and Anna joined James.

"Go with us, brother," Hawk said.

"I'll have to pass for now. I'm sure we will see each other again, though."

"I hope so. We still have a lot of catching up to do. Finish your pirate hunting and come visit, or build a house beside ours."

"Sounds good. Now, I'll need your pistol and dagger," James said, extending his hands.

"Why?" Hawk asked, with some apprehension.

"First, you are no longer a pirate. If you go walking down these streets with weapons like those, everyone here will know what you are. Second, if I'm going to tell everyone I killed you, I'll need proof. The Hawk would never voluntarily give up his prized weapons."

The last part of the plan was for James to say he fought with Hawk and killed him. His body fell off of the small boat and apparently sank beneath the water in the darkness. It wasn't a perfect plan, but James had an exemplary record and was known throughout the fleet for his hatred of pirates. There were also very few that knew Hawk was his brother, and none in the navy that he knew of. There would likely be some questioning, and some doubt, but he thought he could weather the storm.

Hawk shook his head and took off the baldric. He took out the dagger and stared at it reverently. It was his first real weapon. It had saved his life numerous times and was always by his side. He had never really thought about having to part with it as part of the plan. But James was right. And he really didn't need anything tying him to his past. He had enough memories.

He sheathed it and drew the golden pistol. He also loved that weapon. He had made it famous over his year of being a pirate captain. But it didn't have the same meaning as his dagger. It was just a rare and valuable possession. He definitely couldn't wear that on his person in his new life. He finally sheathed it too and handed the baldric to James.

Hawk kept the satchel, which contained a few supplies and all of his gold, silver, and gems. "Treat them well," he said to James with a wry smile.

"Please come visit soon, James," said Anna. "I'd like to get to know you better. And you brothers should stay close now that you've finally found each other again." She hugged James.

"I will, Anna. Now, a quick hug for my brother." James stepped forward and hugged Hawk.

"I'm glad you're telling everyone that you killed me and not hugged me." Hawk laughed after the hug had ended. "Good luck, James."

"You too, Hawk. Enjoy your new life."

"I will. Oh, and it's Henry now. The Hawk is dead."

CHAPTER XX

JOURNEY

Henry turned, grabbed Anna's hand, and they happily walked across the dock and onto the street.

James untied the boat and climbed aboard. It would be tough sailing it back by himself, but he was in no hurry. And more than likely the navy already had ships searching for him.

Pascagoula was a small town. They were on the main dirt lane that led from the docks through the middle of the town. A couple of smaller dirt lanes bisected it. There were only a few of people out at that time of night. Lamps burned at regular intervals providing light, though it was dim, and created large, moving shadows. On the right side of the road, about halfway through town, was a two-story inn.

Henry and Anna walked up the stairs to the porch and through the double doors. A bell that hung in front of one of the doors rang as they entered. A large counter stretched the length of the room on the left. The wall behind was lined with bottle-filled shelves with a doorway cut in the middle. Empty tables and chairs filled the room to the right. A wide flight of stairs in front of them led up to the second story and a balcony that skirted the room they were in. Doors were spaced at regular intervals in the walls. A number of lanterns hung from the ceiling and were mounted on the walls, provided dim lighting for the large room.

After a moment, an older man walked through the doorway. He wore a long white gown and a white cloth hat on his gray head. He had obviously been sleeping and rubbed at his eyes as he reached the counter. "A little late for travelers," he said gruffly.

"A story too long for a night so late," Henry replied. He quickly produced a doubloon and laid it on the counter. "How about a room for the night and no questions asked?"

The man's eyes widened, and the drowsiness instantly disappeared. He quickly grabbed the coin and produced a key from under the counter. He had seen all types come through in his day and even the infamous Jean Lafitte a couple of years back. Money was money, and business was business. "Room thirteen—up the stairs and to the left."

"Thank you, sir." Henry and Anna took the key and quickly climbed the stairs and entered their room. It wasn't much bigger or nicer than the rooms in the Treasure Cove but would do for a few hours of sleep.

Very quickly, they were both undressed and in the firm bed. There were times when they were apart for the long periods that Henry almost forgot the feel of Anna's body, the smell of her perfume, and the taste of her lips and skin. But after only a moment together, it all came rushing back as if they had never been apart. He wondered how he could ever forget the warm, smooth, soft feel of her skin against his and her sweet, flowery scent. Hopefully he would never have to forget again.

"I've missed you so much," Henry said, squeezing her tightly against him.

"Not as much as I have you, Hawk. Or I mean Henry." She kissed him softly. All thoughts of just talking and cuddling for a while instantly vanished. Their bodies were soon on fire as the heat of lust swept them away. The soft kisses quickly grew rough and forceful as they groped each other's body. It was Anna who soon rolled on top of Henry. They made love until early in the morning. Their talking would have to wait until the day, because they both collapsed into slumber soon after.

They awoke at midmorning, washed with the water in the basin, and headed downstairs. There were several patrons gathered around the tables in the common room. An older lady in a worn, faded yellow dress was rushing about serving breakfast. Henry and Anna found a table in the corner and waited for the server. They ordered a meal of chicken eggs—not the turtle eggs Henry was accustomed to—sausage, hard biscuits, and strong black coffee.

They ate mostly in silence and tried to eavesdrop on as many conversations as they could. Most of the stories just dealt with small town affairs, cotton farming, slaves, and other mundane subjects. Word of the pirate's surrender, and Hawk's escape, hadn't made its way to the town yet.

"Ma'am," Henry said when the server came back to check on their meal. "Is there a good town a little further inland where a man and woman could buy a little piece of land and settle down?"

She looked at him for a moment as if gauging his intent. "There are little towns all up the rivers north of here. Traders sail their boats up and down them, pedaling their wares. I've heard a little bit about a town named River Junction a couple of days ride north—not far from where the Leaf River joins the Chickasawhay to form the Pascagoula. It's supposed to be growing pretty fast."

"And land?"

"Plentiful. A lot of land was taken from the Indians all over the state. Just ask around when you get to whatever town you settle on." She turned and walked away, already having spent more time than she'd planned talking with the stranger.

Henry paid for their food, and they left the inn. The day was warm and humid, and the sky was blue above. A thick, salty breeze blew in from the sea. The town was quaint and friendly, but Henry knew it wouldn't be safe for them to stay long that close to the sea. Sooner or later, someone from a visiting ship would recognize him. He hoped the locals would quickly forget them.

They walked down the street, where the wooden buildings were all crowded together in a short stretch. Horses were tied to posts outside many of them, along with an occasional wagon. People walked up and down the street and in and out of the buildings. The general store was a few buildings down. They went inside and Henry quickly gathered up supplies, including food, canteens, rope, a flintlock pistol, a dagger, a blanket, and a canvas tarp. The store owner placed all of their supplies inside of the tarp, except the pistol and dagger, and bound the tarp up with a couple of thin ropes. Henry placed the pistol and dagger sheathes on his belt, threw the tarp roll over his shoulder, and they left the store to find the stables.

They found them at the end of the intersecting street. Henry found the owner and quickly negotiated for two horses—saddled, shoed, and ready to ride. He was sure he overpaid for them, but they were in a hurry, and money wasn't an issue. He picked a large black stallion for himself, whom he named Tempest. Anna chose a gray mare and, after much deliberation, named it Destiny.

They both spent the next half hour getting used to riding the horses. Neither had ridden before. One of the stable hands helped them with the basics. Henry caught on quickly, since he was used to balancing on a pitching boat deck and ratlines. Anna took a little more time. Finally, they both felt ready to begin their journey. Henry tied his bundle of supplies to the back of his saddle, along with his leather satchel. He removed the pistol from his belt and tucked it into a bag on the side of his saddle. He filled their canteens from a nearby well, and then they rode north out of Pascagoula.

The dirt road led out of town and followed the Pascagoula River. The land was wet and marshy, and the road soon deteriorated into just a worn trail. The mosquitoes were buzzing loudly about them, and it was very hot and sticky. After several hours, they finally left the marsh behind and had more solid footing. They began to see cotton farms worked by black slaves. Henry had never liked the idea of slavery. Although a lot of pirates kept them, Bloodstone never had. The old captain and his mother had basically been slaves, so Bloodstone hated the practice. In fact, he freed all of the ones that didn't want to go on account.

They only passed a few travelers, some on foot, some on horses pulling carts of cotton back toward the town. The humidity decreased a little the farther they got from the sea, although so did the breeze.

In addition to the occasional wagon and travelers, they also passed a number of flat-bottomed barges drifting down the river to Pascagoula or the sea. Most had men, sometime slaves, manning oars and poles, in addition to the sails. They seemed to make good time going with the flow of the river and even did OK heading against it. They passed through one small town on this side of the river and saw another on the other side a few miles further up the path. They didn't stop in the one they passed through. Henry didn't want to have any more people pay attention to them than necessary until they were further inland.

As the hours passed, the flat land gave way to some rolling hills. Cypress trees and spruce pines began to appear. They stopped in a little stand of loblolly pines for lunch. They both needed a break from riding in the saddles. Already their legs and posteriors were getting sore. Henry spread out the blanket and meal on the ground, and they sat down to eat.

"Bring back any memories?" Henry asked, making them both a sandwich of meat and cheese.

Anna grinned. "Let's hope there are no alligators. And I don't believe this is private enough for other activities. Even if either one of us were fit for such right now."

"I'm sure there are no alligators. And I can always handle some activity. But you might be right on the privacy." Henry laughed and slapped Anna's hip playfully.

"You rogue!" Anna exclaimed, slapping his hand.

"Retired rogue," Henry said, still grinning.

They packed up and continued their journey up the river. They rode side-by-side where they could, and they talked and laughed. They were both still coming to grips with the reality that, after so many years of dreaming, they were finally running away together. It was slowly sinking in. They were both free, although there would always be a slight chance of Henry being recognized. That chance decreased the further inland they went.

The Mississippi countryside was getting more beautiful as they went. They encountered larger hills and some hardwood forests. Close to sunset, Henry led them a mile or so away from the river and into a small forest of oak and spruce trees. There was plenty of wood and shelter here, and soon Henry had a large fire burning. They heated some beef strips skewered on sticks over the fire and enjoyed a couple of apples. Had they had time, Henry could easily have killed some fresh game to eat. The deer and turkey were plentiful.

He had planned on using the tarp for shelter, but the night was warm and the sky clear, so they slept in the open, wrapped up in their blanket. They didn't make love that night, but they still enjoyed lying together and feeling the heat of each other's body. The noises of the forest animals in the darkness startled Anna some, but she felt entirely safe with her head lying on Henry's chest. An animal or bandit in the dark wouldn't stop the greatest pirate captain alive.

They both awoke very stiff and sore the next day. The insides of their thighs and posteriors were the worst. The thought of another day's ride wasn't appealing, but they had little choice. They ate a cold breakfast, packed their belongings, refilled their canteens in a nearby stream, and mounted.

"I think I'll go back to a ship!" Henry said. He received an immediate scowl from Anna.

The promising sunrise was quickly erased by dark, threatening clouds rolling in from the west. The wind began picking up and thunder could be heard in the distance. It reminded Henry of cannon fire. Large drops of rain began striking them and the ground around them. The intensity picked up until it was a downpour.

Henry had his floppy hat, and Anna wore a white round hat with flowers on one side. The hats helped keep the rain from their eyes, but that was about it. They were riding in an area of open rolling land, with only a few trees, so there was little shelter within sight. Henry wasn't worried about himself. Much of a pirate's life was spent in rain and storms, trying not to be washed overboard to his death. But Anna...she was such a dainty young lady who had barely been out in any weather.

Henry looked over at her. She had her head down, and the rain had soaked her completely. Her brown dress clung to her shapely body. He was glad she hadn't worn a white one. He reached over and grabbed her arm. "Are you OK?"

Anna looked up, the rain now striking her in the face. Then she suddenly burst out laughing. She held her arms over her head, looked up at the sky, and laughed.

"Are you mad?" Henry asked, shaking his head, but also smiling.

"I've never been out on a horse in a downpour!" she shouted above the roar of the wind and rain. "This is most wonderful."

"You're definitely mad."

Henry spurred his horse in front of hers and led them into the shelter of a large oak tree. He quickly jumped off and tied both of their horses to the tree. He then came around to Anna's horse. She looked down at him, still giggling. He reached up, grabbed her waist, and easily lifted her off. With her feet still off of the ground, he wrapped his arms around her and kissed her. Their lips glided effortlessly together, slick from the rain. They were cool, but only for a moment.

"What was that for?" Anna asked when Henry finally let her down so her feet touched the ground.

"For you being so wonderful and happy and beautiful…and to help warm you up."

"Well, aren't you the sweet one today!" She kissed him again and then pushed him away. "Ever danced in the rain?"

"I've seen a few pirates dance a jig on the deck in the rain," Henry said, still marveling at Anna's exuberance.

"Well, then dance me a jig, Mr. Wellington."

"Uh, no thanks."

"Ah, come now. Surely a big, mean, fearless former pirate captain isn't afraid of dancing in the rain," Anna taunted. She then held her dress up, almost to her knees, and began to imitate some of the dancing she had seen on weekend nights when musicians would play at the Treasure Cove."

Henry shook his head yet again. "Do I even know you, Miss. Stevens?"

"Not even vaguely." Anna smiled, twirling around quickly to cause her dress to flare into a wide circle at the base.

"I was afraid of that." He finally laughed and joined her. He figured he could do at least as well as drunken pirates. Both forgot their soreness and danced and laughed and carried on in the rain for some time. Finally their energy wore down. They ate another apple and biscuit, drank some water, hugged and kissed, and then remounted and continued their northward journey in the rain and thunder.

As the day wore on, Anna's fascination with the rain ended. They were both cold and miserable. There were few breaks in the downpour. Several times lightning flashed close to them, frightening their horses. They passed through another small town, again not stopping even for shelter. Finally, near dark, Henry saw a thick grove of pine trees at the top of the ridge to their right. They left the trail and rode into the sanctuary. The pines were so thick that there were actually spots that were not totally soaked.

Henry found a cluster of four trees close together and unwrapped the tarp. He used the two lengths of rope that had been wrapped around it, cut two more from the rope he had bought, and lashed the corners to the trees. He then spread the blanket out on the ground beneath. It was damp, but much drier than out in the open. Anna was a little skeptical, but Henry convinced her to take off all of her clothes. He did the same. He hung their clothes from another length of rope that he tied beneath the tarp. They then lay together on the blanket, folding it over top of them.

Soon their body heat chased away the cold. It was almost dark now, especially beneath the tarp underneath the thick pine canopy. They lay face to face, rubbing the other's back to warm them. Once they were warm, their rubbing gradually transitioned to gentle caressing. Wet passionate kisses joined the touching.

"This looks to be very private," Henry whispered into her ear, gently kissing and sucking her earlobe.

"Indeed it does," Anna whispered back to him, biting and raking his earlobe with her teeth.

Henry rolled on top of Anna. Their now hot bodies pressed firmly together beneath the damp blanket. They could still hear the rain falling around them, but if any drops were striking them or the blanket, they were unnoticed. Anna kept thinking that someday their lovemaking would lose its fire and intensity—that it would become ordinary and mundane. While someday that might eventually happen, that day was definitely not today. She was quickly swept away in a flood of desire and lust. She was pleased as only Henry could please her. They eventually finished and fell asleep in each other's arms, not even realizing they hadn't eaten supper. If there were forest creatures around that night, they were not heard.

They woke early the next morning. They were both relieved to see shafts of golden sunlight penetrating the pine trees in several places. The morning was cool, but the storm seemed to have finally moved through. After dressing in their cold damp clothes, they ate most of the remaining salted beef, cheese, and bread. Henry fed the horses the last two apples to give them a break from only eating grass the past two days.

"How far do you think it is?" Anna asked after they'd packed everything and mounted their horses.

"I would think we should be there before dark. I know we lost some time yesterday, but it looks like a good travel day today."

They rode back to the river and proceeded north. The trail was now barely more than an animal path. There were occasional signs that horses and carts traveled on it, but not recently. The day was very warm and humid, but the sun did dry out their clothes and boots. They were still sore, but there bodies seemed to be adjusting to the riding. They talked and laughed as the rode, enjoying their third day together.

They stopped under a large oak beside the river for lunch. "I hope we reach the town soon. If not, I might have to do some hunting," Henry said as they finished the last two biscuits and scraps of meat. They were both hungry, since they'd skipped supper the night before and had only a meager breakfast. As they relaxed and enjoyed watching the waters of the Pascagoula, they heard a rumble coming from the north.

Anna looked at Henry. He hopped up and walked over to his horse. Anna got up too, and Henry motioned for her to stand behind him. Within a couple of minutes, two horses rounded the bend in the river and galloped toward them. Two large, scruffy men spurred the beasts hard as they rode. One wore old tan linen pants and the other brown.

Both had dirty shirts that appeared to have been white at one time. They had long coats and hats that looked to be made of leather. Knee-high boots completed their outfits. They both wore beards.

They slowed as they noticed Henry and Anna. They stopped their horses when they were beside them on the trail.

"You fellows look to be in a hurry," Henry said, politely.

The larger, tanned, dark-haired man glanced at his smaller, paler, brown-haired companion. The other grinned and looked down at Anna, who was almost hidden behind Henry. "Aye," said the black-haired man, with a grin that was missing several teeth. "Seems we're always in a hurry for one reason or such. But we try to make time for strangers."

Henry nodded. "That's mighty nice of you, I suppose. And just why is it that you stop for us strangers?" He casually leaned back against his horse, his left arm resting on the side of the saddle. His right arm was by his side, hiding the hilt of the dagger sticking out of his belt.

"Ye see, we like to help people," the man said, and he spit brown saliva on the ground beside his horse.

"And just what kind of help are you offering?" Henry asked. He shifted his body slightly to make sure Anna was totally behind him.

"We'll help lighten your load a little." The big man pulled out a flintlock from inside his coat and leveled it at Henry. The other man did the same.

"Thanks, but we're fine," Henry replied. He didn't move.

"Not your choice. Throw that satchel and pack on your saddle over here. Slow and easy like."

"I think you two should keep riding down the trail," Henry said, still not moving.

"Henry, just let them have it," Anna whispered from behind him.

"Look. You can give us your bags now, and you two can live. If we have to take them, you die, and we take your woman with us," the big man replied, leaning forward on his saddle. His finger was on the trigger of the pistol.

"How long do I have to decide?" Henry asked, ignoring whispered protests from behind him. He looked from one man to the other.

"I'll count to three."

"I'm impressed." Henry felt his old bravery and swagger in the face of danger return. These men were no hardened pirates or pirate-hunters though.

The first man growled, and his face reddened. "One, two—"

He never reached three. Henry's right hand suddenly moved at his side. A flash of silver is all the big man saw as the dagger struck him in the chest. The pale man glanced quickly at his partner as the big man gasped and grabbed at the dagger hilt. Before he could turn back to Henry and fire his flintlock, Henry's left arm swung around from the saddle and fired his own pistol. The man looked down at his chest for a moment then tumbled from his horse. The big man now lay slumped over the neck of his.

Henry turned to Anna. She had her face covered with her hands. "Are you OK?" he asked.

She was sobbing now.

He gently pulled her hands away from her face. "It's OK. They're dead."

"Why…why didn't just give them your bags?" she asked between sobs.

"That satchel contains all of our money. What kind of life would we have with no money?"

"We would still…still have each other. We could work." She slowly regained her composure.

"That's not our dream. We've waited too long already. Those men weren't going to take it away from us," Henry said, a little surprised at Anna's reaction.

"Is that money worth dying for?"

Henry shrugged. "I knew I could kill them both without us being harmed."

"How did you know?" Anna asked, wiping away the last of her tears.

"Anna. You know my past."

"And I thought we were leaving that behind."

"We are," he said, placing his hands on hers. "Anna, I'm done killing unless it is to defend my family. And now you're my family. But those men probably would have killed me and taken you anyway."

"My protector, huh?"

"Always."

Henry searched the saddlebags on the strangers' horses. He found a large canvas bag in each full of gold and silver coins. There were also some personal belongings, including jewelry. Anna frowned as she watched Henry. He brought the sacks back over to his horse and tucked them into his saddlebags. He looked at her face and knew what she was thinking. "They are obviously thieves. We'll find someone to turn these into in River Junction. Maybe they even stole the loot from there."

Henry retrieved his dagger from the first man's chest and then pulled his body off of the horse and dragged it down to the river, shoving it into the water. He shoved the second man into the water too. He then tied both of their horses to the oak tree. He opened his satchel and reloaded his flintlock with the powder, patches, and shot within. "We'll tell someone in River Junction where they're at."

Anna finally smiled. They remounted and continued their journey. The trail started to become more defined as they rode, with other trails branching off in different directions. They spotted several houses and fields of cotton and soybeans scattered here and there, most worked by slaves.

After about an hour, they saw another group of men on horseback, riding hard toward them. Henry led Anna off to the side of the trail and positioned himself in front of her again. They waited for the six riders to arrive. The men slowed and stopped their horses on the trail when they reached the couple, just as the other two men had done. Henry was a little nervous this time. Six armed men would be tough to take single-handedly with only a dagger and a flintlock.

The leader of the group walked his horse up to Henry's. His curly black hair, sprinkled with a little gray, stuck out from a floppy hat similar to Henry's. Black sideburns ran down past his ears. He had piercing, hazel eyes, a thin black mustache, and a patch of neatly trimmed hair on his chin. His pale skin was in strong contrast to his black hair. He nodded to Anna and then to Henry. "Begging your pardon, but have you seen two large men riding hard down this trail? Probably came through an hour or two ago." His accent was French.

"Indeed we did," Henry said glancing from the Frenchman to the men behind him. He hoped they weren't the partners of the first two. In case they were, he didn't want to reveal too much information. "What is your business with them?"

The Frenchman stared at Henry for a moment before responding. "They robbed the general store and some patrons in River Junction— killed two innocent people, stole their horses, and headed this way. We're going to track them down, retrieve the loot, and hang them from the nearest tree—along with anyone that aids them."

"So, you are a soldier or lawman?"

The Frenchman scowled and tried to keep his temper even. "No. I run the saloon and inn and kind of help look after the town. I'm John Lafleur. Now, we are obviously in a hurry. Have you or have you not seen these men?"

Henry judged that John was telling the truth. He reached into his saddlebags and produced the two sacks. "Here, this will save you some time," he said, holding the bags out to John.

John's eyes widened as he looked from Henry to Anna and back to Henry. The men behind him also didn't hide their surprise. "And how did you two come by the stolen loot?" John took the two sacks and quickly stuffed them into his saddlebags.

Henry figured there was no use lying at this point. "They tried to rob us. I gave them a warning to ride on. They persisted and threatened to kill me and take Anna. I couldn't allow that. Their bodies are floating down the river ten miles back. Oh, and their horses are tied to a tree beside the river at the same spot."

John tried to stare through Henry with his gaze. "You mean to tell me that you single-handedly killed two vicious killers?" The men behind him whispered between each other and looked at Henry with amazement.

"Well, I don't know about vicious killers. But I did have to kill them."

"What is your name, stranger?"

"Henry. Henry We-Williams. This is Anna Stevens. We're actually heading to River Junction."

"What business do you have in River Junction?" John was still recovering from the news and retrieval of the money.

"We're looking for a place to live. We heard it's a nice part of the country."

John relaxed a little and leaned back on his horse. "Pleased to meet you, Henry and Anna. Oh, it is a beautiful area. We're just a small town. Everyone either farms or logs the pines. We could actually use some young people like yourselves, especially one that can handle himself like you. You're welcome to follow me back into town if you'd like. It's only an hour or so ride."

"That would be great. That is a lot of coin for a store," Henry commented.

"Our town does well in trade." John said with a scowl. "I suppose we owe you a reward for retrieving this money. I'm sure Albert would give you ten percent. Some of the others might chip in too."

"No thank you, John."

"No money? What can we do to repay you?"

"Maybe you could help me find a piece of land. I'll also need a little help building a house," Henry said.

Anna smiled behind him.

"Well, that's easy enough. I just so happen to own quite a bit of land around there. And I'm sure we can find some volunteers to help you build. Follow me, then."

John instructed two of his men to go retrieve the horses. He, the other three and Anna and Henry rode to River Junction.

CHAPTER XXI

RIVER JUNCTION

ᴄ᠍ᴏ

The path continued to transition into more of a defined dirt road. They passed more houses and farms as they went, along with a few travelers here and there. Henry took a liking to John as they rode and talked. John told them about River Junction and the people there. The town had only been around for a few years, and he had helped it to grow and prosper. People traveling up and down the river occasionally stopped in for supplies or to spend the night. Some ended up staying.

Many of the residents worked for the local saw mill, which John owned. They cut pine logs and sold them to the river traders who sailed barges up and down the river weekly. The traders sailed down the river and resold the lumber at Pascagoula, Biloxi, or to larger traders that sailed ships to New Orleans and other cities in the Spanish Main. Others farmed cotton or soybeans, usually with the aid of slaves, and they also sold their products to the river traders. John also had some of his own barges that took lumber, cotton, and soybeans down the river to sell. He brought back supplies and goods in return.

"Do you own everything in River Junction?" Henry finally asked.

"Let's just say I am heavily invested," John replied with a wink and grin as they approached a large wooden bridge that spanned the Pascagoula. "So, where are you and Anna from?"

Henry had been using the time John was describing his town to come up with a story. He knew John, or someone, would be able to tell that he had spent a lot of time on a ship, by his rolling gait, or sea legs as they were known. He also knew that he would have a hard time not slipping up if he made up a story that didn't involve the sea and sailing. "I used to work on a merchantman. Sailed from New Orleans to Boston and everywhere in between. I met sweet, young Anna in New Orleans a year or so ago. She worked in a saloon there. We saved up our money and decided to run off together. I was tired of sea life, and Anna wanted out of the city. So, we caught a boat to Pascagoula and learned of your town." It was a little close to the real story, but at least now he could explain away most questions that might arise.

"Ah, you left the trade too soon," John replied, staring at Henry thoughtfully.

"What do you mean?"

"I hear the end of the pirates is nigh. Word has it that the great Hawk and his crew all surrendered in New Orleans a few days past. The men were to receive pardons, and Hawk was to hang."

It was all Henry could do to keep his face expressionless upon hearing that John had already heard about Hawk. "I hadn't heard that. So, did Hawk hang?"

"I'm surprised you weren't there to see the men surrender. It sounds like the timing was close," John continued to stare at him with his unnerving gaze.

"I guess we left a day or two before. I left out a few details of our voyage. We did make several stops along the coast on the way to Pascagoula. We spent a night in Biloxi while the captain traded goods there. Then we stayed two nights in Pascagoula before our journey up here. So I suppose it's been a week or so since we left."

Anna stared at the neck of her horse as she strained to hear Henry and John's conversation. She liked John but didn't trust him yet. He either knew something or was trying to find out something. She also didn't know how he could have possibly known so quickly about Hawk and his men.

"Ah, I see. Well, anyway, they say this Hawk captured a navy captain, I believe a James Wellington, and sailed off with him in a small boat." John finally turned away from Henry as they crossed over the bridge, their horses' hooves clacking loudly.

"They say that Hawk is a crafty one. Did they find him or James?" Henry's heart slowed a little, but he would definitely have to be careful around John.

"Last I heard, neither had turned up. We get news from the river traders. I suppose we'll hear more in a day or two."

"Oh. Now, what's your story? How does a Frenchman end up running a saloon in River Junction, Mississippi?" Henry asked.

John chuckled. "That is a long story indeed. The short version is that I'm a businessman, and a trader, and have done my share of traveling. I too spent some time on a merchant ship back in the day. In my travels, I saw a good opportunity in lumber and farming in this part of the country where I knew could make a little money and live in a beautiful, quiet, peaceful town."

"I want the long version someday."

"And I yours." John laughed.

River Junction was similar to Pascagoula, only a little smaller. A wide dirt lane passed straight through the town. Two other lanes bisected it. Large wooden buildings lined both sides of the street. They looked to be a mixture of stores and warehouses. Smaller buildings and single-story homes lined the side streets. It looked like a lot of the residents lived in the town.

There was at least one difference from Pascagoula though. Henry instantly noticed armed men standing at the entrance of the town and milling around some of the buildings. He even saw movement on the tops of others. They were trying to blend in with the regular citizens, but they couldn't fool Henry's keen eyes. He wondered if they were stationed in response to the robbery, or a fixture in River Junction. He decided not to ask John about them, at least not yet.

John led them to the largest building, a three-story structure in the middle of town. A short flight of stairs led up to a porch that ran across the front. Posts joined the porch to the overhanging roof. A sign above the door read, "Fleuve Maison." They tied their horses to posts outside, walked up the stairs, and entered through the swinging double doors.

"The River House," John said as they entered. The inside looked similar to most saloons. Round tables and chairs filled the room and a counter ran the length of the far wall with stools in front of it. A few people were spread about the room. An older man tended the bar, and a young, attractive, dark-skinned, dark-haired woman wiped the tables and served the patrons.

"George, prepare our guests a feast of a supper," John called to the man behind the counter. Then he turned to the young lady. "And Madame Rosa, take good care of them."

Henry thanked John for bringing them here and his hospitality.

"I have some business to attend to. I'll be down in a little bit to talk more with you. Enjoy your meal." John turned and quickly disappeared up a flight of stairs in the corner of the room. His three companions followed.

Henry grinned at Anna. She had been quiet on their ride with John, content to listen to the men talk. "What do you think of John?" Henry knew Anna was a good judge of character just from dealing with men as she had all of her life.

"I'm not sure yet. He's definitely not telling us everything. I don't know if I trust him or not. And you?"

"I agree. There's more than meets the eye. He's likeable though. I suppose we'll find out quickly enough if he isn't trustworthy. But if he is honest, we might have picked the perfect town."

"It's definitely a beautiful town and countryside. I cannot wait for a bath and a bed though!"

"We had our bath yesterday. Remember?"

"You might have had your pir—" She caught herself. "Sailor bath. But it was no bath for a lady!"

Rosa brought them large tankards of ale as they waited for their food. Before long, she began bringing out the feast. She brought out bowl after bowl and set them on the table. Then she brought out plates and silverware.

They helped themselves to the food. It was the best meal either of them had ever eaten. There was roast venison, beef, and pork, along with potatoes, boiled greens, and fresh, soft bread with butter. All the food was seasoned and flavored like nothing they had ever tasted. They scarcely talked as they gorged. They hadn't realized just how famished they were. Rosa made sure the bowls, and their tankards stayed full.

As Henry and Anna ate, more people began filing in. It was close to dark, so they were probably coming by for a drink or supper after work. Soon there was a steady buzz in the room. They received some odd glances, but most people spoke to them or smiled. It seemed to be a friendly town. They were both full and feeling good from the drink, but they were also both feeling very tired from their trip. They were relieved when John finally reappeared. His companions were no longer with him.

"So, did you enjoy our food?" John asked, sitting at the table with them.

"The best meal either of us has ever eaten," Anna said.

John raised his eyebrows and then smiled. "That's good. And the ale?"

"Just as good," Henry chimed in.

"Good. Now, would you two like to stay for some entertainment? The musicians will be here soon, and we'll have some singing and dancing."

"That does sound lovely, but begging your pardon, we're both very tired," said Anna with a sweet but tired smile. "It's been a long, rough journey for us."

John smiled warmly. "Ah, but of course. Where are my manners? Go ask George for a room key. I think you'll find the room comfortable. Then in the morning we can go look at some land. There is a tub in your room. Just tell George when you are ready for a bath, and he'll get a couple of our ladies to come fill it for you." He seemed friendlier and more inviting than he had on the trail.

"Let me give you some money for the meal and the room," Henry said, starting to reach for his satchel.

"Nonsense. This is part of your reward. Just a coin in the purse for the money you returned to us. Now, I must speak to my guests. You two have a good night, and I will see you in the morning." John stood and headed off to speak to the people at a table behind them.

Henry and Anna got a room key from George and thanked him and Rosa for their food and service. Their room was up the stairs on the second floor. They pushed the door open and both froze in the doorway. The room within was nicer than any either had ever seen. The floor was covered with a plush red carpet. The wooden walls and ceiling were smooth and painted white. There was a large desk against one wall and a chest of drawers against another. A bathtub was in the near corner, with a table beside it and a mirror behind it. The bed was large and covered with clean, thick white blankets. On the bedside table stood a lit oil lamp. Another lamp stood on the desk, and several candles burned in sconces around the room. A couple of high-backed polished wooden chairs sat in the far corner, with a small table in between. They had red velvet cushions on the seats and backs.

Anna glanced at Henry, laughed, then ran and dove onto the bed. It was as soft as it looked. She rolled over and looked up at Henry. "Can we just live here?"

Henry laughed, shut the door, and ran and dove onto the bed beside her. "Maybe we can ask him who his decorator is and where he got this furniture."

"I'm tired, but I hate to dirty this clean bed. Should we take a bath?"

"Bath?" Henry asked.

"Don't tell me you've never had a bath!"

"Does rain, ocean, or pond count?"

"You silly rogue! Go tell George we'd like our bath drawn."

Henry wasn't sure about taking a bath, but he went downstairs and told George. A few minutes later, a couple of pretty young ladies came in with large metal buckets full of hot water. They poured them into the tub and then went back downstairs for more. After a number of trips, the tub was three-quarters full. They sprinkled some perfumed powder into the water and left the couple alone.

Within seconds, Henry and Anna were undressed and sitting in the tub. Being in a tub of hot water, naked, with his beautiful Anna made Henry forget his doubts. They laughed and splashed and washed each other. After the water had grown cold, they dried each other off with towels that the ladies had left on the table beside the tub. They then climbed naked into the comfortable bed. Despite being tired and sore, they couldn't resist each other. The made love and then slept the best sleep of their lives, not waking until well after the sun had risen.

A knock on the door finally woke them. Henry got out of the bed, slipped on his breeches, and cracked the door open. A young woman stood outside with her arms full of clothing. He wasn't sure if she was one of the ones from last night or not.

"Pardon me, sir, but Mr. Lafleur asked me to bring some clean clothes for you and your companion. We will clean your soiled ones while you are out today."

Henry looked back at Anna, who only shrugged. Then he opened the door wider and took the clothes. The woman smiled and quickly disappeared. Henry brought the clothes in, and he and Anna dressed. His clothes consisted of brown linen pants, a white cotton shirt, leather shoes, and a belt. Anna had a yellow dress with dressy leather shoes and a yellow hat. The dress came to just slightly below her knees, which would help for riding and walking outdoors.

They went downstairs feeling relaxed and refreshed. John was turning out to be a wonderful host. They both just hoped that there were no strings attached. Henry wore his flintlock in one side of his belt and his dagger in the other. He still wore his satchel over his shoulder, not being trusting enough to leave it in the room. John spotted them immediately and came around the bar to greet them.

"Good morning. I hope the room was to your liking?"

"Unbelievable," Anna said.

"And the clothing?"

"The clothes are great too. But you are being much too generous," Henry said.

"Nonsense. You are very important guests. The entire town has heard of your bravery. The clothes and food are nothing compared to the reward you could have had. You can eat a quick breakfast, and then we'll see what we can do about finding you a patch of land."

The breakfast was almost as good as the supper. They had eggs, sausage, bacon, fried potatoes, biscuits, fresh strawberries, and black coffee. John disappeared again and let them eat alone. A half dozen other patrons were also dining. It was obvious that the River House was the main establishment in town. John reappeared just as they finished. They followed him outside, and the three mounted their horses.

"So, Mr. Williams, tell me about this land you seek. Are you wanting to farm cotton? Or soybeans? I can set you up with the land and find you enough blacks to work it for you."

"No. No slaves. And nothing that big. We'd like to just grow enough crops for us to eat. Maybe raise some cattle or hogs. I assume you raise those around here?"

"Cattle and hogs, huh? We raise a few. Not a lot of money in it, though. So you will need some pastureland and water?"

"Water would definitely be good—maybe a creek or river and pond if possible. And some stands of hardwoods and rolling hills. We'd like enough land to ride our horses."

"Hmmm. You might be in luck. Most of the farmers around here want a lot of flat, open land for their cotton. Hills and tress are of no interest. And water is plentiful. A lot of little streams feed the Leaf River. Let's ride a little way and see what we can find."

John led them down the main road and out of the other end of town. The dirt road narrowed a little but was still a good road and obviously well used. The sky was a deep and clear blue, and the day was warm. It seemed less humid than it had down closer to the coast. As they rode, they passed many cotton and soybean fields. They passed an occasional horse-drawn, flat wagon loaded with either bales of cotton or cut pieces of lumber heading to town. John explained that there were docks right in the town where barges came to unload supplies and food from the larger towns and to load up their goods.

Several smaller roads forked off to the left of the main road going to the various farms. When the land around them became hillier and more trees began to appear, John led them off of the main road on a poorly defined trail. After a mile or so, the trail entered a large patch of pine trees. It was a mature forest, and the riding was shaded and easy. It looked like some trees had been cut in the past to make a lane wide enough for a wagon to travel.

The ground gradually rose until they exited the forest. Once out of the pines, the land opened up and sloped down for a hundred yards or so to a flat bottom that was a hundred yards wide and several hundred yards long. The land was grown up with bushes and weeds, and several large trees grew here and there on the upper end. It looked like they might have been left years before after logging. On the west and north sides of the bottom, the land sloped up until it reached a forest of hardwood trees. To the south, the land gradually rose into hills, with one large hill obstructing the view of what lay beyond.

"This land was logged a long time ago, before I got here. It's hardly big enough for cotton or soybeans and a little too far from town. We've got enough logging going on in other places to not need the patch of pines we just passed through. There is a small creek that flows through the trees in front of us. It exits on the other side of that hill, fills a large pond, and keeps going to the southeast. It would take a little work to clear the brush and build a house, but would this work for you?"

"Oh, it's perfect!" Anna exclaimed, riding up between the men. She began gesturing at the various features. "We could build a house between those two big trees for shade. Over there, we could plant a garden. Then we could have animals on the hills and around the pond and creek."

Henry laughed at Anna's excitement. "I guess you have our answer. How much do you want for it?"

"I have some ideas on that. Why don't we head back to town and me and you talk some business?" John said.

Henry felt sick to his stomach. He didn't like the sound of that, and he didn't understand why John wouldn't just give him a price. "OK," he said.

Anna was too excited to care about the delay. She talked to Henry and John about all of her ideas for the land. Henry was still excited too, but a little daunted, both by John's business talk and all of the work that was going to be needed to make Anna's dream come true. When they returned to the hotel, Anna went to the room, while Henry went up to the third floor with John and the same three men that had been with him the day before. The entire third floor was John's living quarters and business office.

"Let's talk, Henry," John said as they all sat down around a large table in the middle of his office. The office was through the first door at the top of the stairs. There were a couple of doors that were closed on two of the walls. The office had a large desk and chair in front of the far wall. A couple of padded chairs stood in front of it. The walls were lined with many book-filled bookcases. A smaller round table was in the far corner, with four chairs around it, then the large table they were at, which could probably seat twenty people. There were a few paintings hung about the walls where there was empty space. All of the furniture was expensive and the room lavishly decorated, with thick blue carpet and white walls. Lamps hung from the ceiling, and candles burned on most of the tables.

"These are some of my loyal men," said John. "Levi, Ferdinand, and Philip. They do various tasks about the town, which I won't bore you with now. Henry, I can use another good man to help run things. Running a town isn't easy business. The incident yesterday with the bandits illustrates that. I am a good judge of character. You can definitely handle yourself and are a sharp, dependable, and trustworthy man. I could use you."

"Those men weren't bandits, were they?" Henry asked, staring hard at John to see his reaction.

John glanced quickly at Philip and then returned his gaze to Henry. "Why would you ask that?"

"I saw the armed men you have scattered about the town. If two bandits just rode into town, stole the money, and rode out, you wouldn't have had time to position that many men throughout town before pursuing. And if all of those men were already stationed in town, two ordinary bandits wouldn't have attempted robbery, or if they did, they wouldn't have escaped."

"I did mention sharp. Very observant, Henry. They were my men. Philip handles matters of…security for me. Those men had apparently plotted for a while to steal the money that came back from a big lumber sale we made in Biloxi, several barge-loads worth. They ambushed and killed two barge pilots on their way from the docks to here. They rode out of town before anyone could get a clean shot at them. That's what also makes your killing them more impressive. They were trained killers, not just hapless thieves. Not bad for a retired sailor and future farmer."

"I've been in a scrap or two over the years," Henry replied flatly. "And why do you say I'm honest and trustworthy? Because I returned the money?"

"You returned *all* of the money. It would have been very tempting to say that it was not all there when you found it. And I would have thought nothing of it. But it was all there, every piece of eight."

"So, what are you asking of me now?"

"Come work for me."

"Doing what?"

"Oh, I don't know. A little of everything. You could help with the security, trade, and business matters. If you did, I could let you have that piece of land for free, plus pay you very handsomely."

Henry looked from John to the other three men. They all smiled and awaited his response. "I am very honored to be asked. But Anna and I have been planning for years to settle down, start a little farm, and maybe a family. Maybe at some point I'll change my mind, but for now I just need some rest and relaxation. If you need my help on something specific, though, let me know. I'm indebted to you already."

John smiled. "Fair enough then. It will still be good having you and Anna around and about town. If you should ever change your mind…"

"So, about the land?" said Henry.

"Tell you what. I'll still give you the land. I'll even provide the materials and labor for your house and farm. But if you sell any of your crops or animals, you have to do it through me. I'll take ten percent and give you the rest upon sale. We need investment. Levi there is my builder, and he's in charge of the logging operation. He can build anything with wood. Ferdinand can help you clear your land and supply you with livestock. He's a German but knows his stuff. He's my head agriculture manager. Do we have a deal?"

Henry rubbed his chin and looked at the men again. "Sounds fair enough. Deal." He stood up and shook John's hand.

"Welcome to River Junction." John replied, grinning.

CHAPTER XXII

HAWK'S DEMISE

ater that night, James anchored the catboat off the north side of a small island. He went below deck and came up with a chicken and Hawk's clothes. He shredded the breeches and threw them overboard with the boots. The items quickly sank. He then wrapped the chicken up inside the white shirt. He tied the shirt to a length of rope hanging from the boom. The chicken squawked and flapped its wings inside of the shirt. James stepped back a few paces and shot the chicken with his flintlock.

James untied the shirt and took out the dead chicken. He cleaned out all of the feathers and entrails and dumped them over the rail along with the carcass. He took some of the excess blood and rubbed it onto his shirt and breeches and put a couple of streaks on his face. He tore the shoulder of Hawk's shirt and ripped all of the buttons off. He made similar cuts and tears in his own. He then lay Hawk's shirt, dagger, and flintlock on the deck and found a place on the deck to get some sleep.

James found some food below deck the next morning and ate a quick and cold breakfast of dried salted beef and hardtack. He had just raised anchor and sailed into the open water when he saw the *Avenger* heading in his direction. The ship immediately spotted him, and within an hour he had climbed a rope ladder up to the main deck, carrying Hawk's remnants with him.

Thomas Smith was the first to greet him. "So great to you see you alive, sir. Did Hawk let you go?"

James gritted his teeth. Something in Smith's tone already grated his nerves. Before he could respond, another man appeared from behind Thomas. He was shocked to see Commodore Cord. "Hawk is dead," he said to both of the men.

"Dead? You killed him?" Cord asked, not hiding his surprise.

"Aye." He tossed the shirt, dagger, and flintlock to the deck. "He finally had to relieve himself off the side of the deck. I saw my chance and charged him. We wrestled for a while against the rail. I managed to take the flintlock from him. He drew his dagger and managed to nick me a few times." James looked down at his cut and bloodied shirt. "I tried to get him to surrender so we could hang him. He insisted on trying to kill me. I finally had to shoot him in the chest. He dropped his blade and leaned back against the rail. I rushed over and tried to grab him so there would be a body. But he toppled over the side, and I ended up with only his shirt in my hand. His body sank."

Thomas and Cord looked at James and then at Hawk's bloodied shirt and weapons. "You are indeed a hero, Captain," Thomas finally said, shaking his head. "You killed the Hawk."

Cord spat onto the shirt on the deck. "I wish we could have hanged the coward. And left his body swinging in the middle of Jackson Square."

"Me too, sir. Me too," James said, acting upset.

"Where did this occur?"

"A few leagues back, near Biloxi I think," James lied.

"And there is no chance that he lived?"

"No. You know me, Commodore. I would tell you if there was a chance he didn't die. Look at the hole in the shirt. I shot him square in the chest from close range. And those were Hawk's prized weapons. He would never voluntarily give those up. Hawk is dead, and his crew and ship are no more. Piracy will soon be over, sir."

Cord stared at him for a moment and finally gave a weak grin. "I'll hold you to that. Let's bring this ship about and head back to New Orleans. I need to inform the governor."

"Yes, sir." James knew there was some suspicion, but as long as Henry truly disappeared into retirement, there wasn't much Cord or anyone else could do. He doubted they would search for a body. It was possible he would send some men into Biloxi, but Henry would never have set foot there. And even if they went as far as Pascagoula, no one would remember seeing two travelers passing through a week or more prior. He just prayed Henry kept his word and didn't return to piracy. He was his brother, and he loved him dearly, but he would have to kill him if that situation arose. "How did you know where to search for me?"

"We didn't. I sent ships in all directions. But I figured he'd hang close to shore with a boat that small and only two of you to man it. And this is close to Bloodstone's old hideout. So I wanted to personally come in this direction."

"I'm glad you did, Commodore."

Cord grunted and walked away.

CHAPTER XXIII

A New Home

ॐ

The next day, Ferdinand and Levi followed Henry and Anna to their land, along with several workers. Ferdinand spoke with a heavy German accent, but they could understand him. They used sickles and then horse-drawn ploughs to clear the land for the house and garden. They decided to leave all but the house and garden area, with a modest clear area around it, grown up. Ferdinand explained that the horses and cattle would eat that vegetation.

They started on the house the next day. Henry had never built a house but had a lot of experience repairing and modifying ships. Once he understood the basics of framing, he got along fine. Levi helped, as did three other townsmen. Henry paid them for their work each day and was generous with the money.

He and Anna stayed at the River House at night. Within a week, the house was finished. Henry hadn't let Anna see it yet, but did take her to visit some of the warehouses in town to pick out furniture. It wasn't quite as nice as John's, but Henry soon had the house furnished and decorated very handsomely. It was small but comfortable.

"OK. Place this over your eyes," Henry said, handing Anna a scarf and grabbing the reigns of Destiny. They were in the pine forest and about to enter their land. Anna hadn't seen it since the first day with John.

She laughed and wrapped the scarf around her head. "I better not fall!"

Henry guided their horses into the clearing so she would be able to get a good view of the cleared land and newly built house. The house set nestled between the three large trees and faced south, toward the hills. It was one story with stairs leading to a porch that stretched across the front, supported by columns leading to a sloped roof. Henry hadn't painted it, but the red cedar logs glowed orange in the sunlight. There were two windows on the front side and one in each of the other walls. A well sat on one side of the house, and a wooden frame built around it supported the wench, rope, and bucket. A privy was built beside a tree in the back yard. A wide, clear path led down the hill from the pines to the house.

"OK. You may remove it."

Anna took off the scarf. Her mouth fell open as she stared at the transformed piece of land and new house. She couldn't speak. She looked at Henry with tears streaming down her cheeks.

"Are those good tears or bad?" Henry asked.

"Oh, Henry! It's wonderful! Even better than I dreamed!"

"There is still a lot of work to do outside. I have to build a barn and put up some fencing. Then we need to work on our garden and get some livestock. But we have a house now and all the time in the world."

Anna nudged her horse next to his and leaned over to give him a kiss. "I cannot believe this day is finally here—the first day of the rest of our lives!"

They galloped down the hill to the house. They dismounted, leaving their horses free to roam, and ran up the steps to the porch. Two rocking chairs sat on the porch beside the door. Henry opened the door and led Anna inside. In one half of the first room stood a large table surrounded by wooden chairs. In the other half were a large plush couch, two padded chairs, and a small table. The couch and chairs faced a fireplace in the far wall to the right. A door on the other side of the big table led into a kitchen with a new wood stove, numerous cabinets, and a basin. A small hallway straight ahead led to the two bedrooms. One was furnished with a bed, dresser, a couple of chairs and tables, a floor mirror, bathtub, and washbasin. The other was made into an office with a nice desk and a large chair behind it, two bookcases, and a small table and two other chairs. Colorful rugs covered a good part of the floors in every room except the kitchen. Lanterns and candles were plentiful in each room. A painting of the ocean was in the main room, and other paintings adorned the walls in the rest of the house. The walls were left unpainted, but the cedar was pretty in its own right.

"Will it do?" Henry asked after the tour.

Anna grabbed him and hugged him tightly, the tears flowing again. "I love you, Henry! It's so wonderful!"

Henry placed his head on top of hers. He even felt a tear or two in his eyes. "I love you too, Anna."

They walked back out onto the porch and sat down in the rocking chairs. The roof blocked the sun, and the hot summer air was made comfortable by the shade and a steady breeze. They held hands and rocked as they surveyed their land.

"I just realized something," Henry said after a few moments.

"What's that, dear?" said Anna, smiling at him.

"This is the first time in my life that I've had nothing to do, nowhere to be, and no one wanting to kill me."

Anna laughed. "Hmmm. And the same for me, except for the killing part. I think I'm kind of fond of it."

"Yeah, me too. I mean there is a lot to be done still, but nothing we can't do ourselves. We have more than enough money to buy anything we need. The farming will just give us something to do."

"You don't think we'll become bored and unhappy, do you?" Anna asked, her smile disappearing.

Henry let go of her hand and lightly brushed the side of her head and face. He then leaned over and gave her a quick, gentle kiss. "Bored being in paradise with you? I don't think so."

"Good answer," Anna said, her smile returning. She kissed him back. "Now we need to start figuring out what all we need for our house."

"What is all of that stuff in there?" Henry asked, raising his voice in feigned displeasure.

"Just furniture, silly. We need food, curtains for the windows, more hangings and paintings for the walls, pots and pans and cooking utensils, soap, perfume, clothes—"

"OK! OK!" said Henry. "You get a list together, and we'll go into town in the morning."

"Oh, and parchment and quills and ink and..." Anna laughed at Henry's scowl.

A little later, they explored the land on their horses. The northern boundary was the forest. The west boundary was the river that flowed about a hundred yards into the woods. The forest was mature and fairly open. Squirrels scurried about on the ground and in the trees, chattering loudly at their intrusion. There were also deer trails crisscrossing the forest. The water could either be called a big creek or small river, ranging from six to twelve feet wide. There were plenty of deep pools that Henry knew had to be full of fish. One end eventually flowed into the Leaf River; the other wound its way through the forest and into the hilly fields to the south.

The river flowed through the hills and fed into a large pond just beyond the large hill that kept them from seeing their house. On the other side of the pond, it continued across the field and into the pine forest. That was their southern border. The eastern edge was about halfway into the pines. It was a perfect piece of land for what they needed, and private. There shouldn't be people coming that way unless they were lost or looking for them.

They made it back to the porch in time to watch the sun set behind the hill and forest to the west. "I still cannot believe we're finally here!" Anna said, the last rays of sun striking her face as she looked at Henry. "I've dreamed about it for so long. Yet as time passed, I had less and less hope that the dream would ever come true."

"I know what you mean. There were so many battles and times when I thought I would die and never be able to share this with you. I think that's probably the main reason I didn't die. I had to see this through."

"It seems like just yesterday when I was working at the Treasure Cove. By this time the sailors and fishermen would be straggling in. I would have to serve and wait on them through their meals and then…"

"There is no more 'and then,'" Henry said. "I'm your only 'and then' from now on."

"You're a very wonderful 'and then,' Henry…Williams." Anna laughed and reached over to rub his thick hair.

Henry grabbed her hand and pulled it down to his face. He looked at her as he gently kissed her fingers and hand. At first it was playful and teasing. Then he started kissing with more intensity. He flicked his tongue against her fingertips and worked in some playful sucking along with the kissing. Anna's cheeks reddened as she watched Henry's lips and mouth work on her hand. He was so romantic and sensual. The innocent boy of six years ago was long gone. Something playful and funny quickly transitioned into something seductive and erotic. A few seconds of Henry's kisses set her body on fire like no man had ever been able to do with hours.

Henry stood and gently pulled her up out of the chair. He scooped her into his arms and carried her into the house, not bothering to lock the door. "I think it's time to spend some time in the bedroom."

"You beast!"

"Retired beast!"

The next few weeks were busy. They first purchased a wagon to pull behind their horses to haul supplies. Then they purchased household supplies, guns for Henry, and posts and boards for the fences, pens, and barn that had to be built. Levi was very helpful and stopped by every day or two to see how Henry was doing and to offer advice. Levi, Ferdinand, and several hands helped to build pens for hogs and chickens, fences around the boundary and pond, and a barn in front of the big hill at the southern end of the land.

While Henry was working in the fields, Anna worked in the house. After everything was arranged and decorated like she wanted, she turned her attention to cooking. Henry showed her what he had picked up from Wesley over the years. She also spent some time with George at the River House when Henry was in town talking business with Levi, Ferdinand, and John. She soon became a very good cook.

Although the work was hard and the days were long, they loved it. They took frequent breaks to sit together and talk and to give a hug or kiss. Many days were spent on the bank of the pond, eating lunch on a blanket as they had so long ago on the island. Some days that was followed by naked swims. In the evenings, they went for walks, rode their horses, or sat on the porch and rocked. Of course, there was always time for lovemaking, pretty much anywhere and everywhere on their land, and especially on the banks of the pond.

Over the past few years, Henry had some doubt about what would happen when he and Anna were together all of the time. After all, they really didn't know each other well. He also thought about the cautionary tales of Wesley and Jack. But so far it had gone even better than he had imagined. Anna was intelligent, quick-witted, and had a good sense of humor. She was also a strong, independent, and spirited woman. She begged to ride to town by herself almost daily, but so far Henry hadn't let her.

It was that spirit that led her to come to Henry one day after lunch and make an unusual request for a woman. "I want to learn how to shoot your guns."

Henry laughed. "That would be scary."

Anna smacked him on the shoulder. "I'm serious! A girl needs to know how to protect herself. What if Indians or bandits attack while you're off in town talking with your men friends?"

Henry still smiled, but it actually wasn't a bad idea. "Are you sure? Those muskets kick hard, and you're just a dainty little thing."

"I'm a strong woman! I can handle your little guns," Anna said, grinning.

"OK. We will go shooting then."

Henry set some empty onion bottles on the fence posts nearest to the house. He started with the musket. He showed her how to measure and pour the black powder, wrap a patch of cloth around a steel ball, and ram it into the barrel with the ramrod. He then showed her how to open the frizzen, pour priming powder into the pan, and close. He handed the heavy gun to Anna. He let her get used to the weight and then showed her how to half-cock the hammer, pulling it back until it clicked in the first notch. He stood behind her and showed her how to aim at one of the bottles. He then instructed her to pull the hammer back one more notch. "OK. Take a deep breath. Place your finger gently on the trigger. As you slowly exhale, squeeze the trigger."

A moment later, the gun roared, and a flash of fire erupted from the barrel. The gun barrel rose up in the air several feet from the recoil, and Anna took a step backward. When the smoke cleared, the bottle was no longer on the fence post. "I hit it! I hit it!" Anna exclaimed.

Henry smiled and gave her a hug. "Let's see if it was luck. Now, load the gun like I showed you and try again." With a little guidance, she quickly had the gun reloaded and ready to fire. She took aim on another bottle and shot again. It was the same result.

"Maybe I can outshoot you, Captain," Anna exclaimed.

"Let's not get carried away." Henry was impressed with her shooting. They shot the musket several more times, until Henry finally had to show off his aim by shooting just the tip off of one bottle. They then moved to loading and shooting the flintlocks, which was pretty much the same procedure. She had a little more trouble aiming them, but quickly caught on.

"Maybe you *should* have been a pirate queen," Henry said as they carried the guns back to the house.

Anna's hand and shoulder were already sore from the shooting. "Don't forget that either," she replied, making a shooting motion toward him with her hand as the gun.

The next phase of their new life was creating the farm. Ferdinand helped Henry pick out a dozen head of cattle, six hogs, and two dozens chickens to start. Two of the cows were milk cows, and the rest were for beef. Ferdinand taught Henry how to feed and take care of the animals and milk the cows. Henry installed a hand pump, similar to the ones on ships, to pump water from the pond to nearby troughs. The hogs had their own pen, as did the chickens. He made a hen house for the laying hens so Anna could gather eggs each morning.

Ferdinand also helped Henry plant several crops in the garden for food, including corn, cabbage, carrots, potatoes, onions, beans, lettuce, and squash. It was only early summer, and Ferdinand assured him that there was time for all of the plants to produce by fall. A month after finding River Junction, Anna and Henry were finally settled into their perfect new life.

CHAPTER XXIV

LOVE AND MARRIAGE

ॐ

*H*enry and Anna were married in a small Christian church at the end of the town. Nearly the entire town showed up for their wedding, even though they hadn't met most of the townspeople yet. Everyone was excited to have new people move to the area, and by now everyone had heard of Henry killing the "bandits." The little church was filled. Some even had to stand in the back. Anna was radiant in a long, billowing white dress, and Henry was dashing in a fine black suit.

The service was quick, with the preacher saying his words and Anna and Henry saying, "I do." After the service, everyone gathered back at the River House for food, drinks, and dancing. Henry couldn't get out of dancing with Anna. Despite his protests, and lack of experience, he moved with ease and grace. He soon forgot about the people watching and just enjoyed holding his new bride.

Anna was introduced to the wives. Ferdinand was married to Caroline, Levi to Lilly, Philip to Elizabeth, and John had a lady friend named Sarah. Anna soon found herself at the table with them as Henry drank with the men. They were all friendly enough and readily shared news and gossip about the town and the people gathered in the room. Anna soon knew much more than she needed to about almost everyone.

The ladies invited her to come have tea with them on Tuesday and Thursday mornings at the small clothing store Sarah owned.

Henry and the men enjoyed themselves and drank a little too much brandy, wine, rum, and ale. They were soon laughing and swapping tales. Henry, despite being drunk, was careful not to say too much. He told a few stories of the sea but tried to keep the talk to general things such as storms, gambling, drinking, and funny things seen and said aboard a ship. More men gradually made their way to the table and soon surrounded the five men.

"How about pirates?" John asked, as Henry finished one story that had everyone laughing hard.

"Excuse me?" Henry asked, suddenly sobering up.

"Oh, surely you ran across a pirate or two in all of your sailing."

Anna had been trying to eavesdrop on the men as much as possible and tune out the chattering women. The more Henry drank, the louder his voice grew. She knew he was talking about the sea and also knew it was a matter of time before he shared too much. She excused herself from the women, saying she would join them for tea someday soon, and quickly made her way to the men's table, pushing her way through the crowd.

"There you are, dear," she said, just before Henry started to reply to John. "Honey, I'm tired, and we still need to have our own wedding celebration."

The men roared with laughter. Henry's face turned red as he got jabbed and playfully punched by Ferdinand and Levi. "Well, gentlemen, I love you all, but not near as much as my beautiful young bride." He pushed his chair back and stood on wobbly legs.

"Come back one evening, Henry, and entertain us with some more stories," John said, tipping his tankard toward him.

When they were on their wagon and heading out of town, Anna scolded her husband. "Henry, you have to watch telling your stories! And drinking that much around those men."

"I know. I'm sorry. I wasn't going to say anything though," Henry replied sheepishly.

"Henry."

"Well, I might have just told a few stories that I've heard," he said, giving a weak grin.

Anna softened a little. "No stories at all are better. Now, you'd better sober up so we can consummate our marriage shortly."

"I think we have done that many times before we were married." Henry laughed. He received a punch on his thigh in response.

The remainder of the summer was great for Anna. She and Henry were as happy as two people could be. When she wasn't working in the house on chores and cooking, she would help him tend to the garden and animals. She just wanted to be close to him as much as possible. He was sweet and caring to her, and she always felt safe and secure with him around. The work was hard, but it kept them busy, and they still made time to relax and enjoy each other's company. Henry even hung a couple of hammocks behind the house between four trees. They laid out there sometimes during the day and on warm nights.

Anna had worried, even before they ran off together, about Henry becoming bored with life away from pirating. He had lived a life that few could imagine, rising to a legendary pirate captain. His name had been known from England to the Spanish Main. He had probably taken more ships, and more treasure, than any pirate who'd ever lived. His life had been pure adventure and excitement since he was six years old. But he seemed content with their new life.

Henry bought some books from the general store and taught Anna how to read. At night, they usually sat together on the couch, by the light of the oil lamps, and read. Anna loved Shakespeare, especially *Romeo and Juliet*. Henry liked *Don Quixote* and *Robinson Crusoe*. They also read frequently out of the Bible, taking turns reading verses to each other. Henry didn't talk much about his religious beliefs, but Anna believed in God and the Bible. She knew they had both committed a lot of sins in their pasts but hoped God would forgive them, especially since they were living well now.

Things slowed down as summer turned to fall. They harvested all of the vegetables from the garden and were done with it until time to plant again in the spring. Henry learned how to slaughter cattle and hogs and process the meat. They added more cattle, hogs, and chickens. They always ate well, with their homegrown vegetables and meat and Anna's blossoming cooking skills. Henry actually spilled out of his lean, pirate body and gained a few pounds around his midsection.

Henry began hunting and fishing with the extra time. Deer, turkey, squirrel, grouse, and rabbit were plentiful and a nice addition to the dinner table. The small game kept Henry's shooting skills sharp. If he wanted more sport, he would take a pistol. If he wanted meat, he would take a musket. Anna wanted to learn how to hunt too, so Henry began taking her with him. She was an uncanny shot. It took her a few tries to get used to hitting a moving target, but she soon picked it up. The river had trout in it, and the pond had catfish and bass. Henry made them both fishing poles, and they became proficient at catching fish too.

They both rode into town at least once a week for supplies and to visit. Henry would go to the River House and Anna usually to Sarah's Clothiers. Sometimes all of the couples got together at the River House for supper. Although they loved being in each other's company every day and night, it was nice to see and talk to other people too. Occasionally, some of the men, with or without their wives, would stop by the farm to visit with them. River Junction was a close-knit town, and all the residents looked out for each other.

Fall gave way to winter, with much shorter, and wetter, days. Henry found himself feeling a little strange. There was a restlessness building inside. There was a tight knot in the pit of his stomach most of the time. He didn't sleep well at night. He became bored with feeding and tending to animals. He even grew tired of hunting and fishing. They had all of the meat they could eat for a long time—salted and cured so it wouldn't spoil. Their piece of land was a good size, but he knew it as well as the back of his hand.

He still loved Anna and being with her, but lately kissing and touching her and making love wasn't the same as it had been in the beginning. Their lovemaking transitioned from every day or two to once or twice a week. It was enjoyable, but her touch and kiss slowly lost some of its effect on him. He longed for the days of tingles, chills, and racing hearts. He tried to feel it again, but no matter how hard he tried, those special feelings were gone.

"Are we going to read?" Anna asked, shortly after Henry came in from feeding the cattle. It got dark early now, earlier still that day, since it was cloudy and rainy.

Henry had taken off his wet boots and sat on the couch in front of the fire, warming his feet. He stared into the flames, his mind lost in their flickering depths.

"Henry?"

He slowly turned to see Anna standing beside him. "Oh, I'm sorry, Anna. Just daydreaming I guess."

Anna frowned and was afraid to ask what his thoughts were about. "So, are we going to read tonight?" She sat down on the couch beside him.

Henry looked at her thoughtfully for a moment, and then turned back to the flames. "I don't think so."

"Oh. Would you like to play cards?"

Henry grunted in a response that Anna took to mean no.

"Would you like to go to bed early and…umm…cuddle?" Anna placed her hand playfully on his knee.

"No," Henry said gruffly.

Anna tried her best to remain cheerful. "My, you're grumpy today."

"Can I not just sit in front of the fire and relax?" he replied curtly.

Anna stood. "Well, I believe I'll go to bed. Come join me soon." She bent over and kissed him. She received only a quick, emotionless peck in return. She walked quickly down the hall to the bedroom, tears in her eyes.

Henry got up and went into the kitchen to retrieve a bottle of rum. He didn't drink much at home, but kept a supply just in case. As the cold, dreary winter set in, he found more and more just-in-case days. He sat back down in front of the fire and drank deeply from the bottle. He drifted in and out of memories and dreams. The flickering flames morphed from lanterns on ship decks, to bonfires at the Rock, to burning ships in battle. He finally woke a couple of hours before dawn. The fire was burned out, and he headed to bed. Luckily, Anna was still asleep. He felt bad after the times that he snapped at her. He knew she was just being kind and supportive. He would try to do better.

His sleep was restless for the next few weeks. Many nights, he would wake up in the middle of the night and couldn't go back to sleep. Occasionally, he slipped out of the bed and went out on the porch. One particular night, he went outside and sat down in one of the rocking chairs. The air was cool and the sky clear. He rocked and stared at the stars in the southern sky. His mind drifted back to so many nights on the sea, sleeping underneath those same stars. He knew which stars could guide him to Nassau or Havana or Hispaniola. He wondered if there were any pirates left sailing the sea, chasing the fat galleons, or if the squadron had slain them all.

Then he thought of James. Was he still in the fleet or had he gotten out? Or was he even still alive? He hoped someday to see him riding through the gate and down to their house. Henry had only been around him a few times but loved him as only brothers can love. How great it would be for James to live close by, along with a wife that Anna could befriend.

"What are you doing?" Anna asked as she came out of the door. "It is cold out here."

"I'm sorry to have woken you, dear. I couldn't sleep. I just came out here to look at the stars."

Anna sat down in the chair beside him, a blanket wrapped around her. She reached over and grabbed Henry's hand and stared at the stars too. A shooting star streaked across the sky, disappearing over the pines. "Remember the first one we saw?"

"Indeed I do."

"And its omen came true. We did head off to a happy and great future," Anna said, trying to see her husband's face in the dim light. Henry stared straight ahead and didn't respond. "You are happy, aren't you?"

"Oh, of course. Sorry, my mind just drifted off for a minute. I am very happy." Henry squeezed her hand and smiled in the starlight.

"Your mind seems to drift a lot lately. Do you want to go back to bed?"

"Sure, let's go."

Two days later he went into town for a few supplies. Anna decided to stay home; she hadn't been feeling well lately. Henry said he would try to be back not long after dark. Neither he nor Anna worried too much about her being alone. She was skilled with a gun. While she had never shot at a person, neither of them was concerned that she could if necessary.

"Ale tonight?" John asked, as Rosa came over to the table.

"Rum," Henry said shortly.

"Rum? Wow, rough day?" John asked, nodding to Rosa to get the drinks.

"Just a rough time in general."

"Animals OK?" Ferdinand asked.

"They're still alive," said Henry, finally flashing a wry grin.

"Hmmm. I bet I know what troubles you," John said. Rosa had returned with their drinks.

Henry swirled the rum in his mug, sniffed it, and then turned it up. He drank half of it in one gulp. "And just what is that?"

"You're bored; restless. You've lived an exciting life as a sailor, traveling the world, visiting many ports, and meeting many people. Your days were never exactly the same. Now, you're cooped up on a small piece of land, doing the same thing every day."

Ferdinand, Levi, and Phillip nodded or grunted in agreement.

"I think you're wrong. I'm with the most beautiful woman in the world, whom I love with all my heart. I don't have to sleep on a foul deck with a hundred unwashed men. I don't have to worry about dying every day. I don't have to wonder where my next coin is coming from. I can work as hard or easy as I want to work, as long as my animals don't starve. I'm living the perfect life." Henry finished his rum and waved at Rosa for another.

"You must just be thirsty for rum then, huh?' John said, staring through him as he was prone to do.

"Aye. Just thirsty, I guess. And tired of rain."

"Well, let me know if you'd like to talk someday."

The men sat and talked and drank for several hours. Henry slowly began to feel a little better and more relaxed as the rum flowed. His companions began drinking to match him. It was Saturday night, and most didn't have to work the next day. They soon began to ask Henry to tell his stories of the sea and his adventures as a sailor.

This time, Henry obliged. He knew it was dangerous, but he found himself wanting to talk about the sea, to relive the memories. He started with some of the pirate tales he had heard about other pirates over the years. And John chipped in his share of stories. It seems that during his life, he had encountered a few pirates too. He was particularly knowledgeable of Jean and Pierre Lafitte. He said he knew of the Lafitte brothers from his time as a merchant in New Orleans.

A few of the other townspeople—mainly Levi, Ferdinand, and Philip—shared stories too. Henry had noticed before that he wasn't the only one in town who walked on sea legs. He didn't inquire into anyone's past though, because he didn't want to share his own. It seemed to be the way in this town. Each person just had a current role, and that was all that anyone needed to know.

Soon, Henry ran out of tales about other pirates and moved on to Bloodstone and Hawk stories—much to the delight of the listeners. Even John seemed to take a keen interest. Henry of course said that he had just heard the tales from other sailors over the years, but the details were amazing, and he was a great storyteller. Gradually, a crowd of men had pulled up chairs around their table to listen. The entire room was near silent when he told of Hawk rescuing Bloodstone and Diablo from the gallows of Port Royal, a story all had heard or read about. Then there was the famous battle with Cord and Kragg, during which Kragg betrayed Bloodstone.

"Some say the Hawk is immortal; that he can't be killed," Jacob, the burly town blacksmith said after hearing about Hawk defeating Kragg. There were some murmurs of agreement.

"Unfortunately not. Word is, Captain Wellington killed him after Hawk's escape from New Orleans," Levi replied, also receiving some support from the crowd.

"Don't think they ever found the body though, did they?" John asked, looking at Henry as he talked.

"I bet the ol' devil is still alive, plottin' and plannin' his next move," Abe said, one of the hired guns that John kept posted about town.

"What do you think, Mr. Henry," asked Bartolomeus, or Bart, as everyone knew him. The Dutchman was John's main riverboat captain. Henry had noticed that there were many nationalities represented here, which was a little unusual for a small town in Mississippi. They all seemed to know John well.

"Hard to say. He definitely had a way of surviving dire situations. But even if he survived, what's he going to do? The time of pirates is done. It's a new day men." Most grumbled in reply and were mostly silent as the story telling wound down. Henry suddenly realized that it must be close to midnight. He quickly stood, excused himself, and walked out with a slight stagger to find his wagon.

It was a long ride home on the dark paths to their house. Luckily, the moon was mostly full and gave enough light to navigate by. When he arrived at the house, he freed his horse from the wagon and let it roam for the night. He tried to walk quietly into the house and to the bedroom. A lamp was burning on the table beside the bed. As he removed his shoes and clothes and gently sat down, a voice behind him spoke.

"Do you know how worried I've been?" Anna asked.

Henry cringed, cursed himself, and slowly slid into the bed. "I'm sorry, dear. There were a lot of men there, and we started swapping stories and drinking a little too much." He finally rolled on his side to face her. Her eyes glistened in the flickering light. They were red from crying.

"Pirate stories?"

Henry swallowed hard. "Ended up with some."

"Henry!"

"I just told them they were stories I had heard. John had his share of stories about Lafitte and other pirates too. It was fine, Anna."

She was quiet and rolled over on her back to stare at the ceiling.

"What's wrong, Anna? I told you I was sorry. I've never stayed out like that before. I guess I just needed to let off a little pent-up energy."

"You miss it."

"Miss what?"

"Pirating. I know you've been restless. You haven't been yourself lately. I've seen how your mind is somewhere else most of the time. I've heard you toss and turn and get up in the night. I saw you staring at the stars the other night." Anna turned her head to look at him again. A tear rolled out of her eye and raced for the pillow.

"Anna, that part of my life is over…forever. I have been feeling a little restless lately, but I guess it's just the winter coming on and all the rain. This is new to both of us. It gets dark early now, and there are no crops to tend. I guess it's just boredom."

"So, you're bored with our new life? And with me?"

Henry sighed. He was still feeling the affects of the rum and really needed sleep. He was also tying to be patient with Anna. But he was not used to being questioned about his comings and goings. He took a deep breath and tried to remember how much he loved her. He reached out and touched her check with his hand, wiped away a tear, and then stroked her hair. "I love our life…and you, Anna."

She smiled weakly and placed her hand on his and squeezed it. He placed one arm under her head, the other around her, and pressed his body against hers. They fell asleep with the lamp still burning.

Henry tried to get his mind back into the farm and his marriage over the next couple of weeks. He tried to find chores about the farm to keep him preoccupied, even if the chores weren't really necessary. He checked all of the fencing and repaired and replaced any damaged boards and posts. He gathered more firewood from the forests and worked on making a more defined trail around their farm. There was enough land that he could usually find something to do.

At night he went back to reading with Anna or cuddling on the couch. He wasn't very interested in making love but tried to initiate it enough to keep Anna happy. He did start staying up later than Anna, though, and enjoyed a few drinks in front of the fire. He found he could sleep better with some spirits in him. Some nights he just fell asleep on the couch. Anna wasn't happy the next morning, but he tried to make up for it during the day and evening.

He went back to town two weeks after his last late night out. After trying to be the good husband and staying busy with chores, he felt a lot of pent-up frustration he needed to let out with the guys. He told Anna he would probably be a little late, but he needed some man time. She seemed OK with it.

He got to the River House just before dark. He bought a bottle of rum from George and headed upstairs to seek John. He thought he would take him up on his offer to talk. It couldn't hurt. Maybe John did know what he was going through. The door to John's office was open, and Henry found him at the table, working through a pile of papers. Henry shut the door behind him and sat down at the far end.

John looked up. He smiled as he watched Henry take a swig out of the bottle. "Another rum night, huh?"

"Aye." Henry tilted the bottle toward John.

John got up and walked around the table to sit beside him. "You might be a bad influence on me." John took a long drink and handed the bottle back. "So, are you ready to talk?"

"I guess it won't hurt."

"I was right, wasn't I? You miss the sea and your former life."

"I guess that's some of it. It's been hard with the winter here and being cooped up inside most of the time. Life on a merchantman was tough, but usually not boring. And the chores and tasks kept me busy all year." Henry took another drink and passed the bottle again.

"Well, it's only your first winter," John said, his friendly smile already making Henry feel a little better. "Those feelings will pass. Give it time. And spring will be here before you know it."

"Yeah, I'm sure you're right."

"But that's not all, is it?" John asked, staring intently at Henry.

Henry looked up at him, debating whether to say more.

"Is it Anna?"

Henry marveled at John's perceptiveness. "I don't know, John. I've loved Anna ever since I met her. All I have thought about for years is being with her. And it's been great most of the time we've been together."

"Most of the time?"

"Until recently. I don't know. It just doesn't feel the same with her. I used to get chills every time she touched me. The hairs on my arms and the back of my neck would stand up with her kisses. My stomach fluttered just seeing her naked. I was content being with her every minute of every day." Henry was surprised he was revealing so much.

"And now...you're bored," said John. "You don't feel the same with every touch and kiss. Lying together isn't quite as...exciting. Sometimes you just want to go out by yourself and not be with her every minute. Sometimes you don't even want to...lie with her."

Surprised, Henry looked at John and shook his head. "How do you know all of this?"

John laughed. "Because it happens to every man and woman."

"It's happened to you?"

"Yes. I met my Madeline some years ago. She was the most beautiful lass I'd ever seen—fair skin, dark black hair, and fierce blue eyes. I thought I had taken ill the first time we kissed, my body shook so. It felt like we had known each other forever. We could talk all day and make love all night—every night. I thought once we married, it would stay like that forever, or even get better." A slight smile of reminiscence played across John's face.

"And it didn't?"

"It did for a while. But with time, some of those feelings faded. I found myself putting more time into work. We had a child together, and the romance declined even more. We didn't talk as much, or do things together, like we did when we were courting. We got along well enough, and liked each other, but I was afraid we had fallen out of love." John took a large swig of rum.

"What happened?"

"I ran a warehouse on Galveston Island at the time and had a decent business going, trading with the Lafitte brothers. But because of

Jean Lafitte, the US Navy sacked Galveston, and my warehouse was destroyed in the process. I could have moved farther inland with Madeline and my son. Or I could have gone back to New Orleans. But I missed the sea and my days on a merchantman. I found myself wanting to captain my own merchant ship. I told Madeline that going back to the sea was my only option to make a living. I helped them move further inland, gave them a little money to get by on, and told them I'd be back to visit as often as I could.

"I bought a large sloop, gathered up a crew, and started trading about the United States and the Spanish Main. I had a successful business. But after being at sea for a good while, I started realizing what a fool I was. I could have gone with Madeline and Jean Pierre and lived a nice, full, family life. I realized back on my ship that I thought about her every free moment, just like the early days. Despite the adventure and excitement of being a captain, my heart was with her."

"So, you fell back in love with her?" Henry asked.

"No. That's my point, Henry. I never fell out of love. Love changes during a relationship. It can't always be like it is in the beginning. It will never stay that way. In fact, those feelings aren't even love. I've had prostitutes in Port Royal make my head swim, heart race, and palms sweat. That's just your physical reaction to an attractive woman and someone new. Once the newness wears off, those feelings fade. Love is much more than that. Love is finding someone you want to spend the rest of your life with and share everything with. It's finding someone who will always be there for you—a familiar, smiling face first thing every morning and last thing every night. To put it in seaman terms, it's like having your first mate, bosun, navigator, and cook all rolled into one. But a lot softer, better looking, and better smelling!"

Both men chuckled.

"It's not always going to be passionate and exciting. But you have to stick it out through the boring times and bad times to appreciate the good times." John said, passing the bottle back to Henry.

"Wow!" Henry said, and he took another swig of rum. "Why did you never go back and try to find them?"

"I guess by the time I realized my error, I figured I'd waited too long. I felt certain she had moved on and found another man. They probably both hated me by then, if my son even remembered me." He paused again. "Well, enough woman talk. Think about what I said though, Henry. If you want to go back to sea and leave Anna behind, then do it. But just make sure it's truly what you want to do. Don't end up like me."

"I've had two other men offer me the opposite advice—to choose the sea over a woman."

"And how did that turn out for them?"

"Well, one is dead, and I'm not sure about the other. But I'm guessing not too well." Henry finished the rest of the rum. He stared at the bottle for a few minutes, his mind wandering far away. Finally, he looked back up at John. "Let me ask you a question, since you seem to be so wise."

"Sure. Anything."

"What is the purpose of our lives?"

John stared at him for a few seconds, as if gauging if he was serious. Finally he laughed. "You are a deep one, my friend."

"So I've been told a time or two," Henry said, but he didn't smile.

"Well, I don't know if I have ever thought about it too hard," John said, leaning back in his chair and placing his hands behind his head. "I do think that the meaning might be different for each person though. If I had to give a broad answer, I would say that it is to give your all and try to be the best at anything you undertake. Strive to make a difference with whatever you do." He paused for a few seconds. "And enjoy the moment—the past is the past and the future may never come. Live your life so you're ready to face death when it comes looking for you."

Henry sat in thoughtful silence for a moment. Finally, he stood. "Enough deep talk for tonight. Let's go show the men how to drink rum."

They ventured downstairs after their talk and spent some time with the other men, sharing stories and drinking more rum and ale.

Henry did his best to act like his normal self for the next few weeks as winter fully set in and Christmas neared. He really wanted to spend more time in town with the men, but he knew Anna wouldn't approve.

He went about his chores with as much gusto as he could muster. He tried to think of new things he and Anna could do. They rode their horses off of their land and explored further west and south. They even did an overnight trip or two. He really wasn't feeling much different inside, but he hid it better.

"Let's go to the sea," Anna said late one night as they sat cuddling, wrapped in blankets by the fire.

The statement startled Henry. He turned to look at Anna, the light flickering on her face making it look as if it shifted and moved. "Really? Are you sure?"

"Henry, I know this move is hard on you and new to you, although I'll never truly understand it. There is no part of my old life I miss. This is enough for me. But I don't want you to be unhappy. Maybe just seeing the sea, smelling the salty air, and watching the ships, will make you feel better. Maybe we could even catch a quick ride on a merchant vessel to Biloxi or somewhere close."

Henry lay back and stared at the ceiling. His heart was racing. That idea appealed to him so strongly it scared him a little. He rolled over facing her and wrapped his arm around her. "That sounds good, but only if you truly want to do it."

"If it will make you happier, then of course I do."

Henry kissed her. Instead of the quick pecks of recent weeks, it soon became passionate. Anna moaned slightly as she kissed him back. Neither had realized how much the desire of old had faded over the past few months. The pent-up hunger and lust quickly reappeared. Their hands roamed as clothes were removed. The heat from the fire warmed their skin, only increasing the heat that their bodies generated. Soon, they were making love in the floor beside the dancing flames.

CHAPTER XXV

A TRIP

*H*enry, I don't think that is a good idea," John said, standing up from his chair and walking to look out of the window. Henry sat at the table in John's office. "I just need a ride down on one of your barges. I can take some cattle and hogs with me to sell while we're down there."

John was quiet for a moment and then turned back around to face Henry. "We both know you're already missing the sea and the life you left behind."

"And that's why seeing the sea again will help refresh me. If you miss something, you go see it, and you no longer miss it," Henry replied, a little aggravated with John.

"This isn't a dog you miss, or a woman. This is your former life. A life of adventure, freedom, glory, fame, fortune…"

"You make being a sailor on a merchant ship sound much too glamorous, my friend," Henry said, trying to hide his shock, sweaty palms, and racing heart.

John glared at Henry and shook his head. "I won't debate you now, Henry. That conversation is for another day. But heed my words. If you want to ride down the river to the coast, then so be it. Bart will set out again the day after tomorrow."

"Thank you, John." Henry stood and walked toward the door.

"But you're a fool if you go," John called out.

Two days later, Henry and Anna met Bart at the docks. The morning was cool, with a steady wind, and the air had the heavy feel of rain to it. Three barges were making the trip this morning. One was loaded with pine logs, another with bales of cotton, and the third with animals. Henry had brought six cows and six hogs into town the night before so Bart could already have them loaded with the others onto the barge. That barge had a large pen for the cattle and a smaller one for the hogs.

A dozen slaves manned the oars and poles of each barge. Once everyone was onboard—with Anna, Henry, and Bart standing on the lead barge with the cotton—the lines were untied, and the boats floated down the river. The wind was gusty and unpredictable, and the current strong, so they didn't raise the sails. The rain started soon after they left town, making it a cold and miserable trip.

They passed by the farms and houses close to River Junction and floated down along the same trail Anna and Henry had rode up so many months before. The boats moved swiftly with the combination of oars and current. They didn't stop at any of the small towns they passed. Once the merchandise was sold in Pascagoula, they would buy the supplies they knew each town needed and peddle them on the way back. John was definitely an astute businessman.

"You two go; enjoy your trip," Bart said after the barges were tied off at the docks in Pascagoula the next morning.

"I need to go sell my animals," Henry said.

"Nonsense. I have these other animals to sell anyway. I'll take care of it. Just meet me here at the same time in four days—if you're ready to go back by then that is."

"I owe you," Henry said, and he shook the man's hand. He and Anna departed the barge.

The rain had stopped, and the sky was finally breaking up. It was still cool and damp though. They walked off of the dock and around the side until they found the white sand beach. The sun had now peaked above the clouds in the eastern sky, and the air began to warm. Henry inhaled the thick, salty air deeply. They just stood and stared out over the water until it merged with the gray clouds on the horizon. He could barely make out the topsails of what appeared to be a three-masted ship in the distance, heading east with the wind.

Anna watched Henry, but didn't speak. She didn't want to know what he was thinking as he watched the distant ship sailing. She just hoped this trip would be enough. She knew that his seeing the sea again could be a mistake, that it might only fuel his discontent, but it was a chance worth taking. If she did nothing, and pretended nothing was wrong, the desire within him would continue to build, until one day he would just leave her. All she could do was support him and hope she was enough.

They removed their shoes and walked along the beach holding hands. "Bet you cannot catch me," Anna said, pushing Henry, and then taking off running into the edge of the water. Henry laughed and ran after her. Anna zigzagged across the beach and through the surf, sending water spraying high around her.

She was quick, but Henry moved like a big cat. He soon caught her and scooped her up in his arms. "Bet I can," he said, and he kissed her salty lips. They spent most of the day walking, looking for seashells and sharks teeth, and frolicking on the beach and in the water. Their clothes were soaked, and it was a little cold despite the sun, but it was a good day for both.

"I take it you've never spent much time on a beach," Henry said, as Anna showed him yet another oyster shell.

"Never!" she replied, laughing and running off to find another.

He smiled as he watched her run about. Sometimes he forgot how young they both were. They both had lived rough lives and were forced to be adults many years too soon. He loved to watch the youthful, playful, energetic Anna. He tried to be as carefree, but he caught himself frequently glancing toward the horizon. When he'd see a ship, he'd size it up. He could tell how many knots per hour it was traveling, if it was loaded or not, its likely armaments, and the size of its crew. He never knew one could be in two places at once, but that's where he found himself now.

They finally made their way back to town after watching the beautiful sunset from the dock. The sunset really brought back a flood of memories. Back in the pirate life, a sunset meant the start of the evening, when the work and fighting were done, and the men could gamble, sing, and talk on the deck beneath the stars. Henry remembered all the nights he spent on the deck with Wesley, talking about life, pirating, and death. And he could almost smell Bloodstone's pipe smoke wafting across the deck behind him like a long tail.

They made their way back to the inn by dark and found a table. There was a decent crowd on hand. Henry and Anna were both pleased to know they served seafood. Soon they were drinking ale and enjoying a meal of fish, clams, scallops, and crab. The room continued to fill up as they ate. A group of obvious sailors made their way in, talking loudly and laughing, and sat at the table behind them. Henry tried his best to talk and listen to Anna, but he found himself also trying to listen to the sailors.

He quickly picked up that they had loaded a load of cotton and soybeans today on a schooner and were heading to New Orleans in the morning. Henry's heart skipped a few beats at the news. Seeing the ocean was great, but to go back to New Orleans would be even better. There he could hear news of pirates and the squadron and maybe even James. The sailors were swapping tales, but he heard nothing of interest or note.

"Henry! You're not even listening to me," Anna scolded.

"I'm sorry, Anna. I guess I'm just a little tired from chasing you around all day," Henry smiled.

Anna leaned over to look past Henry's head. She saw the sailors behind him. "I know what you were doing," she said softly.

Henry leaned forward, so no one else could hear. "Anna, they're going to New Orleans in the morning. Let's go with them!"

Anna stared at Henry coldly and then looked down at her plate. It was a moment before she spoke. "I'm not going back to New Orleans. I have no fond memories of that...that place."

"I understand. But Anna, it would really help me to go there, just for the day. I can catch a ride back the following morning. I just want to hear news of the affairs of the world and maybe find out about James. I would dearly love to see my brother again."

Anna wanted to protest with everything she had. But again she found herself in a no-win situation. If she forbade him, he might resent it and start thinking even more about going after they returned home. If he went, he could end up not returning. But hopefully he could hear what he needed to hear. And it would be good if by chance he could find out what James was doing. "Go."

"Are you sure? I don't have to go."

"You need to go. I'll wait here. I can shop some tomorrow and maybe go down to the beach again."

"I love you so much, Anna! It will be a good trip…for both of us. I promise."

Anna wrinkled her brow. "And you'll be sure to disguise yourself? You haven't been gone that long."

"But of course. I'm just a humble farmer from Mississippi." Henry grinned.

Henry stood on the bow of the schooner with the wind blowing sea spray in his face. The wind was blowing strong from the south, sending waves crashing against the port side of the ship. The boat was still making decent speed, and the trip wasn't long. It was hard for him to be aboard a ship and not either be giving orders or helping with the sails or the helm. It did feel good to be back on the open sea again though. He had hoped it wouldn't. He had hoped he wouldn't feel anything at all. But his heart was racing, palms sweating, and his mind was clear and sharp as he gripped the rail and scanned the horizon.

There were a couple of periods of rain, but Henry's thick wool coat was warm enough. And he had been through much worse while wearing much less. He finally left the bow and paced around the entire deck a few times, checking the sails and rigging, and inspecting the helm. It was a two-masted vessel and designed as a merchant ship. There were only two dozen sailors aboard and very few weapons. There were six cannons, but Henry would wager there was no powder or shot anywhere close by. His first thought was how easy it would be to take a ship like that. His second was how quickly he could convert it for pirating.

He forced his mind to think of other things. He wondered what Anna was doing back in town. He thought about his farm and animals and hoped that Ferdinand would remember to send someone to feed and water them. It would be spring before he knew it and time to plant again. He planned on expanding his crops and growing more corn for the animals. And he wanted to start a hay field. He was also thinking about building a boat for him and Anna to travel up and down the river alone.

Henry sighed. Somehow it was hard to get excited about the farm when he was on the sea aboard a ship. He went and spoke to the captain, an old salty sailor that had spent most of his life on the boat. "Any pirates around these days?"

The captain manned the wheel, now that they approached the mouth of the Mississippi. He didn't trust anyone on his crew to navigate the river up to the city. He took a break from shouting orders to his men to take some wind out the sails to answer Henry. "Nah, not to speak of. Ol' Cofresi was killed earlier this year. He be 'bout the last. I s'ppose there's always a few here and there, but not enough to worry over. The squadron is all over the water now. Good time for halfway honest merchants." He chuckled and then began shouting orders again.

A couple of hours later, they were moored at a dock in New Orleans. The sun had just set behind the city, and the lamplighters were out doing their jobs as Henry entered the square. Not much had changed since he had last been here, except maybe more people, horses, and wagons. He instantly thought back to the pardon of his crew and his "escape." It seemed like that was years ago. He walked around the square, enjoying the sounds and smells. He remembered his first visit there, when Bones guided him through. And then, of course, there was his meeting of Anna shortly after.

He wandered into one of the gaming houses. It was similar to the common room in the inn, only there was no food. There were servers serving alcohol and lots of gaming tables. The room was only about half full at this early hour though. There were many different types of games: dice games like Hazard and Le Bete; card games such as One-and-Thirty; and the board games noddy and backgammon. Henry never had been much of a gambler, but he was familiar with all the games. Many pirates had lost their fortunes on games of chance.

He purchased a tankard of ale from the bar and made his way through the room. If there were pirates left in town, this would a good place to find them. He went from table to table, eavesdropping and starting a conversation or two. There were off duty navy sailors, marines, merchant sailors, and a number of townspeople—but no pirates. Even in the days when pirates dressed nice and took on different names, they weren't that hard to spot, at least to other pirates.

He left after an hour or two and then made his way to the Treasure Cove. He was a little nervous going back there, but in his heavy coat, large floppy hat, and drab farm clothes, he wouldn't be easy to recognize. He had also let his beard grow out since the end of summer. It was dirty blond and made him look much older than Hawk when he was "killed."

The Treasure Cove looked about the same. However, it was a little brighter and looked to have a new coat of paint on the walls and maybe a few newer tables and chairs. There was a bigger crowd here, and three quarters of the tables were full. Henry chose a small table in between some larger round tables that were full of seamen. It looked like naval officers behind him and merchant seamen in front. He scanned the room for Madame Cynthia but didn't see her. A young serving girl came by shortly after he sat down.

"Where is Madame Cynthia?" he asked.

"She left a few months ago—said she was heading west. Madame Rebecca is in charge now. Would you like to speak to her?"

"No thanks, ma'am. How about some hot food and a tankard of ale?"

Henry drank a couple of tankards of ale and ate a hot meal of roast pork, potatoes, and soft bread as he eavesdropped on the table closest to him. The merchant sailors soon began swapping stories of their sea adventures. Henry heard Lafitte's name mentioned a time or two. He was still a legend in New Orleans. Against his better judgment, he switched from ale to rum. He continued listening until he heard a story or two about Bloodstone and then, inevitably, Hawk.

"Mind if I join you," Henry said, sliding his chair over. With the ale, and now rum, he was feeling pretty good. "I might know a story or two."

"About what? Cotton?" one of the men asked, referring to his clothing. The other seven men laughed loudly.

Henry suppressed the anger that instantly coursed though him. He could break the speaker's neck before he even knew he had been attacked. "I heard you mention Bloodstone and the Hawk. I used to sail with a man that had been on account with them for years."

The men suddenly stopped laughing and studied the stranger a little closer.

Henry began weaving his stories, but started off with some of the early battles and deeds of Bloodstone and his crew that most had never heard. Bloodstone normally didn't leave survivors, so only pirates that had served with him knew the tales. Soon, other people were listening to him speak, and a circle of men two and three deep surrounded the table.

The rum kept flowing and his judgment diminished. He didn't pay any attention to one side of the circle parting and allowing some of the naval officers to move in. He got to the infamous stories of Port Royal, Kragg, and then Hawk's final escape, much to the delight of the patrons.

"You think he's still alive?" one of the sailors asked.

"No," a voice behind Henry said before he could respond.

Henry, as well as the crowd gathered around, turned to look at the speaker. He was in full naval uniform and dressed like a captain or other high-ranking officer.

"Captain James Wellington killed him like the cowardly dog he was. I heard it told that he got down on his knees and begged and pleaded for his life before James put a ball in his chest." The officer smirked. His companions, who looked like they might be naval officers too, laughed.

Henry studied the man with his somewhat impaired vision. He looked familiar, but he couldn't place him. He was young, pale, and had a neatly trimmed red mustache and patch of beard. Red hair showed around the edges of his tricorne.

"Is that true, sir?" another man at the table asked Henry.

Henry turned back to face the man who'd asked the question. "From what I've heard of the Hawk, he would never beg or grovel to anyone for anything." He turned back to the redheaded officer. "And unless it was James himself that told the story, I would have to say it is a lie."

The captain pursed his lips in thinly veiled anger. "Either way, the Hawk is at the bottom of the ocean, as are all of the pirate scum. Now, why don't you men tell stories of current things, and real heroes like James Wellington and the members of the West Indies Squadron? Don't waste your breath trying to glorify dead cowards. Although, I do wish there were some left to hang. I do miss them soiling themselves as they flop about on the end of a noose." There was more laughter from the officers.

Henry clenched his fists under the table. He could gut the arrogant captain from belly to neck and be out of the door before his body hit the ground. But he bit his tongue. He had already brought too much attention to himself tonight. He turned back to the table and started asking about local affairs. The officer and his companions seemed satisfied and returned to their table.

Henry eventually asked the men what happened to Captain Wellington. The men said he was still the captain of the *Avenger* and was hunting down the few remaining pirates. He was based out of Pensacola, where Commodore Cord was now headquartered. He was as famous for the squadron as Hawk had been for the pirates.

Finally, around midnight, Henry finished his tankard of rum and stood. He bid his companions good night and turned to walk toward the stairs. The navy officer called out to him before he'd cleared their table. "Ho, farmer, come here for a moment."

Henry gritted his teeth. This man was pushing the limits of his restraint. He slowly turned and faced the table of officers. "Yes," he replied, glaring at the cocky redhead.

"You seem to know a lot about Bloodstone and Hawk. Did you sail with them?"

"No."

"Then how did you come by those stories and in such vivid detail? They didn't leave many survivors to tell tales."

Henry sighed. He was much too drunk and tired for this. "I worked on a merchant ship years ago. One of the crew had served with both of them. I don't recall his name."

The man stared at Henry, studying his face and actions. "And what do you do now?"

"A cattle and hog farmer. Came to town to make some merchant contacts." This night was close to turning out very bad for someone.

"A farmer, eh? And where is your farm?"

Henry knew he should have lied, but he was tired and having trouble standing steady in one spot. "Mississippi. And if that is all, I must go to bed. I'm returning there early in the morning." The officer waved his hand, dismissing him. Henry turned and quickly crossed the room and disappeared up the stairs.

"What was that about, Captain Smith?" an officer beside the speaker asked. He was even younger and more innocent looking than the captain.

"The man is lying. Those stories weren't secondhand," Captain Smith replied, finishing his ale.

"You think he's one of Hawk's pardoned crew?"

Captain Smith stroked his chin thoughtfully. "I don't know. I'm going to find out though. Pack for a trip tonight, Owen. Wear civilian clothes. I've got a mission for you. You can prove if you are worthy of being a first mate."

"Yes, sir!" Owen replied eagerly.

Henry paid for a couple of biscuits and some salted ham on the way out of the Treasure Cove the next morning and headed to the docks. He was relieved to see that the schooner he'd sailed in on was still there. The captain and crew were readying the vessel for sailing. They had loaded clothing, food, and supplies to deliver along the coast until they emptied out in Florida. Henry found the captain and paid for the return voyage.

As he ate his ham biscuits and watched the crew prepare the ship, he noticed another man speaking with the captain. The man carried a large sack over his shoulder and wasn't dressed as a sailor. Henry shrugged and turned away to walk to the stern of the ship to study the river. The day was dawning mild and with a clear sky. There was a decent breeze blowing from the west, which would make it a quick and easy voyage back to Pascagoula. After the ship was untied and the sails unfurled, it moved out into the current of the river, picked up speed, and headed toward the sea. Henry made his way to the bow and watched the water, lost in his thoughts.

"Hello, sir," a voice said from behind him.

Henry cringed and slowly turned his head to the side. The young man that had boarded last walked up to stand beside him. The lad was much too happy for this time of morning. Henry's head wasn't feeling too clear from the night before either. He nodded his head and turned back forward.

"Say, were you in the Treasure Cove last night telling stories?"

He had his attention now. Henry turned back to study the boy's face a little closer. He wore a long gray coat and a hat similar to some worn by businessmen in New Orleans. His face was vaguely familiar, but Henry's memories of last night were a little fuzzy. "I was there."

"I was in the back of the crowd listening. Those were some good tales, sir!"

"Just stories," Henry replied.

"Were you ever a pirate?" the boy asked, his enthusiasm grating hard on Henry's nerves.

"No. Just a seaman and now a farmer."

"Oh, sure sounds like you could have been right there with the Hawk. Ever meet him?"

"No."

"You think he's dead?" the boy persisted.

"Yes. What's your name, lad?" Henry asked, tired of being asked questions.

"Owen, sir. Owen Davis."

"And why are you on this ship, asking me questions?"

"I heard this ship was going to Pascagoula. I have relatives near there. I've been thinking about the farming business. So, you say you're a farmer?"

"Yes."

"What do you farm, if you don't mind me asking?"

"Does it matter if I mind? Cattle, hogs, chickens." Henry replied bluntly.

"Oh, I was thinking about maybe cotton or soybeans. I hear there is money in that. What do you think?" Owen asked, his smile ever present.

"I say do whatever you want to do."

"Hmmm. Whereabouts is your farm located?"

Henry leaned over the rail and rubbed at his temples. The boy seemed innocent enough, but he still had to be careful. He remembered his exchange with the navy officer last night. "North of Pascagoula."

"Oh, where?"

"That, my friend, is none of your concern. Good luck to you." Henry walked away and found the nearest hatch to climb below deck. He hoped Owen would take a hint and not follow him.

The rest of the voyage was fairly uneventful. Henry managed to disappear on the ship as often as he could. Other than a few quick exchanges, he avoided Owen. The return trip felt much different to Henry. The water and salty air didn't feel the same. The searching for sails and daydreaming of the past were gone. He had known since before Bloodstone died that the times were changing. But he had never truly let go. There was always a glimmer of hope. Now, the glimmer had gone dark. Now, he knew that he had let go. His night at New Orleans made him realize that it was truly a different world now—a world of authority and businessmen and pasty-faced, wide-eyed naval officers. The world was civilized now.

But it was more than just that. Something within him had changed. He was truly at peace with leaving his old life behind. Sure, he would still have his memories, but they would be just that. He had lived more in twenty-two years than most would in lifetimes. He had risen to the pinnacle of pirate life and achieved all he ever wanted to achieve. There was nothing left for him to do or prove as a pirate. He had fulfilled Jack's idea of the purpose of a man's life. The legend of the Hawk would live long after he was dead and buried.

His mind turned to his beautiful wife. He imagined touching her, smelling her perfumed skin, and kissing her soft, full lips. He actually found himself missing the nights by the fireplace, talking and reading. He missed their hunting and riding and doing chores together. He couldn't wait for spring. The past year he had gone through the motions of farming. Now, he was ready to embrace it. He thought more about what John had said about his meaning of life. He had been the best pirate. Now, he was ready to be the best farmer, best husband, and best father. And he would enjoy all three roles.

The ship made a quick stop in Biloxi to unload some goods to a waiting merchant and his men and then sailed the rest of the way to Pascagoula, arriving just after sunset. Henry made his way quickly to the inn and to the room. Anna welcomed him with open arms. "You came back!" she exclaimed, hugging him tightly, as well as working in some kisses.

"You doubted me?"

"I'm sorry. A woman's mind can create all kinds of bad thoughts. I just kept seeing you finding your old crew, stealing a ship, and setting sail again."

"Hmmm. I hadn't thought of that." Henry smiled.

Anna struck him hard on the arm. "So, did you find what you needed to find?"

"Let's sit down," Henry said, walking to the bed and sitting. Anna joined him, but tentatively. He told her about his trip, leaving out a few details of the conversation with the officer.

"So, how do you feel now?"

Henry rubbed Anna's back through her dress, causing her to sigh in approval. "Anna, I won't lie to you. I have thought for a while, that if piracy was still going strong, back like when I was first taken by Bloodstone, I might be tempted to return to my old life. But on this trip,

I realized that my love for you would outweigh that desire and any others. This trip just reinforced that the past is in the past. I'm at peace with living in the present and looking forward to the future. I just want to spend the rest of my life with you—farming, doing chores, and raising a bunch of children."

"Oh, Henry, I love you so much!" As Anna kissed Henry, her warm tears spread to his cheeks. "That is all I've wanted!"

"Anna, I love you more than anything in the world. I'm sorry that I even wavered for a moment. I'm totally content now. It won't happen again. I have enough memories and stories to last a lifetime. And now I get to spend that lifetime with the beautiful young woman I love."

After they made love, Anna drifted off to sleep, but Henry lay awake—his arms wrapped around her warm, soft, naked body. He truly felt at peace. He had finished the last chapter of his old life and was content with the new one. Sure, there would be boring days, and their love couldn't always be the wild love affair it had been in the beginning, but their bond would only strengthen. And soon, they would hopefully start a family and have children to raise and love. He'd still entertain John and his men every so often with his stories and tales, but at the end of night, he'd go home to his loving family. And that would be good enough.

They ate a quick breakfast in the morning and left the inn to find Bart at the dock. He was finishing securing the crates and barrels of goods on the barges. There were only two this time. Bart welcomed them aboard with a hearty handshake for Henry and a hug for Anna. Within a few minutes, the lines were untied and the slaves began rowing them away from the dock. "To River Junction!" Bart's voice boomed loudly.

In the predawn darkness, no one had noticed the cloaked Owen Davis, milling about close to the docks, watching the scene intently. "River Junction," he whispered softly.

CHAPTER XXVI

BACK TO THE FARM

⤣

Anna noticed a big change in Henry on the trip back up the river and over the next couple of days. He was as happy and carefree as when they first bought the land and built their farm. He had more energy, and his mind was there, in the present. The days were still cool and rainy, but they enjoyed themselves. Three days later, Henry told her he was going to town to buy supplies. He also wanted to talk to John and tell him about his trip. This time, Anna wasn't worried, even if Henry drank too much and came back late. He was hers now.

Henry finished buying the supplies by dark, secured the wagon, and then entered the River House. Most of the regulars were there, and they all greeted him warmly. He truly felt missed. It might have helped that he bought the entire house a round of drinks. After a while, the musicians straggled in and the music started. Henry, John, Ferdinand, Levi, Bart, and Jacob all sat around a table, drinking some of John's fine brandy. They talked and laughed over light subjects and watched the dancers on the floor.

Henry didn't say too much about his trip to New Orleans. He gave John a look that indicated they would speak later. He shared a few stories of the old days, but this time they were just stories. They did seem almost like tales he had heard, not adventures he had lived. Soon, the crowd gathered around the table once more.

There were always a few travelers and strangers passing through town, and most stopped by the River House for food and drink or a room for the night. A new face or two didn't draw any attention, unless the person drew attention to himself—especially when the music was playing, drinks flowing, and people dancing and carrying on. So it was not unusual that no one noticed the young man dressed in the long black coat with a big wide-brimmed hat pulled down low on his brow. He drank alone at a corner table behind the table drawing all the attention. Several people stood between him and the storyteller.

By midnight, most of the crowd had thinned out. John finally got up and rounded up the rest to either go to their rooms or their homes. The young man drinking alone was the last one to go up the stairs. Henry and John were soon the only two left in the common room.

"All right, Henry, talk."

John walked about the room, gathering up the bottles, mugs, tankards, and dishes and carrying them to the kitchen behind the counter. Henry followed and helped. He told John of the trip to Pascagoula and then to New Orleans.

"Hmmm. So you're done with the sea, huh?" John asked when Henry had finished and the two men stood on each side of the bar, close to the stairs.

"Aye, that I am."

"And you're sure?"

"Yes. I've left the life of pir...merchanting behind me. I'm finally at peace. I'm ready to be a married landlubber. And I'll enjoy every minute of it." He hoped somehow John hadn't caught his slip.

"You didn't start to say pirating, did you?" John asked, and he laughed.

"Blast it!" Henry cursed. The rum had gotten the best of him.

"I know who you are," John replied, matter-of-factly.

"For how long?" Henry asked, shaking his head, still upset with himself.

"Pretty much the entire time. Then your storytelling a few weeks ago erased any doubt." He reached over and clapped Henry on the shoulder. "Don't worry, friend. The Hawk is dead. However, I would like to hear the end of your story, leading up to your death."

Henry looked around the room to make sure no one was lurking. He was hesitant, but John already knew now. It would be the only time he'd tell this story. He told John of James Wellington being his brother, their plot, and the final voyage.

John shook his head and laughed. "You do indeed have a sharp mind. Fine plan."

"Now, tell me how you died," Henry said.

"What are you talking about? Is that the rum?"

"Now, Jean. I've told you."

John Lafleur, or Jean Lafitte as he used to be known, shook his head and grinned. "You dog. How long have you known?"

"About as long as you've known about me. Now, I thought you died off the coast of Honduras?"

"Very close. I attacked what I thought were two merchant ships on a dark, rainy night. Turns out they were Spanish warships. They tore us up pretty good. They ended up sinking my ship and killing most of my men. I was shot twice. A dozen of my mates and I managed to slip overboard into a longboat and rowed till we hit land. We traveled north overland for a while, away from the Spanish forts.

We finally caught passage on a US merchant ship in another town. We told them we had been aboard a merchant ship attacked by the Spanish. They were more than willing to help us out. We ended up going to New Orleans, and we quickly found another ship to give us passage. I knew I couldn't show my face there for long. It just so happened that merchantman ended up going to Pascagoula. I figured that was as good of a time as any to retire. My boys and I traveled up the river, trying to put some distance between us and the sea, and found a little town called River Junction. I had managed to escape with a sizeable stash of coin and decided to grow the town. And, here I am."

"Let me guess. Ferdinand, Levi, Philip, Abe, and Bart were all pirates with you?"

John laughed. "Privateers. They and a few others. We got the word out to some of my former crews on our trading trips to New Orleans and slowly brought more men back. I don't want it to get too big though—no use drawing too much attention to us. There are about two dozen of us here now."

"So, have you ever missed the trade?" Henry asked after a pause to digest the information.

"Pretty bad my first year, like you. But this isn't a bad deal. It's not as glamorous as Baratavia or Galveston, but not bad. I can still trade and bargain and make a little money. And I'm still in charge of men. Like you, though, I know there is no going back. A privateer, or pirate, wouldn't last more than a month or two out there now. Plus the fact that the ships loaded with booty are gone. The Spanish have pretty much milked the New World dry. I can make more money on trade from this little town than a pirate crew could in a year. And I won't be shot or hanged."

"Aye. I agree with that. Well, I better be getting home."

"And, Henry, what say we never speak of this again?"

"Speak of what, John?" Both men laughed, and Henry left.

Owen Davis, who was crouching at the top of the stairs, quickly and quietly slipped off to his room before John, or Jean, came up the stairs heading to his third floor quarters. As he closed the door to his room, he was still shaking with excitement. He couldn't believe what he had heard. He had thought at best that Henry was a pardoned pirate. But he was the Hawk! And James Wellington, the hero of the squadron, was a traitor. Not to mention that Jean Lafitte, possibly even more notorious than the Hawk, was there and alive. Forget being first mate. He would be captain after this, and someday commodore. He would be the true hero of the West Indies Squadron.

Spring came early to Mississippi. The weather soon warmed and the days grew longer. Henry made his garden twice as big as the year before and added some new crops. He also seeded another field for hay.

He bought more pastureland from John on the far side of the pond and added more cattle. He and Anna were happy and content and completely settled into their new life.

They both came to accept the new reality of the physical nature of their relationship. Those special feelings of the early days were gone, never to come back. The frequency of their passion decreased, but to a level both could live with. They appreciated each other's kisses and touches and made sure to try their best to keep each other happy. They were content just being together.

Anna also made a suggestion. She told him that since he had so many great stories and everyone loved hearing them, he should write a book about his life as a pirate. Henry loved the idea, and at night he began writing down the details of his exciting life. He would talk out loud, telling Anna the stories, as he wrote. Within a few months, he had a stack of paper an inch thick, with all of his stories in writing. He named it *The Last Pirate*. Anna told him he should try to get it published someday, when they were sure that pirates, and Hawk, had faded into legend and myth, and no one would come looking for the author.

"Henry, we need to talk," Anna said one day in April after she had arrived back from a trip into town. Henry had finally relented that spring and let her occasionally ride into town alone to spend time with the other women—as long as she had a flintlock with her. She hadn't been feeling well for a while and was frequently sick to her stomach in the mornings. She was going to stop by and see Joseph Barton, the town doctor, while she was there.

"Is everything OK?" Henry said, quickly jumping up from the rocking chair.

"I don't know," she said, looking a little pale.

"What do you mean? Did the doctor find out what is wrong with you?" Henry walked over and placed his hands on her arms.

"Yes." Anna's face was unreadable.

"Anna, please tell me what is going on! Are you OK?"

"It depends."

"On what?" Henry was growing irritated at Anna's behavior.

"If you want to be a father or not."

"A father? What?" Henry stared at Anna, not comprehending until she finally smiled.

"I'm with child, Henry. You're going to be a father!"

Henry's mouth fell open, and he scooped her up high in the air and spun her in a circle on the porch. "I can't believe it!"

"Henry, you might want to be a little more gentle," Anna said, still smiling.

"Oh, I'm sorry! Did I hurt you? Did I hurt the baby?" Henry quickly set her back down on her feet and cautiously touched her stomach.

"No, silly. We're fine. I just didn't want you to get too carried away."

Henry hugged her, being careful not to squeeze her stomach too tight, and kissed her. "This is the most wonderful news ever!"

"I am so glad that you're happy. We're having a child!" Anna looked at Henry, and for the first time ever, saw tears in his eyes.

Henry quickly wiped the tears away. "When? When will it be here?"

"In the winter. Around eight months, he thought."

"Do you need to go lie down and rest?" Henry asked. He was still shaking with excitement.

"For eight months?" Anna laughed. "I'm fine. I can do anything I want to do, at least for most of that time."

"I love you...and our baby!" Henry kissed her again.

It was a month later when Henry looked up from working in the garden to see a man on a horse enter the gate in front of the pines and ride slowly down the hill toward him. He dropped the hoe and placed one hand on the handle of his flintlock and the other on his dagger. He looked quickly to the house to make sure Anna was inside. He occasionally had visitors from town, but this didn't look like anyone he knew.

"Hello, Henry. I'm Owen, in case you don't remember," the man said as he dismounted from the horse in front of him.

Henry recognized the young face of the man that had sailed from New Orleans with him. "What are you doing here? How did you find me?" Henry's face instantly reddened with anger. He involuntarily clinched his fists.

"I mean you no offense, sir. I have news for you."

"What news could you possibly have for me?"

"It's about your brother."

Henry grabbed Owen by his waistcoat with both hands and pulled him close. "I have no brother! And you'd better be riding back from wherever you came."

The blood drained from Owen's face. He swallowed hard. But he continued. "Your brother James is going to be hanged in Jackson Square at dawn two weeks from today. He has been charged with aiding a pirate and treason against the United States."

Henry could barely control his rage. He shoved Owen's chest, sending him sprawling on the ground. He rushed forward and stood over Owen before he had even come to a rest. He bent down, grabbed his waistcoat, and jerked him back to his feet. His dagger was instantly in his hand and an inch from Owen's throat. "Tell me everything, starting from when we landed in Pascagoula!"

Anna had noticed the stranger dismounting to speak to Henry. She walked out on the porch and watched the exchange. She covered her mouth with her hand after she watched Henry shove the man down and then pick him back up again. She didn't know who the stranger was, but something bad was taking place, or about to.

Owen's legs shook as he looked from the point of the dagger to Henry's enraged face. Any doubt of whom Henry used to be vanished. "I bought a horse and followed the river north out of town. I visited my family, who live in a town a few hours north of there. They mentioned a town called River Junction and said it was a good area for farming. So, I came up here a couple of days later."

"Explain the rest!" Henry said impatiently. He touched the point of the blade to Owen's skin.

Owen tried to lean his head back to take some of the pressure off of the sharp dagger point. "I was in the River House having dinner one night. You were there, telling your stories again. I went upstairs to my room when John closed the place up. A little bit later, I started to come back downstairs so I could go out and take a walk, as I was not sleepy.

Halfway down the stairs, I happened to overhear you and John talking. I went back to my room, but not before I heard who you both were."

"Hang me!" Henry shouted, using the phrase that Bloodstone had used so often over the years. "And you went and told the navy!" Henry pulled the dagger back and leveled it at Owen's heart.

"No! No, sir!" Owen shouted back, fearing for his life. When Henry relaxed his arm a little, Owen continued. "After spending a few days here, I made my way back to New Orleans. I still wasn't sure about moving here or the farming. A couple of weeks ago, I was in the Treasure Cove and overheard Captain Smith and his officers talking about James, the Hawk, and Lafitte. I don't know how they found out. I'm guessing if I overheard you, maybe someone else did too. I came back here as soon as possible to warn you."

Henry stared intently at the trembling man before him. Owen's face was covered with a layer of sweat. "You seem to overhear a lot."

"A bad habit, I guess, sir."

"So, you swear to me you had nothing to do with this, and you're not setting me up for a trap?"

"No, sir! You and John seem like nice men that have left your wicked ways behind. I just wanted to let you know. Maybe you can figure out a way to save your brother, like you did Bloodstone at Port Royal."

Henry ignored Owen's attempt at flattery. "Where is James now?"

"I assume they're keeping him in the brig at Pensacola until time to sail to New Orleans. I heard that Commodore Cord would personally be sailing with him and overseeing his hanging." Owen was visibly more relaxed now.

"If you're being honest, I thank you for the warning. If you are lying to me, and had something to do with this, I will personally put a bullet into your skull. Now, please leave my land."

Owen climbed back onto his horse and rode back up the hill and back through the gate. He couldn't restrain the slightest of grins.

Anna walked up to Henry after the man disappeared.

"Did you hear any of that?" Henry asked.

"Yes," she said softly, and she hugged him. "What are you going to do?"

"I don't know," Henry said. His mind was racing. He was almost sure it was a trap. He was also sure that James would die, either way. He had finally found happiness and accepted his new life with the woman he loved. And they had a child on the way.

"You know it's a trap. They'll kill both of you." Tears were flowing down her cheeks.

"It probably is, and that coward Owen probably betrayed me. But it doesn't mean we both have to die."

"The entire navy wants you both dead! You cannot just walk in and rescue James."

"My whole life has been spent figuring ways out of impossible situations. If I do nothing, James will die, and they will come for me. They know where I am, Anna." Henry turned away and cursed under his breath.

"Then we just need to leave now! We can go somewhere else and start over. We have money. They cannot search this entire country. Owen said it was two weeks before they would hang him."

Henry thought deeply as he watched the cattle move lazily about the lower pasture. "James saved my life. He is the reason we are even here. If he hadn't agreed to help us, he wouldn't be facing death. How can I just run off and let him die for saving me?"

Anna cried openly now and covered her face with her hands. "He knew the risks!" she sobbed. "So, you'll get yourself killed, leave me widowed and your child fatherless, for nothing?"

"If I go, it won't be to go to my death. I won't try to save James unless I think we can both survive. I need to go talk to Je...John. I'll be back in a few hours." He quickly kissed her wet cheek and strode to the barn to get Tempest.

John sat at the end of the big table with a couple of stacks of papers in front of him. He saw the look on Henry's face and decided to skip the small talk. "Have a seat. Tell me about it."

Henry quickly told him of his encounter with Owen. John shook his head silently when Henry was finished. "Not a good situation."

"No. I'm not sure if even the Hawk can get out of this one."

"You're not thinking about trying to rescue him are you? You know that's what they want you to do."

"It might be a trap, but I have no doubt they will kill James either way and then come after me. After *us*."

John rubbed his fingers through his thick hair. "Blast! I hadn't thought about that. They could sail a couple of sloops up the river and blast this town to pieces."

"And they will. Unless we do something about it," Henry said.

"And just what could we do?"

"Rescue James. Kill Commodore Cord, Captain Smith, Owen, and anyone else in our way. That will disrupt the squadron for a while. In the meantime, we find another place to settle. They won't find us again."

"Look, I know you have pulled off some daring deeds. But not against the full force of the squadron when they're expecting it," John said bluntly.

Henry stood up and began pacing about his end of the room. A large hand-drawn map of the southern United States and Spanish Main was on the wall beside the table. He walked over to it and studied it thoughtfully. "But what are they expecting?"

"What do you mean?" John stood up and walked over to join Henry.

"Are they expecting me to show up in New Orleans or attack them in route?" Henry pointed to the map. "They're in Pensacola now. They'll probably allow time for a three-day voyage. The quickest route is to pass right along in front of this chain of islands and our old hideout, the Rock. I know every inch of those islands and the surrounding water. I'm betting they're not expecting me to have a crew or ship. They'll think I'll just try a daring rescue similar to the one in Port Royal."

John studied the map. "There would be several good places to hit them, especially with you knowing those islands. But how would you get a ship and crew in two weeks?"

"I'd have to get to New Orleans quickly and see if I could find any of my old crew. I would also like to ask if I could recruit you and your men. We could either buy or steal a ship or two."

John shook his head. "I'm afraid me and my men are too old for that. And my men all have families now. Although I'm sure you'll have a great plan, I just don't know if you can round up enough men to take down whatever they're sailing to New Orleans. Chances are, they'll have more than one ship, and fully manned. I'll talk to the men, but I wouldn't count on our help."

"I'm sorry to hear that. But I have no choice. I couldn't live knowing that I sent my brother to the gallows for giving me my freedom. Can you do two things for me?"

"Anything."

"Look after Anna and my child if I don't come back. And I'll need Bart to get me down to Pascagoula."

"Of course, friend. I wish I could be there with you," John said with sincerity.

"Me too. Me too."

"But I might be able to help you in other ways. Get your thoughts and plan together and come back to see me." He shook Henry's hand heartily and clapped him on the back as he left.

Henry's mind raced on the way back to the farm. If he took a ship, he couldn't do it too soon. If word reached Pensacola, the game was over. He also had to make sure he didn't run into Owen. He felt sure he would be heading back to New Orleans too, if not Pensacola. He'd have to wait until he thought the commodore and James had left Pensacola heading toward New Orleans. Then he'd have to quickly gather his crew, take a ship, and be waiting when they sailed past the islands. He was actually thinking that the cove at the Rock would be a good place to hide a ship. The biggest question now was if he could gather a crew at all.

Anna was in bed but not asleep when he reached the house. She sat up as soon as he entered the room. "Tell me you've decided not to go." Her eyes and nose were red from crying.

"Anna, I have to." Henry took off his clothes and climbed into bed. After he thought about the timing, he wasn't in as much of a rush to leave.

"Then take me with you."

"That's absurd!"

"I can shoot a gun nearly as well as you," she protested.

"First, you are pregnant. Second, shooting is only part of it. I will have to get onto James's ship and rescue him. There will be a lot of hand-to-hand fighting. And a petite, pregnant female is not cut out for swordplay." He tried not to talk down to her.

"Then I'll stay on your ship while you get James. I can handle the helm too, if you recall. Or put me in the crow's nest."

"Anna, I cannot take you. If something were to happen to me, you and our child have your entire lives in front of you. All of us dying would be pointless. They do not want you. You can live anywhere you want. It is just me, James, and Lafitte they want."

Anna was quiet for a moment. She had expected him to say no. "Is Jean going with you at least?"

"It doesn't sound like it."

"Henry, look at me," she said, grabbing his chin and gently turning his head to face her. "Do you think you can save James and yourself too? Or are you planning on dying?"

Henry stared into her beautiful eyes for several moments. Tears were welling up in the corners again, and her lips were quivering trying to fight back crying. "I wouldn't go if I didn't think we had a chance."

"And you'll try to come back to me?"

"If there is any life left in me, I will always come back to you."

CHAPTER XXVII

RETURN OF THE HAWK

❦

*H*awk arrived at New Orleans just after dark three days before James was to be hanged. He and Jean, and many of
Jean's old crew, had worked closely together over the past week and a
half, getting the first part of the plan setup. He was on a midsized, two-
masted sloop. Jean had Bart, Levi, and Ferdinand purchase it in New
Orleans five days prior. It was designed as a small merchantman, with
only ten cannons. That was good though, since no one would suspect
it to be used by a pirate, and it wouldn't be a threat to any of the US
warships.

The sloop slid silently into the dock. Nearby was a large West Indies
Squadron schooner. The second part of the plan had fallen into place.
Hawk grinned as he saw the name of the ship by the torchlight on the
docks: USS *Grampus*. It was the same ship that had nearly foiled his plan
to meet James at St. Thomas. It had also been involved with the defeat
and capture of the last famous pirate captain, Cofresi.

Bart, Levi, and Ferdinand had spent a couple of days in town before
purchasing the sloop and had learned that the *Grampus* spent a lot of
time around New Orleans and was captained by Thomas Smith. Smith
was the same captain who'd questioned Hawk that night at the Treasure
Cove. Hawk had finally remembered Thomas Smith as being James's

first mate in St. Thomas. If he were a betting man, he would say Owen Davis was one of Thomas's officers.

All of the men on the sloop departed and scattered in different directions. There looked to be a number of sailors aboard the *Grampus*, and voices and laughter could be heard from the deck, but no one paid attention to the sloop. Bart and his men were going to kill some time in one of the gaming houses and spend the night in town. The next day, they would return to Pascagoula aboard a barge they had previously left at the docks. Hawk headed to an alehouse he had never been to before. He didn't dare visit the Treasure Cove. He took his time getting to his destination and took many extra streets and alleys. He stopped frequently to make sure he wasn't being followed. After an hour or so, he finally entered The Thirsty Pelican.

The tavern was a little distant from Jackson Square and, as a result, wasn't very crowded. Hawk quickly surmised that the patrons were mostly local regulars. No one paid him much attention as he headed to a small round table in the far, dim corner. His chair was close to a man sitting at the table beside him. The man had a wide-brimmed hat pulled low. But Hawk could see the white hair sticking out from around the sides.

He waited a few minutes until the serving lady had brought him a pint of ale, and checked on the man at the other table, before he spoke. "Hello, old friend," he said softly. Both men's eyes were busy watching the rest of the patrons.

"A sight for sore eyes, you are, for sure," Jack replied.

Another mission Bart and Jean's men had completed was to find Jack. Luckily, he had stayed in the city after the pardon. They gave him a letter from Hawk that told him to round up as many men as he could and have them ready to sail on this night. It also set the time and place for this meeting.

"And the crew?" Hawk knew they didn't have time for pleasantries.

"Got Jimmy, Billy, Charles, Edward, and about seventy-five men. Mort was killed a few months ago breaking up a fight. Bones says he's retired for good."

Hawk silently cursed. He had hoped for at least a hundred. "Gonna be tough."

"Always is."

"Where are they?"

"Scattered about the taverns and gamin' houses. I've got half a dozen runners stationed about. As soon as we're ready, I'll start 'em spreadin' the word. Can you share your plan?" Jack asked, grinning.

"The first part of it. If it doesn't go well, we won't have to worry about the second and third parts."

"I ain't goin' to lie; I'm a little bit excited!" Jack said, a little too loud.

Hawk gave him a scowl, then a wink, and told him the first part of the plan.

It was close to midnight when the first man walked down the dock and boarded Hawk's sloop. The docks were still fairly busy this time of night, since many of the sailors came back from the gambling houses, taverns, and brothels to sleep on their ships. Most couldn't afford a room for the night. Every few minutes, another person boarded the sloop.

The *Grampus* also had its fair share of returning, mostly drunk, sailors. Owen Davis, freshly promoted to lieutenant, was one of these men—although he was cold sober. He walked with a slow, deliberate walk, his chest puffed out. He wore his new promotion well and wanted to make sure everyone knew he was an officer of the squadron. Captain Smith had asked him to keep an eye on the crew and ship, while he and several others stayed at the Treasure Cove. The *Grampus* had been docked at New Orleans with a full crew for the past week, just in case the Hawk showed up early for James's execution. Owen surveyed the dock area for several minutes before boarding the ship. He looked with disdain at the mostly drunken crew, scattered about the deck, talking, sleeping, or passed out. Hopefully, they wouldn't be needed for action this night. He did have several sober soldiers though, who had been forbidden to go into town, keeping watch on the docks. He went below deck to his cabin to get some sleep.

An unusual number of sailors continued to approach the docks, even after a dozen or so had boarded the sloop. The sentries on the *Grampus* took note of the activity, but there was really nothing to report. Most of the men were spread about the docks in small groups, and some milled around the various ships, likely just talking a bit before they boarded for sleep. It was a little unusual, but not against any laws.

An hour later, had it not been so dark, and they had paid more attention, the sentries would have noticed that a wall of armed men had formed in front of the entrance to the docks. They did notice the small groups starting to converge into one large group in front of their ship. The sentry on the bow leaned over the rail. "You men need to disperse!"

A man stepped out of the crowd and looked up at the sentry. "I need to speak to your captain."

"He is not onboard. You may speak to him in the light of day," the sentry replied. He now had his musket resting on the rail, although not pointing at the speaker yet.

"Then get me whoever is in charge—now."

The sentry wavered for a moment, not sure of the best course of action. He finally called out to one of the few conscious sailors and told him to fetch Owen.

Owen quickly left his cabin, scurried up the ladder to the main deck, and strode purposefully across the deck to the bow. "What is the meaning of this?" he demanded.

"Well, well. Mr. Owen Davis," Hawk said. He slid his hand down to the handle of his half-cocked flintlock.

"I am Lieutenant Owen Davis of the USS *Grampus* of the West Indies Squadron. Who are you?" Owen called down, straining to discern the speaker's face. Several other sailors now stood around Owen and the sentry.

Hawk gave a signal with the hand behind his back to the men gathered behind him. "Impressive, Mr. Davis. I'm afraid your career is coming to a tragic end though."

Owen pulled out a flintlock and leveled it at the speaker. "Who are you? And what is your purpose here?" he demanded, shaking slightly.

"I told you a while back that if you had lied to me, or betrayed me, I would put a bullet in your head. Owen, unlike you, I'm a man of my word." Hawk's movement was a blur. In less than a half-second, his flintlock was drawn, cocked, and fired. A split second later, a hole appeared in Owen's forehead. Before his body had hit the ground, the men behind Hawk opened fire with their muskets on the sentry and other visible sailors.

The sailors sitting and laying scattered about the deck of the *Grampus* suddenly came to life, staggered to their feet, and rushed to find weapons. Two loud explosions then rocked the ship, sending many back down to the deck. The sloop beside them had fired two cannons into the hull of their ship, right below the waterline. Before the sailors had recovered, the throng on the dock, led by Owen's killer, charged up the gangplank and onto the deck. Cutlasses flashed as they set about attacking the stunned sailors.

As most of Hawk's men slaughtered the *Grampus's* crew, others set about locking down the hatches that led to the lower decks. Hawk figured at least one hundred sailors were down below. Now they would stay down below, with the hold quickly filling with water. As the battle wound down on the *Grampus*, shots erupted from the dock. Hawk looked over the rail to see the pirates that were blocking the docks firing upon a group rushing toward them. Hawk knew it had to be Captain Smith and his men.

After discharging their muskets and then flintlocks, the pirates fell back onto the docks and headed to the sloop and the *Grampus*. They had killed a number of Captain Smith's men, but the survivors kept coming. Captain Smith and a half dozen of his officers stopped on the dock, some twenty yards from the ships, to reload their flintlocks. "You will finally hang, Hawk, and right beside your cowardly brother! Then I'll deal with your wife and Lafitte!" Captain Smith shouted.

Hawk grabbed a musket from the closest pirate. "Unfortunately, you won't be there to see it. Oh, and say hello to Bloodstone and Kragg for me." There was a flash of fire from the end of the musket barrel. A second later, the ball struck Captain Smith in the chest, just as he had opened his mouth in retort. He fell backward into the men behind him. Before the men could react, two cannons erupted from the starboard side of the sloop, striking the dock right at their feet. The explosions tore through the group, sending them, and their body parts, flying in every direction.

The *Grampus* sailed out first. The sloop followed, but not before firing the remaining three port cannons at the navy sloop that was docked on other side of the *Grampus*. All three shots hit, close to the waterline. A few muskets fired from that ship and from the officers on the dock, but the balls flew harmlessly overhead or struck the water.

Hawk strode over to the first hatch. The men below could be heard shouting and running about. He called down to them. "I'll crack the hatch open, and you will pass all of your weapons through it. Then you will start pumping water and patching holes. If not, we will come down and kill everyone one of you."

"And if we do what you say?" a voice called up.

"Well, if you don't, you will drown anyway. But I'll set you free on the first island we come to and make sure you are picked up soon after. I am the Hawk, and you have my word."

There was whispering and muffled talking down below for a moment. "OK. Open the hatch," said a sailor. The hatch was opened and the weapons were tossed into a pile on the deck.

"What are you goin' to do with them?" Jack asked, as Hawk walked about inspecting the ship and speaking to his old crewmembers.

"Just as I said."

"Set them free? So they can go back to tryin' to kill us?"

"They'll be unarmed. And our fight will be over one way or the other before they're picked up. Remember, Jack, this is a one-time voyage. We're not back in the pirating business."

"Aye, Cap'n." Jack walked away, not hiding his disapproval.

"Good to see you again, Hawk," Billy said, as he and Jimmy came rushing over.

"Same here. You boys been keeping out of trouble?"

"Reasonably so, sir. So, what's the plan?"

"We'll discuss that a little later. First, we need to get to the open sea and make sure this bucket isn't going to sink."

After Hawk felt both ships were under control, he grabbed Billy and half a dozen men and opened one of the hatches. They all had their flintlocks in hand. Some fifty sailors were milling about the gun deck. They all stared at Hawk and the pirates, but none made a move to attack. Hawk and his men climbed through another hatch down to the next deck. Another fifty men were crowded onto this deck. A large group was taking turns manning two pumps, switching off so they stayed fresh. The rest were working frantically repairing the two cannon ball holes in the side. The water was still several inches deep on the deck, and Hawk was sure much deeper in the hold below. The holes were almost patched now, with a mixture of sail canvas, pitch, and boards.

A man dressed like an officer walked up to Hawk. "You are not going back on your word are you?" he asked, his face pale and stressed.

"Of course not. Just making sure you were living up to yours. I am Hawk."

"First mate, Andrew Robinson."

"How's the hold?"

"Better. Most of the water was kept out of the magazine, which I assume is what you're asking."

"Good," Hawk nodded. Despite him being a naval officer, he liked Andrew.

"Sir, may I ask you something?" Andrew said, shifting his feet nervously.

"Go ahead."

"Why did you do this?"

"What do you mean?" Hawk asked.

"Why did you come back to pirating? Why did you steal this ship?"

"To save my brother, of course."

"Your brother?"

"James Wellington," Hawk was getting a little aggravated now. "He is to hang three days from now in New Orleans for helping me escape."

Andrew wrinkled his brows together. "I have heard nothing of this. If Lieutenant Davis knew, he never shared with his crew.

"You weren't stationed there in preparation for the hanging?"

"I don't think so, sir. We were told that the Hawk might be alive and might be heading back to New Orleans. That's all."

"What's that mean?" Billy asked Hawk.

"With snakes like Davis and Smith, it's hard to say. Something is amiss though. Did Owen say anything else about me or James?" Hawk asked Andrew.

"Not that I heard, sir. Just that Hawk wasn't dead and was trying to gather up a crew and ship."

"I appreciate your honesty, Andrew. I'll let you know when we've reached a suitable island." Hawk turned and led his men back to the upper deck. Hawk's mind was desperately trying to figure out what he was missing with the squadron's plan.

Once he was back on the main deck, Hawk quickly sought out Edward at the helm. "Make sail to the Chandeleur Islands. Find one we can get close to so we can drop our friends off." The Chandeleur's were a small chain of islands directly east of New Orleans and on the way to the Rock. Hawk left the navigator to find Jack.

"Grab Jimmy and Billy and meet me in the captain's cabin," said Hawk. "Let's discuss strategy while we have a little time."

A few hours later, the *Grampus* began to slow. Hawk, Jack, Jimmy, and Billy wrapped up their meeting and made their way back to the main deck. The sky glowed in the predawn light, and the sun was soon to rise in front of them. They all noticed the sails being lowered to half-mast as the ship approached a small island. The island was mostly sand with a patch of palm trees and some scrub in the middle. A few minutes later, Jack gave the word to drop the anchor. The ship was as close to the shore as it could get without the risk of getting stuck in the sand. A longboat was quickly lowered to the water, with rope ladders thrown over the rail above it.

Hawk went to one of the hatches and flung it open. "We're here. You may all come up."

The sailors began to climb up the ladder and move toward the starboard rail. The pirates had moved back to open up the middle of the main deck. Soon close to a hundred sailors stood crowded on the deck. First mate Andrew moved through the throng to stand before Hawk.

"I appreciate you saving us from sinking," said Hawk. "I have no issue with any of you. I only took this ship so I can save my brother from hanging. You're free to stay on this island. A number of ships pass by here each day. Build a fire on the beach, and you'll be rescued before dark."

The sailors all stood in place. Most looked toward their first mate, who was in charge since they had no captain or lieutenant. Andrew finally cleared his throat and spoke. "Captain Hawk, my men and I talked below deck. I told them about your situation. We all know and respect Captain Wellington. Most of us have served with him at one time or another. If he is to be hanged, we are not in agreement with it."

"I thank you. But we need to let you off so we can get to sailing. Time is not a luxury we have right now."

"But you misunderstand me. A number of us have decided we want to sail with you. There is definitely some kind of treachery in the works, and Lieutenant Davis and Captain Smith were a part of it. They have misled and used us without our knowledge and agreement. That is something we cannot tolerate. We'd rather sail with you and try to save James than to have to return to Commodore Cord. I don't know about all of your past deeds, but this campaign is a just one."

Hawk turned from Andrew to look at Jack and then Billy. Both men shrugged. Hawk turned back to Andrew. It could all be part of Captain Smith's plan. But Hawk had survived well on his ability to read people. He trusted Andrew. "Any that want to stay are welcome to stay. Just know that this mission is treacherous and many of us won't survive. The ones that do might face the gallows or be forced to disappear forever."

Andrew turned to his crew. "Anyone that wants to leave, leave now." There was a murmur and shuffling amid the ranks. A line slowly formed of sailors that climbed over the rail and down the rope ladders to the boat below. When it was full, the boat was rowed to shore. All got out except the rowers, and they returned to the ship. After several trips, about half the crewmembers were left on the *Grampus* and half were on the island. Hawk grinned. An extra fifty men might just be the break he needed.

The two ships sailed uneventfully to the Rock. The trees that used to block and hide the harbor were long gone. Hawk didn't bother to go up to the old fort. He had heard squadron shore parties had sacked it more than once. The *Grampus* sailed halfway into the harbor and the sloop a little farther in. Both anchored, and pirates and sailors began setting about the many tasks that had to be done—both on the ships and on the shore. It would be sometime that night or the next day when the Squadron ships passed.

After having the name of the USS *Grampus* painted over and *Anna* painted in its place, Hawk, Billy, Jack, and Andrew walked from the beach onto the arm of land that protected the lagoon from the sea. It was slow going, with small gnarled trees and heavy vegetation, but there were a few old trails that Bloodstone's crew, including Hawk, used to use. Behind them, three dozen pirates struggled to move the two large thirty-two pounder cannon barrels, their bases, shot, and powder. Ropes were tied to the barrels and half a dozen men pulled each one. The bases were on wheels, so one man each could push those. The remainder of the men carried the balls, bags of powder, fuses, rammers, sponger swabbing rods, buckets of water, and linstocks. The strip of land was narrow and peaked into a high ridge that ran the entire length, protecting the cove from both sight and storms. An old, overgrown trail followed the ridge. That's where the pirates used to keep lookout for Bloodstone to return from voyages.

"The biggest flaw in my plan is what I don't know," Hawk said to the group as they worked to widen the trail with their cutlasses. "I don't know if they'll be in one ship or two or three. I know they'll pass on this side of the island, but I don't know how far out they'll be. I don't know if they'll sail through today or tonight."

"I assume you got guesses for each?" Jack asked, panting from the exertion.

"Of course. I think they'll be in two ships, just in case the Hawk attacks. Three is doubtful. They know I won't have had enough time to gather a large crew, so I'll either have a medium size ship or two small ones. I think they'll hug these islands fairly close. They may even want to

encourage an attack. Cord is a cocky devil. And I think they'll pass during the day. Night would be too much of an advantage for an attacker."

"How often are your guesses correct?" Andrew asked.

"Have you heard of the Hawk before?" Billy asked, bringing laughter from the pirates.

Two hours later, the two cannons were set in their mounts on top
of the ridge. Shooting lanes were cut, and they were sighted in at about
five hundred yards. The thirty-two pounders had a longer range than
most ships cannons. A crew of four men stayed with each. Lookouts
were stationed at one-hundred-yard intervals, all the way to the eastern
most point of the island. When ships were sighted, each man would yell
to the next, until word had spread all the way to the cannons. The wind
was from the west, so the ships would be moving slowly, tacking into
the wind. The pirates would have time to get back to the *Anna* before it
left the harbor.

CHAPTER XXVIII

FINAL BATTLE

Captain James Wellington stood on the bow of the frigate USS *Congress*. Beside him stood his old captain, the man who had raised him, Commodore Nathaniel Cord. James's mind had been reeling since they had left Pensacola. The commodore hadn't said much to him. He had been getting ready to set sail on his ship, the USS *Avenger*, when the commodore boarded and entered his office. He told him that spies had got wind that Hawk was alive and gathering together a crew. He said that they had to sail right away toward New Orleans, in anticipation that Hawk would steal a ship somewhere between there and Mississippi— Mississippi was where he was rumored to have been hiding out.

The commodore had acted strange to him ever since. He didn't accuse him of letting Hawk go. He just said Hawk must have survived. He also made James ride on his flagship, the *Congress*, explaining that Hawk might come after the *Avenger*, seeking revenge on James. The *Avenger* sailed a few hundred yards behind them. Each ship had a full crew of over three hundred men. Cord said that Captain Smith was on the *Grampus*, watching the docks at New Orleans in case Hawk showed up there. Hopefully, they would catch the pirate somewhere in between.

It wasn't hard for James to act surprised when he heard the news. He was in shock. He couldn't believe Hawk would go back on his word, leave the woman he loved, and go back to pirating. He refused to believe it. Yet something had to be going on for the commodore to have organized the mission. James had risked his career and life to free his brother. If his brother had gone back to pirating, he would have to personally stop him. More innocent men were not going to die because of his mistake and his brother's treachery.

Cord and James shared a spyglass and studied the beginning of the barrier islands off the coast of Mississippi. The first one was just coming into sight on the horizon. It was midday, on a clear, sunny beautiful day. They were tacking into the wind, so their speed was slow and steady. On one of the barrier islands some years ago, they had found an old fort that had most likely been used by Bloodstone and Hawk—the infamous Rock. They had destroyed it, but Cord thought Hawk might come back to that area while he mobilized a new crew.

"Don't you think we're going to be sailing a little close?" James asked, taking the spyglass from Cord.

"If he is there, I want him to attack. Per my sources, he has only had two weeks to try to get together a crew and a ship. He will be no match for two fully armed and manned frigates. If he does not attack, we will sail on to New Orleans."

"A lot of people have died because of underestimating Hawk."

"I am not underestimating him. But bravery and cunning can only carry him so far. He will feel the full brunt of the United States Navy. If not today, soon. And this time, he *will* die," Cord said firmly, and then he turned and walked away.

James spotted the sails in the spyglass about the same time that the lookout in the crow's nest shouted, "sail ho." He saw the main topsail, followed by the slightly shorter fore topsail. There were only two masts on what he could now discern was a sloop. The ship sailed in their direction with the wind in its sails. It was farther south of them though.

Cord quickly rejoined him on the bow. James handed him the spyglass, and Cord studied the approaching ship keenly. "What do you make of it?" he asked James.

"Looks like a merchant sloop, maybe ten guns, small crew visible. Not likely to be Hawk."

Cord quickly scanned the horizon and the islands to the starboard. "Not likely to be Hawk, but could be part of one of his infamous traps." Both of the squadron ships had fifty cannons and full crews. A sloop like the one they were coming upon wouldn't last but a few minutes in a cannon duel. But against the Hawk, they had to be prepared for anything. "Mr. Johnson, have everyone look alive and put the gun crews on standby. Get word to Captain Scott on the *Avenger*."

First mate Isaac Johnson, a middle-aged, burly sailor turned and went about shouting orders to the men on the main deck and to the topman in the crow's nest, and then he disappeared through a hatch. The topman turned to face the ship behind them and gave a series of hand gestures to his counterpart on the *Avenger*. James and Cord continued to watch the quickly approaching sloop. "Should we hail it?" James asked.

Cord was silent for a few seconds. "No. That would just further play into a trap, if indeed this is part of trap. Let's let it make the first move."

The sloop was soon passing by them. Several sailors on its deck waved to the passing naval ship. Once the sloop had cleared their ship, James and Cord finally turned back around, dismissing it as not a threat. They didn't see it ever so lightly alter its course and start sailing at more of an angle toward the *Avenger*.

James and Cord moved to the starboard side of the deck and studied the island they were coming along side. It was the island they thought had been the famous Rock. There was no movement coming from it. Cord was a little surprised. If Hawk were going to make a move before New Orleans, it would probably be here. The island had a protected harbor that was hard to spot from the sea.

Just when the stern of the *Congress* cleared the Rock, and they began scanning farther ahead, they heard a cannon fire. They quickly turned back to the island and saw smoke coming from the bushes on a ridge in front of the harbor. Screams and yells erupted in the distance on the *Avenger*. A few seconds later, they saw a flash of fire and heard a second cannon erupt. Smoke billowed from the *Avenger*.

Captain Daniel Scott had been at the port rail, watching the sloop angle toward them and wondering whether to fire a shot across their bow, when he felt the impact and heard the splintering of wood, screams, and the roar of a cannon. It had come from the starboard side though. He quickly sprinted across the deck to see the smoke drifting from the trees and bushes on the island they were just coming upon. The shot had hit somewhere below the main deck. Before he could even issue an order, he saw the flash of fire, and then felt another impact low in the hull, followed by the boom. "Return fire!" he yelled, which was quickly relayed below deck.

About the time the cannon fuses were lit below on the gun deck, all five cannons on the port side of sloop fired. One ball tore through the mainsail and broke the main boom in half. An explosion set the sail on fire. Another shot hit on the bow, exploding and sending splinters and chunks of wood scattering into nearby sailors. A third shot exploded on the stern, sending bodies flying. One of those seriously injured was the navigator. A fourth shot sailed harmlessly over the deck. The fifth struck a gunport, blowing a hole in the hull and incapacitating a gun crew.

The starboard cannons of the *Avenger* fired, but the rocking of the ship from the four cannon strikes made them wildly inaccurate. They were also shooting at drifting smoke and not hard targets. The balls hit different parts of the finger of land, some throwing up dirt and sand and other crashing through the trees. There was really no way to know if they hit their attackers, unless the cannons didn't fire again. Captain Scott turned to order the port cannons to fire on the sloop, but with the wind and ship's speed, it was already past. They had some good gunners to have hit them traveling at that speed.

A moment later, he had his answer. The first cannon on the island fired again, once more striking right at the waterline, below the gun deck. A few seconds later, the second one fired, striking toward the bow of the gun deck. The balls didn't explode, but were large and heavy and did damage.

"They're club hauling!" Scott's first mate, Alexander Nelson, yelled. He now manned the helm for the injured navigator.

The captain rushed back to the stern to see the sloop drop an anchor and come about hard to port. The sloop turned 180 degrees, until its starboard cannons faced the back quarter of his ship. He knew none of his cannons could hit it unless he turned the entire ship. He ordered all available hands to fire at the sloop with their muskets, a mostly ineffective strategy with only a handful of sailors on the main deck of the fast-moving sloop. The five sloop cannons roared, raining more explosive and ball and chain shots onto his ship. One shot missed and landed harmlessly in the sea. Two exploded on the main deck, causing more injury and death. One tore through the main mast rigging, further debilitating the vessel. The last shot was the most serious—apparently striking the rudder. Alexander confirmed it a moment later. "Blast it, I can hardly steer!"

"Come about!" Cord yelled, sprinting from the bow of the *Congress* to the helm. "Come about hard!" By this time they were well past the Rock and the battle behind. The *Avenger* had apparently suffered damage to her sails too, only increasing the distance.

James followed quickly after him. They didn't know exactly what was happening on the *Avenger*, but they knew they were being attacked from the shore and apparently from the sloop. It took several minutes for the large ship to turn all the way around and start heading back toward the battle.

As the big ship turned, James and Cord rushed back to the stern so they would know what they were sailing into. "Hang me!" Cord shouted. James quickly spotted the cause of his curse. A large schooner had emerged from the harbor, apparently just after they had passed, and was now turned leeward, quickly approaching the *Avenger*. The *Avenger* had reloaded and just fired again at the cannons on the shore. Reloading again would take a minute or more, and they didn't have that much time before the new foe reached them. The schooner changed direction slightly, sailing directly toward the bow of the larger frigate. The sails were still mostly full, and it moved swiftly.

Captain Scott was quickly overwhelmed. He normally sailed a much smaller ship, and he had limited combat experience. His few encounters had been against single foes that he clearly outgunned. The commodore had asked him to captain the *Avenger* only a few days before. The plan had been for both ships to attack Hawk, who would most likely be on a much smaller ship. Now he was being attacked on two fronts. The sloop was small, and there were apparently only two cannons on shore, but he was paralyzed. He couldn't steer the ship now, so he couldn't turn to get his cannons aimed at the sloop. And even if he could, he then wouldn't be able to fire back at the shore.

"Captain, enemy schooner, coming hard to bow!" Alexander shouted.

Captain Scott's problems just got worse. He rushed across the body-littered deck to the bow. He stared in shock at the ship that approached. It looked like one of the squadron's own schooners. His ship was hardly moving into the wind, with the loss of the rudder and so many sails. The schooner, on the other hand, was fully rigged and with the wind. It was coming at an angle so that Scott couldn't hit it with any of the cannons. He finally shouted orders to ready the starboard cannons and prepare for a broadside against the schooner. At least with the schooner beside them, the cannons on shore wouldn't be a threat.

Hawk stood aboard the bow of the *Anna*, a musket in hand. All of his men were either on the running rigging lines or lining the starboard rail, except for Edward, who was at the helm. Hawk could have sailed right beside the big frigate and fired a point blank broadside. It might have even sunk the ship. But that wasn't the plan. He needed the larger ship to face the *Congress*.

"Fire!" Hawk called as soon as the ship was in range. All of the pirates and the newly joined navy sailors fired muskets into the sailors rushing to the bow of the *Avenger*. The musket balls tore through the scrambling sailors, most balls finding targets. A few of the remaining sailors returned fire, but only one pirate was wounded in the arm. "Drop anchor and strike the sails!" yelled Hawk.

A number of pirates rushed to drop the anchor off the stern of the ship. Others furled the sails, greatly slowing the speed of the schooner. Edward steered directly into the frigate, the two bows scraping together until the *Anna* ground to a halt against the *Avenger*. Hawk shouted one last command. "Granadoes and grapple!" He lit and tossed his own granado onto the deck of the frigate. It was joined by a couple of dozen more from his crew. Explosions and screams rang out across the deck of the *Avenger*.

There were no sailors available to stop the grappling hooks from catching the railing. The pirates on the deck pulled the smaller ship against the frigate and tied the lines off. Pirates were already swinging and dropping onto the deck of the *Avenger* as others scampered up the grappling lines and climbed over the railing. The sailors tried to rush forward to stop the attack, but the pirates opened fire with their flintlocks and then charged with their cutlasses.

No one was left on the stern of the ship to see the two dozen pirates, led by Billy, climb from the sloop over the stern rail of the *Avenger*. The sloop had raised anchor, caught the floundering ship, and threw their grappling lines over the rail and boarded. The pirates spread out and sought out the hatches. Each of them tossed a stinkpot onto the gun deck below, shut the hatches, and quickly chained them shut. They then fired their flintlocks into the sailors that were trying to hold off Hawk and the other pirates.

"Take some wind out!" Cord shouted onboard the *Congress*. He had just watched in horror from the bow as the schooner sailed into the *Avenger* and the pirates boarded. He knew that Captain Scott was greatly overmatched. However, he had to plot his own plan of action. The pirates had killed a fair share of sailors, but there were probably still two hundred alive on the ship. If he opened fire with his cannons, the already damaged ship could sink, killing all aboard. Plus, he couldn't be sure Hawk didn't have any other tricks up his sleeve. As they got closer, he recognized Hawk's schooner. It was the *Grampus*. That probably meant that Captain Smith and Lieutenant Davis were dead, as well as their crew.

"I hate that pirate!" said Cord.

"What's your plan?" James asked, watching in disbelief as Hawk and his men attacked the *Avenger*.

"I think we sail to the port side of the *Avenger* and pick off as many pirates as we can with muskets. If we see the pirates are taking the ship or its cannons, we sink it."

"Sink it even with sailors still alive?" James asked in surprise.

"If need be. Hawk will not win or escape today."

Hawk fought like a man possessed. As he feared, James and Cord were on the other ship. He knew they had to take the *Avenger* as quickly as possible. His hope was to get as many of the crew as possible to surrender. That would keep Cord from sinking the ship. He would have to come aboard, try to kill the pirates, and retake it. That's where the plan became murky. The pirates would be greatly outnumbered, and Hawk had no idea where James would be or how to get to him. He thought he might try the same move he did in the first battle with Cord, climbing in through the cannon port. But he was fairly certain Cord would be ready for it. All he could do now was fight and hope that fate, or God, would give him some assistance.

"Commodore, we cannot fire upon our own ship while there are still over a hundred sailors alive onboard," James said as the *Congress* neared the bow of the other frigate. "Word of that would spread straight to the president. I say we fire a few volleys and then board the *Avenger*. We have three hundred men, plus whoever is left over there. It looks like Hawk barely has one hundred."

Cord swore under his breath. He would just as soon sink the *Avenger* if it would guarantee that the Hawk would die. Then he could deal with his brother. But James did have a point. There would be too many witnesses for the word not to get out. He could end up on the gallows himself.

Then another idea came to him. "Very well. Bring all hands to the main deck except for two dozen. They'll stay below in case anyone tries to climb in through a gunport. And James, I have a special task for you."

The orders were given for the *Congress* to sail broadside to the *Avenger*, close enough to grapple and pull the two ships together when the time was right. Sailors began streaming up through the hatches. Soon, the deck was packed by most of the three hundred men, musket's ready. Cord and James watched the battle rage on the other ship for several minutes. The pirates were outnumbered, but they were skilled and vicious fighters. The full naval crew wasn't on the main deck however. Something must be keeping the men below deck. They also noticed the sloop moored against the stern of the *Avenger*, apparently now empty.

"There's the coward!" Cord cried out, pointing to the blond-haired pirate currently engaged with Captain Scott. He and James stood against the port rail, surrounded by their armed crew. Hawk's blade was a silver blur as it rained down upon the severely overmatched captain. "Give me your musket," Cord demanded of the closest sailor.

James stared at Cord in surprise. Cord had never been much of a hands-on commander, preferring to stay back and direct the action. Then Cord handed the musket to him.

"When Scott falls, kill Hawk. That's an easy shot for you. Hit him in his cold, black heart. You can redeem yourself for letting him escape last time."

James took the musket. He stared at it, then at Hawk, then at Scott. It would be an easy shot, especially if he rested the barrel on the rail. He had sworn to himself that he would kill Hawk if he ever returned to pirating. But although Hawk had apparently returned, and would send a lot of innocent men to their death's today, he couldn't bring himself to shoot him. First, Hawk had no chance to defend himself. He deserved better than to be shot unaware from a distance. Second, he still wondered if there was more to the reason Hawk had returned. He wanted a chance to talk to his brother face-to-face and hear what he had to say before he issued a death sentence.

"What's the matter, James? You tried to kill him once before, correct?"

"Yes…sir. It's just…I don't like the idea of just shooting him from a distance. Let me board and face him man-to-man."

"You've tried hand-to-hand before. Obviously, that didn't work. Let me put it to you a different way. Shoot and kill your brother, or you will hang for treason for aiding his escape the last time and now for refusing a direct order. And Hawk will still die by one of these other sailor's bullets."

James realized that Cord did suspect he let Hawk go. He also surmised that this was probably part of Cord's plan all along—to make him kill his brother. If he didn't shoot him, he had no doubt he would die, as well as Hawk. Reluctantly, he placed the barrel of the musket on the rail and cocked the hammer. He leaned down behind it and placed the bead on the front of the barrel onto the back of Scott. Scott's body was blocking all but Hawk's head. But Hawk was wearing Scott down, and it was only a matter of time before he fell. Then Hawk would be an unobstructed target.

James's heart pounded as he watched Hawk leap back to dodge a desperate swing from Scott. As Scott's sword swung harmlessly past, Hawk stepped forward, jabbing his blade forward. The tip of the blade appeared through the back of Scott's blue jacket momentarily. The captain looked down at the blade, and then the tip disappeared as Hawk withdrew it. The captain dropped to his knees, and then slowly toppled forward. Hawk stood over him for a second, bloody sword in hand, presenting a dream shot for any marksman.

"God be with us both," James whispered. He slowly exhaled as he squeezed the trigger. The shot hit Hawk high in his left breast, knocking him backward a step. He looked up and his eyes instantly found James's eyes, even among all of the sailor's surrounding him. Hawk's face was one of total shock. But something made James think it was shock for more than just being shot. James mouthed a final word to his brother and then watched him collapse onto the deck.

"Now, was that so hard?" Cord took the smoking musket back from a shaken James. "Men, take this traitor and lash him tightly to the main mast," Cord ordered to the sailors close by. He turned back to James. "We'll talk later."

James couldn't move or even speak as his cutlass and flintlock were quickly removed, and the rough hands of four nearby sailors half dragged him to the main mast. They quickly wrapped a thick rope around him and the mast, from his neck to his waist, and tied it so tightly that he couldn't move his upper body at all. He could only helplessly watch the battle unfold.

Jack and Jimmy grabbed Hawk's body, dragged him back through their ranks, and laid him against the rail. They had no time to see if he was still alive. Blood soaked the left side of his shirt from his shoulder to stomach. They quickly went back to fighting the sailors. Ordinarily, a pirate crew could be demoralized by the loss of their captain, especially one like the Hawk. But these pirates and sailors knew that defeat would mean their deaths, either by sword or noose. There would be no quarter given.

Soon, the three ships—*Anna, Avenger,* and *Congress*—plus the sloop, were all lashed together. The sailors on the *Avenger* were losing the battle with the desperate pirates. It hurt that so many of their companions were still trapped below deck. Their captain had been killed, and they would probably have surrendered if not for the *Congress* and its fresh soldiers streaming onboard. Very quickly, the deck was packed with sailors, and slowly the ebb of the battle changed. The mass of bodies pressed the pirates back toward the rail.

Jack panted heavily as he dispatched yet another sailor only to see two more take his place. He had watched Hawk fall from the bullet from his brother. He realized, as did all the men, that this had indeed been a trap. His hope all but disappeared as he saw the fresh wave of sailors storming aboard the deck. He also saw sailors start coming up from below deck as they had finally shot or hacked through the chains. His crew were better fighters, and more desperate, but they were also only human. "To the death!" his voice rang out. He knew some of the crew had to be thinking about surrendering and taking their chances with the court. But he also knew there was a good chance that Cord would kill them all even after they dropped their weapons. "We lived like men, fought like men, and will die like men!" The pirates let out a cheer and dug deep for another rally.

No one from either ship noticed yet another sloop approaching fast with the wind. It had rounded the western edge of the Rock about the same time that the *Congress* had come alongside the *Avenger.* It lowered its sails and coasted silently alongside the *Congress.* A small group of men quickly threw their grappling lines and climbed over the railing of the larger frigate. There were still a hundred sailors on board, but all were pressed around the far rail, either looking for musket shots or waiting their turn to enter the fray.

The men crouched and ran to the main mast. The leader took out his dirk and quickly cut the ropes binding James. James looked at the man in stunned silence. "James Wellington?" the man asked, with a French accent.

"Uh, yes. But who are you?"

"Jean Lafitte, sir. Here to rescue you."

Hawk opened his eyes. He halfway expected to find he was in hell, or possibly Heaven. But instead he was staring at the feet of his crew, scampering about the bloodstained deck, battling against a horde of sailors. Hawk's chest and shoulder ached and throbbed, and his left arm felt like it was probably unusable. He looked down at his blood soaked-shirt. He wasn't sure why he was still alive, or how long he would be, but he was. The shot must have hit above his heart. He slowly climbed to his feet, grasping the rail for a moment until the deck quit spinning and the darkness in his eyes retreated.

He reached down and grabbed a cutlass lying on the deck. He realized that the sailors from the *Congress* had apparently boarded the ship. His crew had been decimated, with only a small, bloody, exhausted group left surrounding him, being pressed from three sides. He took a deep, painful breath, tried to ignore the pain, and charged into the battle. "The Hawk lives!" he shouted.

The pirates rallied one last impossible time at the sight of their bloodied leader. Hawk's left arm hung uselessly by his side, but the cutlass danced in his right. For a moment, the pirates pushed their attackers back—but only for a moment. The sheer weight of the sailors once again pressed against the pirates. Soon, not more than two dozen pirates remained.

Then, a loud sound rang out over the battle. It was a horn. The combatants continued to battle, until the horn sounded two more times. Slowly, the swordplay ceased, and both sides looked for the source. The navy sailors slowly parted, all the way back to the deck of the *Congress*.

Commodore Cord dropped the horn and strode confidently through the middle of his troops. His lip curled up as he stepped over bodies and pools of blood. His uniform was still pristine, and he looked more like he was at a formal ball than in the middle of one of the greatest battles in the history of piracy. He casually drew his rapier as he headed straight toward the bloodied pirate captain.

The pirates also moved back along both sides of rail, leaving the two men facing each other. "You seem to have many lives, Mr. Hawk," Commodore Cord said loudly, stopping six feet from the famous pirate captain.

"Never enough, apparently," Hawk replied wearily. He leaned forward with his right fist resting on his right knee, sword still in hand.

"No. Unfortunately for you, this will be the last. I will finish the job your bungling, traitorous brother, has failed at—twice. I do propose a deal though."

"Let's hear it."

"I don't want any more bloodshed. But you and your men know you have no chance to win this battle. You all will definitely die. So, I propose that you and I duel to the death. If I win, your remaining crew, and your brother, James, will stand trial for their crimes. A fair judge will decide their fate."

"And if I win?"

Cord laughed. "If you win, my crew will let you, James, and your remaining men go free. If any of you return to piracy, I'm sure my successor will see you all receive a quick death."

Hawk looked over at Jack, who stood bloodied from head to toe. Jack looked at him weakly, with no expression. Hawk then looked from Billy to Andrew on the other side. They looked about the same as Jack and were also too exhausted to give a response. Hawk didn't trust Cord. But Cord was right. There was no chance any of them could survive much longer. And he had no more "Hawk miracles." He also knew that if Cord had any skill with his rapier, the naval officer would probably kill him. Hawk only had one good arm and was exhausted. But that was the best chance he could give his crew. He thought of Anna and his unborn child for a moment. He silently told Anna he loved her and that she should take good care of his child. Then he told her goodbye.

"Let's do it," Hawk said to Cord.

James stared incredulously at the dead man that had just rescued him. Lafitte and his men were pirates, but he faced certain hanging if he stayed aboard the *Congress*. He let the men escort him to the far rail, and they all climbed back down to the deck of the sloop. There was one pirate high up in the crow's nest and only a handful on the deck. He assumed more were below deck manning the cannons.

"Ready the guns!" Lafitte yelled through the closest open hatch. The grappling lines were quickly removed and the sloop was pushed away from the frigate.

The two combatants circled each other for a moment. The sailors were loud in their cheers for their commodore. The pirates were mostly silent, using the time to catch their breath. Cord looked at Hawk's useless left arm and sneered. This would be over quickly. It was just a matter of how much pain he wanted Hawk to experience before he died. Although Cord did not participate in many battles, he was an expert fencer and sparred frequently. Had Hawk been healthy, and had two good arms, he could probably have shattered the long, thin rapier. But with only one arm and being tired and weak, he would be no match for the quicker blade.

Hawk attacked first, suddenly swinging an overhand blow down at Cord's head. He hoped Cord would try to block it with his thin blade. But Cord nimbly leapt to the side, jabbing his sword out as Hawk's blade swung harmlessly past his other side. The rapier blade jabbed Hawk in his good shoulder. The stab was quick and not very deep, but it hurt and drew blood. Hawk tried a quick backhand slash, but with the same result. Cord jumped back and flicked his blade out into Hawk's injured left shoulder, bringing a grunt from Hawk.

Hawk fought valiantly, but ineffectively. The commodore was quick, skilled, and most importantly, fresh. His blade darted in and out, leaving bloody holes behind. Hawk was soon bleeding from half a dozen wounds, his shirt soaked with blood. Each wound not only hurt, it sapped more strength. He became slower, and wilder, with his attacks. He was too slow just to stay on the defensive. For the first time in his life, he knew he couldn't win a fight—or even survive it. He faced a death he couldn't escape. The worst part, of course, was never being able to see his beautiful wife again or see and raise his unborn child. The next worse part was dying at the hands of Cord.

Cord continued to circle Hawk. He was impressed with Hawk's strength and determination, but the pirate was slowly dying with each jab. But Cord also wasn't a fool. He knew in a battle, anything could happen. If he were to slip and lose his footing, Hawk could change the fight with one swing. He had inflicted enough pain. It was now time to finish the job. He stepped forward and rained furious blows down upon Hawk. Hawk was forced to move his sword side-to-side to try to keep up with parrying. As soon as Cord had a clear shot at Hawk's chest, he would run his rapier through his heart.

The opportunity soon came. Hawk was slow in bringing his cutlass back from his right side after a parry. Cord quickly drew back and prepared to plunge his blade through the pirate captain's body. Then, he suddenly felt pain and fire erupt in the back of his shoulder blade. A gunshot rang out from somewhere behind him. He screamed out as the blade dropped out of his hand from the pain and shock of the shot. *Treason?* Forgetting his foe, he quickly looked back over his shoulder. The sailors behind him had all turned to look back too. Cord saw what they were looking at—another ship on the other side of the *Congress*, mostly blocked by the sails and rigging. A tendril of smoke was still floating in front of the crow's nest on the new ship, which was just visible between furled sails. A pirate with a large floppy hat and a large bulky brown cloak stood there holding the smoking musket.

Cord realized his mistake, but much too late. He quickly turned back around to see Hawk's blade rushing toward him. He could only stare in horror as the blade transfixed him. He looked from the blade up to Hawk's blood-and-sweat-covered face, unable to speak. Hawk pulled his blade free, and Cord collapsed to his knees. His ears began to ring and the ship spun beneath him. Darkness rushed in from the edges of his eyes. A moment later he fell forward dead onto the deck.

The sailors were thrown into a state of shock and confusion. There was a new pirate ship to face now, their muskets had been left behind on their ship, and their flintlocks had been fired. They had tied their captain to the mainmast of the *Congress* and the commodore was dead. Then, some noticed that James was no longer tied to the main mast. Many sailors started rushing back to the *Congress*, while the remainder turned to see what Hawk and the pirates would do. Johnson, the battered and bloodied first mate, tried to maintain order. He stayed aboard the *Avenger* to make sure they didn't surrender it to Hawk.

"Fire!" Lafitte yelled, as soon as the deck of the *Congress* had filled with returning sailors. From this angle, he and his crew couldn't see who had been shot from the crow's nest. They knew Hawk and Cord had been in a duel and hoped Cord lay dead. The sloop was almost at point blank range to the frigate when the five cannons fired into its side. The sloop sat much lower in the water, and the cannons had been angled down. There was only one way to defeat a ship that big with only five shots and not enough pirates to reload.

As the sailors arrived back on the *Congress*, some went for the muskets, while others poured down through the hatches to prepare the cannons. Suddenly, explosions ripped through the side of their ship as the cannons erupted from the sloop. The sloop had fired explosive shot into the hull from extremely close range. The first four explosions opened up huge holes in the hull and caused powerful explosions in the hold. The fire from those shots, and the water rushing in, might have been enough to sink the ship. But the fifth ball found the magazine. One explosion turned into another. Soon a series of explosions ripped through the ship.

First mate Johnson and the sailors remaining on the *Avenger* had resumed the battle with the pirates when they heard the explosions behind them. They turned in horror to see the fireballs tear through the other ship. They stood and stared, not caring about the pirates behind them.

Hawk motioned for everyone to go back to the *Anna*. Quickly, they climbed over the rail and slid down the grappling lines back to their ship. Hawk was last to arrive. "Push off and hoist the sails!" He shouted hoarsely.

The anchor line and grappling lines were quickly cut and the sails furled. Only a dozen pirates had made it back to the *Anna*, not enough to load and fire the cannons below. The wind had started to shift during the battle, but the sails still filled with enough wind to start the schooner moving down the length of the frigate. The pirates were too tired to cheer, but all were amazed to have survived. Once they passed the stern of the *Avenger*, they were free. Hawk wasn't sure who had shot Cord, or whom the other ship belonged to, but he would find out soon.

They never cleared the hull of the *Avenger*. The cannons on the frigate, nearly point blank to the *Anna*, opened fire. Many of the cannon crews were never able to join the fight above deck. When the gunner heard the cannons firing from the sloop, he ordered the gun crews to man the cannons again and prepare for a cannon battle. The gunner saw the *Anna* sailing past and ordered the starboard crews to open fire. The smaller schooner was torn to shreds by the explosions. The pirates were bombarded both by metal fragments and chunks of wood.

Hawk stared in horror as the cannons fired on the ship beside them. The sound was deafening. He turned to run toward the far deck as the first explosions hit. A large chunk of the rail struck him in the back of the head just as he left his feet to dive overboard. Blackness took him even before he felt the cold water.

Johnson and the sailors remaining on the *Avenger* realized the pirates had disappeared. Then they saw the *Anna* destroyed by the cannons below. The *Congress* was totally in flames and starting to break apart and sink. Johnson couldn't see what had happened to the other sloop through the flames and smoke, but he had had enough. The Hawk and his crew had most likely just been killed from the broadside, or would die soon enough in the water. His ship was still badly damaged, rudderless, and much of the mainsail was useless. But he ordered what sail they had to be raised. He could try to repair the rudder en route. Luck was with them, and the wind now blew from the east. The two cannons from the shore fired again, striking the gun deck in two places. That only helped to validate Johnson's decision. The wind caught the remaining sails and the boat slowly limped toward New Orleans, leaving fire and death behind it.

James helped lower the longboat from Lafitte's sloop. They had been too close when the magazine on the *Congress* blew. Their ship had nearly capsized and was now ablaze. Flying pieces of wood and debris had killed several pirates and seriously wounded others. They had just enough time for the ones who could still walk to climb into the longboat before the sloop sank. There were only seven of them total now.

They started rowing around the sinking remains of the *Congress* to try to see what had happened to Hawk and his crew. They had heard the cannons fire from the *Avenger*, and had seen it set sail, so they knew it was not likely to be good news. James looked at the thin pirate with the large floppy hat and long, loose cloak. He was the one who'd fired the musket from the crow's nest and had barely made it to the longboat in time.

"Did you kill Cord?"

"No. I hit him in the back of the shoulder, but caused him to drop his weapon and turn to look at me. Hawk finished him off."

James's mouth dropped open when he heard the feminine voice of the speaker—a voice he knew. He looked at Lafitte, who merely grinned and shrugged. The pirate removed the floppy hat, letting her long brown hair fall about her shoulders.

"Anna?" said James.

Hawk vaguely knew he was floating. It was dark and there was no sound. He wondered if he was finally dead. He didn't know how long he floated. He didn't know if he floated in the water, or in the air, or somewhere in the heavens above. After some time, he saw a faint, blurry glow. The blur began to clear and the glow came into focus. He heard voices, either coming from a great distance or just muffled. The glow slowly materialized into a pale face. He blinked a few times and realized it was Anna. She smiled to him—her warm, sweet smile. She spoke, but her words were too muffled to understand. He noticed her clothing in the dim light and realized she was dressed as a pirate. He realized this must be death. He tried to tell Anna he loved her one last time, but wasn't sure if he actually spoke. Anna's face blurred and the glow faded, and then darkness took him again.

CHAPTER XXIX

THE LAST PIRATE

❦

"The end."

"The end?" the young blonde-haired boy asked in dismay. "Did the Hawk live? Did Anna have her baby? What happened to James? And Lafitte and the pirates?"

The man laid the large hardbound book, *The Last Pirate*, on the table beside the rocking chair. He looked down at the six-year-old boy on his lap and laughed. "That, young Peter, is for you and your imagination to decide."

"Awe! I bet they did. I bet the Hawk and Lafitte are still out there capturing ships!"

"Now, Peter, there are no more pirates," a woman said, entering the room from the kitchen.

Peter climbed off the man's lap and ran over to hug her legs. He looked up and flashed a mischievous grin. "Wait till I get big, mother! I'll be Peter the Pirate King!"

"You'll do no such thing! Now go get ready for bed, or you'll be Peter the red-bottomed young boy!"

Peter put his hands behind his back, covering his bottom, and ran squealing down the hall to his bedroom.

"Do you think he might be a little young for that story?" she asked the seated man, shaking her head and failing to suppress a slight grin at Peter's antics.

"I'm beginning to wonder," the man replied, shaking his head. "At least we're in Tennessee and not close to the sea or a ship. He's the spitting image of his father. The memories he conjures up..."

"Don't you think he'll get suspicious of our names being in the book when he gets older?" Anna asked.

"I bet his little head is pondering that right now. If only his father was here to go explain it to him," James replied.

Anna nodded silently.

"Explain what to him?" Henry asked, just coming in the front door of the house. He carried a musket over one shoulder and a pair of grouse in the other hand. He held the grouse up in front of him. "A hard day of farming, followed by a successful hunt. Life is good!"

ABOUT THE AUTHOR

C. R. Sturgill was born in 1970 in Ashe County, North Carolina. He moved with his family to Marion, Virginia, in 1972. After high school, he attended college at Virginia Tech and graduated with a BS in management. He's worked in the transportation and logistics field ever since. After moving around for ten years with his job, he ended up back in the mountains of Southwest Virginia in 2001. He has one teenage son.

C. R. developed an interest in writing as early as third grade after writing a short story that earned the praise of his teacher and parents. He went on to place in the teenage division of the Sherwood Anderson Short Story Contest in high school. He wrote his first novel, a fantasy, at sixteen but never tried to publish it. After writing many short stories, poems, and starting a few novels, he finished his second novel at age twenty. *Blood Tides* is actually a rewrite of that book. He set aside his writing after college for almost fifteen years to focus on career and family.

He was inspired to publish his first book, *Dreams From the Heart: Tales of Hope & Love*, in 2013, in honor of his mother—his biggest supporter and fan—after she died of pancreatic cancer in 2012. The book is a collection of short stories written over a period of several years that explore love, romance, family, hope, and dreams. In addition to dedicating the book to his mother, he's donating a portion of the proceeds of the book to the Pancreatic Cancer Action Network in her name.

Made in the USA
Charleston, SC
28 February 2014